Incomplete Strangers

LAURA-ELISE BISHOP

This book is dedicated to everyone who has ever felt afraid, and to those who helped them feel safe again

Contents

Chapter One

October 2014, Canterbury, Kent, England

Molly's fingers trembled as she zipped up her boots and slipped on her coat. She focused on her breathing, trying to dispel the nausea swirling in her stomach.

'Ready then?' Saskia pushed a hand through her tangled blonde hair.

'You're going out like that?' Molly ran her eyes over her black pencil skirt and cashmere sweater, then her sister's neon pink pyjama trousers, T-shirt with a sweary slogan, and woolly cardigan with frayed cuffs.

'I offered you a lift to the station. I wasn't planning to get out of the car. This is how I'm leaving the house, take it or leave it.' Saskia shrugged.

Molly sighed and handed her car keys to her sister. Today was hard enough as it was without getting into a fight with Saskia. 'Should I drive us to the station?' she asked. 'I know the best way to go at this time of the morning and you're never up at this time.'

Saskia pushed Molly gently out of the house, locked the door behind them, then unlocked the car. 'Molly, you need to relax. The station is five minutes away. It'll be fine.' She waved her hand airily.

Molly climbed in and put her seatbelt on. 'I hate feeling so needy, but I couldn't do this without you.'

'You aren't needy. You need me. There's a difference. This is what we need to do today. Accept it.' Saskia's tone was firm.

When Saskia parked in the station car park, Molly fiddled nervously with her seatbelt.

Saskia leant over, unclipped it for her and squeezed her hand. 'It's going to be OK. You're so brave. You can do this.'

Molly smiled weakly at her sister, then checked her make-up in the mirror, running her finger over the scar on her face. Despite the amount of blusher she had put on, her skin was still deathly pale, and her ice-blue eyes were still bloodshot from the lack of sleep. Smoothing her pale blonde hair behind her ears, she smiled at Saskia. 'Thanks, Sas.'

Her eyes landed on Saskia's messy bun. They were such opposites; Molly was petite, and Saskia was tall and leggy. Molly was shy, anxious, and introverted. Saskia was fearless, and right now Molly longed to be her.

Saskia glanced at the clock on the dashboard. 'Come on Molly. It's time to go. You've got ten minutes until the train leaves. You can definitely do this.'

'I know. Thank you for being here today.' Molly's voice trembled as she spoke.

'Do you need me to come with you?' Saskia asked. 'I meant it when I said I would.'

Molly shook her head. 'No. I said I would do this by myself, and I will.' Her legs felt like jelly and her palms started to sweat as she got out of the car.

Saskia got out too, shutting the door behind her. 'You have your purse and your phone, right? And that little alarm thing we bought?'

'Yes, I have all the things.'

The alarm had almost deafened her last night when she'd tested it, but it made Molly feel safer. Also tucked into her bag was the book that Saskia had lent her. A saucy romance wasn't her usual choice, but it would distract her on the train journey.

Saskia gave Molly a thumbs up. 'Text me when you get there. I'll do the food shopping after I drop you off, like a good little housewife.' She smirked.

'You're the best.' Molly gave Saskia a hug. 'Thank you. I'll put my half of the money in your account later.'

'Thanks,' Saskia said, then let Molly go. 'Love you.'

'Love you too.' Molly smiled at her sister. Saskia wouldn't have hidden at home for two weeks. She would have got right back on the train the next day.

Inside the station Molly swiped her ticket through the barrier and made her way onto the train. I did it, she thought to herself as the train pulled out of the station.

When the train arrived at London's Victoria station, Molly's nerves returned. On the train, she felt safe. Now she was back into scary territory again. She got off the train, her breathing heavy and laboured. Ahead of her, a noisy crowd of women laughed with each other, and she blended in with them, keen not to be singled out as being alone and vulnerable. She followed them out of the station and into the street, the bitter wind blasting her skin and blowing her hair around her face. Starting her journey to work, she passed a coffee shop. Her stomach rumbled, and she longed for a coffee and croissant, but it was full of people in suits and coats shuffling towards the counter, all of them with blank, resigned faces. A wave of nausea washed over her, spurring her on towards her office.

As the giant toucan on the top of her building appeared in front of her, she started to feel apprehensive. People were going to ask questions. Her fingers flew to her eyebrow again, hoping the concealer was still covering her scar. She pushed the revolving glass door firmly and walked across the lobby towards the receptionist sat at the large desk.

'Molly, darling, you're back. How are you?'

Taking a deep breath and focusing on Sue's grey, elegantly styled hair, Molly managed a short response. 'I'm OK. How are you?'

'I'm fine, darling. I'm so pleased you're back.' Sue paused, as if trying to find the right words. 'If you need to talk about anything, love, you know where I am. Just take it easy today. Be kind to yourself.'

Molly nodded, afraid that if she stayed here any longer, she might burst into tears. 'Thank you. I really appreciate it.'

'You are so welcome darling.' Sue smiled. 'I won't keep you. I know that Karl's keen to see you.'

'I'm keen to see him too.' Molly smiled as she thought of her boss, a gentle Nordic giant. 'Thanks again. See you later.'

She walked through the reception area, and into the lift. Her office was on the fourth floor and although the thought of being squashed into the lift for that long made her feel slightly sick right now, her heels were too high to walk that far. Without them, she felt small, and vulnerable, not tall, and graceful, like her sister.

As the lift rose, Molly fiddled with one of the buttons on her coat. The doors opened and, keeping her eyes down, she walked to her desk, sitting down and breathing a sigh of relief. Switching her computer on, her eyes drifted to the window, and the commuters outside marching along the pavement. Her desk was one of ten in the large open plan office, all neatly marked with large blue dividers. Photos of her, Saskia, and their friends covered her desk. Her collection of clay cactuses, flamingos and llamas congregated underneath her large monitor. She slipped off her heels and put on the blush pink leather slippers that lived under her desk, then turned on her computer. While it came to life, she opened her planner, selected a pen from the large fish shaped jug in front of her and started to plan her day. Once that was done, she pulled her phone out of her bag and sent Saskia a photo of the cloudy skies that loomed outside her office.

I'm back! X▨

So proud of you Mole! :)

Molly smiled and typed a reply.

What are you up to?

I'm at the supermarket hunting for a lil treat for you. Disappointed at the lack of talent here. Rom coms have a lot to answer for. I was expecting to meet my future husband here. What a load of shit! X

Molly covered her mouth to stop herself laughing. Saskia had a filthy mouth and absolutely no filter.

Rom coms are a complete waste of time.
Please get the stuff on the list. I would love
a treat, but we do need the essentials. Love
you. X

Another message arrived, this one from her best friend, Liz.

I'm thinking of you today LOVE YOU!!!
Martha and Jacob send their love too. X

Liz would have dropped her daughter, Martha, at pre-school, then raced across the city to get to her job as a veterinary nurse that morning, and Molly's eyes filled with tears , touched that her friend had remembered her.

Thanks love. I was so scared this morning
but I did it!!! Saskia even got up to take me
to the station! X

Molly put her phone back in her bag and opened her emails. Nothing new had come in since last night. On her desk were two unopened manuscripts. She ripped open the envelopes and checked through the pages.

These were the manuscripts that were supposed to be delivered to her house last week. She picked up the piece of paper from the bottom of the envelope, recognising April's scrawly handwriting.

Molly,
Here's the third draft. I'm sorry, it's late. There's not too much to change. Give me a call if you need to.
April x

She rolled her eyes, squashed the note into a ball, and with a carefully aimed shot, threw it straight into the bin. She opened her desk drawer, finding her mug and a box of her favourite teabags; rooibos straight from South Africa. The spicy scent reminded her of the dusty, hot landscape. She peered over the top of her cubicle. It was quiet. Time to run the gauntlet. Sliding out of her chair, she hurried into the kitchen, tapping her scarlet nails on the counter as she waited for the kettle to boil, praying no one came into the kitchen.

Back at her desk, with her cup of tea, she started to feel relaxed for the first time that day, even during a frustrating phone call with one of her authors.

'Karl asked you to send over the second draft last week and I've still not received anything.'

Eric's tone was apologetic. 'I'll have it over to you by tomorrow at the latest, I promise.'

'Before lunch would be ideal,' she replied tartly.

'I'll do my best. Have a good afternoon, Molly.'

Such a charmer, she thought to herself as she hung up and went back to her emails.

Over the last four years, her open plan office at Toucan Publishing had been a noisy, friendly environment. Today was different though. Today no one wanted to meet her eyes and offered her nothing more than a gentle smile. It was just like when her mum died. No one knew what to say and was too scared they would say the wrong thing.

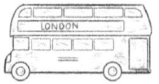

After working on the new manuscript for what felt like eternity, Molly removed her tortoiseshell glasses and checked her watch. It was lunchtime. She peered outside and decided she couldn't face elbow barging a wall of suits out of the way in the sandwich shop today. She decided to see what the canteen had to offer. Before she could slip out of her cubicle, Karl was right in front of her. He was tall, with light blonde hair, and pale blue eyes. He was a gentle giant who considered every word before he spoke. He leant against her desk, studying her intently.

'Molly, sorry I didn't come in this morning. I've been in a meeting. How are you doing?'

'It's good to be back.' She plastered a smile onto her face, hoping it was convincing.

'I almost believe you.' He smiled. 'If you need anything at all please come and talk to me. I know how strong minded you are, but please be kind to yourself.'

'Thank you.' She lowered her voice. 'This morning wasn't as bad as I thought it would be. Saskia came with me to the station and she's going to pick me up later.'

'Good. I'm glad you've got her to support you.' He stood up. 'I'm just going down to the canteen. Do you want to come with me?'

'Sure.' She locked her computer screen and stood up. 'I only managed a piece of toast for breakfast and I'm starving now.'

He shook his head. 'I bet you are, but I understand. I would be the same.' As they walked into the lift, he turned to Molly. 'I've briefed the team not to ask you any questions. I didn't want you to feel pressured into going over it again when you got in today.'

'I thought you had,' she said. 'I got some very polite smiles, but no one's actually said anything to me.'

'Oh.' He wrinkled his nose. 'That wasn't quite what I meant to happen.'

'Don't worry, I appreciate what you were trying to do.' She sighed. 'It's just that when these things happen, people don't know what to say or do. It was so quiet in there you could have heard a pin drop this morning. I'll talk to them this afternoon and make sure they know that they don't have to hide from me.'

'That's so typical of you. You want to make them feel better.' He gestured to her to go first as the lift doors opened. 'Sometimes you need to put your own wellbeing first, Molly.'

Her own wellbeing was something she hadn't considered for a while. Her job, her family, and her friends took up most of her headspace.

As they walked into the canteen she felt anxious again. The tables were all full, and there was a long queue of people carrying trays loaded with everything from sandwiches to noodles, fries to salads.

She browsed the hot dishes at the Asian food counter, ordered a Nasi Goreng, and joined the queue behind Karl.

'I'll get these.' He pulled out his card and handed it to the cashier before she could say anything.

She felt her cheeks colour. 'Thank you. You didn't need to do that.'

He waved his hand. 'It's nothing. Call it pay back for that cake you made me for my birthday. I can't imagine that lingonberry jam was cheap, and it took me right back to my childhood.'

'Ah, you're so welcome.' She followed Karl to a table and sat down opposite him. 'I'd never tried it before, but I liked it. Saskia polished off the last of it on toast the other day. She nearly choked when I told her what it cost.'

'Well, I appreciate it, and I'm glad you're back,' he said.

After she'd eaten, Molly felt a little braver and made her way across the office to speak to Ed, Leslie, and Charlie, her teammates. She briefly explained what had happened to her, knowing they wouldn't ask any difficult questions, or push her for more information. They were, as she had expected, sympathetic and supportive.

Returning to her desk, she scrolled through the playlists she'd made for every mood, before choosing the drum and bass one, made up of remixes of some of her favourite songs. She put her ear buds in, unlocked her computer and returned to her manuscript.

Karl's cheery face appeared at her desk as the clock hit five, and Molly pulled out her ear buds. 'Hi,' she said. 'Do you need to see me?'

'I thought I'd walk you to the station.' He paused, studying her face. 'If you'd like me to.'

She smiled. 'Oh, that's sweet of you. You don't need to do that.'

'I know,' he said softly. 'But I thought it might make you feel a bit safer. The offer's there if you want it.'

She remembered what her therapist had said about allowing people to be there for her if she needed them and took a deep breath.

'Actually, yes, that would be good, thank you.' She took her slippers off and put her boots back on, then grabbed her coat and walked to the lift with Karl.

When she left the building, with Karl by her side, the city had transformed from the grey gloom of the morning. A mixture of neon and fluorescent lights guided her through the darkness, and back to the train station.

At the arched entrance, Karl stopped and turned to Molly. 'Do you want me to see you onto your train?'

She nodded, hating how vulnerable she felt right now. 'I'd like that, thank you.'

'Come on then.' He led her to the gate for her platform. 'I'm afraid I can't come any further, but the train is there. All you need to do is get on.'

'Thank you for everything today, I really appreciate it.' She looked up at Karl.

His brow furrowed. 'It was nothing, Molly. I appreciate you. You are one of our family, no? We are all here to support each other. I'll see you tomorrow.'

'You will,' she said. Today had been a thousand percent better than she had imagined it would be. 'See you tomorrow.'

She gave him a cheery wave and fed her ticket into the barrier, then stuffed it back into her pocket. Karl's kindness, and the kindness of her team had been overwhelming. She was used to having to fight her own battles, and they'd swooped in to support her. The train doors opened in front of her, and she climbed on, scanning the carriage for an empty seat. Even better, there were two empty seats a few rows ahead. She sank into the window seat and let out a sigh of relief as the train doors shut.

Just before the train pulled away from the station, the seat next to her was claimed. A smile crept across her face. It was Cute Train Dude. He had started getting on the train a couple of months ago, and she had been struck instantly by him, like being hit by lightning. He had smiled at her, a single smile in a sea full of glares, or eyes that never met hers. Sometimes he wore glasses. Sometimes he didn't and his grey blue eyes, framed by dark lashes, stared right into her soul. His hair was a dark blonde, and the perfect mixture of styled and tousled. Fine, sandy stubble ran along his jaw, giving him a slightly rugged look, but the suit that he sometimes wore indicated that he had a desk job. Tonight he wore jeans paired with a black t-shirt and a navy blue bomber jacket. She could imagine how soft the fabric would feel between her fingers.

They always exchanged a smile, and it made her heart skip a beat. Then the guilt set it in. If he only knew that she thought about him sometimes when she was in the shower or talked to her sister about how perfectly his jeans clung to his toned legs. Saskia had christened him Cute Train Dude, even though she'd never seen him. Molly's description of him had been more detailed than her police statement two weeks ago. Seeing him tonight had completely distracted her from thinking about that night.

She tried to focus on her book as her thigh pressed against his, but the raunchy content was not helping her at all. She was sure she'd caught him smile at the cover, which featured a muscular man in a tight shirt ravishing a buxom woman, and she was cringing.

He pulled out his Kindle and she tried her best to sneak a peek but couldn't quite see what he was reading. Working in publishing and being obsessed with books had made her nosy. A loud screeching sound made her jump, and the train lurched to a stop before plunging into darkness. A sea of mobile phone screens lit the train carriage as the train remained stationary. She gripped the armrest next to her in panic and heard a sound coming from next to her.

'Ouch! That's my arm!'

'Oh God, I'm so sorry.' Molly clapped her hand to her mouth and looked down. It wasn't the armrest she was gripping; it was the arm of Cute Train Dude.

Chapter Two

OCTOBER 2014, LONDON, ENGLAND

Chris was looking down the train carriage, trying to figure out what was going on, when he felt his arm being grabbed. The emergency lights came on, and he turned, looking into the icy blue eyes of his neighbour.

'I'm so sorry,' she said.

'Don't worry. Are you alright?' He noticed the terror in her wide eyes, and wondered what was going through her mind. He had seen her before on the train. She was heartbreakingly beautiful, but he'd never managed to work up the courage to speak to her. The smile that he exchanged with her was one of the best parts of his day and made the long commute slightly more bearable.

'Uh, I...' A flush of embarrassment spread across her cheeks, but her grip on his coat sleeve didn't loosen.

He didn't know what she was dealing with, but he wanted to calm her down.

'It will all be fine,' he said gently. 'They'll fix whatever's going on and we'll be on our way.' He smiled at her. 'I'm Chris, by the way.'

'Molly,' she said. 'Nice to meet you. So sorry about grabbing you.' Her grip loosened on his coat sleeve, and she winced.

'It's not a problem,' he said mildly.

The lights flickered on, and off again. When they came back on, he noticed that the colour had drained from her face. She was breathing heavily, and frantically scanning the train carriage. On her forehead he noticed a small scar, still purple, indicating it was fairly recent. What had happened to her?

'Everything's going to be just fine.' He spoke slowly, trying to calm her. 'Take a deep breath.' He found himself breathing in sync with her.

An announcement blared through the train, making all the passengers jump.

'We are deeply sorry for the unscheduled stop. We hope to get on our way very soon.'

After what felt like a lifetime, the lights came back on, and the train rushed off as if nothing had happened.

'Molly, are you OK?' he asked. Her chest was still heaving, and her breathing was still heavy.

'I will be,' she said quickly. Her eyes met his, and he held her gaze for a few seconds, before she returned to her book, and he to his, but he couldn't concentrate on it. He was too fixated on her.

When the train arrived at the station in Canterbury, he put his Kindle back into his battered Star Wars satchel.

Molly shoved the dog-eared book she was reading into her own bag and buttoned her coat up. 'Um, I'm sorry, can I get out?' she asked, her face colouring again.

'Sure.' He slid out of the seat. 'This is my stop too.'

'I'm sorry I made your journey home weird. I just...' she trailed off as she got off the train.

He stepped onto the platform after her. 'Hey, it's no big deal. You didn't make anything weird. I've never seen that happen before.' He was reluctant to leave her. Although she'd plastered a smile onto her face, she seemed vulnerable, afraid.

'At least it didn't delay us too much,' she said.

He nodded. 'I know. That's a relief. The commute is long enough as it is.' As he reached the door of the station, he turned back. 'It was nice to meet you, Molly. See you again.'

'Same. And thank you. You really helped me.' She clutched the strap of her satchel tighter and gave him a huge smile.

'Anytime.' He walked out of the station, into the cold, dark air, changing direction as his apartment building appeared in front of him, and walking into the city. He needed company. And advice.

Molly watched Chris walk out of the station, trying to process what had just happened. She had just grabbed a complete stranger! And even though her head had been screaming at her to let him go, she just...couldn't. His voice had been calming, almost meditative and the way that his grey blue eyes had locked onto hers had made heat pool in her lower stomach.

She'd always thought he was handsome, but up close, he was stunning. And she had been close. So close that she could study the neat line of his jaw, the sweep of his dark blonde hair. She'd gone from terrified to intrigued in a matter of seconds. He hadn't objected to her clinging onto him like a limpet. Rather than pushing her away, he'd comforted her, something that had caught her off guard. He was a stranger, yet she felt like she knew him. And now, after tonight, he wasn't a complete stranger. He was someone she wanted to get to know more about. The bitter evening air whipped her hair across her face as she loitered by the station entrance, scanning the car park, hoping that Saskia hadn't forgotten to pick her up.

A few minutes later, Saskia appeared, wearing a leopard printed furry coat, paired with flip flops and tracksuit bottoms. Her damp hair was pulled into a messy bun on the top of her head and her cheeks were flushed. 'Evening, gorgeous. How are we doing then?'

Molly threw her arms around her sister, breathing in the strawberry scent of her shower gel. 'I'm alright.'

'I'm sorry, I'm a bit wet,' Saskia said. 'I forgot the time and had to dash out of the door before I was totally dry.'

Molly laughed, then followed Saskia across the car park to her car, and got in, her breathing slowing back to normal. 'Are those my tracksuit bottoms?'

'Yes. Sorry.' Saskia winced as she drove out of the car park. 'I couldn't find mine.'

'Doesn't matter. I'm so glad you're here.' Molly paused. 'I spoke to Cute Train Dude. I feel like such an idiot though, I've totally embarrassed myself.'

Saskia's eyes widened. 'What did you do?'

'I'll tell you when we get in. I need to make sense of it all,' Molly said.

'Was he wearing a navy bomber jacket?' Saskia asked. 'I'm sure I saw him walking into the city when I drove past the Westgate Towers. Dark blonde hair, fancy beard. That sound like him?'

Molly nodded. 'That's him,'

'I can't wait to hear about it. I knew you'd be stressed out when you got in, so I've started dinner.' Saskia grinned. 'I've made a ragu from scratch for spaghetti Bolognese. I used Ezio's recipe.'

Ezio was the head chef at the restaurant where Saskia worked and his authentic Italian food was as good as she'd eaten on holiday in Rome the previous year. He frequently sent Saskia home with foil trays of food for her and Molly.

'Yum! I'm looking forward to it already,' Molly said. 'He's like the Italian dad we never had.'

Saskia laughed. 'Yeah, unlike the French dad we do have who never cooks for us.'

'Very true. We do eat out a lot when we go over to see him,' Molly said.

'Yes, and why do you think that is?' Saskia asked. 'He loves all the attention he gets in the restaurants. Signing autographs, meetings fans, that's his thing.'

Molly nodded. 'He's like you. He was born to be famous.' She could remember the hard times, before her dad's career took off, when they had little money, when winters were cold, and he was never at home. Fame came with a price though. Now, when she saw her dad, she was slotted into his busy schedule, and it was always far too brief.

'Food shopping is all done too,' Saskia said, bringing Molly out of her thoughts. 'Today I'm the domestic goddess. Don't worry, I'll be handing the mantle back to you tomorrow.' She drove slowly down their narrow road, looking for an empty space to park in.

'Impressive. What was it like doing the food shopping?' Molly asked, then winced as she watched Saskia complete a very cavalier parallel park.

'As hideous as expected.' Saskia unclipped her seatbelt. 'Come on, I'm starving.'

The porch light came on as Molly unlocked the door, breathing in the familiar scent. Home. Her favourite place. She and Saskia had grown up in this Victorian end of terrace, taking their first steps across the wooden floorboards of the hallway.

'Now, will you tell me what happened with Cute Train Dude?' Saskia raised an eyebrow.

'Maybe. Let me get changed first. These clothes aren't meant for spaghetti bolognaise,' Molly said. Her body had relaxed now she was home, in her safe space.

Saskia studied Molly's knee length pencil skirt. 'No, that skirt alone probably cost more than my whole outfit.'

Molly laughed and followed Saskia into the kitchen, the scent of tomatoes, basil and garlic hitting her. The tiles were cold underneath her feet, and she grabbed her slippers which were by the back door.

The kitchen hadn't changed in years. The white butler's sink sat below the sash window with a view over the decking, all the way to the pond at the bottom of the garden. The marble worktops were covered in onion skins, splodges of sauce and a variety of knives and spoons, which she pretended not to notice. The chaos was worth it as Saskia's cooking was so much better than hers.

Leaving Saskia tending to her sauce, Molly went upstairs to change. After their mum died, Molly and Saskia stripped the threadbare carpet off the stairs and sanded them, so that they matched the floorboards in the hall. It had taken them longer than either of them expected, but they had needed something to keep them occupied.

She went into the bright pink bathroom, and washed her hands and face, before tying her hair into a ponytail. Walking past Saskia's bedroom, the door half open, she wrinkled her nose. There was no way she could function in that mess. Next to Saskia's room was their mother's bedroom, perfectly preserved. Her clothes still hung in her wardrobe, and her photos still stood on her dresser.

Molly's bedroom was the last room on the corridor. It was immaculate, with everything organised, clean and tidy. Her wardrobe was organised by colour, every outfit picked out ready for the next day. Thick velvet curtains draped onto the floor, but they were never drawn, allowing her to gaze at the stars, and imagine that her mum was watching over her. It was her sanctuary away from the chaos and disorganisation of the living room, which Saskia covered in magazines, abandoned craft projects, and scripts. She sat down at her dressing table, taking off her rings and necklaces and putting them back into her jewellery box.

Opening her make-up bag, she smoothed some moisturiser onto her skin, smiling at the tiny, framed photo of Molly and Saskia squished in their dad's arms, which stood on the top of her dressing table, along with her collection of make-up brushes and bottles of perfume. She picked up the other photo on her bedside table, the one of her mum.

'I did it, Mum. All they keep saying is how brave I am, but I still feel scared. I miss you so much, but Saskia is being a good mother hen. She's looking after me, just like you did.'

She studied her mother's smiling face, feeling a familiar tug of sadness in her heart. She put the photo down, then changed into a pair of leggings, and an oversize t-shirt, then followed the smell of the rich pasta sauce back into the kitchen.

'Ah, now you're ready for spaghetti bolognaise. Let's do this.' Saskia grinned at Molly. 'I got your biscuits today.' She nodded to a packet on the counter.

'Thank you. They remind me of staying with Papa.' Molly put the packet of palmier biscuits into the cupboard and frowned. 'Saskia, seriously?' She shook her head. 'You bought more sweets?'

Saskia winced. 'I might have got a few bags. Don't nag me about it. I picked up some of that beer you like as well.'

'Great, I need one after today.' Molly pulled two cold bottles out of the fridge and popped the tops off, handing one to Saskia.

Saskia took a gulp of her beer. 'Now are you going to tell me about Cute Train Dude?'

Molly turned to face her sister. 'Yes, but it's so cringey. We'd left London when the train just stopped, and the power went out. The whole train was just darkness, apart from a million phone screens obviously.' She took a swig of her beer.

'Just what you needed today.' Saskia shook her head.

'I know, right?' Molly rolled her eyes. 'Anyway, I was sitting right next to Cute Train Dude, and I jumped and grabbed what I thought was the arm rest, but it wasn't, it was his arm. I just grabbed it.'

'No!' Saskia shrieked, thumping her beer bottle down onto the worktop, sending bubbles everywhere.

'I was so embarrassed, but he could clearly tell I was absolutely petrified and just talked to me, told me to take a deep breath, and he just held my gaze until I felt calmer,' Molly smiled at the memory. 'Then the train sprang back to life again, like it had never happened.' She passed Saskia a cloth

'Then what?' Saskia stared at Molly as she wiped up the spillage.

'Then we just read out books until we got back to Canterbury.' Molly paused. 'His name's Chris, although I still like Cute Train Dude. It's so accurate.'

Saskia was transfixed. 'You weren't wrong about him. He's an incredibly unique kind of hot, the kind that just hits you like a truck.'

Molly laughed. 'I know! I agree with you. He's stunning. Tonight started off as a nightmare, but it ended up feeling like a weird dream.'

'What about moron Mark?' Saskia raised her eyebrow.

Molly gulped down the rest of her beer. 'Just because I have a boyfriend doesn't mean I can't appreciate a beautiful man.'

'Maybe you could do a swap. I feel like Chris would be a serious upgrade.' Saskia cocked her head to the side while stirring her sauce.

Molly frowned. 'Saskia. He's my boyfriend, and I love him.' She opened the cutlery drawer and got out some knives and forks, taking them into the dining room and laying the table.

'You love him. He makes the bare minimum of effort with you!' Saskia shouted through to Molly. 'I mean, has he even contacted you to ask you how you got on today?'

'He's working late tonight.' Molly said defensively, walking back into the kitchen. 'I'm sure he will once he finishes work.' She gripped the cutlery more tightly.

'Has Liz messaged you today?' Saskia got another beer out, popping the top off and taking a gulp.

'Twice. Once on the way in and once on the way home.' Molly sighed. Saskia had got a point. Her best friend had been far more supportive than her boyfriend, but she wasn't exactly surprised by this.

Saskia drained the pasta, before turning back to Molly. 'Liz works twelve-hour shifts, dealing with sick animals, and she has a toddler, and still managed to text you twice today.'

'Fine. You know what, he didn't text me and I am annoyed about it, but I'm dealing with enough right now, I don't want to start an argument with him.' Molly leaned against the worktop, tears pricking at her eyes. 'I just wanted to get through today without any drama and I didn't even manage that.'

'Woah, hold on, Molly. You did get through today without any drama. You were so brave this morning to get on that train.' Saskia put the pan of pasta on the stove and wrapped her arms around Molly. 'You handled the power cut as best you could. There was no drama. Yes, it sucks that Mark didn't text you, but that's what he's like. The important thing is that you did it, and tomorrow you're going to get back on that train and do it again.'

Molly nodded. 'I feel bad for Chris now. He didn't know why I freaked out and he got caught in the middle of it all today. It's not his fault and I'm not going to drag him into my mess.'

Saskia squeezed Molly tightly. 'I do want to continue this conversation, but I also need to serve the dinner, so I'm going to let go of you for just a second.' She pulled away from Molly and scooped the spaghetti onto their plates. 'Stop worrying about everyone else. You know what the commute is like; every man for himself. This guy clearly wanted to help you. If he didn't, he wouldn't have. So, move on.'

Molly smiled and wiped her eyes with her sleeve. 'You're the best, you know that?'

'I love you more deeply and more fiercely than anyone on this earth.' Saskia spooned the Bolognese sauce onto the plates of pasta. 'I'm here cheering you on every step of the way.'

'You are so dramatic, and I love that.' Molly picked up the plates and took them into the dining room.

Saskia followed and sat down opposite Molly. 'You should be proud of yourself. I bet Karl was so pleased to see you back today, wasn't he?' Saskia clumsily twirled her pasta around on her fork.

'Yeah, he was so sweet. He bought me lunch today, and walked me to the station,' Molly said.

'He's a total DILF,' Saskia giggled through a mouthful of pasta.

Molly put her head in her hands. 'You're never coming to my office again.'

'Sorry, Mole. These things just slip out.' Saskia shrugged.

'I stand by what I said. You're banned.' Molly shook her head. 'You can help me make some cookies to take in tomorrow, though.'

'Count me in,' Saskia said. 'You know I'm your best taste tester.'

Chris threw open the heavy glass door of the bar and walked over to an empty stool at the counter, sitting down. He'd only been there a few minutes before Scott appeared.

'Alright mate, want a beer?'

'At least two,' Chris said, sighing heavily as he sat down.

'Good day?' Scott wiped his hands on his apron.

'Weird day.' Chris took a deep breath.

Molly was something else. He could still feel where her scarlet nails had dug into his arm. He hadn't been able to think about anything else for the entire walk here.

'Huh?' Scott frowned at him. 'Hold on.' He gestured towards a couple at the end of the bar. 'I'll be right back.'

Scott came back with a bottle of beer and handed it to Chris, before leaning his hands on the bar, the rolled-up sleeves of his shirt revealing his tattooed arms. 'Tell me what happened today, why was it weird?'

Chris pulled his wallet out of his pocket and handed a note to Scott. 'I'm still trying to figure it out myself.'

Scott rolled his eyes and took the money, checking the note before putting it into the till and handing Chris his change. 'Let's go out the back for a minute, I'm due a break.' He turned to the pink haired barmaid. 'Jo, I'll be back in ten.' She nodded and gave him a thumbs up as he grabbed his water bottle.

Chris picked up his beer, took a gulp and followed Scott out to the back door of the bar. He sat on one of the stone steps, watching the stars in the darkness.

'Tell me about today then.' Scott leant against the brick wall and lit a cigarette.

Chris took a sip of his beer. 'I spoke to her today.'

Scott smiled. 'Cute Train Girl? What happened?'

'On the way back from London I sat next to her, and we had some kind of power cut. The train stopped and the lights went out. She panicked and grabbed my hand, thinking it was the armrest,' Chris said.

Scott's eyes widened. 'No way? What did you do?'

'I talked to her, just like Mum used to do with you when you were scared.' Chris replied. 'The train started moving again and she seemed a bit calmer, so we talked a bit. Her name's Molly. She lives in the city too.'

'What happened when you got back here?' Scott asked.

'We just said goodbye. Then I came here. I...' Chris sighed. 'I can't stop thinking about her.'

Scott stubbed his cigarette out on the wall and flicked it into the bin. 'You like her, right? But you couldn't ask her out because it wouldn't have been the right thing to do and now, you're wondering what to do next.'

'Very good. You got it in one.' Chris rubbed his hand over his chin. 'She's obviously dealing with something pretty huge.'

Scott rolled his eyes as he shoved a piece of chewing gum into his mouth. 'Let me guess, you think you've worked out what it is.'

Chris nodded. 'I think she was mugged. Last time I saw her was a couple of weeks ago. I noticed her bag, it was one of those super expensive ones like you bought for Angela, before she dumped you...'

'Thanks for reminding me,' Scott said, shaking his head. 'Please continue, Sherlock.'

'I haven't seen her until today. She pretty much jumped out of her skin when the train broke down, and I saw a new scar and a faded bruise on her face, as well as a new bag, which she clung onto for the entire journey.'

Scott considered this for a minute. 'You're wasted in IT mate. You should be a detective.' He chewed furiously on his gum. 'It's those books you read, I'm sure of it.'

'I agree.' Chris picked up his beer bottle and took a gulp. 'There was one where Inspector Rousseau was training a recruit and was teaching him how to notice things that everyone else misses. Those techniques kind of stuck with me.'

'If you're planning to ask her out, then "did you get mugged" is not the best opening line,' Scott deadpanned.

'I can't ask her out, Scott. Not until I know what she's dealing with.' Chris stood up and launched his empty beer bottle into the bottle bin.

'I agree,' Scott said, pulling the door open. 'Don't rush it.'

'That's not my style.' Chris followed Scott back into the bar. 'You know that.'

'I know.' Scott let out a long exhale. 'If I'd stayed out there any longer, I'd have had another smoke.' He shook his head angrily.

'You've cut down. It's a start.' Chris sat down on the stool as Scott walked off, reappearing behind the counter of the bar.

'It's not good enough,' Scott said as he passed Chris a menu. 'I'm guessing you're eating here tonight?'

'Yeah, Alex is coming down later to talk about this weekend.' Chris replied, studying the menu.

'I'm excited for you, mate.' Scott lowered his voice. 'The last DJ we had in here was absolutely shit. You and Alex will smash it.'

'It's a different crowd than we're used to.' Chris bit his lip and scanned the room. 'Are these guys ready for two drum and bass DJs?'

'Don't start doubting yourself.' Scott frowned at Chris. 'I've seen enough DJs to know that you guys will go down a storm here.'

'Thanks, mate,' Chris said. 'I needed to hear that.'

Scott shrugged. 'You've put me back on my feet enough times, about time you let someone do the same for you.'

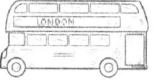

Saskia wrinkled her nose at the dining table which was splattered with sauce and crumbs from their garlic bread.

Molly followed her gaze. 'I'll clear up. You've been so good to me today.'

Saskia smiled. 'You should be proud of yourself. I know Mum would be. I can't imagine how scary it must have been to go back into the station again.'

'Ah, please stop it. I'll start crying.' Molly tucked her head inside her T-shirt so that Saskia couldn't see her face. She didn't want to admit how hard today had been. She pulled her head back out, wiped her eyes and got up, collecting the plates and cutlery, and taking them into their tiny kitchen.

'It's alright to cry, Mole.' Saskia appeared behind her. 'Let it all out.'

'No, thank you. I don't want to have to stuff it all back in again.' Molly gave Saskia a teary smile.

'I get what you mean.' Saskia leant against the fridge as Molly loaded the dishwasher. 'But you do have to get this stuff out. I just channel it into my characters.'

'What characters?' Molly raised an eyebrow.

'I'm going to get back into acting.' Saskia eyed up the cookies on the cooling rack. 'I just need to find the right part.'

'I hope you do,' Molly said. 'You need to be on the stage.'

Saskia nodded. 'I know. It's just been...hard.'

Molly slid her arm around Saskia. 'You're the most fearless person I know. The perfect part is out there for you. Just promise me that if you find it, you'll fight for it.'

'I will.' Saskia rested her head on Molly's shoulder.

'Good,' Molly said. 'Now clear off and let me clear up.'

'I know better than to get between you and your cloth.' Saskia bowed dramatically and left the room.

Molly put her phone on the worktop and turned the volume up, scrubbing the counters, the sink, and the stove, while singing at the top of her voice. She couldn't sing as well as Saskia, but singing made her happy.

Once the kitchen was clear, Molly pulled out a tin and put some of the cookies into it, and a couple onto plates for her and Saskia. She put the kettle on and stared out of the window at the stars twinkling above her, wondering where Chris was right now. Did he go home to a family, did he have kids and a wife? How old was he? The kettle clicking off as it boiled made her jump, and her stomach lurched with guilt. She wanted to push him out of her mind, but the way he'd allowed her to cling to him, and the concerned expression on his face as he'd comforted her had stuck with her.

She took Saskia's tea and a plate of cookies into the living room.

'Ooh, thanks love.' Saskia was curled up on the sofa, reading a book. The gentle light of the lamp glinted off her nose ring, and a splodge of sauce nestled on her cheek.

'You're very welcome.' Molly put the plate and mug down on the coffee table and went to get her own mug and plate. 'Are they any good?' she asked as she sank into the sofa next to Saskia.

'So good,' Saskia said through a mouthful of cookie. 'Do you have to take them into work tomorrow? Can't you just leave them here?' She fluttered her eyelashes.

Molly shook her head. 'No, I'm taking them in. Karl and my team have been so kind, so no, they're coming in with me. I'll make you some more.'

'Fine. In that case I'll allow it. You can take them.' Saskia took a large gulp of her tea.

Before she went to bed, Molly stacked the last cups and plates into the dishwasher and switched it on. Saskia had fallen asleep on the sofa and would never remember to do it. She was about to go and wake her sister up when her phone started ringing. She picked it up, smiling.

'Mark, hi! Where are you?'

'I'm at the bar. I'm having drinks with our clients. How are you?' He sounded drunk.

She sighed. 'I'm fine, thanks. The train journey was a bit...rough, but I got through it.'

'Of course. It was your first day back today, wasn't it? I'm sure you smashed it.'

He hadn't remembered. That's why he hadn't rung earlier. She gripped her phone tightly and gritted her teeth.

'Yep. It was fine. Karl walked me back to Victoria.'

'Ah, he's a good man. I like Karl,' he said, raising his voice over the cheering in the background.

'Sounds like you're having fun.'

Her skin felt hot and prickly. If he had time to party with his clients, why hadn't he had time to contact her?'

'We have to show the clients a good time, Molly. I'm glad you've got back into the swing of things. I knew you would. You're tough.'

'I have to be.' She had to be tough so that she could support everyone else. 'I'll see you when you get back. Love you.'

'Love you, babe.'

She hung up, walked back into the living room and sat down next to Saskia, giving her a gentle shove. 'Come on, love, you need to go to bed.'

'I'm up.' Saskia pulled herself upright. 'What time is it?' She rubbed her hands over her face.

'It's ten thirty. I'm not letting you fall asleep here again. You won't sleep properly if you do.' Molly held out her hand and pulled Saskia to her feet.

'You're right. As always.' Saskia traipsed upstairs. 'Night, Mole.' She kissed Molly on the cheek. 'You did an awesome thing today. Be proud.'

'I'll try,' Molly said. 'Night.'

In the rosy glow of the bathroom, she cleaned her teeth, then went back to her bedroom and changed into her pyjamas, climbed into bed, and gazed out of the window. Instead of thinking about the night she was mugged, as usually did before she fell asleep, she thought about Chris, remembering the strangely calming effect that he'd had on her, and the feeling of contentment that washed over her as he spoke to her. Whatever it was that had passed between them, she knew she would never forget it.

Chapter Three

October 2014, Canterbury, Kent, England

After a restless night's sleep, Molly dragged herself out of bed, and into the shower. She put her make-up on, covering the scar on her eyebrow which was still a dark purple. Opening her wardrobe, she decided on a blue dress printed with teacups and saucers, thick black tights, and her navy ankle boots.

She poked her head into her sister's bedroom. Clothes were strewn over the armchair in the corner of the room. Piles of paper, which Molly assumed were scripts, were strewn across the dressing table. Her wardrobe door hung open, revealing numerous hangers pressed tightly against each other, a riot of clashing colours and textures. At least her bed was empty, which meant her sister was awake. She shuddered at the mess, and pulled the door shut. When she got downstairs, she nodded approvingly at the dining table. A china rack was full of toast. There was butter, jars of jam, and a floral teapot, with cups, saucers, and plates. Saskia appeared from the kitchen, where the radio was playing, carrying a jar of peanut butter.

'Morning, Mole,' she said. Breakfast's ready!'

'You made me breakfast?' Molly tried not to sound surprised, but it was usually the other way around. She sat down opposite Saskia and poured her a cup of tea before pouring one for herself.

'Of course,' Saskia smiled. 'You had to stuff your toast down yesterday because we were both rushing around, so today I wanted to make it more relaxed for you.'

'Thanks, love, I appreciate it.' Molly spread her toast with butter and jam, touched by Saskia's gesture. 'I'll be back at seven tonight if you're free to come and get me.'

She took a glance at her sister's outfit. Today it was an oversized yellow hoodie, luckily with no sweary slogan, and a zebra print cardigan. Her eyes were heavy. This time of the morning was not Saskia's favourite.

'I swapped my shifts this week so I could come and get you,' Saskia said. 'Ezio understands. He wanted to come and escort you to the station himself.'

'That doesn't surprise me. I still remember his colourful response when you told him what had happened to me.' Molly shook her head.

'I hope that the police catch the guy who mugged you before Ezio does.' Saskia cackled, taking a sip of her tea. 'Did you speak to Mark last night?'

'He called while you were asleep on the sofa.' Molly's eyes remained fixed on her cup.

'And how did that go?' Saskia said drily. 'Did he ask you how you were? Let me guess, he hadn't even remembered you were going back to work yesterday.'

'You're right again.' Molly winced. 'But once I reminded him, he did at least manage to ask about it. So that's something. He just doesn't do feelings. I never know what he's feeling. He's a mystery to me.' She finished the last of her tea and put her empty mug down on the table.

Saskia snorted. 'He's something Mole, but I'm not sure it's a mystery. More like a shitty boyfriend who pretends not to do feelings so he can get away with the bare minimum.'

'You don't have to date him, Saskia.' Molly continued eating her toast. She loved her sister, but she had no filter.

Saskia licked a smear of jam off her finger. 'No, but watching you date him makes me furious. If I was dating him, I would have told him to fuck off a long time ago.'

Molly ignored Saskia and checked at her watch. 'I think we should get going. The busy train will have left, and if we go now, we can make the slightly less busy one.'

She didn't want to talk about Mark, and she knew Saskia would move on to something else if she didn't respond to her.

'Fine,' Saskia said, standing up and clearing up the empty plates. 'I'm sorry, I shouldn't argue with you. You're probably nervous enough as it is.'

'It's a good distraction.' Molly took their empty mugs into the kitchen.

'I just think you deserve better, Mole.' Saskia followed Molly into the kitchen and put the jam back into the fridge. 'He snaps his fingers, and you go running off to see him, but he's never there for you when you need him.'

'It's not like that, Saskia.' Molly wiped the toast crumbs off the worktop, then turned round to face Saskia. 'I appreciate your concern, but this is not a situation that I need or want you to get involved in.'

'Noted,' Saskia said and pulled Molly in for a hug. 'I love you and I am here for you. Let's get you to the station.'

Chris's alarm woke him up and he groaned, rubbing his face. It was still dark, and it was so early, too early to have to get up and go to work. He and Alex had stayed at Mimosa last night until midnight planning their set and when he'd got home, he hadn't been able to sleep. He'd still been awake when Scott got home at two am.

He dragged himself into the shower and got dressed, before quietly leaving the flat, carefully shutting the door so that he didn't wake Scott. It was dark as he walked to the station, where the bright lights blinded him as he swiped his ticket and walked through the barrier.

When he got on the train, he scanned the carriage, wondering if Molly was there but there was no sign of her. He put his headphones in and pulled out his book, trying to concentrate on it, but his eyes kept closing. His phone buzzed and he pulled it out of his coat pocket.

Is your train girlfriend there? Is she the reason you couldn't sleep last night?

Maybe... I can't stop thinking about her. She's not on the train this morning.

Chris's stomach rumbled as he walked to his office, so he picked up a granola bar and a couple of bottles of fruit juice from a café. When he reached the vast glass and steel structure where he worked, he pushed open the door, walking into the marble lobby and over to the receptionist.

'Morning Penny! How are you doing?' He smiled at her.

'I'm fine thank you sweetheart, how are you?' she asked, her brow furrowed. 'Are you alright?'

'I didn't sleep very well.' What else could he say? That he'd fallen for a complete stranger on the train last night and couldn't sleep because he was thinking about her? He handed her one of the bottles. 'I got you a watermelon and pineapple juice. That's the one you like, isn't it?' He'd picked up one for her before, when she couldn't leave the desk to get her lunch.

She took the bottle. 'Yes, that's my favourite, thank you, that's so sweet of you.'

'No problem.' Chris stuffed the other bottle into his satchel and yawned.

'Why don't you go for a nap in the server room? I won't say a word.' She mimed zipping her lips. 'If you get an hour now, you'll be right as rain by lunchtime.'

'You sound pretty confident about that. Have you done that before?' Chris whispered, afraid he would burst out laughing. Penny was as straightlaced as they came. She would definitely not sneak off for a nap.

'Of course not,' she insisted, folding her arms, and nodding at the bottle on her desk. 'Thanks for the juice.'

'You're welcome. See you later.' He walked through the reception and into the lift to get to his morning meeting with Kevin, the MD. He had no idea why Kevin liked him so much, but he suspected it was because of Chris's intimate knowledge of his browser history.

As darkness enclosed the city that evening, Molly's palms started sweating as she thought about walking to the station. It had been a pretty standard day. She'd eaten her packed lunch at her desk, watching the suited commuters marching down the road with their paper bags full of sushi, wraps and noodles, and scowled at them, wishing she was brave enough to go out there herself. The crowds, and traffic unnerved her though, and she was glad of the sheet of glass that separated her from them.

She put her coat on and stuffed her phone, book and almost empty box of cookies into her bag. A voice beside her made her jump.

'Molly, I'm catching the train from Victoria tonight, do you want to walk together?'

It was Ed, one of the other editorial assistants. His soft brown eyes fixed on her as she put on her coat. He wasn't much taller than her and as she stood up, she finally felt able to respond.

'Did Karl ask you to do this?' She knew he couldn't lie and would crumble under the gentlest of interrogation.

He squirmed. 'Well, he didn't directly ask me, I mean, I wasn't asked to...'

She cocked her head to the side and raised her eyebrow.

He held up his hands. 'Alright, he asked all of us if we would take it in turns walking you to the station after work. He knows you'll never ask. You're too bloody independent.'

'I'll be fine, Ed,' she said, despite being rooted to the spot.

'You're in here pacing like a tiger because you know you've got to go out there and you don't want to. Why don't you let me walk you there?' He shifted his bag on his shoulder.

She sighed. 'You're right. Thank you.' She followed him to the lift. 'I'm not that independent. I could be living on my own by now, but I'm not, I'm still living with my sister, clinging to her like a limpet.'

He laughed as the lift doors opened and they got in. 'More like the other way around. Has Saskia got a job yet?'

'Yes, she's waitressing, not reading scripts and forgetting to go to auditions.' She shook her head.

'I think you like mothering her.' He raised an eyebrow. 'I think part of you doesn't want her to get her big break in case she moves out.'

Her eyes widened. 'Maybe. Anyway, what's happening with you and Samuel, have you found somewhere to live yet?'

'We're trying to find somewhere in Kent; rent is ridiculous here,' he said.

The lift doors opened, and they walked across the lobby, waving goodnight to Sue on the way out. As Molly stepped out of the door, she froze. The darkness seemed to amplify the sound of the traffic, and the sirens. The neon lights on every building highlighted the crowds of people jostling their way back to the station. Her body started trembling and she turned back, towards the bright lights of the lobby.

Ed offered her his arm. 'You can do this. I'm with you, alright, and I'm staying right with you until we get back to the station. It's OK to be scared. I would be.'

She nodded and slid her arm into his. 'I hate this. I hate feeling like this, so completely trapped and afraid.'

He steered her towards the crowds of commuters. 'I bet you do. I won't pretend to understand, but I do know that you won't feel like this forever.'

'I hope not.' She kept her eyes focused on the road ahead of her, and her arm tucked into Ed's.

'When are you going to move in with Mark?' he asked.

She sucked in a breath. 'I don't want to live in London, and he doesn't want to live in Canterbury.'

'One of you has to give in at some point,' he said, pulling Molly across the road with him.

'It's not going to be me,' she replied as she hurried to keep up with him.

'Sticking to your guns. I like it.' He gestured theatrically to the station entrance. 'We're here already! It wasn't so bad asking for help, was it? We had a nice little walk and a catch up. It was fun, right?'

She gave him a friendly squeeze as they walked across the concourse. 'It was fun. Thanks, Ed.'

'I'm not going anywhere until you're through the barrier.' He let go of her arm as they got to the gate for platform three.

'You're a good friend.' She gave him a hug.

'It's nothing.' He waved a hand airily. 'But if you wanted to make some more of those cookies for us, I definitely wouldn't complain.'

'Of course.' She pulled her ticket out. 'Á bientôt, mon cher.' Waving to him, she swiped it through the barrier and ran towards the train, which was leaving any minute now.

Please let him be on the train. I need him, she thought to herself, scanning the carriage, before taking the nearest empty seat, next to a woman with a collection of shopping bags tucked between her legs.

She pulled out her novel and started reading. The beeping of the train doors made her jump, and she looked up, her eyes meeting Chris's. He was a few rows ahead of her, and he nodded to her. She smiled at him, and wished she could swap seats with the woman next to him, but she didn't want to make it totally obvious that she wanted to be sat next to him. He smiled back at her, then pulled his Kindle out of his bag, so she got her book out and started reading.

A while later, she was so engrossed in her book that the woman next to her had to practically shout at her to ask her to move. She apologised and stood up to let her out, taking the window seat for herself. A flood of people got off the train, and a smile spread across her face as Chris appeared in front of her.

'Is this seat taken?' he asked.

'It is now,' she said as relief washed over her. Her breathing slowed; her body relaxed. She had no idea why he had this effect on her. Mark didn't. He was always calm, but tightly wound.

He sat down next to her. 'No dramatic power cut tonight then?'

'It's been incredibly boring.' Her eyes ran over the hint of light brown stubble on his jaw and his bloodshot eyes. He'd clearly slept as badly as she had.

'Apart from your saucy novel that is.' He smirked and gestured to her book.

She laughed. 'It's my sister, Saskia's. What do you read?'

'Oh, mostly crime stuff, detective novels. Do you know Gaspard Millot? I love his stuff. I found one of his books at home when I was a kid, and I became obsessed with reading them all.'

She flinched, her eyes not meeting his. 'Uh...Yes, I've heard of him.' She changed the subject quickly. 'I prefer historical fiction, but I'm trying something new today. Yesterday was rough. Saskia thought it would help.'

'I could tell.' He smiled at her. 'Do you want to talk about it?'

'I guess so.' She'd practiced speaking about it without any emotion. No feelings, just words. 'Two weeks ago, I was mugged outside the station. I'd got a late train home after drinks with my workmates, and some guy grabbed me in the car park. He punched me so hard I fell over, and then he stole my handbag.'

His eyes widened. 'Molly, I'm so sorry. Did anyone help you? There must have been other people in the car park.'

She shook her head. 'It was over so quickly. I went to the police, but the guy had a hood, and I couldn't give a good description of him. I drove home and didn't leave the house for two weeks. Yesterday was the first time I got on the train again after it happened.'

Her stomach lurched, and she dug her fingernails into her palms. One day it wouldn't hurt so much to talk about it. But today was not that day.

'You're so brave,' he said. 'That must have been so hard, and the power cut yesterday probably didn't help.'

'It wasn't ideal, but you helped me through it. I'm so sorry I grabbed you.' She felt her cheeks flush again at the memory.

'I could tell you were going through something,' he said. 'My mum used to sit with my brother when he was scared or upset and just talk to him, get him to focus on his breathing. It always calmed him down.'

'Your mum sounds wonderful,' she replied, and a pang of sadness enveloped her. Her mum had always been there for her when she was afraid.

He nodded. 'She's a counsellor, and very good at reading people. She seems to always know what they're thinking or feeling, and what they need, especially my brother.'

'Are you still close with your family?' she asked.

'Oh yeah. I live about twenty minutes from my parents. My brother and I live together,' he replied. 'We've been inseparable since we were five.'

She frowned, puzzled, but before she could speak, he continued.

'Scott was my best friend at school, and he turned up at my house one afternoon after school in tears,' he said quietly. 'He'd run away from home. His dad was an alcoholic. We had no idea until Scott told us what was going on. My parents adopted him a year later.'

'What happened to his mum?' she asked.

'She died when he was two,' he replied. 'He doesn't remember her.'

'Oh wow, that must be so hard.' She sucked in a breath as a familiar stab of pain, of sadness and loss, coursed through her chest.

He nodded. 'He's always seen my mum as his mum, and when we adopted him, he got two new aunts too. Now he's surrounded by mums.' He laughed. 'They can be a bit full on, but they mean well.'

'They sound lovely. They've taught you well. You helped me so much yesterday.' She wished that she had aunts, some female figure that she could turn to, but both of her parents were only children.

'You don't know this, but you helped me.' He lowered his voice. 'When I first started my job a few months ago, I was so nervous, and your smile was the first thing I saw when I got on the train. No one else even noticed me, but you gave me the biggest smile. I've never forgotten it.'

'A smile doesn't cost anything.'

Her heart skipped a beat at his words. *I've never forgotten it.* That was adorable. She was saving those words for when she needed a pick me up.

'I'd never seen you before and you were like a deer in the headlights, you know? I figured a smile might help. What do you do?'

'I work in IT for InvestTech. Do you know it?' he asked.

She nodded. 'I know it, the building is just around the corner from mine.'

'What do you do?' he asked.

'I'm an editorial assistant at Toucan Publishers,' she said, finally meeting his gaze. Even in the horrible fluorescent lighting of the train, he was ridiculously good looking. 'I work in children's books. It's kind of my dream job. I loved books as a kid.'

She smiled. It wasn't love. It was an obsession. While Saskia loved to perform and entertain, Molly had loved to hide in the corner with a book.

'That sounds like a very cool job. Is it stressful? I bet there's loads of deadlines.'

'It's stressful sometimes, but my team are brilliant and have been so supportive over the last few weeks.' She remembered the box at the bottom of her tote bag and pulled it out. 'I made these cookies for the guys I work with to say thank you, would you like one?'

His eyes lit up as she offered the tin to him. 'You made these? They look incredible.'

'I did. Help yourself,' she said.

'Thanks, Molly.' He picked up one of the cookies and took a bite. 'Mmm, these are good.'

'Thank you.' She beamed at him. 'I have some more at home, well I did this morning, but Saskia seems to run on sugar and caffeine so I reckon she'll have eaten them all.'

'Do you guys live together?' he asked.

'We do. We're complete opposites, so it's kind of... interesting.' She laughed. 'She's quite chaotic and messy, and I'm neat and organised.'

He laughed. 'You sound like me and Scott. He's exactly like your sister, a whirlwind of chaos. I like calm.'

'Same.' She nodded. 'And Saskia doesn't understand that. I feel like I have to parent her. I remind her about auditions, I make her poached eggs on toast at the weekends. That and pancakes are about the only things I can cook.'

He shook his head. 'You made those delicious cookies.'

'No, that's baking.' She smiled. 'I can bake, I just can't cook. Saskia can cook, but she doesn't always want to. She waitresses in an Italian restaurant and her boss is like our unofficial dad so he sends care packages home for us.'

'Italians are all about family. It sounds like he looks after you guys,' he said. 'I love cooking. I taught myself at university and Scott's hates cooking, so it always falls to me. Asian food's my favourite, I make a good pad Thai.'

'I love pad Thai.' Her eyes lit up. 'We used to go to this Thai place all the time with my mum. It's called Lotus Thai. I don't know if you've been there?'

'I have.' He was interrupted by a loud announcement. The train had reached Canterbury already.

'I'll wait until Saskia gets here,' Chris said to Molly as they reached the station entrance.

'Thank you. I always get nervous as she's driving my car, and she's not the best driver.' She laughed. 'I should be grateful, right? It's only that she crashed it into a bollard not long after I got it.'

'I get that,' he said. 'I don't let Scott drive my car. He's a liability.'

'They sound very alike. Oh, here she is.' She waved as Saskia ran up to the station.

'Evening, Mole!' Saskia said, beaming and unashamedly eyeing up Chris.

Molly stifled a giggle. 'Saskia, this is Chris, we met on the train yesterday. Chris, this is Saskia, my sister.'

Saskia held out her hand. 'Pleased to meet you. Thank you for looking out for my sister.'

'I think we're looking out for each other.' Chris smiled at Saskia.

'Good.' Saskia nodded and her eyes flicked from Chris to Molly. 'So, we should get going then.'

'Right.' Molly smiled at Chris. 'Maybe see you tomorrow then?'

'See you,' Chris said.

Chapter Four

October 2014, Canterbury, Kent, England

Molly drove to the Chinese takeaway and ordered far more food than they'd eat. She handed Saskia the hot paper bag, which she cuddled all the way back to their house.

Saskia waited until Molly opened the front door before she exploded at her. 'What's going on?'

'What are you talking about?' Molly took off her coat and picked up the takeaway bag from the floor, where Saskia had left it while she pulled her coat off.

'I'm talking about me standing there like a lemon while you two were staring at each other like something out of those shitty rom com films.' Saskia put her hands on her hips.

'Saskia!' Molly shook her head at her sister and took the bag into the kitchen.

'I'm serious. What the hell happened on that train?' A smile crept over Saskia's face.

Molly rolled her eyes, then washed her hands and got two plates and two sets of chopsticks out of the cupboard. 'It's not like that.'

Saskia rummaged in the fridge, pulling two bottles of beer out and opening them, handing one to Molly. 'Then what is it like?'

Molly opened the foil containers and put them on the dining table, then came back into the kitchen, face to face with Saskia, whose arms were folded. 'I told him the story of how I got mugged, then we shared my cookies. Not very erotic, is it?'

'Disappointing.' Saskia picked up the plates and chopsticks, and Molly took their bottles of beer, following her sister into the dining room

'Can we talk about why you're wearing my spare glasses?' Molly asked Saskia as she sat down.

'I lost mine and I needed to do some reading.' Saskia shrugged.

'You've not got a job, have you?' Molly's chopsticks paused before they reached her mouth.

'Maybe. I have an audition soon, but I don't want to say anything in case I mess it up,' Saskia replied, before dipping her spring roll into the sweet and sour sauce.

'Have you actually been home today? It's so tidy in here.' Molly asked.

'Hilarious.' Saskia rolled her eyes. 'I worked the lunchtime shift, but I also cleaned the kitchen when I got back. I'm going to turn over a new leaf, become tidy and organised. Maybe you can help me tackle my bedroom at some point.'

Molly shuddered. 'I've been desperate to get my hands on it for ages. It won't be this weekend though. We'll be out Saturday so we can write Sunday off and next weekend I'll be at Mark's.'

Saskia made a face as she spooned some lemon chicken onto her plate. 'Did you tell moron Mark about Chris?'

'Nope,' Molly said through a mouthful of noodles.

'Did you tell Chris about moron Mark?' Saska pressed Molly.

Molly avoided her sister's gaze. 'Nope.'

A piece of spring roll plopped into Saskia's lap. She picked it up and put it in her mouth. 'Molly, this is so unlike you,' she said, through her mouthful. 'What's going on?'

'I don't know.' Molly shrugged. 'When I'm with Chris, my anxious brain just slows down. Something in him makes me feel calm. But don't read too much into this. We're just friends.'

'Right,' Saskia said slowly.

'We are just friends, Saskia,' Molly replied. Even thinking about Chris made her happy, but she wasn't going to tell Saskia that. 'Don't give me a hard time, it's not like I was making out with him on the train, we were just talking.'

'Methinks you are a little defensive.' Saskia raised an eyebrow. 'So you haven't made out with him in real life, but I bet you have in your head.'

'Saskia! We really connected. Emotionally. Not physically.' Molly wiped her mouth with a napkin. 'As two people offering each other some understanding. That's all. I don't need to tell Mark as there's nothing to tell.'

This wasn't exactly true. Chris overwhelmed her senses and made her feel calm at the same time. He was something else and until she figured out exactly what, she wasn't sharing anything else with Saskia.

'Fine, I'll butt out.' Saskia stuffed the last of her spring roll into her mouth.

Molly breathed a sigh of relief. Right now she didn't want to get into what she felt for Chris, or why.

'Are you sleeping any better?' Saskia asked.

'No.' Molly started stacking up the empty foil containers. 'I either can't get to sleep, or I get off to sleep, but I have a nightmare, then I can't get back to sleep. I don't know what to do.'

'Think happy thoughts,' Saskia replied and stood up, picking up their empty plates.

'Thank you.' Molly rolled her eyes. 'That's very helpful advice.'

'I know it seems basic, but when you focus on the good stuff, it's harder for the anxiety to get in,' Saskia said, taking the plates into the kitchen.

Molly closed her eyes, telling herself to think happy thoughts. The first thing that came into her head was Chris, and his smile. The murmur of pleasure that escaped him as he tried her cookie. It gave her a little thrill of happiness, a buzz. She opened her eyes. Maybe this wouldn't be so hard after all.

Molly's alarm woke her up the following morning. At six thirty am it was still as dark as it had been when her eyes finally shut sometime around one. Creeping downstairs, she rolled out her yoga mat. She loved this quiet time to herself, hearing the world starting to come to life, and did her sun salutation, before lying down for meditation, absorbed in listening to her breathing.

After her meditation, Molly went into the kitchen to make breakfast, spooning yoghurt and granola into two bowls, before chopping apples and bananas into slices and putting them on top of the yoghurt and granola. She'd just put the bowls on the table when Saskia appeared in the dining room.

'Did I make it in time? We need to leave in half an hour, right?' Saskia was out of breath, her face bare, her hair in a damp messy bun on the top of her head.

Molly laughed. 'Yep, you made it. Breakfast is ready.'

Saskia smiled. 'Nice work, Mole.' She sat down and picked up her spoon. 'Thank you.'

'I aim to please.' Molly sipped her tea, keeping her eye on her watch.

At the station, Molly scoured the train for Chris, but he wasn't there, and she started to feel anxious. With him by her side she had felt safer, and alone, she felt vulnerable. She got on to the train and as it sped towards London, she pulled out her phone and sent Mark a message,

> How's it going in Belgium? X

> It's full on!!! I was expecting to come back to London tomorrow night, but I've been asked to go to Luxembourg for two weeks. I've blocked out the whole weekend for you when I get back though X

> Can't wait! Love you X

She put her phone away, already excited to see him again. After her mum died, Mark was the only constant in her life. He booked tables in the best restaurants for their dates. He took her to art galleries and rooftop bars. He was polite, and intelligent. But even after four years together, she still felt like she didn't know him.

Molly couldn't stop the smile from spreading across her face as she saw Chris walking down the train carriage towards her.

'Hey!' she called. 'I hoped I'd see you.' She gestured to the window. 'Window or aisle seat?'

'I don't mind.' He sat down next to her. 'Aisle is fine.'

'How was your day?' she asked.

'Long. It involved explaining to people twice my age why they can't put paper clips in USB ports.' He rolled his eyes. 'How was yours?'

'Oh, pretty much the same, just less paperclips.' She yawned. 'I'm sorry. I'm so tired.'

'Me too. I didn't sleep very well.' He rubbed the back of his neck.

'Me neither,' she said looking down at her lap.

'You can catch up now if you like. Here.' He patted his shoulder. 'I'll wake you up when we get to Canterbury.'

'That's sweet of you, but I snore, and you don't deserve that,' she whispered. 'I once fell asleep on a guy and when I woke up, I had dribbled down his shoulder. I was so embarrassed.'

'No! That's awful!' He burst out laughing.

'I know. The thing is, I did the same thing about a week later!' she said, giggling.

He shrugged. 'He chose to sit next to you again, he knew what he was letting himself in for!'

Somehow sharing that story didn't make her cringe. His quiet acceptance of her meant more than she was willing to admit. She opened her bag and got out a small square tin.

'I sneaked the last few cookies out of the house this morning. Saskia will be fuming, but I figured we could share them.' Taking off the lid, she offered the tin to him.

'Thank you,' he said, taking one of the cookies. 'I appreciate you feeding my sugar addiction.'

'I appreciate you sitting next to me.' She lowered her voice. 'I feel safe with you, Chris, and I didn't think I would ever feel safe on the train again.'

'It's no problem. You bring the snacks and I'll be your bodyguard.' He smiled at her.

At the station, Molly cringed as Saskia drove right up to the station entrance and slid down the window, grinning at them.

'Evening guys.' Saskia smiled at Chris. 'You want a lift?'

'No, I only live a few minutes away, but thanks.' He smiled at Saskia, then turned to Molly. 'See you tomorrow, maybe?'

'Sure,' Molly said and nodded, her throat feeling strangely dry.

Molly climbed into the car next to Saskia and burst out laughing when she saw that she was wearing her pyjamas. That was why she hadn't got out of the car.

'Well, that's charming, isn't it?' Saskia huffed drove out of the car park. 'I come to get you and you laugh at me.'

'It was the fleecy pyjamas. I'm sorry.' Molly bit her lip.

'I had a shower when I got in from work and I couldn't be bothered to get dressed again, it's such an effort, isn't it?' Saskia wrinkled her nose.

'It is. I can't wait to get into my pyjamas.' Molly glanced over at Saskia's bare face and glowing skin, wishing hers had a healthy glow rather than a pasty sheen.

A waft of garlic hit Molly as she unlocked the front door. She turned to Saskia. 'Whatever you're cooking smells delicious.'

'Lasagne. I'll be honest, I didn't make it. Ezio sent it home for us. He sends his love, by the way. And some tiramisu, but I ate that earlier. Sorry.' Saskia pulled off her boots and put on her fluffy slippers.

Molly shrugged. 'Don't worry, I'm making brownies to take into work tomorrow. I can sample one of those.'

'Yes! Brownies,' Saskia wandered into the kitchen. 'You need an impartial taste tester, Mole, for quality control.'

Molly followed her. 'Quality control? Really? You'll try to snaffle them all.'

'I'll be good. I promise,' Saskia assured her.

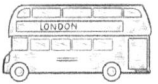

Chris let himself into his flat. It was cold and dark. Scott wouldn't be home for a long time, and he couldn't be bothered to go to the bar tonight. He got a beer from the fridge and sat on the sofa, staring out of the window. From his living room he had a stunning view of the city that he never got tired of. There were curtains on the windows, but he never pulled them, as he liked to watch the changing skies over the city. He thought about Molly. It had been a long time since he'd felt that kind of connection with anyone. And it had come out of the blue.

The minute their eyes met he had wanted to know more about her. The more he learnt, the more he wanted to know. The urge to protect her, to shield her had got stronger the more they'd talked. She'd told him that he made her feel safe, and he would do everything in his power to ensure that she was safe. Although he was attracted to her – more so than he had been to anyone before – there was no way he would jeopardise their fledgeling friendship by revealing that.

He made himself some roasted vegetable pasta for dinner, putting the leftovers into a glass dish for Scott to have when he got in later. The flat was quiet without him, and the large dining table was far too big for one person, but with his family and friends always dropping in, it was a necessity.

After he'd eaten, he put a film on, and tried to concentrate on it, but when Scott came in at one am, he was still awake. He couldn't stop thinking about her.

'Are you alright mate?' Scott asked.

'Yeah, I'm fine. Just couldn't sleep,' Chris said.

'What's going on?' Scott sat on the edge of the sofa. 'Is it work?'

Chris shook his head. 'No, work's fine.' He wondered whether to tell Scott what was actually going on.

'Molly then?' Scott raised his eyebrow. 'Is the problem that you did ask her out and she's not OK with it, or that you didn't, and you want to?'

'The latter. She said I make her feel safe, and that's what's important. I need her to know that she's safe with me, and asking her out will just make it seem like I've been there for for that reason alone, which isn't the case.'

Scott nodded. 'Is she someone you could just be friends with?'

'I don't know, but I'm going to try because she needs me.' He rubbed his face. 'That's the plan, anyway.'

'Solid plan.' Scott nodded. 'I hope it works out. You never know, she might feel the same way.'

'She hasn't given me any indication that she does.'

Apart from the discreet glances he had noticed her sending his way. And the way she smiled when she saw him.

'Well, either way, you can't stay up all night,' Scott said. 'If you keep missing out on your sleep, your migraines will come back.'

'Good point.' Chris stood up and yawned. 'Thanks, mate.'

'Hey, I'm here for *you*.' Scott patted Chris on the back.

Chapter Five

Molly made extra overnight oats for Saskia, adding frozen fruit and a dollop of honey. Even though Saskia was twenty-three, Molly was very protective of her. Saskia's brain worked differently to hers. While Molly had excelled in school, got good grades, and gone straight to university, Saskia had struggled through school before eventually deciding on a performing arts degree.

After she graduated, Molly secured an internship at a publishing house in London, which led to a permanent job, and a long commute from Canterbury. Saskia had wanted to move to London too, as she'd always longed to be on the stage, but her plans were derailed by her mum dying in the second year of her degree. She'd had roles as a TV extra, and in the Canterbury city pantomime, but had fallen into a waitressing job rather than pursuing her dreams.

Saskia flew by the seat of her pants, while Molly had a plan and a timescale for everything. Everything except meeting Mark. In her last semester at university, she'd literally bumped into Mark in the library. With dark hair, olive skin, and deep brown eyes that burnt into hers, she was attracted to him instantly. He'd asked her out for a drink, and she'd fallen for him even more in the swanky bar that he'd taken her to. He'd made it clear how much he liked her, and they'd been together since that night.

He worked in international finance, and a year ago, he'd got a new job, which took him abroad a lot. She'd learnt to make the most of the time that they did get to spend together. He always arranged the best dates, in fancy restaurants or cool bars, before taking her back to his luxurious apartment in Canary Wharf. She'd had a message from him last night, with photos from Oslo, where was currently, meeting, or most likely partying, with clients. She was already looking forward to seeing him. After finishing her breakfast, she sent him a message.

> Can't wait to see you next weekend! Can we try the new Lebanese place? X

> Sure. Can you stay the whole weekend? You can go to work from mine on Monday morning X

This was Marks's subtle way of trying to convince her to move to London, but there was no way she was giving up her mum's house for his box of steel and glass. When they'd moved to England from France, she was only five, and her parents had little money. They'd struggled for the first few years there, until her dad's career suddenly took off. Her whole life was in Canterbury, and the house contained a lot of her memories of her mum, Nancy, who had died three years ago.

When she died, Saskia was still a teenager and struggled to even talk about it, so Molly had squashed her grief and taken care of Saskia as well as making sure the house, and all of the paperwork was taken care of. While their friends rallied around them, Mark was notably absent and didn't attend Nancy's funeral, saying it was too hard for him. Molly hadn't thought much of it at the time, but Saskia had never forgiven him for not supporting her.

Mark frequently told Molly that Saskia was wasting her life, and her performing arts degree by waitressing, but her mum's death had hit Saskia hard. Being caught in the middle was difficult. She loved them both. Saskia was fun, chaotic, and wild. Mark was steady, sure, and reliable. She hoped that one day he would change his mind about moving to Canterbury, and they would get married and bring their children up here, watching them learn to walk on the ancient floorboards just like she and Saskia had.

As the years went on, that dream was becoming less and less likely. Mark's job and his travel abroad took up most of his time, but she didn't like to think about the possibility that he wasn't her person. It was too painful. It was much easier to go on dates with him, to sink into his bed at the end of the night, and not think about the future.

She checked her watch and sucked in a deep breath. It was time to go. She put her bowl in the dishwasher, then picked up her bag and car keys, wondering if she'd ever be able to cycle to the station like she had for the last four years.

Her sister appeared, bleary eyed, still in her pyjamas.

'Sorry, my alarm didn't go off. Come on, let's go.' Saskia threw a coat over her pyjamas and pulled on her thick fleece lined boots.

Molly packed some of her brownies into a box, breathing in the heady, rich, chocolate scent, and got her umbrella. She ushered Saskia out of the door, her words all flying out in a nervous flurry.

'There's overnight oats in the fridge, you can take my car to work, but you need to fill it up and if you are able to pick me up tonight, I'd be super grateful.' She unlocked her car and climbed in, fastening her seatbelt.

'I may be working tonight. Ezio hasn't let me know yet, but I'll keep you posted.' Saskia put on her seatbelt. 'Let's go.'

The train was packed again as usual, but Molly read her book and didn't make eye contact with anyone. Her phone buzzed and she pulled it out of her pocket, smiling as she read Liz's message

> How's the commute going? I'm sending you all the love X

> I'm fine! I've made a train buddy. I make him cakes and he sits with me. X

> What a hero! I'd do anything for your cakes. X

Molly laughed and put away her phone.

That afternoon, Karl called Molly into his office, and her heart started pounding.

Karl smiled kindly at her. 'Sit down. It's nothing to worry about.'

Molly sat down on one of the leather chairs in front of his desk, which was littered with photos of his family, scribbled on manuscripts, and his giant notebook.

'I just wanted to check on you. I know you hate anyone asking how you're doing but it's important. You've been through a lot.' He rested his chin on his hand.

She bit her lip, then chose her words carefully. 'I know it'll take time for the anxiety to settle. Especially because anxious is my natural state anyway.' She laughed. 'I've been seeing a counsellor, the same woman I saw after my mum died, and she's been so helpful. I'm seeing her tonight when I get back to Canterbury.'

'I'm glad you've got someone to talk to,' he said. 'If we can do anything, if you need anything, just ask.'

'Thank you. I don't find it that easy to ask for help.' She smiled, and shifted in her seat, as a nagging voice in her head told her she was being a burden on him and her team. 'I'm used to just kind of getting on with it.'

'You don't have to just get on with it here, Molly. I hope you know that. Why not split your time between working at home and in the office?' he suggested. 'That would mean less commuting for you.'

'I'd love that, thank you.' Not having to worry about the commute every day would be a weight off her mind.

'How about we leave early tonight? What time's the next train?' he asked.

'Four thirty I think.' She checked her watch. 'I think we can make it if we leave now.'

'Get your things and I'll go with you,' he said. 'If you're seeing your counsellor tonight, then having some time to decompress before you get there would probably be good, right?'

'It would. Thank you.' Now she wouldn't have to stuff her dinner in before she went to see Colette. She stood up. 'I'll be ready in two minutes.' Hurrying out of Karl's office, she sent Saskia a message letting her know that she would be coming back early.

When she left Karl's office, her whole body felt lighter, like a weight had been lifted from her. The commute was long, and stressful, and the combination of that and her disrupted sleep made her feel permanently exhausted. The split between working at home and in London would allow her nervous system some time to regulate itself. She quickly grabbed her coat and bag, then followed Karl to the lift, and out into the neon lit cityscape.

'Any plans this weekend, Molly?' Karl asked as they walked to the station together.

Molly smiled. 'Uh yes, Saskia's hired Halloween costumes for us and we're going out in the city with some friends. How about you?'

His brow creased. 'My plans are slightly different to yours. I'm still doing up our bathroom, so I'm going to spend it tiling.'

'Wow, you're going to be busy.' Her weekend was going to be chaos, she knew it. Saskia and her friend Jess were both liabilities, and she had no idea what costume Saskia had got for her to wear. 'Part of me wishes I was tiling instead of going out.'

'Part of me wishes I was going out in a Halloween costume instead of tiling,' he said. 'It might be a bit scary for you to start with. but you'll have your friends with you and they'll look after you, right?'

She thought about this for a second. Saskia and Jess would look after her, but only until they were drunk. Then the tables would turn. Liz, her own best friend, would be far more reliable, and she was going to stick to her side all night.

When they reached the station, Molly scanned the board for her train and Karl followed her to the gate. 'See you on Monday,' she said as she pulled her ticket out of her pocket at the barrier to the platform. 'Thanks for, well, everything.'

'No problems,' he said. 'Have a drink for me, won't you?'

She nodded and swiped her ticket through the barrier, waved to Karl and made her way to the train. She didn't bother trying to find Chris. He wouldn't be there. It was too early. The seat next to her was soon taken by a man in a suit who immediately got a laptop out and spent the entire journey to his station typing.

She got off at Canterbury, spotting Saskia in her leopard print coat walking towards her.

'Evening! Check you out sneaking out early.' Saskia high-fived Molly.

'I'm not. My boss said I could leave early, and he came with me,' Molly said as Saskia drove them home.

'Either way that's a result.' Saskia raised an eyebrow. 'Only it isn't, is it? You're miserable because you didn't get to snuggle up with the lovely Chris all the way home.'

'Not true. I'm just tired.' Molly felt embarrassed about lying to Saskia. She had missed Chris on the train tonight, but it made her feel guilty, like she was cheating on Mark.

Saskia let them into the house and pulled off her leopard print coat. 'We need an early night tonight, Mole. Tomorrow night's going to be mayhem.'

'Wow, that's very sensible of you.' Molly nodded at her sister. 'I'm impressed.'

Saskia rolled her eyes. 'I have my moments.'

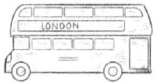

Chris spent the whole journey home worrying about Molly. He felt sick. Why wasn't she on the train? What if something had happened to her? He felt strangely responsible. He'd told her that he would be her bodyguard and she wasn't there. As the train pulled into Canterbury, the storm intensified, lashing him with rain as he walked back out of the station.

The walk back to his flat was cold and wet, and he shivered as he let himself in. After a hot shower he felt better, but Molly was still on his mind. He opened up his laptop, then the set list that Alex had sent to him. As he ran his eyes over it, he thought about Molly again, wishing her had her number, or some way of contacting her. His stomach lurched as he imagined her being hurt, or lonely, or afraid. Shit. His feelings for her were stronger than he thought. Her beautiful face, her kind nature. Her slightly snarky sense of humour. He was hooked on all of those things.

Telling himself that the next time he saw her, he would ask for her number, so that he would never feel like this again, he tried to focus on the set list. Once tomorrow night was over, he could relax. He had no idea if Alex was nervous. If he was, he would never let on. Chris sent him a message to let him know that he had checked the set list, and he replied almost immediately.

Thanks for that, mate. Are you wearing a costume tomorrow night?

No way! Are you?

Wait and see

He shook his head. His cousin had always been mysterious and didn't like revealing his feelings. Or at least that was how he had been, until he met Kate, his girlfriend, who didn't believe in holding anything back. He was more open now, but he still hid behind a carefully constructed emotional coat of armour a lot of the time, and particularly when he was on stage. Performing live was hard for him as he preferred to stay out of the limelight.

Chris felt exactly the same way, but they'd been DJing together for the last couple of years at Alex's family's hotel and taking it to another venue was the next step. It just made him feel sick with nerves. At least it was Scott's bar, somewhere he knew. He debated walking down there for a beer, but the rain was still lashing down outside, so instead, he shut the laptop and switched on the TV, trying to distract himself from thinking about tomorrow night.

Chapter Six

October 2014, Canterbury, Kent England

Every surface in Molly's bedroom was covered in clothes and make-up, but for once, she was ignoring the mess. She was having fun. As she slid the long black wig onto her head, she giggled at Saskia, who had somehow transformed her long blonde hair into short black hair, with a very convincing wig. Her sister was putting the skills she'd learnt on her performing arts degree to good use.

'Mole,' Saskia said, 'try not to smudge your make-up.' She finished adjusting her own wig and came over to Molly, helping her to get hers in the right place.

Molly looked at herself in the mirror, and gasped. 'Oh my God! You can't even tell that it's me. I look totally different.'

Saskia had whitened Molly's already pale skin, drawn delicate flicks of black eyeliner over her eyelids, and coated her lips in bright red lipstick.

'That's why I like acting. You can be whoever you like.' Saskia adjusted her black bow tie.

'I wouldn't have guessed you'd go for Gomez and Morticia Addams, but then I can never guess what's on your mind.' Molly blotted her lips on a tissue.

'I like it that way.' Saskia smoothed Molly's wig. 'It gives an air of mystery.'

Molly sipped the last of her drink, making sure not to smudge her lipstick. 'You can say that again.' She looked at Saskia, who was slipping on a velvet smoking jacket. 'You make quite a handsome man.'

Saskia cackled. 'It'll be a brave guy that hits on me tonight.'

'It will. Now can you help me into this dress?' Molly held out the skin-tight black dress that Saskia had hired for her. The sleeves tapered to a point and the back was scandalously low, with a short, flowing train.

'Of course, come here,' Saskia said, stuffing the cigar she was holding into her mouth.

Molly lifted her arms and Saskia helped her in, squeezing the tight fabric over her head and down her body.

'Hold on, Mole.' Saskia put the cigar in her pocket and picked up her phone. 'Pose for me, caramia.'

Molly burst out laughing and picked up the silk rose that Saskia had got for her, clutching it to her chest, and staring moodily into the camera. 'That any good?'

'Oh yes.' Saskia showed Molly the photo. 'Now put your arms around me and gaze longingly into my eyes.'

Just as Saskia took the photo, the doorbell rang.

'Oh shit, the taxi's here already,' Saskia said, grabbing her patent leather brogues and putting them on. 'We've got to go.'

Molly nodded and followed her down the stairs, then put on the scarlet stilettos that she had borrowed from Saskia. They were far too high for her, but the dress was too long without them and the last thing she wanted to do was to fall over in it.

Before Saskia opened the door, she turned to Molly. 'Mole, if you need to leave at any point, you say, and we go. Got it?'

'Got it.' Molly nodded.

Strangely, in her costume, she felt braver. Tonight, she was someone else. She started to understand why Saskia loved acting so much.

'I need to get back out there. I can't hide in this house every night. I need to remind myself that I'm not going to get mugged every time I go out in the dark.'

'Of course you won't. Stick with me and you will be just fine.' Saskia gave her a salute and opened the front door.

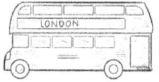

Molly was drunk. More drunk than she had been in a long time. It hadn't been her idea to do shots, but she was enjoying herself. Her arm was wrapped around Liz, and the two were singing at the top of their voices. Liz was Molly's sensible friend. They'd met at high school, where they were the studious ones, who always got their homework done.

Liz pulled Molly towards her, twirling her under her arm.

Molly laughed, stumbling over the hem of her dress. 'Ugh, not so fast,' she said. 'The room is spinning.'

Liz shook her head. 'Your sister's a bad influence.' She adjusted her witch's hat, and smoothed down her long purple wig, which concealed her natural dark hair. She was also wearing a long black dress, but hers was velvet and less revealing.

'What are you talking about?' Saskia wobbled over to Liz. 'I'm a great influence.'

Jess, Saskia's best friend let out a loud cackle. 'No, you're not,' she said.

Her pink hair was pulled into bunches on the side of her head, and she wore a nurse's white dress, splattered with fake blood. She and Saskia had dated for a while and had somehow stayed the best of friends after they broke up. They either flirted with each other, or bickered, and the more they drank, the worse it got.

Jess folded her arms. 'We're both as bad as each other.' She put her arm around Saskia.

Molly laughed. 'She's right,' she said to Saskia. 'You guys egg each other on.'

'Thank you,' Jess said.

As the song finished, Molly dragged her friends over to the bar, ordering them all bottles of water, handing them out like the mother hen she was. 'Drink this,' she said. 'You'll thank me tomorrow.'

Liz laughed. 'Molly, I'm not drinking. I'm driving you all home, remember?'

'Ah yes,' Molly said, giggling. 'I do now.' She looked at Liz's bottle of water. 'Well, drink it anyways, it's important to stay hyderatated.'

'Do you mean hydrated?' Liz asked, stifling a giggle.

'Yes, that too. Molly took the cap off her bottle and guzzled it.

'How do you manage to remember to do this, even when you're this drunk?' Saskia slurred.

'I don't know, it's like a reflex.' Molly shrugged.

'Are you OK?' Saskia put her arm around her sister.

'I'm fine, just a bit drunk!' Molly shouted over the music. 'Who's playing tonight? I've loved their entire set.'

'No idea,' Jess said, 'but I want their set list.'

The music changed from drum and bass to remixes of some of the 90's hip hop classics that they'd grown up with. As they danced in front of the DJ booth, Molly did a double take. Was that Chris behind the decks? She tried to focus but it was too dark to pick out his features. Her head felt fuzzy, and she felt like she was either going to burst into laughter or tears. Closing her eyes, as the bright lights streamed over her body, she forgot her fears. Flanked by her friends, and in her disguise, she felt safe, and for the first time in a while, brave.

When she came out of the ladies bathroom a while later, her eyes locked onto someone sitting on a stool at the bar. *Chris.* She turned to Saskia, who was beside her, hoping she hadn't seen him. They were both far too drunk to talk to him right now. It was too late though. Saskia had followed her gaze.

'Mole!' Saskia bellowed. 'It's Chris.' She pointed at him, before bursting out laughing.

Molly put her hand over Saskia's mouth. 'Don't come over,' she said to her, 'unless I look like I'm embarrassing myself, in which case, promise you'll drag me away from him.'

'I don't make promises, Mole, you know that,' Saskia replied, before smoothing Molly's hair. 'Go get him, tiger.'

'Hello,' Chris stared blankly at the woman in front of him. She'd just said hello to him, but he had no idea who she was. She had long black hair, a white face and deep, blood red lipstick. Not only was she ridiculously sexy in her tight black dress, but she knew his name.

'Chris, it's me, Molly.' She burst out laughing.

'Molly? I didn't recognise you.' Chris gulped. The dress clung to every curve, and she was taller than usual, her eyes almost level with his. 'I would never have guessed it was you.'

Molly twirled. 'Pretty weird, huh? I keep jumping when I see myself in the mirror.' She moved closer to him, wobbling slightly in her heels. 'Was that you I saw up there on the stage?'

He nodded and took her arm to steady her. 'It was me.' His heart started pounding faster as she gripped onto his arm. Her glacial blue eyes sparkled under the bright lights. 'I'm not the famous one, though. My cousin Alex is Celestial, I don't know if you've heard of him?'

Her eyes widened. 'No way!' she said, laughing. 'I love him. He's amazing. What about you? Have I heard of you? What's your stage name?'

'Sub Zero. I doubt you would have heard of me. I've not been doing it as long as Alex.' He smiled as Alex walked over. 'Alex, come and meet one of your adoring fans.'

He relinquished his grip on her arm as Alex joined them.

Alex smiled at Molly and raised an eyebrow. 'Nice to meet you…uh Morticia.'

'This is Molly. We met on the commute,' Chris said to Alex.

He hadn't told Alex about Molly, as his cousin was incredibly perceptive, and he was afraid Alex would know that he had feelings for her.

'I'm just fangirling right now,' she said, smiling at Alex. 'I love your remixes. They're so good.' She pulled out her phone. 'I've got your Nero and Wilkinson remixes on one of my playlists.'

'Ah, wow, you've made my night. Tonight's our first night here. I don't do live sets very often.' He looked up at the stage, where another DJ had taken over. 'I loved it, but I'm glad it's over.'

'Well, it was *phenomenal*,' Molly said. She ran her eyes over Alex's jacket, which was embroidered with silver skulls.. 'I love your jacket. It's so spooky.'

'It's my nod to a Halloween costume,' Alex replied. 'My girlfriend embroidered the skulls onto this jacket for me.'

Chris felt a pang of jealousy. Alex was taller than him, with dark hair and a general air of mystery which seemed to have a magnetic effect, drawing women to him.

'Alex is too cool for fancy dress.' Chris smiled.

'Where's your costume?' Molly asked Chris.

'Playing live makes me nervous enough. I couldn't face doing it in a costume,' Chris said. 'Although at least if I was shit, no one would know who I was.' He looked up as Alex's girlfriend, Kate, dressed in a black catsuit and velvet cat ears walked over, wrapping herself around Alex. He nodded to Molly. 'As you can see, Kate isn't afraid to get dressed up.'

'Any excuse,' Kate said, kissing Alex on the cheek. 'Banging set, guys.' She turned to Molly. 'I love your costume! Chris, who is this beautiful woman? Is she with you?'

'This is my friend Molly. We catch the train together.' Chris took a deep breath. He loved Kate, but sometimes she had no filter. 'Molly, this is Kate, Alex's girlfriend.'

'So good to meet you,' Molly smiled at Kate. 'I love your outfit.'

'Thanks, it's fine until you have to go to the bathroom.' Kate laughed, making Molly laugh too.

Chris's jaw dropped as someone walked up to Molly and slid an arm around her.

'Loved your set, Chris.' She turned to Kate and Alex. 'Who are you two?'

'Saskia?' Chris frowned, certain it was her.

'Call me Gomez.' Saskia smirked at Chris.

Molly and Saskia exchanged a look, one that Chris couldn't interpret.

'This is Alex, my cousin, and his girlfriend, Kate,' Chris said. 'You liked the music tonight then?'

'Definitely,' Saskia said. 'You guys were awesome.'

Scott appeared behind the bar. 'Can I get anyone a drink?'

'No thanks,' Molly said. 'We're just leaving.'

'Molly, Saskia, this is my brother, Scott,' Chris said, noticing that Saskia and Scott were gazing at each other.

'Hi there,' Saskia said to Scott. 'I'm Saskia.'

Scott studied her face. 'Hi Saskia. Your make-up is really good.'

'Thank you, I'm an actress, so I've got a little bit of experience with stage make-up. I don't usually look like this.' Saskia's blush was still visible underneath her white make-up.

'The moustache suits you,' Scott said drily.

'Thank you,' Saskia smiled. 'You're cute.'

Chris rolled his eyes. Typical. He and Molly had been talking to each other for what felt like weeks, and he hadn't even asked for her number. Scott had only just met Saskia, but she was clearly already enamoured with him. He let out a long exhale and turned back to Molly, who was trying to climb onto the stool next to him. He held out his hand and she took it, sliding onto the stool.

'Thanks,' she said. 'These heels are a nightmare.' She looked up at the stage and wrinkled her nose. 'I don't love these guys. You were so much better.'

Even with all of the make-up, he could see that her eyes were glazed, and she was giggling far too much. 'Are you alright, Molly? Have you guys been drinking tonight?' He glanced at Saskia, who was laughing hysterically at whatever Scott was saying.

'We might have had a *few* drinks,' Molly said. 'You are so beautiful, Chris. Do you know that?' She squeezed his hand tightly, her scarlet nails pressing into his skin.

'You're beautiful too, Molly,' he said. The feel of her hand against his was making his heart rate rocket, but she was drunk, and he was worried. 'How are you guys getting home? Do you need a lift?'

She shook her head. 'Oh no, my friend Liz will take us home. She's our designated driver tonight. There she is! Liz!' She called to a woman in a long purple dress, who walked over to her.

'Is this guy bothering you, Molly?' The woman folded her arms and narrowed her eyes.

'No, silly,' Molly said, giggling. 'This is Chris. You know, my train buddy.'

'Right.' Liz nodded. 'Cake boy.'

Chris snorted with laughter. 'Cake boy?'

'Yeah, you protect Moll, and she brings you cake,' Liz said. 'Lovely to meet you.'

'Same.' Chris smiled at Liz. 'I hear you're the one that's got to get this lot home tonight.'

'Yep. That's the plan. They're all staying at Molly's so I'll just open the door and throw them in. They can fend for themselves.' Liz rolled her eyes.

Chris laughed. 'Good luck.'

'We have to go,' Molly said to Chris. 'It was so good seeing you.' She planted a scarlet kiss on his cheek.

'See you on Monday,' he replied, breathing in her sweet coconut scent. As she turned away from him, the low cut back of her dress revealed a tattoo across her shoulder blade. In fine black lines, it was a galleon, sailing through choppy water. It was exactly how he felt about tonight.

The following morning, Chris lay in bed replaying the previous night. The nerves that had plagued him before his set had disappeared once it had started, replaced by adrenaline. The best part of the night had been seeing Molly in her costume. She'd told him he was beautiful, then disappeared, leaving him with nothing but a glimpse of her tattoo. A knock at his bedroom door interrupted his thoughts.

'Come in!' he shouted.

Morning mate.' Scott opened the door and walked in, wearing a hoodie and a pair of checked pyjama bottoms. He put a cup of coffee on Chris's bedside table.

'Thanks,' Chris said and picked up the coffee, taking a large gulp. 'I needed that.'

'What's up?' Scott sat down on the armchair next to Chris's bed, drinking his own coffee.

'Last night.' Chris shook his head. 'I'm so confused.'

'You smashed it.' Scott nodded approvingly. 'The crowd loved it. You guys had more bootlegs than a noughties jeans factory.'

'Nice reference.' Chris laughed. 'The set was great. It's just everything else that was confusing.'

'I see what you mean about Molly. She's gorgeous *and* she's vulnerable. When she arrived at the bar, she was clinging to Saskia like her life depended on it. Did you swap numbers?' Scott asked.

'No, she'd had too much to drink. We didn't really talk much,' Chris said.

What she had said had stayed with him though. Why had she called him beautiful? Was it the alcohol or was that how she really felt?

'Saskia's pretty hot too. Even dressed like Gomez Addams, she was stunning.' Scott laughed.

Chris glowered at Scott. 'Don't fuck around with her, Scott. Do not pull your hot barman shit with her.'

Scott shook his head. 'I did try. But she called me right out on it. I've asked her out. On a date.'

Chris groaned. 'You don't do relationships.'

'I might for her. She's something else. I couldn't really see her face, but I know she's hot, and she's so funny.' Scott took a sip of his coffee. 'What are you going to do about Molly?'

'I don't know,' Chris replied. 'I've been out of the game so long that I don't know the rules.'

'Time to start playing, my friend.' Scott stood up. 'Get up and get yourself showered. We're going to Mum and Dad's for breakfast.'

Molly opened her eyes and groaned. Her head was pounding, and the light streaming in from the open curtains hurt her eyes. She was in her own bed, but she wasn't alone. And her roommate was messy. Her bedside table was covered in an assortment of random items. A black wig, a pint of water, half a lemon, and a half eaten packet of gummy bears.

'Is it morning already?' Saskia croaked as she opened her eyes.

'Saskia,' Molly hissed. 'I kissed him.'

'What?' Saskia mumbled, rubbing her eyes. She was still wearing the frilled shirt from the night before, and the sleeve flopped over her face.

'I kissed Chris last night. Oh shit, this is bad.' Molly lay back on the pillow.

'You kissed him on the cheek!' Saskia retorted. 'What's wrong with that?'

'I've never done that before. He'll think it was weird.' She covered her face with her hands.

'Can you noisy bitches keep it down?' Jess stumbled into the room, her pink hair sticking up.

'Morning, love.' Saskia smiled at Jess. 'Molly shove over. Make room.'

Molly frowned as it all came back to her. After they'd got back from the bar last night, Saskia had offered Jess her bed, so Molly had let Saskia share hers. And Saskia being Saskia, had got into bed with a bag of sweets. They'd obviously both fallen asleep before they could take Molly's pre-emptive hangover cure of painkillers, water and lemon. That would explain why she felt so awful. She shuffled over, and Jess, still in her nurse's outfit, climbed into the bed next to Saskia.

'Well, this is cosy.' Jess shut her eyes. 'Three pissheads in a bed.'

'Don't lump me in with you two.' Molly sat up, regretting it instantly as her head started swimming. 'I've not been that drunk for ages.'

Jess shrugged. 'It's a normal Saturday night for us.'

'Ignore her.' Saskia said to Jess. 'She's just mad at herself because she kissed her *friend* last night.' She turned to Molly. 'Mole, you can't hide it. I could feel the chemistry between you.'

'But...I can't have feelings for him,' Molly croaked. 'I feel so embarrassed.'

'He did not look like he was complaining.' Saskia started giggling.

'This is some dramatic love triangle shit,' Jess said. 'And I'm totally here for it.'

Chapter Seven

November 2014, Canterbury, Kent, England

'Morning Chris.' Molly smiled at him as the train pullled into the station.

She was feeling proud of herself. Yes, her hangover had wiped out most of yesterday, but she had got up this morning to catch the early train. However, she had just come face to face with Chris, and she cringed as she remembered kissing his cheek and holding his hand on Saturday night. This was why she didn't drink. She always ended up embarrassing herself.

'Morning, Molly,' he said, smiling back at her.

They got onto the train and sat down next to each other.

'I'm so sorry if I embarrassed you at the weekend.' She was sure he was thinking about it, but he was too polite to say anything. 'I hadn't drunk that much in such a long time.'

'I'm beautiful, am I?' He raised his eyebrow.

She wasn't afraid. She was going to own it. 'You are beautiful. You're not just handsome, you're kind, and caring. Beautiful.'

'Well, that's a glowing review.' His cheeks flushed, and he rubbed the back of his neck. 'You're all of those things too, you know.'

'I am?' she squeaked. Now she was caught off guard. She could feel her own cheeks flushing. 'That's so sweet. I... I had a bit too much to drink and I was worried I'd embarrassed you, or me, or both of us.' She was rambling, but she couldn't stop herself.

'You didn't embarrass anyone. I had a great night.' He paused. 'So did Scott. He can't stop talking about your sister.'

'Saskia's the same,' she said, lowering her voice. 'I knew from the minute they met that she'd fallen for him. She might be an actress, but she's so obvious.'

He laughed. 'So is Scott. You always know what he's thinking. He's not like you.'

'What do you mean?' she asked.

'You're like an onion. There are so many layers. I feel like I've only seen a few of them.' He raised his eyebrow.

'Same.' She smiled. 'You didn't tell me you were a DJ.'

He shrugged. 'I don't tell many people. Alex is also super private about it. What did you think of our set?'

'I loved it,' she said. 'I've already downloaded the playlist from his website. I listen to music all the time, and my playlists are so varied.'

'Which one do you listen to the most?' he asked.

'Don't judge me, but it's this one.' Scrolling through her phone, she pulled up her favourite playlist. 'Fall Out Boy, Green Day, Panic at the Disco, I love them all so much.'

His eyes widened. 'I would not have guessed that at all. You are a mystery.'

She handed him an earbud. 'Let me drag you away from the drum and bass, over to the dark side.'

'I'd let you lead me to the dark side any day, Molly,' he said, raising his eyebrow.

Her heart pounding, she held his gaze. The effect he had on her was mesmerising. She couldn't tear herself away from him. But she had to. He put the earbud in his ear, still holding her gaze and she smiled.

'Let me know what you think. I won't be offended if you hate it,' she said, forcing herself to break eye contact with him.

She pulled her book out of her bag and opened it. She was playing it safe today, with a travel book by one of her favourite explorers. Reading smut with him sat next to her was too dangerous a game.

'So far so good,' he said as the first song started playing.

He got out his own book, and Molly breathed a sigh of relief. She could immerse herself in her book and try to ignore the warm, contented feeling that washed over her as his arm pressed up against hers.

When the train arrived in London, Molly stuck closely to Chris's side as they walked across the concourse together.

'Can I walk you to your office?' he asked. 'Mine is just around the corner, and I figured you might want some company.'

She wondered what expression was on her traitorous face. She'd been aiming for brave, steely determination, but in reality, she was probably displaying wide-eyed fear.

'Of course.' She nodded. 'I'd like that.'

When they reached her building, he leant towards her, and she kissed him on the cheek, before jumping back in horror as his cheeks coloured. 'I'm so sorry, I thought we were cheek kissing.'

He pulled a piece of fluff from her hair. 'I was just going to grab this. Don't worry about it, I don't mind.' He smiled.

She shook her head. 'My dad's French. I'm so used to kissing on the cheek. It just comes naturally to me.'

'You didn't mention that.' He raised his eyebrow.

Yes, and there's a very good reason for that, she thought to herself.

'Ah well, like you said, many layers.' She pushed open the glass door of her building, then turned back to Chris. 'Au revoir, mon ami.'

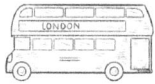

That evening, Molly unlocked her front door and threw her keys onto the table in the hall. She pulled off her boots and coat and walked into the living room. Saskia was stretched out on the sofa watching a film.

'What's up, Mole?' Saskia frowned at her. 'I thought you'd be buzzing. You were up and out on the early train. I'm so proud of you.'

'When I got to London, it felt great.' She slumped onto the sofa next to Saskia. 'Then I had a shit journey back and it rattled me a bit.'

'What happened?' Saskia narrowed her eyes.

Molly debated lying to her sister or at least concealing some of the truth but decided against it. Saskia would know. 'I missed my usual train, and therefore, Chris. The only seat was in a group of four, with three men who leered at me and made obscene comments about my dress. It was peeking out of my coat, and they were amused by the cat print.' She looked meaningfully at Saskia.

'Ohhhhh. Ew! What arseholes. Did you report them?' Saskia asked.

'To who? And what would anyone do about it?' Molly sighed. 'I didn't let them get to me. I just put my earbuds in and ignored them.'

'You were so brave today. I'm proud of you,' Saskia said. 'A few weeks ago that would have had you in tears. How do you feel now? I've got a date tonight, but if you need me to stay in, then I will.'

Molly shook her head. She needed Saskia to stop being so nice. She was too close to tears. 'No, it's fine. I'm going to see Colette. I'll talk to her about it.'

'Are you sure?' Saskia frowned. 'I can totally postpone.'

'No, I promise you, I'm fine.' Molly smiled. 'Are you excited about seeing Scott again?'

'I am. He intrigues me.' Saskia grinned. 'Most of the time guys feed me cheesy lines and expect me to fall at their feet. He tried that and I called him out on it straight away. He liked that, and I like him. Can you come and help me choose an outfit?'

'Sure.' Molly pulled herself to her feet and followed Saskia to her chaotic bedroom.

When Saskia finally left the house, Molly was exhausted. Saskia had emptied most of her wardrobe onto her bed to find an outfit for her date, then almost talked herself out of going before eventually getting dressed and leaving the house in a taxi. Having waved goodbye to her at the door, Molly spotted Saskia's house keys on the table in the hall. She shook her head and sent her sister a text to let her know that she had forgotten them.

As she went to stuff her phone back into her pocket, it rang. She answered it and Mark's handsome face filled the screen of her phone.

'Hey. How are you?' he asked.

She could see his hotel room in the background, and the plush white bedding on the bed he was lying on.

'I'm good. Work's fine, I'm getting braver with the commute, and I went out with the girls for Halloween.' She giggled. 'I'm still recovering actually.'

'I knew you'd bounce back. You're so strong.' He smiled at her.

'I don't know, it's still tough...'

'I'll be back on Friday,' he said, interrupting her. 'You're still coming to stay for the weekend, right?'

'Of course,' she replied. 'Can't wait.'

'Me neither. I've got to go. I've got dinner with clients tonight. See you on Friday. Love you.'

'Love you.' She hung up.

She was already looking forward to the weekend. They would go out and eat the kind of food she wouldn't dream of cooking at home, then when they got back to his apartment, he would show her with his actions, not his words, how much he had missed her.

After eating some leftover lasagne, she put a film on and wrapped a blanket tightly around her. Saskia had got a fire going in the living room before she went out, so the room was warm and cosy, and as she tried to concentrate on the film, she felt her eyes closing.

Molly's eyes shot open, a loud knocking sound disturbing her from her sleep. Her heart started pounding.

'Molly! Are you there?'

A shout came from outside the house. She breathed a sigh of relief. It was Saskia.

'I'm coming, hold on.' She pulled herself to her feet and walked to the door, grabbing her keys, and unlocking it.

'I've been out here for ages!' Saskia's eyes were fiery, and she had her hands on her hips.

'I'm so sorry,' Molly said. 'I locked the door after you left and then I fell asleep. How did the date go?'

'Mmm.' Saskia closed her eyes. 'He's the best.'

Molly laughed. 'Are you going to elaborate?'

'We went to Forno and had pizzas and frozen margaritas. He didn't try any cheesy lines and he kept his hands to himself. Who would have thought that the tattooed, gorgeous barman would be a gentleman?' Saskia shrugged.

'Oh I had a feeling he would be.' Molly beamed at Saskia. 'I'm so happy for you.'

'He's asked me to see him again.' Saskia paused. 'That's the tricky part. I want to see him too, but I'm waiting for a call back from an audition and if I get it, I won't be in the city much longer.'

Molly's eyebrows shot up. 'What's the job? And where is it?' She started to feel anxious.

Saskia wrinkled her nose. 'It would be in London, and I'd have to go up there for at least a month. That's all I'm saying.'

'London?' Molly's voice came out higher than she'd intended it to. She tried to keep her tone, and her face neutral as she spoke. 'That's incredible. I'll wait to hear more when you want to tell me, and I'll keep everything crossed for you.'

'Thank you,' Saskia said. 'I know you've always got my back, and I love you for it.'

'I love you too.' Molly smiled.

She was happy for her sister, but there was a sadness creeping over her. The thought that Saskia might leave her, and not come back. She pushed it to the back of her mind, determined not to let her true feelings show.

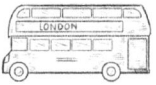

The following morning, Chris was making a cup of tea when Scott walked into the kitchen.

'Morning, mate.' Scott grinned at Chris.

'I'm guessing last night went well.' Chris raised an eyebrow. He slid the mug over to Scott, got another one out of the cupboard and made himself another cup of tea.

'Are you going to tell me about it?' Chris took a sip of his tea.

Scott nodded. 'It was good. We really clicked.' He held up his hands as Chris raised his eyebrow at him. 'Not like that. I don't do one night stands anymore. We just talked. No bullshit. Just two people actually talking to each other. She loved the pizza and the cocktails. Obviously, they weren't as good as mine.' He smiled. 'I really like her.'

'Happy for you, mate.' Chris put his mug down. He was happy for Scott, but at the same time, he felt jealous. Scott had gone for it with Saskia, and he was still working up the courage to ask Molly out.

'Thanks. It just went too fast,' Scott said. 'She doesn't stop talking. I think I heard her whole life story last night. I'm seeing her tomorrow night, so I'll get part two.'

Chris laughed. Saskia was such a contrast to Molly, whose layers he was still unpeeling.

'Did you know that their mum died three years ago?' Scott asked. 'That's got to be so hard. I mean, I didn't even know my mum and I still get upset thinking about her. Saskia said that Molly kind of took over from her mum when she died and looks after her.' He paused. 'Like you do with me.'

'I didn't know that. She doesn't talk about her parents. Did you tell her about your parents?' Chris asked.

'No,' Scott said. 'I don't think it's first date conversation material. I need to figure out if it's going anywhere before I casually drop the fact that my alcoholic dad used to hit me and I ran away from home when I was five.' He paused. 'Does Molly know?'

Chris took a sip of his tea. 'She knows your home situation was rough, and that Mum adopted you. I didn't tell her the whole story. It's not my story to tell.'

'I wish it wasn't my story. I didn't tell her much about me at all. She obviously knows I'm your younger brother and that we live together.' He smirked at Chris's raised eyebrow. 'I know I'm only a few months younger, but it still counts.' He paused. 'It's late. Aren't you usually leaving by now?'

'I'm not going into work today. I've got a doctor's appointment at ten.' Chris bit his lip.

'The migraines?' Scott frowned.

'Yeah, I'm struggling to keep on top of them.' Chris ran his hand through his hair. 'They've been getting worse over the last few weeks, and last night's one was bad. I've barely slept.'

'I don't start until midday. You want me to come with you?' Scott finished his tea and took his mug over to the sink.

'No, but I appreciate the offer.' Chris finished his tea. 'Do you want some breakfast? My painkillers have just kicked in.'

'No. You sit there. I'll do it.' Scott walked over to the fridge and opened it. 'As I said to you the other night, you've got to stop thinking about everyone else all the time. Let someone be there for you.' He pulled out a box of eggs. 'Scrambled eggs on toast?'

'That would be great.' Chris smiled at Scott.

On Friday morning Molly lugged her scarlet red suitcase down the stairs and stuck it into the hall. She'd packed a couple of dresses and pairs of heels, as well as some very revealing underwear. After almost three weeks apart, she was ready to reconnect with Mark. She hoped that she could get away with eating her breakfast and sneaking out of the door before Saskia woke up. She wasn't the best in the mornings but would be even worse if she spotted the suitcase. Her hatred of Mark knew no bounds.

She made herself a bowl of granola, fruit and yoghurt and sat down at the dining table. It felt strangely quiet without Saskia, and tomorrow morning she would wake up in Mark's sleek, modern apartment. She already knew how the weekend would go. There would be drinks at a fancy bar, dinner at an expensive restaurant, and then he would take her back to his apartment and show her how pleased he was to see her. The only thing that was missing was an emotional connection, but he didn't seem to want that, and she had Saskia and Liz to have deep and meaningful conversations with. Mark was just for fun.

Knowing that Saskia had a long shift at the restaurant ahead of her, Molly made her a granola bowl and left it in the fridge, before checking her watch and realising she needed to leave. She'd just put her coat on when Saskia came down the stairs in her pyjamas.

'You're off early.' Saskia spotted the suitcase next to Molly and rolled her eyes. 'Oh yes, moron Mark has allowed you to go and spend the weekend with him in his box of glass in London. How delightful.'

Molly didn't bother arguing with Saskia. She wasn't going to get anywhere. 'I'll be back on Monday evening.' She gave Saskia a cheerful smile. 'Enjoy your date with Scott tomorrow night.'

'I will.' Saskia ran her hands through her hair. 'Have a good weekend too.' She ambled over and gave Molly a hug. 'I'm sorry. I'll try and keep my feelings about Mark to myself.'

'Maybe just tone it down a little?' Molly sighed. 'I hate that you two don't get on.'

'Sorry, Mole.' Saskia shrugged. 'I can't help how I feel. He's not good enough for you.'

Molly's eyes flicked to the clock on the wall. 'We'll have to carry this on another time. I'm going to miss my train.'

Saskia huffed and put her slippers on, picking up Molly's suitcase and following her out of the door. She put the suitcase on the pavement and gave her a hug. 'See you on Monday.'

'Keep me posted on tomorrow night.' Molly kissed Saskia's cheek. 'Be safe.'

'Always. Love you,' Saskia replied.

Molly opened the door of the waiting taxi and put her suitcase into it. 'Love you too. Go inside, you'll freeze out here.' She climbed into the back of the taxi and waved at Saskia as the driver pulled away.

On the train, Molly struggled to concentrate on her book. She hadn't seen Chris all week and it worried her. She should be thinking about Mark, but Chris was comforting, and strangely familiar. These were all things that she couldn't tell anyone else, especially Liz and Saskia, and definitely not Mark.

Mark was the only thing in her life that had been constant, and stable, but a horrible nagging feeling that maybe he wasn't the best partner for her lurked in the pit of her stomach. Maybe dates in fancy restaurants and cocktails in swanky bars weren't enough to keep them together. Pushing that thought to the back of her mind, she hurried off the train.

'Ooh, someone's off for a nice weekend.' Sue raised her eyebrow as Molly walked up to the reception desk.

'Morning, Sue. I'm staying at Mark's this weekend,' Molly said, adjusting her bag on her shoulder.

Sue raised an eyebrow. 'Very nice, what have you got planned?'

'No idea, he likes to surprise me.' Molly laughed. She thought it would be a relaxed laugh, but it shot out as a hideous cackle that echoed around the huge lobby.

Sue's eyebrows shot up. 'I've not heard you make that sound before.'

Molly shook her head. 'I'm sorry. It usually only comes out when I'm nervous.'

'Are you nervous?' Sue frowned at Molly. 'Haven't you two been together for a while?'

'Oh yes. We've been together for four years. I'm definitely not nervous.' Molly gripped the handle of her suitcase. She was sure that her guilty secret was written across her face.

I'm cheating on my boyfriend in my head with the guy from the train.

'Right.' Sue's frown dissipated and she smoothed down her blouse. 'Hope you have a wonderful weekend together, love.'

'Thank you, you too,' Molly said, hurriedly and she walked away, she felt her cheeks burning. Why did she feel so guilty when she hadn't done anything wrong?

Chapter Eight

Molly arrived at Mark's flat after staying late at work, then taking an expensive taxi ride to Canary Wharf.

'Evening, gorgeous,' Mark said as he opened the door to her and ushered her inside.

She beamed at him, her stomach fluttering as he slid his arms around her. 'Right back at you.'

He was a good few inches taller than her, and she had to stand on her tiptoes to kiss him, running her hands through his dark hair. She breathed in his woody aftershave and squealed as he lifted her up, running his lips down her neck.

'Wow, you're pleased to see me, huh?' she murmured.

'I always am.' He took her coat from her and hung it on the hook behind her, then wheeled her case into his bedroom.

She went into the living room and tried to make herself comfy on the boxy leather sofa, then pulled her phone out of her bag to send a message to Saskia.

> Got to Mark's safely. Hope work was OK, and you got some good leftovers. Love you X

Mark walked back in with two glasses of wine, handing one to her, before sitting down next to her. 'Santé.' He clinked his glass against hers. 'Glad it's the weekend?'

'I'm glad that I get to spend it with you.' She took a sip of her wine.

'Same.' He frowned at her canvas satchel. 'That bag is hideous.'

'Are we going to go there again?' She rolled her eyes.

He pushed up the sleeves of his cashmere sweater. 'You didn't get mugged just because you were carrying a £600 handbag.'

She shrugged. 'I was mugged the day after you gave it to me. No one was ever interested in *this* bag.'

'I said I was sorry, and I meant it. That bag was a gift. I had no idea that would happen.' His jaw tightened.

'Maybe we should just stop talking about it,' she said. 'I appreciated the gift, and the sentiment behind it.'

He nodded. 'So you're over it now?'

'I don't know about over it.' She paused. 'I'm seeing Colette again, and Ed and Karl have been so supportive. I made a friend on the train too.'

'What's she like?' he asked.

'*He* is very nice,' she said. 'He works in IT at Invest Tech. Do you know it? Their building is near mine.'

'Yeah, I know it.' He stood up, frowning at her. 'So, this guy has randomly decided to sit next to you every night, for no reason. What's he expecting in return?'

'Cake!' She burst out into nervous laughter. 'I'm the baker, he's my bodyguard.'

'Right.' He nodded. 'That's all he wants. Cake?'

'Yes. He's my friend. He's helped me through a difficult time.'

She wanted to say that Chris had shown more concern for her than Mark had, but now was not the time. It would only make things worse.

He took her hands in his. 'I'm jealous, Moll. I've been away for ages, and I don't like thinking about you with another man.'

'I'm not *with* another man,' she said.

'I didn't mean it like that.' He took a sip of his wine. 'How do you know you can trust him?' he asked.

She hesitated. How *did* she know?

'I just know. My gut tells me he's a good guy. And Saskia's dating his brother, so I've got to know him too.'

'How nice,' he remarked. 'If this guy is genuinely helping you and he doesn't have some ulterior motive, then that's great, but I know what guys are like.'

'That's a pretty damning review of your own sex,' she said.

He shrugged. 'I'm just being honest. I love you, Molly, and I want to protect you.'

She had never seen him envious of anyone before, and she wasn't sure she liked it. She didn't want to be *claimed* like a possession, but she also didn't want this weekend to end in an argument.

When he kissed her, she sank into him, and pushed her thoughts to the back of her mind. Their relationship wasn't perfect, but who had the perfect relationship?

Molly woke up in Mark's dark bedroom, realising the bed was empty next to her. She pulled his bathrobe over her floral pyjamas and walked into the kitchen.

'Morning Moll.' Mark smiled at her, as he spread butter on his toast, under the glare of the spotlights in his high tech, minimalist kitchen. 'I didn't want to wake you. Do you want a coffee?'

She frowned at him. 'You know I don't drink coffee.' After four years why didn't he remember that? 'Do you still have some of my tea bags here?'

'Of course. In the cupboard.' He nodded to the cupboard behind him.

She flicked the kettle on and slid her arms around him, kissing his cheek. 'What's the plan for today?' She stole a piece of his toast and sat on one of the stools tucked under the end of his kitchen island.

He put another slice of bread into the toaster. 'They have an exhibition of pirate and privateer artefacts at the Maritime Museum. I thought that you might like to go to that.'

'I would!' Molly said. 'You know how much I love pirates.'

'I do. My mum's asked us to go over for dinner.' He paused. 'But we don't have to. I can book a restaurant.'

'I'd love to see your mum.'

She wished she could pop round to see her own mum for dinner. It annoyed her that Mark was so blasé about his mum. His dad was another matter. She would gladly go a long time without seeing him, and so would Mark.

He handed her a jar of apricot jam - her favourite - and she spread it onto the plate of toast that he passed her.

'I'll let her know we'll be coming over.' Picking up his own plate of toast and coffee, he sat down next to her. 'She sends me all these messages all the time. I don't think she's got used to me not being around so much now that I've got this job.'

'I don't think I have either,' she said softly as she ate her toast.

His expression was unreadable, and she wondered what he was thinking. He said nothing, just sipped his coffee and ate his toast.

Once he'd finished his breakfast, he picked up his phone and typed out a message. His phone buzzed almost immediately and he smiled. 'Mum's excited that we're coming over. She's going to make some baklava for us.'

'Yum! I love her baklava.' Molly smiled. 'When did you last see them?'

He rubbed a hand over her chin. 'Not since we all went out for dinner a couple of months ago.'

She frowned. 'You haven't seen them since then? Do you ever see them if I'm not with you?'

A pattern was starting to emerge, and this was something she had never brought up with him before.

'I take Mum out for lunch sometimes,' he said, somewhat defensively.

'And your dad?' She raised an eyebrow.

'He's always working.' He stood up and picked up her empty plate. 'Do you want any more toast?'

Nice deflection, she thought to herself.

'I'm good, thank you,' she said.

The conversation was obviously over.

'Sorry that I don't have any fruit or granola for breakfast,' he said as he stacked the dishwasher.

'It doesn't matter,' she replied. 'I didn't realise I was so predictable.'

'I could set my watch by you. You have fruit and granola for breakfast. You go to yoga on Thursday evenings and Sunday mornings. You always get Chinese takeaway on a Tuesday night.' He raised an eyebrow. 'Do you want me to go on?'

She groaned. 'I am that predictable, so boring. You're spot on.'

'Maybe one day you'll do something totally out of character, and you'll surprise yourself.' He kissed her cheek.

'Unlikely. Saskia is the unpredictable one. I had to be the boring one, so that she could be the fun one.' She stared out of the window at the boats going down the Thames.

'She's a bit more than unpredictable. Is she still working at the restaurant?' He brushed the crumbs off his fingers.

'She's waiting for a call back for an audition.' She clutched her mug tightly as she spoke. 'I don't know any more than that. Whatever it is, I hope she gets it. She's been stuck in a rut for so long.'

'You worry too much about her. She's an adult. She can make her own choices,' he said.

She glared at him. He didn't understand at all. 'She's all I've got. I have to take care of her.'

He frowned. 'That's not true. What about your dad? What about me?'

Her eyes narrowed as she responded. 'Papa lives in France; I see him four or five times a year. I see you a couple of times a month when you're not abroad somewhere. I *live* with Saskia. I see her every day. I'm bound to be overprotective, I'm her big sister.'

'You could live here, then we could see more of each other,' he said.

'How would we see more of each other?' Her chest tightened. 'You work abroad for most of the month.' She looked around the room. 'I'd just be here on my own all the time.'

'We'd have more time together when I'm here. You wouldn't be two hours away.' He took a sip of his coffee. 'I'm not trying to pressure you into anything. It's just a suggestion.'

She nodded. He said he wasn't trying to pressure her, but every time she was here, they had the same conversation. Could she be happy here? She stared out of the window. 'I suppose I could get used to this view.'

He ran a hand through his messy dark curls. 'What, you mean me in the morning?'

She gave him a playful shove. 'No, silly, the one from the window. I love watching the boats. Although...' She turned her face up towards his. 'I suppose you're not that bad to look at either.'

He stood up, his hands on his hips. 'Not that bad? Is that all you can manage?'

She laughed as he scooped her up and carried her down the hall to his bedroom, throwing her onto the bed. He climbed on top of her, kissing her neck.

She squealed as his teeth grazed her skin. 'Aren't we supposed to be going out?'

'It can wait,' he said.

The sun shone as Molly walked hand in hand with Mark away from the Maritime Museum.

'So, was that what you'd expected? They seemed to have some good stuff. As soon as I heard it was pirates, I knew you'd love it.' Mark slipped his hand into Molly's.

'I did love it. I love the history of piracy, the support from the monarchy, the double crossing.' Her eyes lit up. She'd appreciated Mark's patience as she'd pored over the endless glass cases in the exhibition.

'What about the violence, press ganging, and the scurvy?' He frowned. 'I think you're kind of glamorising it.'

'All of history is grim at points. I still like pirates,' she said.

He laughed. 'I don't understand it.'

'My dad is descended from some famous French pirate.' She wrinkled her nose. 'I can't remember his name. Maybe that's why, maybe there's some kind of connection there. Thank you for taking me, I know it's not your thing.'

'Maybe not, but you always come to the Oval with me.' He kissed her cheek.

'That's true. And I can't stand cricket. Do you want to stop for a drink before we go to your mum's?' She nodded to the pub across the road.

'Sure. Double rum, is it?' He grinned.

'Very funny. I'll have a beer, something in a bottle. I don't mind what,' she said as they walked through the door.

He frowned. 'We always have wine. Since when did you drink beer?'

She lowered her voice. 'I don't love wine that much, Mark. I pretended to like it when we met to impress you.'

'Right.' He bit his lip. 'Two Peronis please,' he said to the barman.

They took a table in the window and Molly zoned out as she drank her beer. Maybe she wasn't as predictable as Mark thought she was. While he wasn't there for her, she was always there for him. When he wanted to go out, she was by his side. She'd never seen it from his perspective before. Maybe she was his constant. He had been fiddling with a bar mat for a while now, slipping it between his fingers. He was obviously nervous about going over to his parents' house. He always was. His mum was kind, sweet and caring, but his dad was an aggressive bully, who Mark was terrified of.

When she'd finished her beer, she returned their empty glasses to the bar, then slid her arm into Mark's, as they walked down the road to his parents' house.

When they reached his parents' house, Molly turned to face Mark. 'Are you alright?'

'I'm fine.' His expression said otherwise. His brow was furrowed and his jaw was tight.

'If you need to leave at any point, just let me know.' She took a deep breath. 'I know things can get...tense between you and your dad.'

'I said I was fine.' Mark snapped and rang the doorbell. 'Can you just leave it?'

Molly swallowed the lump in her throat and plastered on a smile as Mark's mum, Elisa, opened the door.

'Habibi!' Elisa said, putting her arms around Mark before he even got in the door. She kissed his cheek. 'It's been so long.'

'Mama' he said, smiling. 'Ana asf.' He kissed her cheek and squeezed her tightly. The frown had disappeared from his face, replaced by a broad smile.

Molly plastered on a smile. Mark had snapped at her, but of course the first thing he said to his mum was that he was sorry. 'Ahlaan, Mama,' she said, embracing Elisa.

She called Elisa Mama, just like Mark did. She always had. Elisa had insisted on it, and Molly found it comforting after her own mum died. She squeezed Elisa's tiny, bird-like frame. Her olive skin smelt of rosewater and her dark, almost black curls brushed Molly's cheek as she pulled away from her.

'Come in,' Elisa said, ushering Molly inside and closing the door behind her.

Molly walked into the hall of Mark's parents' house, immediately comforted as the house was so like hers, a Victorian terrace with a narrow hallway. She took off her coat and hung it on one of the crowded coat hooks and tucked her shoes onto the rack below the coats, stuffed with Mark's teenage sibling's shoes.

'I was starting to forget what you looked like.' Mark's dad, Greg raised an eyebrow at Mark as he and Molly walked into the living room.

Molly squeezed Mark's hand tightly. She didn't like the way that Greg's eyes were always slightly narrowed at Mark.

'Hi, Dad.' Mark sat down on the cracked leather sofa and smiled at his dad who was sunk into his armchair.

'And Molly too. Nice to see you, sweetheart.' Greg gave Molly a tight smile.

'Is everyone hungry?' Elisa hovered by the doorway. 'Greg, the lamb's ready, can you come and carve it?'

'Duty calls.' Greg stood up and nodded to Molly and Mark before following Elisa out of the room.

'Should we go and help?' Molly whispered.

'No, you know Ummi won't let us.' Mark squeezed Molly's thigh. 'I'm glad you're here.'

'I hate the way he talks to you, Mark.' She kept her voice low.

'I'm not discussing this now.' He let go of her leg and stood up, walking out of the room.

She sighed and twiddled her ring around on her finger. He would never discuss it, no matter where they were.

'Dinner's ready.' Elisa walked back into the room. 'Where did Mark go?'

Molly's heart sank. 'I uh...' She heard footsteps upstairs. 'I think he went to the bathroom.'

'Well, come and have a seat.' Elisa smiled broadly at Molly.

As she walked into the dining room, Mark reappeared. He offered her a tight smile and sat down at the dining table, nodding at her to do the same.

'It's quiet without the kids here, isn't it?' Elisa smiled at Mark and Molly. 'They're out with friends tonight.'

'That's a shame, I've got some good book recommendations for Riya,' Molly said. Mark's younger sister was as much of a bookworm as she was.

'I'll let her know,' Elisa replied. 'She loved the last ones you suggested. How's everything going with work, still busy?'

'As always.' Molly grinned. 'How was Morocco?'

'Wonderful.' Elisa's eyes crinkled as she smiled. 'Much warmer than it is here.' She rolled her eyes at the rain lashing the windows. 'Mark, you must come out with us next time. You too, Molly.'

Mark nodded. 'We will, Ummi.' He glanced at Molly. 'It's been a while since we last went.'

Molly could picture the ornate, tile covered courtyard of Elisa's family riad. She'd spent many hours there with Mark's family. They spoke predominantly Arabic, but also French, and a little English. Every time she went, Molly learnt a little more Arabic, but they hadn't been for the last year as Mark's job had kept him out of the country so much.

After they'd eaten, Molly helped Elisa to clear the plates away into the kitchen.

'Molly, I made some baklava.' Elisa proudly showed Molly a decorative ceramic plate filled with delicate pastry squares.

Molly's eyes lit up. 'It smells amazing.'

'Thank you. You and Mark love it, so I wanted to make it for you.' Elisa smiled and got some small plates out of cupboard, handing them to Molly. 'Can you take these in for me, and I'll bring the baklava?'

'Of course,' Molly replied and picked up the stack of plates.

She followed Elisa back into the dining room, where the atmosphere between Mark and his dad was so tense she could almost feel it. She set the plates down and Mark helped himself to a piece.

He took a bite, and when he swallowed, he smiled at his mum. 'It's great, thanks, Mama.' He turned to Molly. 'Have you ever made this?'

Molly shook her head. 'No, but I'd love to have a go.'

'It's not too difficult. I will give you the recipe.' Elisa picked up a small fork and took a bite of the baklava. 'I'll make some more for Christmas. Will you be here then?'

'Of course,' Mark said.

Molly's eyebrows flew up. It was their turn to be with her family this year. He ignored her gaze and continued talking to his mum. She took a deep breath and continued eating her baklava. She knew why he had said they would both be there. He didn't want to face his dad without her at his side. She wouldn't tackle him about it in front of his parents. It could wait.

'I can't wait to have you both here for Christmas again,' Elisa said, 'but you're welcome any time, you know that.'

'I do.' Mark took a sip of his wine. 'I'd love to come over more often, but I'm away so much with work.'

'Ah yes, the mysterious job.' Greg gave a hearty laugh. 'Explain what you do again, Mark?'

Mark gave him a tight smile. 'I manage the European contracts for a global investment company.'

'Right,' Greg said. 'Still doesn't mean anything to me.'

'I could explain it to you, if you'd like?' Mark's tone was tentative, and he took a sip of his wine, fixing his eyes on his father.

'Don't worry, son. I'm not as clever as you. I don't have a fancy degree. I'm just a greengrocer.' Greg picked up his glass and took a long gulp.

Elisa stood up and clapped her hands. 'Right. Who would like a cup of tea?'

'I'll help you.' Mark shot out of his chair, picking up the empty plates, and walking out of the room.

Elisa followed, leaving Molly alone with Greg.

'And how are you getting on then, Molly? Have you made editor yet?' He narrowed his eyes.

'No.' Molly's breath caught in her throat.

Why was this man so terrifying? He clearly knew the effect he had on people. She held eye contact with him but didn't say anything else. She was determined not to be scared of him.

Greg cracked his knuckles and sat back in his chair, studying her. 'You career girls. I thought that was what it was about these days. Getting to the top, smashing the glass ceiling.'

'I'm in a good position where I am,' Molly said mildly. 'I wouldn't necessarily say I was a career girl. I mean someday I want a family too...' She trailed off as Mark walked back in, putting a cup of tea down in front of her.

'What are you two talking about?' Mark asked, sitting down.

'Ah, Molly was just wondering when you were going to do the decent thing and propose,' Greg said. 'She's just told me she wants a family, and I assume you'll want to get married first.'

'Someday,' Molly replied, her heart racing, as she tried to keep her voice steady. 'Someday I would like a family.'

Mark's face was pale as he gripped his own mug tightly. 'Exactly. There's no hurry is there?'

'Hurry for what?' Elisa asked, bringing in more cups of tea, putting one down in front of Greg and sitting down with her own.

'A family, Mama,' Mark said. 'There's no hurry for a family.'

'Oh, but you don't want to leave it too long,' Elisa replied. 'You're both heading for thirty already, aren't you?'

'Mum, I don't think this is an appropriate conversation.' Mark flicked his eyes at Molly. 'You're embarrassing Molly.'

'She was the one who brought it up,' Greg said, his eyes also fixed on Molly.

Molly swallowed a gulp of tea and wished that the ground would open up and swallow her.

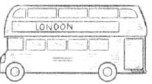

'You should see more of your mum. She misses you,' Molly said as they walked back to the Tube station.

Mark rolled his eyes. 'I see her as much as I can.'

'I would love to be able to spend more time with my mum,' she replied, her voice cracking.

She swallowed hard, hoping Mark wouldn't notice. The warm hug that Elisa always gave her reminded her of her own mum.

'I'm sure you would,' he said. 'I'm sorry that she died, Molly. But your relationship with your family is very different from mine.'

She thought about Mark's dad and winced as she remembered his laser-like stare. 'That's true. But their house is so cosy and welcoming, like my house. I want my children to grow up in my mum's house, just like Saskia and I did.' She paused. 'I don't know if that's what you want though.'

They'd barely discussed the future over the last four years. Both of them had been focused on their careers.

'I don't know what I want right now,' he replied. 'As I said, there's no hurry.'

She nodded. 'Sure.' A tiny seed of doubt was growing in her mind. Mark was perfect for right now, but was he the person she wanted to spend the rest of her life with?

He slid his arm around her, and they walked together in silence until the glowing lights of the Tube station appeared in front of them.

When they arrived back at Mark's apartment, Molly felt full, warm, and sleepy. She slid off her coat and shoes. 'Tonight was good. Your mum's cooking is incredible.'

Mark unzipped his coat and hung it next to Molly's. 'I guess I should appreciate it more, I grew up with it.'

'My mum couldn't cook at all,' she said, smiling wistfully. 'She tried her best, but it just wasn't her thing. Just like me.'

'Just as well I can then, isn't it?' He went into the living room and sat down on the sofa.

'Can we talk about Christmas?' she asked, sitting down next to him. 'It's actually our turn to be with my family this year.'

'I'm sure we were at your house last year,' he said. 'Why don't we do Christmas Day with mine, then Boxing Day with yours. Then we can still see both families.'

'I guess so.'

She wanted to tell him that actually, she wanted to spend Christmas Day with her family, but she didn't want to cause an argument. She still felt rattled from Greg's interrogation and was desperate to put it behind her. She tried to get comfortable on his boxy sofa, unsuccessfully, and sighed.

'Come here.' He held out an arm to her.

She hesitated, then deciding she couldn't face any more drama tonight, moved closer to him.

He wrapped his arm around her waist, his fingers sliding under the hem of her top. 'My dad's a real mood killer, isn't he?'

Surprised at his willingness to be reflective, Molly looked up at him. 'He was...hard work tonight.'

'I'm sorry.' He turned so that he was facing her, then cupped her face in his hands and kissed her.

'It's not your fault,' she said quietly as she pulled away from him.

The tightness of his jaw, and the lack of sparkle in his eyes told her how much his dad's behaviour was hurting him too.

'Why don't we focus on the gorgeous meal your mum made and the box of baklava she gave us. We can polish that off tomorrow.'

'You always see the positive in everything, Molly.' He brushed her cheek with his thumb. 'Do you want another drink, or shall we go to bed?'

Squashing her lingering resentment of him, and his dad, she nodded. Maybe connecting physically would be good for both of them. 'I've had enough to drink.'

He stood up and held out his hand, pulling her to her feet. 'Then let's go to bed.'

She followed him into the bedroom, where he unzipped her dress and slid it down her body, before tossing it onto the armchair next to his bed.

Slowly, she unbuttoned his shirt, sliding it off and running her fingers over his toned torso. He threw her onto the bed, climbing on next to her. The tense, pained expression he'd had on earlier had disappeared. As he removed her underwear, his eyes lit up, and she squashed the nagging doubt that he wasn't right for her, in favour of climbing on top of him. It always worked, and this time was no exception.

Molly was struggling to keep her eyes open. She was sat opposite Mark in a tiny café in Greenwich, where they'd gone for breakfast, but having hardly slept the night before she was having trouble concentrating on what he was saying. She tried to hide a yawn behind her hand, but judging by the cloudy expression on Mark's face, she'd failed.

'Am I boring you?' Mark asked.

'No, sorry, it just took me a while to get back to sleep last night.' She fiddled with the handle of her cup.

Her dreams had taken her back to the station car park again, back to her bag being snatched, the photos of her mum in her purse, taken away. She had fought furiously, and then in the middle of the night freezing cold, woke up, realising that she had thrown the duvet off the bed, annoying Mark. He had been angry, with her, the sharp tone of his voice bouncing off the bare walls of his bedroom.

She'd stared at the plain white ceiling, listening to his breathing, and thought about Chris, his concerned face and the gentle touch of his hand in hers. It was a contrast to Mark's sharp tone and lack of care. These thoughts had sent her back to sleep, and when she'd woken up this morning, the memory of her nightmare had been replaced with the memory of Chris, and the comforting feeling that rushed through her when he'd offered her his hand on Halloween.

She picked up her cup and took a sip of her tea. 'Did you go back to sleep?'

His face showed no signs of disturbed sleep, unlike hers, which had required a lot of concealer this morning.

'Eventually,' he said. 'These nightmares, are they a regular thing?'

She nodded. 'More regular than I'd like.'

'I thought you were seeing a counsellor.' He frowned. 'Can't she help you?'

'I have been seeing Colette, but she hasn't got a magic wand,' she said. He just didn't understand. 'I don't think about it as much during the day, but at night it's obviously still on my mind.'

'You look exhausted.' He brushed her hair away from her face. 'I hope this counsellor knows what she's doing.'

She bit her tongue. There were so many things she wanted to say to him, but she didn't have the energy to argue with him. She was exhausted. It was more than a feeling. He had already moved on and had his head buried in a newspaper while he drank his coffee. He clearly had absolutely no interest in carrying on the conversation, or trying to understand how much being mugged was still affecting her.

Chapter Nine

November 2014, Canterbury, Kent, England

'I had a good time this weekend,' Molly said, sliding her arms around Mark. 'Have you got time to come to Victoria with me? I'm still not that confident on the train on my own.'

They were stood at the entrance to the station in Canary Wharf. The familiar gnaw of anxiety had taken hold of her stomach at the thought of travelling alone.

Mark brushed her hair away from her face and kissed her cheek. 'You've got nothing to be afraid of. Hold your head up high and face your fear. It's the only way.'

'Right.' She nodded. 'I'll see you when you get back from Copenhagen then?'

'Sure.' He tipped her chin up so that her lips met his. 'I'm back Thursday evening, so I could meet you after work on Friday?'

'Sounds good to me. I'll speak to you later. Love you.'

She kissed him again and he pulled away, not replying. He walked off down the road and she closed her eyes, letting out a long exhale, a pang of rejection stabbing at her chest. Just for once, she wanted to know that he cared about her as much as she cared about him.

At lunchtime Molly gazed out of the window at the café over the road. Today was the day. She wasn't going to back out. She pulled on her coat, twiddling the button between her fingers.

'Ed,' she hissed. 'I'm gonna do it.' She flicked her eyes towards the window and the café.

'Do you want me to come with you?' He stood up.

She shook her head. 'No, I need to do this on my own. Thanks for the offer though.'

'Can I get you anything?' She paused by his desk.

'I'm alright, thanks,' he said. 'I'm meeting Samuel soon. I just thought I'd offer to come with you.'

'I appreciate you, as always.' She smiled at him, clutching her bag tightly, before marching purposefully down the office to the lift.

In the lobby she got out and waved to Sue as she passed the reception desk. She pulled the glass door open and pushed the button at the pedestrian crossing just down the road. She crossed the road, buffeted between groups of commuters, and walked up to the door of the café, pulling it open.

She browsed through the fridges, clutching her bag tightly against her chest and chose her favourite hoisin duck wrap, then took it to the counter to pay.

'Is that everything?' The cashier said with a strong American drawl, and smiled at Molly as she handed over the wrap.

'Uh, yes, thank you.' Molly pulled her purse out of her bag and tapped her card on the card reader.

The cashier put Molly's receipt and her wrap into a paper bag and handed it to her with a smile. 'Have a nice day,' she said.

'Thank you. You too.' Molly took the bag from her and made her way quickly to the door.

She crossed the road and hurried towards the giant toucan on the side of her building, pulling open the glass door and colliding with Ed in the foyer.

'You did it!' he said. 'Good work, Molly.'

'Yep.' Molly nodded. 'Nailed it.'

'I knew you could do it.' He smiled at her. 'Would you like me to come with you next time? We could eat in if you like. It'll give you a break from this place.'

'I could do that.' She smiled back at him. 'Say hi to Samuel for me.'

'He keeps asking if you and Mark want to come out for a drink with us.' He raised an eyebrow.

'Sounds good. I'll ask Mark,' she said.

As she got into the lift, her stomach sank. She wasn't being honest with Ed. She'd asked Mark so many times to come out with her and Ed and Samuel and he'd made an excuse every time. She pushed her thoughts of him to the back of her mind and focused on her lunch, and the tiny victory she'd had today.

When she'd finished her lunch, she picked up her phone, remembering that Saskia had gone on a date with Scott at the weekend. Saskia had been uncharacteristically quiet, probably because she knew Molly was with Mark.

> Just checking in. Are you still on a post-date high? X

Saskia replied quickly.

> Yes!!! On cloud nine. Have you escaped from moron Mark's supervillain lair? X

Molly rolled her eyes.

> Yep, still in one piece. Just. It was a mixed bag. He took me to a pirate exhibition but dinner with his parents was awkward AF x

> Quelle surprise. Let me guess - his dad caused a scene? xx

> Got it in one! x

Molly laughed and put her headphones in, today choosing a classical music playlist and focused on her latest manuscript, a fantasy story featuring dragons, fairies, and elves. As the music played, she lost herself in the magical world as she read and edited.

Chris ran across the platform and jumped onto the train just as the whistle blew. The doors shut behind him and he breathed a sigh of relief. He made his way through the train, hoping he would see her again. As he walked into the third carriage, he spotted a blonde head and a green coat. The seat next to her was taken, so he sat on an empty seat a few rows back and pulled out his book.

Two stations later, after Molly's seat neighbour got off, Chris slid into the seat next to her. 'Hey. Long time no see.'

'Hey yourself. How are you?' She smiled at him.

'I'm fine,' he said, and held her gaze for a few seconds. Just long enough for the world to stop. She didn't look away. Was she as into him as he was her?

'How was your weekend?' he asked, his heart pounding.

'I stayed with my boyfriend for the weekend,' she said. 'He lives in Canary Wharf so we spent the weekend in the city.'

Her words were like a punch to the gut. She had a boyfriend? *Shit*, he thought to himself. *Of course, she's got a boyfriend*. She's pretty, kind, and funny. He unzipped his coat and tried to keep his face neutral as she continued talking.

He cleared his throat. 'Oh right. Did you guys have a good weekend?'

'We did. We went to the Maritime Museum, and went to his parents' house for dinner,' she replied. 'How was your weekend?'

He studied her face. She'd just spent the entire weekend with her boyfriend. Why didn't she look happier about it? Puzzled, he rubbed the back of his neck. 'Alex and I did another set at Mimosa on Friday, but I spent the rest of the weekend in bed with a migraine.'

'Oh no, I'm so sorry,' she said. 'That sucks.'

'Yeah, it does suck. I got some new medication though and it's helping,' he replied. 'What did you see at the Maritime Museum?'

'They've got an exhibition of pirate related artefacts at the moment.' She lowered her voice. 'I've been obsessed with pirates since I was a kid. Apparently, my dad is descended from a famous French pirate. Most girls dress up as princesses and plan their weddings. Not me, I had an eye patch and made Saskia walk the plank.'

His laugh echoed across the silent carriage, and he covered his mouth. 'Sorry, that's hilarious.'

He suddenly remembered the galleon tattoo. It all made sense now.

'Saskia's always been theatrical, even before university,' she said. 'We used to put on these little plays for our parents. Then after they got divorced, Papa went back to France, and we used to force mum's friends to watch them.' She laughed. 'They were always encouraging, but my acting was terrible. It makes me cringe thinking about it now. Mum was always so supportive of both of us.'

This was the first time she'd mentioned her mum and he wondered whether to ask any more, or whether to just let her talk. Before he could say anything, she continued.

'She died three years ago.' She took a deep breath. 'I don't talk about her very much. It makes people imagine losing their own parents and they don't know what to say. She had a stroke. Saskia and I were with her.' Her eyes filled with tears.

He squeezed her hand. 'I'm so sorry, Molly. That must have been so hard. It must still be so hard. I know grief isn't linear and some days are easier than others.'

She nodded. 'You're right. How do you know? Have you lost someone?'

'My uncle, Alex's dad, was killed in a car accident when I was a kid.' He paused. Almost twenty years later it was still painful to talk about. 'It was such a massive shock for our whole family. We're all very close.'

'I can tell,' she said. 'You, Scott, and Alex seemed close on Halloween.'

'We are,' he replied. 'Alex and I used to spend every summer together and Scott's been part of my family since he was five. It's the same for you, isn't it? You and Saskia are close, right?'

'Very. I sometimes feel like her mum, rather than her sister.' She rolled her eyes. 'I worry about her so much.'

'I saw her this weekend,' he said. 'She stayed over at our place on Saturday night.'

She looked surprised. 'Really? Seems like it's getting serious between her and Scott. She's very definite about people, she either loves them or hates them.'

'Really?' He raised his eyebrows. 'I'd better be careful what I say.'

'You're fine.' She smiled. 'She likes you.' She bit her lip, as if she was trying to hold something in. 'Are you seeing anyone?'

He shook his head. 'No. I broke up with my ex-girlfriend a few months before I moved back here. She didn't want to move down here, and I did. She didn't want to leave her family, and I missed mine. We're still friends. We went travelling together when we graduated, so we have some good memories together.'

'That's sweet. Where did you go?' she asked.

'We covered a lot of Southeast Asia,' he replied. 'Bali was my favourite. It's so beautiful.'

'I'd love to go. Sounds dreamy.' She pulled out her water bottle and took a swig from it. 'Before I started university, my friend Liz and I travelled around Africa for the summer. I fell in love with Morocco, and weirdly my boyfriend's family are Moroccan, so I've been back there a few times with them.'

He tried not to think of her boyfriend, or how close she might be with his family.

'I've never been,' he said. 'I'd like to go, though. Do you speak Arabic?'

She shook her head. 'Not much. I can rattle off a few words, but his family speak French and some English too, so we make it work. Mark speaks much better Arabic than me. We met at university, but we worked out that we'd been in Morocco at the same time that summer. Another weird coincidence.'

'Sometimes life is like that,' he said. 'I met my girlfriend on the first day of my first term university. We were both lost on campus.'

'That's adorable.' She smiled. 'A meet cute. Where did you go to university?'

'Leeds. I only moved back here a few months ago when I got this job,' he said.

'I wondered why we'd never met. That'll be why.'

'I loved living in Leeds. It's such a cool city. Scott came up in my second year and we got a flat together.' He paused. 'We missed each other. We'd been together every day since we were five. He got a job in a bar, and within two years he was managing it.'

'Sounds like you had a great time there. Why did you come back to Canterbury?' she asked.

'I got headhunted for this job in London,' he said. 'I knew I could do it and live here so I could see more of my parents. Scott and I agreed that we'd only move back here if it made sense for both of us and he found the job at Mimosa a week after I was offered mine.'

'Fate strikes again!' she said, her eyes widening. 'I love that!'

'I think so,' he replied. 'We didn't have anywhere to live, so we had to move in with my parents while we tried to find a place. We went from a tiny flat on the outskirts of the city in Leeds to a shabby old farmhouse in Bridge.'

'Your parents live in Bridge? How posh.' She raised an eyebrow.

He laughed. 'Not as posh as you think. We have a regular sized house, no helipad, no horses. Just a very grubby old farmhouse.'

'I love old houses. Mine is a Victorian terrace,' she said. 'When my parents first moved into it, they didn't have much money. We spent most of the winter huddled in front of the fire. The house has changed a lot since then, but it's still pretty shabby. Saskia and I like it that way. We're drawn to vintage stuff.'

'I got that impression from your clothes,' he said, then realised that might sound rude. 'I mean, they're all vintage style, not saying they're old or anything.'

She put her hand on his arm, sending a jolt of electricity through him. 'It's fine. I know what you mean.'

The train pulled into Canterbury West station, and Chris remembered what he'd been planning to ask Molly. Knowing she had a boyfriend made him wary, but they were friends, right?

'Would you be happy to swap numbers?' he asked. 'Then you can let me know if you want me to save you a seat.'

'Sure. I'd like that.' She pulled out her phone and handed it to him.

He put his number into her phone. 'See you tomorrow maybe?'

She pulled on her coat and zipped her bag up, putting it over her shoulder. 'See you then. I'll bring some treats. It's been a while.'

He walked her to her car and waved as she drove off, before going back to his flat feeling completely miserable. He'd been planning to ask her out and now he felt like a complete idiot.

When Scott got home about an hour later, Chris was still wearing his suit, his tie and collar undone. Usually, he couldn't wait to get into his sweatpants, but tonight, he'd got in, drank a beer, and sat on the sofa, staring out of the window, watching the rain lashing down.

'Are you alright, mate?' Scott called as he walked in.

'Molly's got a boyfriend.' Chris took a swig of his beer. 'She's been off in his fancy flat in Canary Wharf for the weekend. I was planning to ask her out tonight.'

Scott winced. 'I'm sorry, mate.'

Chris groaned. 'Did you know about this?'

'Saskia told me.' Scott sat down next to Chris. 'Apparently, he's a complete douchebag. I wouldn't worry about him. I've seen you and Molly together. She definitely likes you.'

'Doesn't matter.' Chris frowned. 'She's got a boyfriend, so she's off limits.'

Scott shrugged. 'Saskia hates him. Her dad hates him. What did she say about him?'

Chris put his bottle down on the coffee table. 'She didn't say much. She'd just spent the weekend with him, but she didn't seem that happy about it.'

'Bide your time, my friend.' Scott patted Chris on the arm.

'Not my style.' Chris finished his beer. 'She'll be a good friend, but that's it.'

'And you'll just swallow your feelings for her?' Scott raised his eyebrow.

'I'll have to,' Chris said, through gritted teeth. 'Did you see Saskia today?'

Scott nodded. 'I did. She got the part! She's going to be in Peter Pan in the West End.'

Chris grinned. 'That's brilliant news.'

'It is, she's wanted this for years,' Scott said. 'I'm so proud of her. It's the first role she's had since her mum died. She's so brave, I'm kind of in awe of her.'

Chris nodded. 'Me too. There's no way I could do it, she's fearless.'

'She is.' Scott paused. 'And she moves to London next week.'

Chapter Ten

NOVEMBER 2014, CANTERBURY, KENT, England

Molly raised her glass in the air. She'd only been home a few minutes before Saskia had pounced on her to share her good news. Saskia had poured them both glasses of Champagne, and turned the radio up loudly in the kitchen, where they were now both dancing around excitedly.

'You got the job!' Molly shrieked at the top of her voice.

'I got the job!' Saskia turned the radio up. 'I've got my first role in the West End! I love doing pantomimes.'

'Think about how many people will see you. Hundreds, maybe thousands.' Molly's eyes widened. 'I can't wait to see you on the stage again.'

Saskia grinned. 'I can't wait to be up there.' She took a swig of Champagne. 'How was your weekend with the lovely Mark?'

'It was good.' Molly nodded enthusiastically 'We saw his family and he took me to the pirate exhibition at the maritime museum.'

'Then he told you he's going away again and he'll see you next week.' Saskia rolled her eyes.

Molly laughed. 'Saskia, it's his job.'

Saskia narrowed her eyes. 'There's something else. What aren't you telling me?'

Molly sighed and put her glass on the worktop. 'Every relationship is complicated, right? It's good and bad. It's like he just doesn't get how traumatic this was for me. He thinks I can just forget about it like that.' She snapped her fingers.

'He doesn't get it Molly. He's never got it.' Saskia put her glass down a little too hard on the worktop and put her hands on her hips. 'I don't know if I want to leave you right now, I don't know if he'll be there for you if you need him.'

'You need to do this, Saskia,' Molly said. 'You can't come back here every night, and living with the girls from the cast makes sense. I'll be just fine.' She sloshed more Champagne into Saskia's glass, then topped up her own.

'You're right. It's just going to be weird not seeing you every day.' Saskia took a swig of her Champagne.

'I know,' Molly said. 'What did Scott say? I mean, you guys have only just got together.'

A smile spread across Saskia's face. 'He's just as excited as you are. Even though it means me moving away and not being able to see him as much, he's still happy for me.'

'I've never seen you click with someone so quickly.' Molly smiled.

'Oh we connected.' Saskia waggled her eyebrows. 'In all kinds of ways. He's so like me. Chaotic, unpredictable and up for anything.'

'I don't want gory details,' Molly said firmly. Saskia's sex life had always been wilder than hers. 'Chris told me you stayed over at their flat.'

'I like Chris. *He's* a gentleman.' Saskia stared defiantly at Molly.

'I get your not-so-subtle hint, but we're just friends.' Molly rolled her eyes.

After they'd had dinner, Molly was hit by a pang of sadness. Soon, she would be on her own in the house she had grown up in. Telling Saskia that she was going to bed, she went upstairs into her mum's bedroom and pulled the door closed behind her. Turning on the lamp, she opened the wardrobe and ran her fingers along the clothes hanging there, each piece bringing back a different memory. Sliding a denim jacket off the hanger, she slipped it on. It smelt like her mum, of perfume and sunscreen. Slipping it off, she put it away again. Her fingers closed around the hanger of a navy-blue velvet jumpsuit. She rubbed the soft fabric between her fingers, clutching it to her as she sat down on her mum's bed.

'Mum, she's going away. She's doing it at last, following her dreams.' Molly lowered her voice. 'I'm so proud of her, but I'll miss her so much.'

'I'm going to miss you too.' Saskia appeared at the door. 'Sorry to interrupt.'

'Come here.' Molly held out her arms to Saskia who came and sat next to her on the bed.

Saskia pulled Molly in for a hug. 'We'll still see each other loads, I promise, I mean you work in London, right?' She let Molly go.

'I know.' Molly nodded. 'I didn't want to say anything to you, I didn't want you to think that I wasn't happy for you.'

'You can be happy for me and sad for you.' Saskia brushed Molly's hair away from her face. 'You're not rationed to just one feeling at a time.'

'I know. I am happy for you. You're going to be Tinkerbell.' Molly beamed at Saskia. 'You were made for that role.'

'I hope so.' Saskia laughed. 'We'll soon see. The director is taking a big chance on me so I need to prove I can do it.'

'You can. I've seen you do it a thousand times before,' Molly said firmly.

Saskia smiled at the jumpsuit laid out on the bed. 'She looked beautiful in that, didn't she? You should try it on.'

'I can't.' Molly shook her head. 'It's hers and it reminds me of her. I couldn't wear it.'

Saskia ran her fingers over it. 'Maybe it wants new memories.'

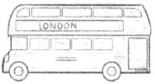

'I would like to make a toast. To me and my brilliant acting skills,' Saskia said, raising her glass.

Molly laughed, then glanced at Jess and Liz, who were also laughing. All thre of them held their glasses up.

'To Saskia and her brilliant acting skills,' they chorused.

Molly took a sip of her Champagne, and picked up her dessert menu. To celebrate Saskia's new job, she and her friends had just devoured a feast of Thai food. Despite this, she was sure she had room for something sweet. There was always room for something sweet.

'I won't forget my humble beginnings,' Saskia said. 'I'll remember you all when I'm a mega famous movie star.'

'You better. Remember all the things I know about you,' Jess retorted.

'Very good point.' Saskia laughed. 'All of you know way too much about me. I need to keep you on side.'

'We expect front row seats,' Liz added. 'We need to get the best view of you flying through the air.'

'I'm slightly nervous about that part,' Saskia admitted. 'I did audition for Tiger Lily as well, but the girl who got the part is so much better suited to it. She has this gorgeous shiny dark hair and olive skin.'

'You guys suited dark hair at Halloween,' Liz said. 'I'm so used to you with blonde hair, but it worked.'

'It was so much fun,' Molly replied. 'Not as much fun as seeing Saskia dressed as a man, wrapped around Scott.'

Jess and Liz laughed, and Saskia blushed. 'Shut up, you lot. I am a lucky girl. He fancies me no matter what I'm wearing. He's seen the good, the bad, and the ugly. I'm sure he would still want to be with me, even if I was still doing adverts for cold sore cream.'

'Hey, that advert paid for our decking,' Molly said. 'This role is huge, and I know it's going to lead to other things that will be just as good.'

'Thanks, love.' Saskia blew Molly a kiss. 'And all of you, you've always been my best bitches. I'm going to miss you all so much, but I keep telling myself it's only a month.'

Molly smiled wistfully. This role would only be a month, but once Saskia was in London, among other actors and actresses, she'd be sure to make contacts. Her career could take off, pulling her away from Canterbury. She remembered Saskia's words and allowed herself to feel both happy *and* sad.

'It might only be a month, but I know it'll lead to even better things for you,' she said. 'I'm cheering you on all the way.'

Saskia nodded, her eyes full of tears. 'I know you are.'

Molly dragged herself out of bed the next morning. She picked up her phone and read the garbled message from Liz.

> Can't make yoga. Can't leave my bed. Too much Champagne! X

She laughed and typed out a reply.

> Uh oh… Hope you get some rest! X

> It is baaaaaad. Jake has taken Martha to the park. Can barely open my eyes. X

Molly laughed and put her phone on her bedside table. She peeked into Saskia's room on her way to the shower and grinned at her sister, sprawled across her bed, fast asleep. She showered and went downstairs, and with her stomach still swirling from the Champagne the night before, made herself some tea and toast.

Once she'd eaten it, she returned to the kitchen, made a strong coffee, and took it back upstairs with her.

'Sas? Can I come in?' Hearing a muffled groan, Molly nudged Saskia's door open.

Expecting to see her sister still spread out on her bed, she was surprised to see her sat on the floor in her pyjamas, surrounded by the contents of her wardrobe. Molly handed her the coffee. 'Thought you might need this.'

'Thank you. You're a lifesaver.' Saskia took the mug and sipped it. 'How do you feel this morning?'

'A bit rough to be honest.' Molly sat down, leaning against Saskia's bed. 'I'm not used to drinking so much Champagne. How about you?'

'Same.' Saskia groaned as her eyes ran over the chaos around her. 'This seemed like a good idea ten minutes ago.'

Molly cast her eyes over the room. The wardrobe doors hung open, and the drawers were open too, clothes spilling out of them. 'Want a hand?'

'Uh yes.' Saskia nodded vigorously. 'I need all the help I can get.'

'I'll be right back.' Molly went downstairs and fetched some rubbish sacks. She opened the cupboard under the stairs and got out a large suitcase which she dragged up the stairs and into Saskia's bedroom 'The suitcase is for whatever you want to take to London, and everything else we'll either donate or put away. Got it?'

'Thank you.' Saskia stood up and hugged her sister. 'You're always here for me.'

'And I always will be.' Molly squeezed Saskia tightly. Her hangover was only amplifying the tide of emotions washing over her. As hard as she tried to tell herself that Saskia was doing what she was born to do, she still didn't want to let her go.

'Alright, enough already.' Saskia wriggled out of Molly's grip 'I'm going to start crying. We need to focus, and sort this mess out.'

'Good plan.' Molly nodded and held up a pair of black faux leather trousers.

Saskia let out a wicked cackle. 'Oh, those are staying. They bring back a lot of good memories.'

Molly dropped them. 'They've been washed though, right?'

A few hours later they had sorted through all of Saskia's clothes. Molly had stopped feeling sick and had kept Saskia focused with a steady stream of soda, sugary sweets and crisps.

Saskia picked up a pile of books and put them in a bag for the charity shop. She waggled the filthy novel at Molly. 'This should give someone else a bit of a laugh.'

'Well, I enjoyed it,' Molly said, shrugging. She shook her cloth out of the empty window, recoiling at the amount of dust on it. 'It was like chewing gum for my brain, I just switched off.'

Saskia nodded approvingly at the immaculately tidy room. 'I'd love it to be this tidy all the time.'

'In order for that to happen, you would have to actually tidy it. And clean it.' Molly grimaced. 'I'm not going to even think about what kind of hellhole your bedroom in London will end up like.'

'Maybe I'll turn over a new leaf.' Saskia raised her eyebrow. 'I'll be like you, obsessively tidy.' She paused. 'Are you going to be alright here on your own?'

'Yes of course, I'm twenty-six years old. I'm not a child.' Molly rolled her eyes, but she wasn't looking forward to being on her own in the house, especially now, when the mornings and the evenings were so dark.

'I'm not suggesting you are,' Saskia said. 'You're way more grown up than I'll ever be. I just worry about you.'

Molly folded her arms. ' You don't need to worry about me. I won't be alone. I have Liz, remember.'

'And you have Chris too.' Saskia smirked.

'I do. He is a very good friend,' Molly said firmly. 'I think Mark might come here more often if you aren't giving him the death glare.'

'Will he though?' Saskia's eyes narrowed. 'I can't help feeling like he's just paying you lip service. How likely is it that he's actually going to come over?'

'I don't know,' Molly huffed. 'I can't keep having the same conversation with you about him.'

'Fine. I'll say no more.' Saskia jumped off the bed and went back to tidying her make-up. 'This is the lipstick I used on you on Halloween. It suits you much better than me.'

Molly applied it using Saskia's mirror, then turned to face her. 'Does it still suit me without the black hair?'

'Oh yes. Keep it.' Saskia nodded.

Molly took the lipstick back to her bedroom and put it in her make-up bag. She wasn't sure if it was the alcohol last night, or Saskia leaving, but she had spent the whole day trying not to cry. She took a deep breath and twisted the gold rings around on her fingers.

When she went back into Saskia's room, she could finally see the progress they'd made. The wardrobe, dresser and bedside table were all spotless. Saskia was sitting on the bed sorting through the last of her things.

'We have one last job. We need to take these bags to the charity shop. Are you ready for that?' Molly asked.

Saskia shook her head. 'Not really. I don't think I will ever be though. Can we go to the drive through on the way back? I need a burger.'

'That's the best idea you've had all day.' Molly wrinkled her nose at her dusty clothes. 'Let me have a quick shower.'

'That's not a bad idea. I still have crisp crumbs all over me.' Saskia cackled and Molly rolled her eyes.

Chapter Eleven

Molly wasn't alone on her commute on Friday morning, but it wasn't Chris beside her. It was her sister, clad in her leopard print coat and leather trousers, with a huge suitcase and her floral handbag.

When they arrived at Victoria, Saskia flew out of her seat and off the train, with Molly close behind her.

'I'm meeting Caro outside the station and she's going to take me back to the house. I'll never find it otherwise,' Saskia said as they walked across the concourse.

Saskia wasn't known for her sense of direction, and she was very unfamiliar with London.

'There's Caro.' Saskia's eyes lit up.

A woman in a tight navy-blue dress and a white cashmere coat was walking towards them and waving at Saskia.

'Good morning, darling,' Caro said to Saskia and then turned to Molly. 'And this must be Molly. So nice to meet you.'

'Same.' Molly smiled at Caro. She oozed glamour, with her strawberry blonde curls neatly falling over one eye, and a collection of gold chains around her neck. Her lips were coated in a deep cerise pink lipstick and her long lashes framed her emerald eyes. 'You're Mrs Darling, is that right?'

'That's right.' Caro nodded. 'I wanted Wendy, but it wasn't meant to be.' She shrugged and turned to Saskia. 'You ready for this? The house is super cute, if a little snug. I've had my things dropped off there this morning.'

'I can't wait!' Saskia squealed as they walked along the road together.

Molly stopped at the crossing. 'I'm heading this way.' She jerked her head towards the street on the left, then pulled Saskia in for a hug.

'Look after yourself,' Saskia whispered to Molly.

'You too,' Molly said, swallowing the lump in her throat, and hoping she didn't burst into tears in front of a stranger.

Caro smiled. 'Molly, you must come over to the house once we're settled in.'

Molly nodded. 'I'd love that.'

'I'll call you later,' Saskia said.

The lights at the crossing turned green, and Molly hurried across the road, turning around as she heard her name being called.

Saskia was grinning at her. 'Love you!' she shouted.

Molly laughed. 'Love you too!'

She walked towards her office, clutching her bag and her suitcase. Sitting down at her desk, she tucked her suitcase underneath it, and pulled her phone out of her bag. There was a message from Mark. She smiled as she opened it, wondering which restaurant or bar he'd booked them into tonight.

> Hey babe, I totally forgot about Lewis's stag do this weekend. Maybe see you next weekend? X

She let out a long exhale. He was cancelling on her at the last minute? Angrily, she typed a response.

> So glad I dragged my suitcase across the city for nothing. I'm busy next weekend.

Molly let herself into her dark, cold house after work, and switched on the hallway lights before locking the door behind her. The house was tidy and calm, and this unsettled her. As much as she found Saskia's aura of chaos irritating, it was scarily quiet without her.

Her coat was wet, as she'd got caught in the rain on the way back to her car. She peeled it off and put it on the radiator to dry. Dragging herself upstairs, she had a hot shower, then dressed in a comfy shirt, her mum's old woolly jumper, some black leggings, and fluffy socks.

She went into the kitchen and turned the radio on to cut through the silence and put a piece of leftover lasagne into the microwave to heat up. While it cooked, she made a salad, then took her dinner to the sofa, needing the noise of the TV for comfort.

After she'd eaten, she lit some candles, and got out her blanket, then picked up her phone. Mark had replied. She smiled to herself. He seemed apologetic for once.

I'm sorry. I forgot. I'll make it up to you. X

She didn't reply, as the prickle of anger was still lurking in her body. If making it up to her meant taking her to an overpriced restaurant and banging on about his job again, she wasn't interested. Her phone started ringing, and she sighed, but it wasn't Mark. It was Chris.

'Hi,' he said. 'I hope you don't mind me calling you, but you didn't reply to my message earlier and I wanted to check that you were alright. You weren't yourself on the train tonight.'

Her stomach lurched. Had he sent her a message? She'd been so preoccupied with Mark, she hadn't noticed.

'I'm sorry, I must have missed it. I'm sad about Saskia leaving, but I didn't want to tell you. I didn't want you to think I was pathetic.' She wasn't going to tell him about Mark. She didn't want to go over it again.

'I don't think you're pathetic.' He paused. 'Do you want me to come over?'

'No, don't worry,' she said firmly, feeling the heat rising in her cheeks. Why did the thought of seeing him make her instantly feel better? 'I'm fine.'

'You don't sound fine,' he replied.

'Well maybe I'm not totally fine, but I will be.'

Why was she protesting so hard? Why couldn't she just admit that she wanted to see him?

'Text me your address. I've just left the gym so I'll be with you as soon as I can.' His response was immediate, his tone as firm as hers.

'Thank you. See you soon.'

She hung up and sent him her address, then the flood of worst case scenarios started flooding into her head. What if he robs you? What if he assaults you? He's a stranger. You barely know him. The last thought hit home the hardest. What if you can't fight your feelings for him? She scrolled through her messages, and there was the message that Chris had been talking about.

> Hey, I just wanted to check in on you. You were really quiet on the train.

He was being friendly. That was all it was. He knew her too well for her to hide her feelings from him. She sucked in a breath, and went upstairs, pushed the door to her mum's bedroom open and sat on her bed. Her hands shook as she picked up the photo on her bedside table.

'Mum, am I so wrong to just want to see a friend tonight? He makes me feel safe. He comforts me. He knows me.' She knew her mum would say the same thing she had always said. '*Follow your heart. It won't steer you wrong.*'

But her mum was more like Saskia than Molly, more emotional than rational.

'I need him, Mum, and I don't know why, and it feels so scary, but I can't run away from it, or him.'

The doorbell rang, making her jump. She put down the photo.

'Thanks for the talk, Mum. I love you.'

She hurtled down the stairs to open the door, her breath catching in her throat as she stared at Chris. He was wearing navy tracksuit trousers and a tight grey t-shirt which emphasised his toned body. His hair was damp, and she could smell the citrus aftershave she was so used to.

'Thank you so much for coming over.' She chewed her lip. 'Was I that weird on the train?'

'No.' He paused. 'It wasn't what you said, it was what you didn't say.'

'Right,' she said. 'I forget how perceptive you are.'

Over the last few weeks that they had been travelling together, she'd picked up on his knack for spotting tiny details that other people would miss. He pointed out secret trysts, private meetings, hidden glances. Just like her dad. He'd told her he had learnt this skill from the Gaspard Millot thrillers that he was addicted to, and she'd changed the subject immediately.

She could see a thin silver chain around his neck with a circular pendant and leant forward to look at it. 'I've never seen that before. What is it? I can't read the writing.'

'It's a St. Christopher,' he said. 'Patron saint of travellers. I was named after him. My parents were travelling when they met.'

She grinned. 'Patron saint of travellers? Well, you've been positively saintly to me.'

'You've been pretty good to me as well. Are you going to let me in?' he asked.

She was still gripping his pendant. She let go and stepped back. 'Oh yes, sorry.' She put her hand to her forehead. 'I'm a terrible hostess. Would you like a drink? Tea, coffee or something cold? We have endless soda thanks to Saskia's sugar addiction.'

He followed her into the kitchen. 'Tea please.'

'Regular or herbal? I have rooibos. That's my favourite.' She pulled a box out of the cupboard.

'Never heard of it.' He shrugged. 'I'll give it a go, though.'

'It's kind of smoky and spicy. It's from South Africa, I drank loads of it when I was travelling.' She took two mugs out of the cupboard and put the rooibos teabags in, followed by the freshly boiled water. Handing the mug to him, she waited while he sipped it cautiously.

'I like it.' He nodded approvingly. 'Do you have it with milk, or not?'

'I do, but you don't have to.' She added a small amount to her mug before handing it to him. 'Try it with milk.'

He put his mug down on the counter and took hers. 'It's better with milk, I think.'

It felt strangely intimate sharing a drink with him in her kitchen, but she tried not to think about it.

'That's what I think.' She added a slosh of milk to his mug and handed it back to him. 'Let's go into the living room, it's warmer in there.'

She sat down next to him on the sofa and sipped her tea.

'Are you OK with me being here?' he asked. 'I know I was a bit...forceful on the phone, but you sounded like you needed me but you didn't want to say that.'

'I did need you,' she smiled. 'And I didn't want to admit it. I don't love being here on my own, but I don't like asking for help.'

'You let me help.' He frowned. 'Why?'

She put her mug down on the coffee table and turned to face him. 'You make me feel safe.'

She didn't want to elaborate. He made her feel safe, but he also made her feel other things too. He made her pulse race, her heart pound. He made her want to tear his clothes off. But she wouldn't tell him that. Her phone rang and she grabbed it, glad of the distraction from Chris's imperceptible expression. She mouthed a quick 'sorry' and walked into the hall to answer it.

'Saskia! How are you doing? How did it go today?'

'It's pretty full on,' Saskia said. 'It doesn't feel real at the moment. The others are chaotic clutter bunnies like me, so we're going to live in a pigsty with no bossy sisters telling us to clear up.'

Molly felt a pang of sadness. Was this it now? Was her sister going to leave her for good? 'That's great. I'm so glad you're alright. I'm missing you already.'

'Why don't you ask Jess or Liz to come over?' Saskia asked.

'Maybe,' Molly said. 'I've got yoga with Liz Sunday morning.'

'What else have you got planned? You hate spending the weekend on your own.'

Molly took a deep breath. 'I'm not on my own.'

'I thought Mark was away?'

'He is away.' Molly could almost hear Saskia's brain working. She paused, waiting for it.

'Oh my god! You didn't? You did? Is Chris there? Molly! You little beast.' Saskia's cackle blasted into Molly's ear.

'He was on his way home from the gym, and he dropped in to check on me.' Molly hissed.

'Are you naked?' Saskia asked, giggling.

'No, I am not.' Molly retorted. 'We're just having a cup of tea on the sofa.'

'You know what, I'm glad he's there. I trust him with you. He's good for you, Mole. You've been a totally different person these last few weeks. He's put the smile back on your face. Listen, I've got to go, but I'll speak to you tomorrow.'

'Wait, Saskia? Are you still there?'

She had already hung up.

Shaking her head, Molly stuffed her phone into her pocket, and walked back into the living room , sitting down next to Chris. 'Sorry, that was just Saskia updating me. She's having the time of her life.'

Chris laughed. 'I bet she is. And I know it'll be hard for a while, adjusting to not being with her.'

'You're right. At this time of year, we just hole up in here and watch TV, it's lush.'

She would usually be wrapped in a blanket with Saskia and her mind wandered, imagining being wrapped in a blanket with Chris.

'I don't blame you,' he said. 'That's what we do. But our place doesn't have half as much character as this.'

'Thank you. 'We hung onto as many of the original features as we could. Do you want to have a look around?' She stood up, wanting to put some distance between them. The candlelight flickering in his eyes was making the butterflies in her stomach do somersaults.

'Sure.' He stood up, following her into the dining room.

'The dresser is an antique,' she said, gesturing to it, 'and my mum collected all of these old plates, which we still use.' She led him into the kitchen. 'The kitchen's too narrow for more than two people to be in here, but I hate cooking anyway, so it works out just fine. I use it to bake and Saskia cooks.' She laughed. 'I might have some treats for us once I've shown you the rest of the house. You have to see the pink bathroom.'

Leaving the kitchen, she walked up the stairs, with him right behind her.

'Oh wow, it is very pink,' he said as he stood in front of her in the bathroom.

'I know. We found the brightest pink we could, it makes me smile every morning.' She walked along the corridor to her own room, pushing the door open. 'Here's my room.' She noticed him trying to hide a smile as he walked inside.

'What's up?' she asked. 'What's funny?'

'When you offered to give me a tour, I thought that your room might look like this. Very neat, mostly antique furniture, loads of books.' He gestured to the wardrobe door. 'I bet everything in there is colour coordinated and ironed.'

She groaned. 'Am I that predictable?' Yet again, she was outed for being boring. Staid. He was right, but for some reason it stung.

'Maybe, I don't know.' He shrugged. 'You seem really organised. Everything you wear is always immaculate. So why wouldn't your wardrobe be?'

'Correct again, Poirot,' she said, smiling.

'It's weird, isnt it? Noticing all of this stuff about people, assessing their characters.' He looked away from her.

'No, it's not weird. I like the way your brain works. I wish I noticed these details about people.' She gave him a playful nudge and paused outside the next door. 'This is Saskia's room.'

'I bet that room's not tidy,' he said.

'You're wrong. We blitzed it while we were hungover on Sunday.'

He made a face. 'That sounds terrible.'

She nodded 'It was terrible. I was nearly sick twice. We rewarded ourselves with burgers in our onesies.' She let out what she thought was a laugh, but instead one of her cackles shot out.

He burst out laughing. 'What was that?'

'My awful cackle,' she said, cringing. 'Saskia and I both have them. They always sneak out when I least expect it to embarrass me.'

'It's hilarious. Can I make you do it again?' A smiled pulled at the corner of his lips.

'I hope not.' She paused at the next bedroom door. 'I can't show you this room. This is my mum's bedroom. We haven't changed it at all since she died. It's exactly how she left it.'

'There's nothing wrong with that,' he said, his voice low. 'Grief is unique to the person experiencing it.'

'Wow,' she replied. 'That's deep.'

She was standing too close to him now, close enough that she could lean forwards and rest her head on his chest. She stepped back slightly. 'Saskia and I both go and sit in there sometimes, just to feel her.' She saw a tear plop onto the wooden floorboards and wiped her eyes, her cheeks burning with embarrassment. 'Oh, for God's sake. I'm so sorry. Come on, let's go downstairs.'

'What were you watching?' he asked as they sat back down on the sofa.

'Ocean's Eleven, for the hundredth time,' she replied. 'I love heist films. Either heist films, or big musical productions from the 50s and 60s. Grace Kelly's my favourite actress and I love her in High Society.'

'I've never seen it,' he said.

'It's a classic. She's a glamorous socialite called Tracey Lord. She's dramatic and fiery, and she's torn between Bing Crosby, Frank Sinatra, and John Lund.' She pulled the DVD case out of the cabinet and handed it to him. 'What's your favourite film?'

'Star Wars.' A smile spread across his face. 'I'm a huge Star Wars fan.'

'Your bag.' She smiled. 'You have a Star Wars bag.'

'That's right,' he said, nodding. 'See, you pick up on the small details too.'

'Sometimes.' She shrugged and picked up the TV remote. 'Do you want to watch the rest of this?'

'We could...' He paused and waggled the DVD at her, 'but you've sold me on High Society. Let's watch that.'

'Sure' she said, touched that he wanted to watch her favourite film. 'We need snacks. How does rocky road sound? I'll go and make some more tea as well.'

'Sounds good to me,' he replied. 'Can I help?'

'No, I'll be right back.' She went into the kitchen and sang to herself as she made the tea and plated the rocky road slices, putting them onto a tray and taking them back into the living room.

His eyes lit up as she walked in and put the tray down on the coffee table. 'Thanks, Molly.' He took the plate that she handed him and took a bite of the chocolatey square on it.

She picked up her mug of tea and took a sip from it, almost choking as she heard the moan of pleasure come from his mouth.

'These are great,' he said, taking another bite. 'I love the little marshmallows.'

She picked up her own plate and took a bite, allowing each of the textures and tastes to flood her mouth. 'Hmmm, they're not bad. They need another texture, maybe some chopped hazelnuts.'

'That would work.' He nodded appreciatively. 'If you need any taste testers, I'm always happy to help.'

'I'll keep you in mind.' She picked up the TV remote and pressed play. 'Especially now that my chief taster is in London, living her best life.' She nodded to the TV as the opening credits finished. 'Here we go, I can't wait to see what you think.'

A few hours later, Molly woke up with a jump. The TV screen was black and next to her Chris was sprawled out. She giggled at his long body hanging off her tiny sofa and debated whether to wake him. Instead, she wrapped him in a blanket. She blew out the candles, then cleared up the mugs and plates.

When she returned to the living room, Chris was still asleep, so she sat a glass of water on the coffee table for him and went upstairs to her bedroom. As she washed off her make-up and changed into her pyjamas, she felt comforted by the thought that she wasn't alone in the house. Even though they'd only just known each other for a short time, she felt closer to Chris than she did most of the people in her life.

Chapter Twelve

November 2014, Canterbury, Kent, England

Molly strode off the train and over the bridge onto the platform the other side. She swiped her ticket through the barrier and walked to her car. In the dark car park, she felt a thump on her arm. She struggled as the hooded figure tried to grab her bag, before hitting her in the face. She screamed at him, but no sound came out. He pulled the bag from her shoulder, shoving her onto the cold ground. Shards of gravel scratched her palms as she tried to stop herself from falling onto her face. Clutching her bleeding hands, she screamed again but the man was already gone. She ran to her car crying, fumbling in her pocket for her car keys. A voice was calling her name, but she couldn't see where it was coming from.

With a thump she woke up. She was laying on her bedroom floor, and her duvet was in a heap next to her, along with her pillow.

'Molly, are you OK?' Chris was standing in her doorway, his eyes bleary, his hair sticking up. The light from the moon shone through the window, illuminating him.

'I had a nightmare. It happens sometimes.'

She felt her cheeks colour, a wave of embarrassment flooding over her.

'Here. Take my hand.' He held out a hand to her, pulling her to feet.

She pushed her hair off her face. 'I'm so sorry for waking you up.'

'You don't need to apologise,' he said softly. 'I was worried about you.'

He glanced at her duvet, which was laying in a heap on the floor and picked it up, putting it back onto the bed.

'Thank you.' She swallowed hard, fighting the combination of fear and embarrassment flooding through her. 'I haven't had a nightmare for a couple of weeks, but this one was a bad one.'

'Will you be alright now? Do you want me to stay?' He leant against the doorframe, his brow furrowed with concern.

'No, it's fine. I'll go right back to sleep.' She sat down on the bed and rubbed her face.

He nodded to the heavy velvet curtains. 'I don't pull my curtains either.'

She yawned. 'I like to look at the stars.'

'Me too.' He smiled.

She felt like she was still dreaming. The moonlight bathed Chris in a soft glow, and she fought the urge to wrap herself around him. Her heart was still beating so fast she thought it would fly out of her chest, and although she'd told him that she didn't need him to stay, the thought of him leaving the room made her chest tighten. She stood up and straightened the duvet out, smiling as he picked up the other end and helped her.

'Thanks,' she whispered.

'No worries.' He cleared his throat. 'So, I uh, should go.'

'Yes. Of course. Thank you for checking on me.' She sat down on the bed. Every time she blinked she was back in the station car park on the floor.

As he reached the door, she found her voice. 'Chris. I'm scared.'

He turned around. 'Do you want me to stay?'

She nodded. 'Is that OK?'

'Of course it is.' He sat on the other side of the bed, stretching his legs out in front of him. 'I'll stay here until you fall asleep.'

Her heart rate slowed as she climbed back into the bed. She wasn't quite sure why his presence comforted her so much, all she knew was that she didn't want to fall asleep unless he was next to her.

'Thank you.' She lay down, closing her eyes and listening to the rhythm of his breathing. 'Goodnight Chris.'

Molly opened her eyes, and rolled over, bumping into something solid. Chris's arm. 'Shit!' she squeaked.

It came flooding back to her.

The nightmare, his calm, patient tone, his reluctance to leave her. He hadn't got into the duvet, he was laying on top of it, his arms folded across his chest. Her breath caught in her throat. After last night, she wasn't sure if she saw him as a friend anymore, or if she ever had. His eyes opened and she froze, not wanting to get caught staring at him.

'Morning,' he said, sleepily. 'How are you doing?' His brow creased with concern.

'I'm fine,' she said, and a pang of guilt and embarrassment washed over her. 'I'm so sorry about last night. Did you get any sleep?'

'Yeah, I slept really well.' He climbed off the bed. 'I should uh, let you get dressed.'

'Let me get you a towel, so you can take a shower.' She hurried down the hall to the bathroom and pulled a large towel out of the airing cupboard, hanging it on the heated towel rail and then went back into the bedroom. 'I've put a towel out on the rail to heat up for you. Help yourself to whatever you need in there.'

'I've got shower gel and a change of clothes in my gym bag; I'll just go and grab them. Are you sure you don't want a shower first?' he asked as he climbed off the bed.

She shook her head. 'No, I'm good. Help yourself.'

The quicker she could get him out of her bedroom, the better. His aftershave lingered in her hair and on her skin, and she couldn't stop staring at his toned arms, imagining them wrapped around her.

While Chris showered, Molly went downstairs, and cleaned and tidied every bit of the kitchen, trying to distract herself from the embarrassment she felt about the previous night. When she heard the shower switch off, she put the kettle on, and she had just finished making them both a cup of tea when he walked into the kitchen. His hair was still damp, and the hoodie and sweatpants he was wearing looked cosy and warm. Again she fought the urge to put her arms around him.

'Hey,' she said. 'Did you enjoy the pink bathroom?'

He smiled. 'It was like showering in Barbie's dream house. It's cool.'

She laughed. 'It *is* cool. I love it. I made you a cup of tea,' she passed him the mug. 'What would you like for breakfast?'

He looked thoughtful. 'It's Saturday, right? You said you make poached eggs for Saskia at the weekend. Would you let me do that for you?'

She gazed up at him. 'You don't have to do that. I invited you over here and ruined your sleep.'

'I slept just fine,' he said. 'Don't worry about me. You had a rough night. Why don't you let me do this for you?'

It had been a long time since anyone had taken care of her, and the kindness of his gesture took her by surprise.

'I'd like that. Shall I show you where everything is?'

'Sure.' He looked around the kitchen. 'I get the feeling that everything has its place in this kitchen.'

'You would be right.' She got out a pan from a large drawer under the hob, and took the eggs out of the fridge.

While he cooked the eggs – more expertly than she ever could – she made some toast. Slowly her embarrassment about last night dissipated as he talked and cracked jokes. He was so easy to get on with, and this little domestic scene felt natural, not awkward.

'We're good to go,' he said, carefully putting the poached eggs on top of the toast. 'Where's the cutlery?'

'I'll get it,' she replied and pulled some cutlery out of the drawer, as he took the plates to the dining table.

'Thank you so much for this,' she said as she sat down opposite him. She cut into the egg, the yolk running down over her toast. 'Wow, these are miles better than the ones I make Saskia.'

'I've had a lot of practice. Scott likes poached eggs too.' He cut into his own eggs, nodding approvingly. 'These are decent actually. I've had a lot of disasters.'

'Me too.' she shook her head. 'We usually just laugh it off and try again.'

'Same!' He smiled at her.

'I'm so sorry about last night, I must have scared the life out of you.' She chewed her lip.

'Don't be sorry. You didn't scare me. I heard you fall out of bed and I was worried abot you.'

Her chest tightened. He was worried about her. Even though they were fully clothed, being sat here with him felt very intimate. They'd spent the night in the same bed and he'd cooked for her. Alarm bells started ringing in her head, but she ignored them. 'I was so glad you stayed with me. I was so scared to go back to sleep.'

His eyes locked onto hers. 'I couldn't have left you. I was worried about you.'

You're so selfless,' she said, her heart pounding.

'Not always,' he replied, 'but I knew you needed someone to look out for you last night.'

'Why isn't it awkward between us?' she asked. 'It's like we already knew each other.'

He shrugged. 'I dont know. I feel the same way. I felt comfortable with you from the moment I met you.'

She held his gaze for just a second, admiring the flecks of blue in his eyes. She still thought he was hot, but now that she actually *knew* him, his good looks weren't the only thing that was drawing him to her. Frightened by her feelings, she picked up his empty plate and stacked it on top of hers.

'When I spoke to Saskia last night, she wasn't even surprised that you were here. I would never ask anyone to come over ordinarily. I'd just pretend I was fine, even if I wasn't.'

'You don't have to pretend with me,' he said.

'I don't feel the *need* to pretend with you.' She knew why. 'You listen to me, rather than telling me to get over it.'

'I'd never treat you like that.'

The look in his eyes unnerved her. They had darkened, and his need to protect her made her heart skip a beat. But he wasn't hers, and she wasn't his.

'I know you wouldn't,' She couldn't tear her eyes away from him.

He broke eye contact with her first, and finished his tea. 'Can I help you clear up?'

She shook her head. 'Thank you, but that's my favourite part. I might hate cooking, but I love cleaning.'

'Why doesn't that surprise me?' He laughed. 'I'm gonna go, but if you want me to come back later, I can.'

'Don't feel like you have to,' she said. 'I'm gonna clean the house, go to the supermarket, you know, all the boring stuff that Saskia doesn't like doing.'

He smiled. 'That sounds familiar. Scott seems to think that food should just appear in the fridge.' He paused. 'Do you want go out for a drink tonight?'

She considered it for a second. 'Yes, I want to go out. I'm sick of being afraid to do anything. I've not been out since Halloween.'

'Right.' He sipped his tea. 'That was an interesting night.'

'I don't want to get that drunk.' She grimaced. It had taken her far too long to get over that night and she'd also further embarrassed herself with Chris while dressed in her slinky costume.

'You don't have to drink anything,' he said. 'We can go to Mimosa if you want. Alex messaged me earlier asking to meet up tonight. Kate's coming too. If you'd rather do something else – or nothing – that's also fine, obviously.'

She stared into his slate grey eyes. 'No, I'd like to come, that sounds good.' She would just keep her distance from him.

He put his empty mug down on the table. 'Do you want to get dinner too, or just go straight to Mimosa?'

She bit her lip. The city would be full of people, and it would be dark, and cold, but she wouldn't be alone. She would be with someone who would protect her. 'I think we should get dinner too.'

'Great. Do you want to book somewhere?' he asked.

'You like Thai, right? How about Lotus Thai?' This was a good bet as the owners knew her. She would be somewhere she knew, with someone who had made it clear that he would protect her.

'Sounds great.' He stood up and walked out into the hall, picking up his bag. 'Let me know what time to come over.'

'I'll see you later,' she said. 'If you get a better offer for tonight, don't worry, I've got a ton of films to watch.'

'I've made plans with you.' He put on his jacket. 'Even if I was inundated with offers – which I'm not - I've said we'll go out and I always keep my promises.'

I bet you do, she thought to herself. She knew him. He was honest, kind, and good. As he opened the front door, the sun's rays streamed in, bathing him in a golden glow. She sighed. It was fitting. He was her guardian angel.

'I'll see you later.'

She waved him off and shut the door, walking into the living room, and flopping onto the sofa, which still smelt of his aftershave.

She picked up her phone and rang Saskia, wondering if she was awake.

Saskia answered, a mumbled hello. 'Morning Mole, how are you doing today? How was last night?'

Molly could imagine her sister wiggling her eyebrows suggestively.

'It was nice. We watched a couple of films, he fell asleep on the sofa, and he's just left.'

She didn't tell Saskia about her nightmare. Last night's one was the worst one she'd had so far. She'd never thrown herself out of bed before.

'How boring. I was hoping you were going to tell me you lured him into your bedroom and had your wicked way with him.'

'Saskia! We're friends.' This was a blatant lie, but Saskia couldn't see Molly's face and so she hoped she would get away with it.

'Hmmm. Are you though?' Saskia's reply was blunt as usual.

'Yes. We're friends. He's funny and kind and we just get on.' Molly kept her tone as neutral as possible.

'What have you got planned tonight?' Saskia asked. 'We're going out for drinks after the rehearsal and getting sushi.'

'That sounds brilliant! I'm going out for dinner with Chris, then meeting Kate and Alex at Mimosa,' Molly said.

'Oh man! That means you'll get to see Scott,' Saskia said, her voice heavy with sadness. 'Can you give him a squeeze and a kiss from me. No tongues though.'

'Hilarious. Of course I will.' Molly smiled. 'Have a great time. I'll come up for a night out once you're settled in.'

'Yes, Mole! You'll love it.' Saskia squealed. 'Caro is desperate to get to know you. We've hit it off big time. We're so similar. I think she's actually more chaotic than me.'

'I'm so glad.' A pang of jealously stabbed at Molly's chest. She and Saskia had always been inseparable, but they were nothing alike. 'Count me in. I'll speak to you tomorrow. Love you. Be safe.'

'Love you too. I know that if you're with Chris, you'll be safe.'

Molly smiled. 'He's a good guy.'

'A very good *friend*. See you later, Mole!'

Saskia hung up and Molly sat down on the sofa. She probably shouldn't be going out with Chris tonight. It wasn't a good idea when she so obviously had a crush on him, but he was her friend, and she wanted a night out. She *needed* a night out.

Chris left Molly's and drove straight to his parents' house. He parked on the gravel drive and walked up to the front door. The bricks were old and faded, and a honeysuckle bush curved into an arch around the porch. The front door swung open just as he reached it.

'Hello mate, I saw your car. How are you?' His dad, Bill, ran a hand through his light grey hair as he let Chris into the house.

'Good, Dad, how are you?' Chris took his shoes off.

'Oh, same old. Have you been to the gym?' Bill asked, eyeing Chris's crumpled tracksuit.

'Uh, yes,' Chris said. He didn't like lying to his parents, but the truth was too complicated.

Bill shook his head. 'So predictable.'

If only you knew, Chris thought to himself. He walked into the living room. 'Hi, Mum.'

'Morning, darling!' His mum, Anne, was sat on the rug in front of the fireplace, doing a jigsaw puzzle on a wooden board. 'I'm still stuck on your birthday present.'

'Want a hand?' he asked.

'Of course.' She smiled and shifted over so he could sit on the rug too. 'Bill, are you helping?'

'Not right now.' He walked out of the room.

He sat down next to her and picked up the box, studying it.

'I didn't know you were coming over.'

Chris looked up to see Scott walking in. 'Same. What are you doing here?'

'Brought some beer samples up here for Dad. He's now making room in the fridge in the garage.' Scott sat down on the sofa. 'And he made me breakfast.' He gestured to the plate of toast he was holding, then sat down on the sofa. 'Did you eat at Molly's, or do you want some breakfast?'

Anne looked up. 'Why did you stay at Molly's?'

Scott gave Chris a meaningful look, then took a bite of his toast.

'She uh, she needed a friend. Saskia's gone and she's still pretty vulnerable.'

Chris had made it clear that he and Molly were just friends, but he got the impression they didn't believe him. He'd sent Scott a message before he went to bed last night, letting him know where he was, and he regretted that too. With his parents and his brother, his private life never stayed private.

'She's lucky to have such a good friend,' Anne said.

Chris wasn't fooled. He knew her words weren't as innocent as they seemed.

He sighed. 'Yes, and so am I. We ate rocky road and we watched an old film, High Society. Do you know it?'

'Oh yes.' Anne nodded. 'Seems pretty apt if you ask me.'

Scott frowned. 'What am I missing?'

'Nothing.' Anne stood up. 'I'll go and put the kettle on.'

After she left the room, Chris groaned and turned to Scott. 'Why are you trying to make my life harder? I don't want Mum knowing about Molly and me.'

'So there *is* a Molly and you, is there?' Scott raised his eyebrow. 'Has she split up with her boyfriend?'

'I didn't mean it like that,' Chris said. 'I meant I don't want them interfering. They won't understand and they'll think there's more to it than there actually is.'

'I'm going to ask you one question.' Scott folded his arms. 'Where did you sleep last night?'

Chris ran a hand through his hair. He couldn't lie to Scott. He never had, but telling the truth would provoke a lot more questions.

'I slept on her bed. I was asleep on her sofa, then she had a nightmare and fell out of bed, which woke me up. When I went upstairs, she looked terrified so I stayed with her and slept on her bed.'

Scott nodded. 'You want to look after her. It's what you do, but you're going to get hurt.'

'I won't,' Chris said. 'Molly's having a hard time right now and she needs a friend.'

'She's got a boyfriend.' Scott blurted out. 'I'm worried about you.'

'You don't need to worry about me,' Chris said, just as his mum walked back into the room holding two mugs.

Anne eyed them with suspicion. 'Well, this is a lovely, tense atmosphere. What's going on?'

'I feel like I'm watching a train crash happening right in front of me.' Scott turned to Chris. 'This isn't like you. Molly has a boyfriend, and you are *far* too involved in her life.'

'Yes, and he isn't.' Chris said through gritted teeth. 'He's never there for her. I am. I make her feel safe. She needs me. I can't get hurt if she never finds out how I feel.'

Swallowing his feelings for her was painful, but he would do it because she needed him to.

Anne's bright blue eyes locked onto Chris's. 'Darling, is this what you want? You deserve to be happy, not breaking your heart over someone you can't have.'

It's too late, he thought to himself. 'It doesn't matter how I feel about her because she can't ever know.'

'Do you think she's got feelings for you?' Scott asked.

'I don't know.' Chris shrugged. He had a feeling that Molly felt the same way, but he was too scared to consider what that might mean. 'I know what I'm doing.'

This was a complete lie. He'd never felt so out of control in his life.

'I should be keeping out of this,' Anne said, 'but I just want to say that relationships are complicated, and sometimes the lines between friends and lovers become blurred before you even realise it. You might know what you're doing, but does Molly?'

'I'm sure she does. Last night we watched a film and fell asleep on her sofa. It was all totally above board,' Chris insisted.

It *had* all been totally innocent. Apart from the thoughts he'd had of pulling her into his arms and holding her so tightly she forgot her fears.

'Fine.' Scott held up his hands. 'I won't say anything else. Are you coming out tonight? Alex messaged me earlier. Has he contacted you?'

'He did,' Chris said. I'm getting some dinner with Molly first, then we'll come to the bar.'

Scott put his head in his hands. 'This is such a dangerous game you're playing mate. I hope you know that.'

Chapter Thirteen

November 2014, Canterbury, Kent, England

Molly spent the rest of the day scrubbing every surface of the flat, washing the blankets on the sofa and tidying up the piles of books. She got her outfits ready for the week ahead and unpacked the suitcase full of clothes that she'd packed for the weekend. She wondered what Mark was doing, and where he was. What would he say if he knew that someone else had slept in her bed last night? Or that she'd thought about nestling her head on Chris's chest and letting him hold her? Ruminating would get her nowhere, she decided, and she needed to get ready before Chris came over.

She took off her pyjamas and threw them on the bed, catching sight of herself in the mirror inside the open wardrobe door. Slowly, she turned, studying her curvy figure. She and Saskia had never been self-conscious about their bodies. Their free-spirited mum had made sure of that. As she stared at herself in the mirror, an image flashed into her mind, one of her and Chris together in her bed, her fingers trailing across his cheek.

Where did that come from? she thought to herself. She shook her head and walked into the bathroom.

She ran herself a bath and lay back in the hot, bubbly water with a new book. It was the sequel to the steamy romance novel that Saskia had lent her. Her mind drifted off as she read, imagining that Chris was the main character, a spy who had been tasked with protecting a wealthy heiress from a mysterious enemy who wanted her dead. Her pulse raced as the bodyguard and the heiress finally gave in to their feelings. Every sound, every touch was laid out for her on the page.

As she read, she hoped that this would get him out of her system, that she could leave her crush behind her in the pages of the book. The female main character murmured with pleasure as her spy turned lover satisfied her every desire. As she clung to him tightly, her body drenched with sweat, she whispered to him.

'You make me feel safe.'

Shit. She shut the book and tossed it onto the tiled floor. This hadn't helped. It had just made things a hundred times worse. She took a deep breath and sunk her head under the water.

When she surfaced again, her heart was still pounding. Through the bathroom window she could see the sun setting over the houses on the other side of the road. Chris would be back any moment now. She pulled herself out of the bath and wrapped herself in a towel.

As the sky outside darkened, Molly put her hair into rollers and went through her wardrobe trying to decide what to wear. She didn't do low cut or revealing. She felt sexier with a boat neck and a midi dress than she did in a tube of Lycra. The doorbell rang and she ran downstairs in her bathrobe to answer it. Her breath caught in her throat as she swung the door open.

'Chris! Hi.'

He was wearing a navy silk bomber jacket, the one she'd seen on the train, a dark blue t-shirt, tight fitting black jeans and black desert boots.

She swallowed hard. 'Come in.'

'I like your outfit.' He smirked.

She stepped back to let him into the hall. 'I'm not going out like this, I just lost track of time.'

Thanks to that book, she thought to herself.

She tried to avert her eyes as Chris slipped his jacket off, revealing his toned arms. Now the feelings were out there, in her head, she was struggling to stuff them away again. Every time she shut her eyes, she could see him, wearing a suit, shutting her in his bedroom, telling her he would protect her.

'I've booked us into Riad for dinner,' she said. 'The Thai place was fully booked.

His eyes lit up. 'The new Moroccan place? I've been wanting to go there since it opened, just haven't had time.' He locked eyes with her. 'If at any point you want to leave, we go. No questions asked.'

'Thank you,' she breathed, feeling overwhelmed.

He was too handsome, too kind. Too caring. She needed to put some space between them so that she could sort her head out.

'I'll just go and get dressed. Do you want a drink? I've got some beers in the fridge.'

'Do you want me to drive?' he asked.

'No, let's get a taxi, then neither of us has to drive,' she said quickly. Being in his car somehow felt too intimate.

'Then yes, I'd love a beer,' he said.

'Coming right up.' She pulled her robe around her and walked into the kitchen.

As she pulled the fridge open, she groaned. Saskia had put the bottles of beer on the top shelf, and she couldn't reach them.

'Chris!' she called. 'Can I borrow you?'

He appeared in the kitchen doorway. 'What's up?'

'I'm too short, and I can't reach the beers,' she said with a resigned sigh.

If he found this funny, he didn't let on. He simply reached up to the top shelf and passed two bottles down to her.

'Thank you.'

She slid the cap onto the edge of the worktop and smacked the top of the bottle with her hand, releasing the cap, before handing the bottle to Chris.

'I've never seen it done like that before,' he said, taking it from her.

'That's what he said.' She burst out laughing and opened her own bottle of beer. 'My dad taught me to do this.'

He laughed too. 'Yet another layer, Molly. Santé.' He tapped his bottle against hers.

'Santé.' She took a sip of her beer and then led him back into the living room.

Even sat on the sofa next to him in her bathrobe, and with a head of rollers, she didn't feel awkward. 'I'll go and get ready, I won't be long.'

'Sure,' he said. 'Shall I order a taxi?'

'That would be great, I'll be back in ten minutes.' She smiled at him and hurried out of the kitchen, taking her bottle with her.

She flung her wardrobe open and ran her eyes over the contents. Jeans would be good. Jeans and a jumper. She was only going out for dinner with a friend. Her fingers ran over the soft fabric of the green dress she'd planned to wear on her date with Mark. It seemed like it wanted to be taken out tonight. Ignoring the voice in her head telling her it was a bad idea, she slid it off the hanger and put it on. The bodice clung to her curves and the full skirt flared out from the waist, stopping just below her knees. The Bardot neckline showed off her neck and shoulders but hid her cleavage. It was elegant, not revealing. It was perfect.

Sliding out her rollers and putting them back in their box, she smoothed out her curls and added a coat of the blood red lipstick that she'd worn at Halloween. As she stared at herself in the mirror, she noticed that the haunted, scared expression had left her eyes, which now sparkled. Her face was no longer pale and drawn, instead her cheeks were pink and flushed. She slipped on her rings, a simple gold band, and a cocktail ring studded with a ruby, her birthstone. They had been her mother's and she felt comforted by wearing them.

Just be his friend, she told herself firmly as she studied her reflection.

Taking a deep breath, she picked up her black peep toe stilettos and clutch bag and went downstairs.

Chris sucked in a breath as the living room door opened and Molly walked in, sat on the edge of her sofa, and put on her heels.

'Wow,' he said, 'it's Tracey Lord herself.' He smiled, but his heart rate had ramped up, and the shy smile she gave him in return was almost more than he could handle.

She laughed. 'Thank you. I like this.' She ran her fingers down the sleeve of his jacket. 'It's so soft.'

He shivered, her touch like a bolt of electricity down his arm. 'Thanks.' He picked up his phone. 'The taxi has just arrived.'

'Can you fasten the hook at the top of my dress?' she asked.

He nodded. 'Sure, hold on.' He rubbed his hands together so that his fingers weren't cold.

She turned around and brushed her hair to one side, then he fastened the hook, his fingers brushing her soft skin. Her scent enveloped him, and he stepped away quickly as his feelings threatened to overwhelm him. 'You're all good.'

'Thank you. On y va!' she replied.

Inside the taxi, Chris glanced at Molly. Her eyes were shut tight, and her breathing was heavy. He knew this would be hard for her, but he also hoped it would help her to heal. As her eyes opened, he held out his hand to her and she took it, her scarlet nails digging into the skin on the back of his hand. He gave her a smile and she smiled back, just as the taxi stopped at the rank on the Burgate, the ancient, cobbled street that ran towards the cathedral.

'You good?' he asked, turning to her after he'd paid the driver.

'I'm good,' she replied, though she looked unsure.

He slid out of the taxi and offered her his hand, helping her out.

'Thank you,' she said, smiling at him.

He wanted to hold her hand as they walked into the city together, but he reminded himself that she wasn't his, and he wasn't hers. They were friends. He did watch her closely, though, and noticed that as they got closer to the restaurant she seemed more relaxed. The sounds of cutlery clinking and laughter floated through the air as they walked through the narrow backstreets, full of restaurants and bars.

When they arrived at the ornately carved wooden door of the restaurant, he opened it for her. 'After you.'

'Thank you.' She smiled at him and he followed her inside.

'Good evening and welcome to Riad.' A waitress greeted Molly and Chris. 'Let me show you to your table.'

As they sat down, she handed them both drinks menus. 'I'll be back in a moment to take your orders.'

After she left, Chris looked up at Molly over his menu. 'What do you recommend? I've never had Moroccan food before.'

He thought it was a strange choice considering her boyfriend's mum was Moroccan but he didn't say anything. He didn't want to ruin the evening before it even started.

'It all sounds good,' she said studying the menu. 'I would go with flatbreads, houmous, dips, and olives to start and then a tagine. That'll give you a good introduction to the flavours.'

'Sure.' He nodded. 'I'll try anything.'

When their starters arrived, Chris followed Molly's lead and tore off a strip of flatbread, dipping it into the houmous.

He nodded appreciatively. 'This is good.'

'It is.' She gestured to a small bowl which contained a thick red sauce. 'That's harissa and it's very spicy, just to warn you. I can't tolerate spicy food at all.'

'Well now I want to try it,' he said, taking a piece of flatbread and dipping it into the bright red sauce, before taking a bite. His eyes watered immediately. 'You're right. That's spicy, but it's also delicious.'

She laughed. 'You're welcome to it. I've learnt my lesson. It's not for me.'

When the lamb tagine arrived, piled on top of fragrant couscous. Molly spooned some of it onto her plate. 'If we were in Morocco, we would be eating this with our hands.'

'I always try and do what the locals do when I go abroad, but I'm glad we have cutlery tonight.' He paused. 'Do you eat with your hands when you're over there?'

She nodded. 'I do, and I make such a mess, but Mark's family are used to it. I use a big napkin.'

'Big napkin for the win.' He smiled. 'Do you go over there a lot?'

He needed to get a feel for how close she was with his family. She talked about them and his mum more than she talked about him.

'I've not been for a year or so,' she said. 'Mark is always too busy to go. It's a shame. His family are lovely. They're very close, and it reminds me of how my family used to be before Dad moved back to France and Mum died.' She took a sip of her drink. 'That's what I want one day. A family, a noisy, chaotic family. How about you? What do you want out of life?'

'Wow. That's a big question.' His eyes met hers. 'I want a family. I'm very close with mine, and I want to be with someone who shares the same goals.' His mind drifted for a second, imagining him and Molly together, but then he remembered Mark. 'Does Mark want a family too?'

She paused. 'I think he does. He's just very focused on his job right now.'

He could read her like a book. Whatever the situation was with her and Mark, she wasn't happy with it. He could tell from the way she nibbled at her bottom lip, as if she was afraid to talk about it. He didn't want to push her. Changing the subject was the best idea, he decided. 'Do you think Scott and Saskia are a good match?'

'I don't know Scott that well, but what I do know, I like.' She put down her cutlery. 'Saskia is smitten with him. I've never seen her fall so hard for anyone.'

'Same with Scott,' he said. 'He's fallen for her big time. I like her, and I think she's good for him.'

'I guess we have to be very grateful for that power cut.' The sadness had left her eyes now, and the light from the candle on the table flickered in them as she spoke. 'You and I are such good friends, and Scott and Saskia are inseparable.'

He repeated Molly's words to himself. *We're such good friends.* And that was how it would have to stay. 'I know. It worked out well for all of us.'

Molly put her card down on top of Chris's when the bill arrived. The food had been incredible, and although the restaurant had only been open a few months, it was packed. She wasn't surprised. The food was as good as it had been in the small village just outside Marrakech where Mark's family lived. Was it slightly weird that she'd brought Chris here, when her boyfriend's family were Moroccan? Possibly. But it reminded her of somewhere comforting, safe, and where she belonged. So she pushed her thoughts to the back of her mind.

'Thank you,' she said to the waiter as she tapped her card on the card reader. 'The food was incredible.'

He smiled at her. 'You're very welcome. We hope to see you again.'

'I'll definitely be back.' She returned his smile.

'Me too,' Chris added. 'I've never had Moroccan food before, but I'm a huge fan.'

'I'm so pleased to hear that. Enjoy your evening.'

As the waiter walked away, Chris slipped on his jacket. 'Are you ready to head to Mimosa? Kate and Alex are there already.'

'Sure. Let's go.' Molly put her coat on, then followed Chris through the bustling city streets to Mimosa.

'What do you want to drink?' Chris asked her as they walked into the bar.

'A rum and Coke would be great, thank you.' She fought the urge to grab Chris's hand. The bar was packed and without the alcohol fuelled bravery from the last time she was there, she felt vulnerable.

'Sure,' he said, then turned to the barmaid. 'Hi Jo. Can I get two rum and Cokes, please?'

'Hey, Chris. How are you?' She took two glasses down from the rack above her, putting a scoop of ice and a measure of rum into them.

'I'm good thanks,' he replied, then nodded to Molly. 'This is my friend, Molly.'

'Hey, Molly. Good to meet you.'

'Same.' Molly greeted her with a smile. 'I love your hair.'

Jo patted her pink curls. 'Thanks, love.' She topped their drinks up with Coke and added a slice of lemon, then put the glasses on the counter in front of Chris, then took the note that he handed her. 'I'll be right back with your change.'

'Is Scott working tonight?' Molly asked, picking up her glass and taking a large gulp. The rum warmed her throat and calmed her nerves.

'No, he's off tonight. He'll either be asleep already or out with friends and he won't turn up until three am.' He laughed.

'I can believe that,' he said, taking another sip of her drink.

Jo came back and handed Chris some coins.

'Thanks.' He picked up his glass. 'See you later.'

Molly scanned the room, and spotting Kate and Alex in a booth at the back of the bar, tapped Chris's arm. 'Looks like your cousin's trying to keep a low profile.'

'He's not a fan of the limelight, despite being a famous DJ.' Chris smiled. 'They look far too cosy there, let's go and interrupt them.'

She giggled and slid her arm into his as they walked over to their table.

'Hey, Molly,' Kate said. 'Cute dress.'

'Thank you.' Molly felt her cheeks colour. Was the dress too much? She slid her arm out of Chris's and sat down opposite Kate.

Chris sat down next to her. 'You OK?' he whispered.

She nodded. 'I'm fine.'

Could he tell that she felt awkward?

Where did you guys go for dinner?' Alex asked

'We went to Riad. The food was so good,' Chris said. 'We weren't going to have dessert but the waiter persuaded us.'

'And now I want to go to sleep,' Molly admitted. 'Have you guys been?'

Kate shook her head. 'No, but I want to.'

'You should,' Chris said. 'I had never had Moroccan food before, but Molly chose all the right things.'

'Are your family from Morocco?' Kate asked Molly.

Molly shook her head. 'No, my mum was English, and my Dad's French. My boyfriend's family are Moroccan, so I know the food pretty well.'

'Ah, I see.' Kate nodded. 'Where does your Dad live?'

'He lives in Provence,' Molly said, 'in a secluded little farmhouse, miles from anyone, which is perfect for him.'

For his job, solitude, peace, and space for reflection were key, he had always told her. That's why life in Canterbury had never worked for him. She could remember him leaving when she was barely a teenager.

'That sounds dreamy.' Kate smiled. 'My aunt live in Nice, in a villa in the hills and it's idyllic.'

'I love Nice,' Molly said. 'Dad's taken us there plenty of times.'

Alex checked his watch, then drained his glass. 'Right, I'm up. See you guys on the dancefloor?'

'I didn't know you were playing tonight,' Chris said.

Alex rolled his eyes. 'I wasn't supposed to be, but one of the DJs cancelled, so I got roped in.' He stood up and walked across the bar to the DJ booth.

Molly had almost finished her drink already, and she could feel her cheeks warming from the rum. She looked up as a woman with dark hair walked over to the table.

'Mia!' Kate said, sliding out of the booth and giving her a hug. 'You made it! Do you want a drink?'

Mia shook her head. 'I'm good. I came to dance.' She smiled at Chris. 'Hey! Long time no see.'

Chris stood up and kissed Mia on the cheek. 'I know. Good to see you. This is my friend, Molly.'

'Hello, Molly,' Mia said as Kate knocked back the last of her drink. 'Are you joining us?' She gestured to the dancefloor which was already packed.

Molly nodded and finished the rest of her drink, following them through the crowd.

A pang of sadness swept through her as she watched Kate and Mia dancing. She thought about Saskia, and how much she wished she was here too.

'What's wrong?' Chris shouted to Molly over the music.

'Just missing Saskia,' Molly said. 'Ignore me.'

'Come,' he said, and held out a hand.

She took it and he twirled her under his arm, before pulling her back towards him. She could smell his citrusy aftershave, mixed with rum, as he locked eyes with her. *He's my friend*, she told herself. Yet every time her eyes met his, she kept wondering what it would be like to kiss him.

When the last track of Alex's set finished, Molly felt the hot, sweaty trickle of anxiety running down her spine. The bar was packed, and she could barely see her way out. Everything felt too loud and hot. She felt Chris's arm around her waist, and she turned to face him. He guided them through the crowd, and back to their table.

'Hey,' he said. 'You're really pale. Are you alright?'

'I am now. I felt overwhelmed. It was too crowded,' she said.

'I could tell. Do you want to go?' he asked.

She nodded. 'Is that OK?'

'Of course,' he said. 'I'll sort out a taxi.'

She sunk into the soft velvet booth and sucked in a breath. Her skin felt clammy, but the anxious feeling had passed.

'Hey love, are you OK?' Kate appeared next to her.

'I'm fine,' Molly said. 'Just needed some fresh air.'

'Tell me about it.' Mia slid into the booth opposite Molly. 'It's too hot and everyone keeps bumping into me.'

'Do you want some water?' Chris asked Molly.

Molly shook her head. 'No, I'm fine.'

When their taxi arrived, Chris guided her out of the bar, tucking her arm into his. The cold night air cooled her hot skin, calming her, and she sucked in a deep breath as she got into the taxi. After putting her seatbelt on she laid her head back against the head rest. She'd done it. She'd proved to herself that the city was safe. Even without her sister with her, she was safe.

'How are you feeling now?' he asked as the taxi drove out of the city.

'Absolutely fine,' she said. 'Sorry for cutting your night short.'

'You didn't,' he assured her. 'Alex's set had finished, and I would be heading off now myself if I had been there without you.'

She nodded. 'I had a great time tonight.'

'So did I,' he said. 'If it helps, I was nervous too. I was worried that Alex would want me to do a set. I get so nervous beforehand I want to throw up.' He shook his head. 'I didn't sleep for two days before the last one.'

'Oh no, that's awful,' she replied. 'You've got nothing to worry about. Everyone was dancing for the whole of your set.'

He seemed to consider this before he responded. 'True. I couldn't do it every weekend though. I'd hate the pressure and having everyone staring at me.'

'Me neither, I don't like being the centre of attention, unlike Saskia, who likes all eyes to be on her.' She smiled and thought of Saskia, wondering if she was still in rehearsals, or whether she and Caro were out drinking. She hoped she was safe, wherever she was.

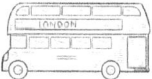

The taxi headed out of the city, and Chris turned to Molly. 'Do you want me to stay at yours tonight?'

They hadn't discussed where he would be staying, but his car was at hers, and he'd drunk too much to drive. The taxi could of course take him back to his place, but he was worried about Molly being alone.

'I don't want to make you sleep on my sofa again,' she said. 'You're too tall.'

'I fall asleep on my sofa most nights, and it's smaller than yours,' he replied. 'Honestly, it's fine.'

She nodded, and he saw her let out a long exhale. He wondered how much of her true feelings she hid, how much of her own discomfort she squashed, so as not to inconvenience anyone else.

'My car's at yours, and I've drunk too much to drive, but I can ask the taxi driver to take me home after he drops you off,' he said. 'I just need to know what you want.'

He had a feeling he knew, but he needed to hear her say it.

'Would you stay?' Her teeth pulled at her scarlet coated bottom lip. 'I'm worried about having another nightmare.'

He nodded. 'Of course I can.'

The taxi pulled up outside her house, and before she could get her purse out, he handed the driver some money, thanking him. He climbed out of the taxi first, then held his hand out to Molly. As she took it, their eyes met, and he felt the familiar prickle of electricity between them. Had she felt it too? Hiding his feelings for her was getting harder.

Molly unlocked the door, gestured to him to go in first, then followed him in, locking it behind them. She leant against the wall to unbuckle the straps on her high heels. She tossed them onto the floor and glared at them. 'So pretty, but so fucking painful.'

Laughing, Chris shook his head. 'I've never heard you swear before.' She never failed to surprise him.

'Layers, baby,' Molly smirked at him. 'I'm an onion, remember?'

'Of course, you are. Are you a bit drunk?' His head felt fuzzy, and he couldn't remember how much they'd had to drink. After taking his shoes off, he followed her through the darkened house to the kitchen.

She switched on the light, frowning at him. 'We didn't have that much to drink, did we?'

He leaned against the worktop. 'We had a beer before we left here, then a beer and a mint tea in the restaurant, and two mojitos in the bar. More than I'd planned on drinking. I wanted to stay sober so that I could look after you. I'm sorry.'

'Don't be. I had a great time. Kate and Mia are so funny. They remind me of me and Saskia.' She looked away from him, and he knew she was feeling sad again.

'Hey,' he said gently. 'Don't be sad. Saskia will be back here soon.'

'Will she?' Her eyes glittered with tears. 'This might be it for her, her big break. She might move to London and I'll hardly see her.'

'I know things are changing so fast right now, and it's hard to keep up, but that bond that you and Saskia have, it's so strong.' He fought the urge to put his arms around her. 'That won't change. You'll always have it.'

'You're probably right, as always.' She looked up at him. 'Why are you so good to me?'

He held her gaze. 'I care about you, Molly.'

'I care about you too.' Her voice cracked as she spoke, then she cleared her throat and opened one of the cupboards on the wall, taking out two glasses.

He watched, puzzled as she added some water to the glasses, then took a small plastic tub from the fridge, and opened it, taking out some lemon slices and putting them into the glasses. She handed one of the glasses to him. 'This is my hangover prevention cure.'

He took a gulp of the water. 'Mmm, lemony.'

'One more thing.' She got a packet of paracetamol tablets out of the cupboard and handed it to him. 'Take a couple of these. You'll wake up tomorrow with no hangover.'

'Thanks.' He took the tablets and washed them down with the water. 'You want to watch another film?'

He wasn't ready to go to sleep yet, and he had a feeling she wasn't either.

'Sounds like a plan.' She picked up her glass. 'It might be a little cold in the living room, though. I'll switch the heating on.' As she walked back through the hall, she stopped by the thermostat and turned it up.

He shivered as he walked into the living room, then glanced at her bare legs. She would be colder than him. He spotted a blanket on the back of the sofa, and as she sat down, he picked it up. 'You must be freezing. Here.' He wrapped the blanket around her.

She looked up at him. 'You must be cold too.' She held out one end of the blanket and spread it across both of their laps. 'We'll have to share, is that alright?'

Nope. Worst idea ever, he thought to himself, but he didn't say that. 'Sure.'

'What do you want to watch?' she asked.

He rubbed a hand over his chin. 'Why don't we finish the rest of Ocean's Eleven.'

She switched the TV on and put the film on. 'Let's see who's still awake at the end of it.'

He laughed. 'Probably not me.' He rested his head back against the cushion, trying to focus on the film, not the effect that her proximity was having on him.

Chapter Fourteen

Molly left the train and walked over the bridge, laughing at one of Chris's jokes. They swiped their tickets through the barrier and walked out of the station. She turned to say goodbye to him, but a hooded figure, dressed in black, had grabbed him, punching him in the stomach. She screamed, grabbing onto the man, trying to push him away. He lay on the cold, hard ground, his face covered in blood. Again, she screamed, but no one came. She knelt down next to him and shook him. 'Chris! Chris! Wake up, please wake up.'

'Woah, Molly, calm down.'

Molly opened her eyes, to find that she was lying on her sofa, pressed up against Chris, her fists balled up in his t-shirt. 'Oh no!' she said, releasing her grip. 'I'm so sorry.'

'It happened again, right?' He sat up on the sofa, rubbing his eyes.

'Yes.' She sighed and sat up. 'Again. I'm so sorry, are you alright?'

'I'm fine,' he said. 'Are you?'

She nodded. 'I am now. This time it wasn't me getting attacked in my dreams, it was you. I was trying to protect you.'

His face fell. 'That sounds awful. What can I do?'

'I'm not sure. I think I should go to bed.' She stood up and ran her teeth over her tongue, which felt fuzzy. 'I need to clean my teeth.'

'Me too.' He smiled. 'I'll let you go first.'

She stood up and fumbled her way to the staircase in the darkness, walking up to the bathroom. As she washed her face and cleaned her teeth, she remembered Chris's terrified expression as she woke up, gripping his t-shirt. She walked to her bedroom and pulled back her duvet, grabbing her pyjamas, then groaned, remembering the tiny hook on the back of her dress that she couldn't undo. She heard Chris's footsteps on the stairs, and the bathroom light being switched on. She paused and waited until she heard the door open again and went out into the doorway.

'I'm so sorry for grabbing you and screaming at you,' she said. 'You didn't need that.'

'Don't be embarrassed,' he said softly. 'It doesn't matter. Are you alright now?'

'I'm fine,' she said firmly. 'I'll sleep it off.' She turned around. 'Can you just undo this hook for me?'

'Sure,' he said.

His fingers were soft and warm on the skin on the back of her neck, sending her heart rate soaring as he slid the hook out of the clasp.

'Thank you,' she said and turned to face him. He was close now, so close she could study the length of his eyelashes, and the flecks of blue in his eyes.

'I, uh, should go,' he said. 'You need to get some more sleep. I'll take the sofa.'

She nodded. 'Thank you.'

As she looked at her bed, the thought of closing her eyes and being back there on the station again, crying over an injured Chris made her heart sink.

'You're scared it's going to happen again, aren't you?' he asked.

She nodded.

He ran a hand through his hair. 'Let me go and put my sweatpants on and I'll stay with you for a while.'

She let out a long exhale. 'Thank you.'

She closed her door, slid off her dress and underwear and pulled on her pyjamas. Her head was a swirling mess of emotions. She still felt slightly drunk, scared at the idea of shutting her eyes again and exhausted by the nightmares.

He knocked on the door just as she'd climbed into her bed. 'Can I come in?'

'All good! Come in!' Molly shouted.

As he walked in, she knew she was in trouble. He was dishevelled, but in a sexy way, his hair sticking up, his t-shirt crumpled, probably where she'd had her sweaty hands clung to it, and a blanket stuffed under his arm. He walked over to the empty side of the bed and lay down on it, wrapping the blanket over him.

'Thank you for this.' She felt comforted by his presence, but as she lay down next to him, the urge to nestle herself into his chest got stronger.

'Not a problem.' He paused. 'You're dealing with a lot right now. You're adjusting to being back in London again, to Saskia leaving, and tonight was the first time you'd been out without her.'

She nodded. 'You're right. As usual.'

'I'd rather not be,' he said. 'I'd rather you weren't going through any of this. I wish I could make it better.'

'You are.'

She felt as if he could protect her from the world. As she lay with him and listened to his breathing, she could feel her fear dissipating. She rested her head against his shoulder and shut her eyes.

Chris woke up again a while later. Moonlight was still streaming in through the window. It wasn't morning yet. He shifted on the bed, wrapping the blanket around him. At that moment, Molly's eyes opened and his heart sank. Had she had another nightmare?

'Hey,' he whispered. 'Are you alright?'

'I'm fine,' she said. 'No nightmare, I'm a very light sleeper. I felt you move.'

'Sorry. Go back to sleep, it's still early.'

'Thank you,' she whispered, 'for being there for me.'

'I'll always be there for you,' he whispered back.

He wanted to tell her how much he cared about her, how he never stopped thinking about her, but he didn't get a chance as her lips met his.

Desire flooded through him, as her hand slid to the back of his neck, pulling him towards her. This was everything he'd ever wanted and everything he was afraid of all at the same time. Her lips were soft, and her perfume enveloped him. He kissed her back, softly at first, but then her murmur of pleasure spurred him on. His hands slid around her waist, pulling her closer to him. She pulled away from him, sliding his t-shirt off and running her hands over his chest, touching the small silver pendant resting in the dip in his collarbone. 'I was right, you are beautiful.'

'You are the most beautiful woman I've ever met in my life.'

'Really?' Her voice was a whisper.

'Yes.' He nodded. 'I've never had a friend like you.'

'Me neither, Cute Train Dude,' she murmured.

'Cute Train Dude?' He frowned.

'That's what I nicknamed you,' she said.

He laughed. 'I nicknamed you Cute Train Girl.'

How was that possible? They'd both given each other the same nickname. He imagined them both on the train next to each other on Monday morning, and how bad he would feel if this went any further. They'd both been drinking tonight. She had a boyfriend. He had to put a stop to it, even though every fibre of his being wanted her with a ferocity that he'd never experienced before.

'Molly, I can't do this,' he said. 'You have a boyfriend, and we've both been drinking. I think you'll regret this.'

'Oh shit.' She put her head in her hands. 'I'm the worst person ever.' She peeked at him through her fingers. 'I've never done this before. This isn't who I am...'

'I believe you.' He caught her eye. 'Do you want me to go?'

'No, of course not,' she said. 'I just feel so...I'm sorry. I shouldn't have kissed you.'

'Hey.' He took her hand, holding it tightly. 'It's OK. Let's go to sleep and figure everything out in the morning.'

And like that, his dream came crashing down. She regretted kissing him. That brief moment where his stars had aligned had faded. If he had dared to hope that they could be more than friends, she had confirmed that it wasn't meant to be.

She lay her head down on the pillow, and closed her eyes. 'I'm sorry.'

'I'm not.' He whispered. He shouldn't have kissed her. But he would never regret it.

Molly squinted as the bright sunlight streamed in through her window. Her head was nestled against Chris's shoulder, and her leg was wrapped across his body. She studied his sleeping face, from his dishevelled hair to his chiseled jaw. He was beautiful. And last night she had not only told him that – again – but she had kissed him. She closed her eyes and let out a long exhale. Their relationship wouldn't ever be the same, and it was all her fault.

He opened his eyes and smiled at her. 'Morning,' he murmured.

'Morning.' She moved her leg off his thigh. 'I'm sorry. I got too close...'

'I think we both got too close,' he replied. 'I'm so sorry about last night.'

'No, don't be sorry, I kissed you.' Her heart sank. He regretted it. *Obviously,* he did, it was such a bad idea.

'I kissed you back,' he said. 'You were scared, and hurting, and you needed a friend. I shouldn't have kissed you.'

But I wanted to kiss you, she thought to herself. *That's what makes this even worse.*

She sat up, needing to put some space between them. 'You didn't do anything wrong.'

In fact, she couldn't stop thinking about how *right* it had felt.

'We can just forget it, can't we?' She bit her lip. 'I don't want this to ruin our friendship.'

'It won't.' He sat up and turned to face her, taking her hands in his. 'No one has ruined anything. We're going to be fine.'

She nodded furiously, his tone soothing her, as it always did. 'OK. We should, uh, get up.' He wasn't wearing a shirt and she was all too aware that this was because *she* had taken his t-shirt off last night. 'Do you want a shower?'

He shook his head. 'Ladies first.'

'Such a gentleman.' She climbed of out bed, feeling self-conscious in her t-shirt and shorts. 'I guess it's true what they say about nice guys coming last, right? That's because they're always putting everyone else first.'

He smirked. 'I guess so.'

Realising what she'd implied, she cringed. 'Oh my goodness, I didn't mean... It's just that you said I should go first.' She paused by the door. 'I'm gonna take a shower. I'll be right back.'

While Molly showered, Chris went downstairs and sent a message to Scott. He wouldn't be awake right now, but he needed to tell him what had happened before he convinced himself not to.

> I've done something I shouldn't have. I kissed Molly last night and now I don't know what to do

Last night had felt like a dream, but it was one that he knew could easily turn into a nightmare. When Molly had kissed him, she had set his whole body on fire, and he wanted to tell Molly how he actually felt about her, that he saw a future for them, but he was certain that if he did, she wouldn't want to be his friend anymore. He sat on the sofa for a minute, afraid to go back upstairs. He didn't need to see Molly in a towel, or worse, naked. His phone buzzed with a message, and he picked it up, groaning as he read it.

> Looks like the train's crashed...I'm home and I'm awake. When you get back, we'll talk

> I'll be there soon. Go easy on me

He put his phone down on the coffee table, and picked up his car keys, then went out to his car to get his gym bag. When he came back in, he listened for the sound of the shower, and hearing nothing, went back upstairs. The bathroom door was open, and it was empty, so he went inside, locking it behind him. It smelt of her coconut shampoo, and it reminded him of wrapping her in his arms last night. She'd seemed so genuinely upset about their kiss this morning, and while a tiny part of him had been hoping she would tell tell him that it was him that she wanted, he'd put that thought to the back of his mind, to make sure that she knew they could still be friends. He couldn't imagine not having her in his life.

He pulled off his clothes and switched on the shower. Time to wash away last night and start afresh.

When he went into the kitchen, Molly was stood at the counter making tea, her damp hair curling around her shoulders. She wore a pair of leggings, and an oversize t-shirt, and she looked so cute that he had to jam his hands into his pockets so that he didn't wrap his arms around her.

She startled, and he held up his hands. 'Sorry, I didn't mean to make you jump.'

She waved a hand. 'Don't worry. I've always been super jumpy.' She handed him a mug of tea. 'Are you hungry?'

'Thank you.' He took a sip of the tea. 'I could definitely eat. Do you want me to make some poached eggs?'

'Let's go for something different. Shall I make you one of my granola bowls?' she offered.

'I'd love that,' he said.

She took two bowls out of the cupboard, and began methodically adding granola, yoghurt, and berries to them. 'Peanut butter?' She took a jar from the cupboard. 'I like a little drizzle on the top of mine.'

'Sounds great.' The bowls were, as he expected, beautifully arranged, with a neat swirl of peanut butter on the top.

'There you are.' She handed him a bowl and a spoon. 'Let's go sit down.'

He slid into the chair opposite her at the dining table and took a mouthful of the granola. 'Wow, that's good.'

She shrugged. 'It's nothing fancy, it's only a hastily assembled breakfast, but it's what I eat most days.'

'It's great. Much better than coffee and toast, which is what I usually have. We never seem to have any time to do anything else.' He studied her face, looking for any sign that she still felt awkward, or anxious about their kiss.

'I can get this on the table in less than five minutes, which is good when you live with an agent of chaos, who rocks up ten minutes before we need to leave the house.' She rolled her eyes. 'I'm sure you know what I'm talking about.'

'I do, but remember that my agent of chaos works nights, so he doesn't get up until I've gone to work most days.' He paused. 'Unless it's the weekend, and then he's up early to go to the gym with me. His competitive nature is the only thing that gets him out of bed.'

'I noticed that you're, uh, *toned*. I'm guessing you're a regular at the gym?' Her cheeks coloured as she finished talking, and he couldn't ignore the way her eyes roamed over his arms.

'I am,' he said. 'I was the small, quiet, skinny kid. I got picked on, so I started going to the gym and just kind of got hooked on it. I feel better, not just physically, but mentally when I've had a good session in the gym.'

'I'm sorry that you had to deal with that. Kids are so mean.' She paused. 'If it helps I was a small nerdy kid too. I'm still the small nerdy kid in my head.'

He smiled. 'Nerdy kids are the best.'

'I even got a nerdy tattoo.' She giggled. 'It's an accurate replica of a 16th Century galleon, a tattoo for history nerds.'

'I saw a glimpse of it on Halloween,' he said. 'It's cool.'

'That dress was so low cut at the back *and* the front.' She shook her head. 'Trust Saskia to find me the most revealing outfit.'

'It suited you,' he said. 'You looked so hot, and when I saw the tattoo I had to do a double take. I didn't expect it. You told me you were the sensible one and Saskia was the wild one.'

He clamped his mouth shut. Calling her hot was *not* a good idea, but it had slipped out. He took another mouthful of granola, hoping she would gloss over it.

'Saskia would never get a tattoo,' she said. 'She has no tolerance for pain and she wouldn't sit still long enough. She did come with me when I had mine done and she held my hand. I was sure I would back out, but it didn't hurt as much as I thought it would.'

He smiled. 'You're a lot braver than you think you are.'

His voice soothed her, and she smiled. 'That's kind. Sometimes I don't feel very brave.'

'Maybe you don't, but you are.' He caught her eye. 'Last night you were so brave. Even though you'd had a nightmare, you still went out. You didn't let the fear get to you.'

'True.' She caught his eye. 'Thank you for not judging me.'

'Judging you?' He frowned. 'Why would I judge you? We *both* did this, and if you want, or need, to tell Mark about what happened, I'll take the blame for it.'

She shook her head. 'I'm not going to tell him. There's no way I would throw you under the bus.'

He nodded. 'So we're good then?'

The doorbell rang, making them both jump. 'I should...get that,' she said, walking out to the hall.

He heard the door open, and Molly talking to someone. A few minutes later, she came back into the dining room, with Liz, and gave him an apologetic smile. 'I totally forgot about my yoga class today. I'm sorry...'

'Don't worry,' he said, finishing the last of his granola. 'I need to go to the gym anyway.'

'Right.' She gestured to the door. 'I'm just gonna get changed.'

After Molly had gone upstairs, Liz sat down opposite Chris. 'I know you and Molly went out last night. I don't know what has or hasn't happened between you. I just need to know that you've got her best interests at heart, as the last thing she needs is another selfish arsehole in her life.'

Chris almost choked on his tea. 'Her happiness is the most important thing to me, I assure you.'

He wondered who the selfish arsehole that Liz was referring to was. Was it Mark? Or the dad she never talked about?

'She's been through a lot, and she doesn't like asking for help.' Liz paused. 'She seems to be able to talk to you, though.'

'She does,' he said. 'I said to her that I would always be there for her, and I mean it.'

'I believe you.' She lowered her voice. 'How's she doing?'

He wondered how much to share. If Liz was her best friend, then she needed to know the truth. 'She's had two nightmares this weekend, but she still insisted on going out for dinner and drinks last night. She's still scared, but she's also facing all of her fears. I didn't take my eyes off her last night, I promise you.'

'I don't doubt it.' The hint of a smile pulled at her lips. 'I'm glad she met you.'

Before he could reply, Molly appeared, her cheeks flushed red. 'I'm sorry to chuck you out,' she said to Chris.

'Honestly, it's fine. I need to go anyway.' He stood up and took their empty bowls into the kitchen. 'I'll speak to you later.'

'Sure.' She smiled at him, then kissed his cheek. 'I'll call you later.'

He could feel his cheeks burning, and Liz's intense stare. 'Enjoy your class, ladies.' He walked into the hall and picked up his bag.

As he turned around, Molly was behind him. 'Are we OK?' she whispered.

'We're fine,' he whispered back, then kissed her cheek. 'À bientôt.'

Chapter Fifteen

Molly followed Liz out of the front door, locking it behind them, then climbed into Liz's car and put her seatbelt on.

'Are you going to explain?' Liz asked as she pulled out of the parking space.

Molly winced. 'He stayed over.'

'Yes, I kind of got that impression.' Liz rolled her eyes.

'He called me on Friday night, and then he came over,' Molly said. 'Nothing happened, then last night we went out for dinner and ended up in my bed. We kissed, but we both stopped it. It was like nothing I've ever felt before. It was *so* good.'

Liz's eyes remained focused on the road, but she let out a long exhale. 'Wow. What happens now, then?'

'We both agreed that it can't happen again,' Molly said firmly.

'Is that what you want?' Liz parked outside the yoga studio and turned to Molly. 'He clearly cares about you a lot. You know how I feel about Mark, but Chris, I like.'

Molly frowned. Of all her friends, Liz was the last person she would have expected to say that. 'You do? Even though I've *cheated* on Mark with him?'

'I've spent ten minutes with Chris and in those ten minutes he has indicated that he cares more about you than Mark has in years,' Liz said. Her eyes locked onto Molly's. 'What's actually going on between you two?'

Molly put her head in her hands. 'I don't know. I'm so confused. When he said we were just friends, I didn't know whether I was happy about it or not. It's made me rethink my whole relationship with Mark. Something must be wrong if I'm kissing someone else.'

'Is it possible that you were a bit drunk, and you just got carried away?' Liz suggested.

'Yes.' Molly breathed a sigh of relief. 'That's probably it. You're right. Did you ever have a situation like this with Jacob?

Liz checked her watch. 'I'll tell you on the way home. We need to go.'

When they returned to the privacy of the car, Liz took out her water bottle, took a long drink then turned to Molly. 'A few years ago, a hot new vet started at my practice. He was so sweet, and it threw me off guard a bit. I went home and told Jacob about it, and he just shrugged and told me he'd worry about it when I said I was in love with him. I quickly worked out that it was a crush. He moved to another surgery a year later and I wasn't even that sad. That's just my experience though.' She paused. 'How would you feel if you didn't see Chris again?'

'Bereft. I would be a mess,' Molly replied immediately.

Liz sighed. 'In which case, you need to work out what to do next.' She put her seatbelt on. 'Do you want to come back to my place for lunch?'

'I'd love to, if you don't mind,' Molly said.

'Of course not. You're always welcome.' Liz pulled out of the car park, and Molly chewed her lip, wondering where Chris was, and what he was feeling.

They arrived at Liz's house just outside the city, and Jacob, her husband swung the door open.

'Molly!' he said. 'This is a surprise. Good to see you.' He pulled Molly in for a hug. He was a huge, bear of a man, with a dark beard and big brown eyes.

She squeezed him back, her head barely level with his chest. 'Fine, how are you?'

'I had a bit of a beating at rugby this morning, but other than that, good.' He kissed Liz on the cheek as she walked into the house. 'Hello, love. How was your class?'

Liz gave Molly a discreet smile. 'We covered a lot today.'

That's an understatement, Molly thought as she followed Liz and Jacob into the living room and sat down on the floor next to Martha, who was doing a jigsaw puzzle. 'Want a hand?'

Martha smiled. 'Yes, please. Can you find the cow?

Molly sorted through the pieces, which were all covered in farmyard animals.

'I'll go and give Jacob a hand with lunch if you're ok here, Molly,' Liz said.

'Oh I can help if you need me!' Molly put down her jigsaw piece.

'No, you're good.' Liz smiled at her.

Martha had just slotted the last jigsaw piece into place when Liz came back into the living room. 'Lunch is ready. It's vegetable curry, but it's super mild.'

'Sounds delicious.' Molly let Martha direct her to a chair next to her own, and as she breathed in the fragrant scent of the curry, her stomach rumbled. Jacob served her an enormous plateful of curry, rice and naan, and she dug in, hungrily, pausing only to tear Martha's naan up for her.

After they'd eaten, Molly and Liz walked Martha to the park. The autumn air had turned wintery, but she was heated from the inside from the curry.

'Are you alright now?' Liz asked. 'Are you still trying to figure out how you feel?'

'I know how I feel,' Molly whispered. 'Guilty, and scared, and angry with myself.'

Liz glanced at Martha as she went down the slide, then turned back to Molly. 'I'm going to be totally honest with you, because I'd want you to be honest with me. If you tell Mark you kissed Chris, it's going to to end well for anyone. It was a drunken kiss, and both of you are on the same page about it. The guilt will fade, and there is no point being angry with yourself. What are you scared of?'

'I'm scared of losing them both,' Molly said quietly. 'I love Mark, and what I feel for Chris is so complicated, but I don't want to lose either of them.'

'Then that kiss can't happen again,' Liz replied. 'Only you and Chris can decide whether you *are* just friends, or if there's more. And if there is, then you can't keep them both.'

When Molly got home, she lay on the sofa watching TV until her stomach started rumbling. She made herself a toasted sandwich for dinner and ate it cross legged on the sofa. Wondering what Chris was doing, she picked up her phone, then put it down again. Distance was what she needed right now, so that she could figure out how she felt. Her phone buzzed with a message, and she picked it up, then almost dropped it when she saw that it was from him.

> I hope you're alright. Last night hasn't changed anything for me. We're still friends and I'm still here for you :)

> Thank you! I needed to hear that. I'm here for you too. Maybe see you tomorrow?

It should have been a relief, hearing that Chris wanted to be friends, but it wasn't. In her head, images of Chris and Mark swirled around, leaving her feeling unsettled. She turned the TV up, hoping to drown out her thoughts. Her phone ringing made her jump and she glanced at it cautiously before picking it up.

'Hey Mole.' It was Saskia. 'Are you alone?'

Molly started laughing, and before long, her whole body was shaking. 'I'm alone. Oh Sas, I've done a bad thing.'

'Is this the bit where I pretend be surprised?' Saskia asked. 'How bad are we talking? Because you were freaking out about kissing him on the cheek. Did you accidentally touch his butt?' She laughed.

'I knew you'd find this funny. No, I didn't touch his butt. I kissed him. On the face. I mean, the lips. And we were in my bed and his hands...'

'Really?' Saskia shrieked. 'Oh, Mole, it was so obvious that was going to happen. You two are drawn to each other.'

'No, no, no, it was a mistake, we both agreed it was a mistake.' Molly swallowed hard. 'It's what we both want.'

Saskia scoffed. 'Sure, and I'm the Pope.'

'Not helping.' Molly closed her eyes. 'I shouldn't have told you.'

'I would probably have found out anyway,' Saskia said. 'I bet Chris will tell Scott and he is the worst at keeping secrets. And then I would have been mad at you for not telling me. So, spill it. I want all of the details.'

After filling Saskia in, Molly started to feel slightly calmer. She had kissed him, but he had stopped it. So as long as she squashed whatever feelings she had for him, they were all good.

'So you're not going to tell Mark, and you're just going to pretend this didn't happen?' Saskia sounded doubtful.

'No, I'm not telling him, and yes, I'll just pretend this didn't happen. It'll be our secret.' Molly paused. 'Well, a secret that all four of us know.'

'If that's what you want, then that's what we'll do. Hey, can you meet me for lunch tomorrow? I miss your face.'

'Same,' Molly said. 'What time and where?'

'Twelve, and I'll text you.'

'Á bientôt,' Molly said. 'Love you.'

'Love you more,' Saskia replied.

Molly hung up, and wandered around the house, checking the doors were locked before she went to bed. As she climbed inside the duvet, she inhaled Chris's scent, mixed with her own perfume.

Molly didn't see Chris on the train the following morning, which was probably for the best. She had thrown herself into her work that morning, determined to take her mind off him and the weekend, but when her phone buzzed with a message from Saskia, she knew that her whole weekend was about to be dissected. As she walked into the lobby, her sister was the first person she saw. She ran over to her and flung her arms around her.

'I've missed you so much and it's only been one weekend!'

'Sounds like it's been...eventful.' Saskia slipped her arm through Molly's. 'Come on, let's get some lunch and you can fill me in.'

Molly took Saskia to the café over the road from her office. 'You have to try the hoisin duck wrap,' she said as they browsed the giant fridges. 'It's the best.'

'I'll get these.' Saskia took the wrap from Molly's hand. 'You've treated me enough over the years. Go and grab that empty table.' She pointed to the corner of the café.

'Thank you.' Molly smiled and sat down at the table, putting her bag onto the other seat.

'So,' Saskia said, as she sat down opposite Molly. 'I need all of the details.'

Molly took a bite of her wrap, while she decided what to tell Saskia. She swallowed and wiped her mouth with a napkin. 'Why don't you tell me about how the rehearsals are going?'

Saskia gave her one of her no-nonsense looks. 'You *know* how the rehearsals are going, we speak at least twice a day. I need to know what happened when you saw Chris this morning.'

'I didn't see him.' Molly lowered her voice. 'There can't be anything between us,' Molly said firmly. 'I've got a boyfriend, and Chris is my friend.'

Saskia's eyes locked onto Molly's. 'Would you have kissed Chris if you were really that in love with Mark? And can you be just friends with someone that you've kissed?'

'I'm literally the worst person ever, aren't I?' Molly whispered.

'Nope. Mark has won that prize for the last four years in a row.' Saskia cackled. 'Look, if you want to be friends with Chris, that's fine. I'm just worried about you. I don't want to see you get hurt.'

'I don't want anyone to get hurt. So, I'm not telling Mark about the kiss and whatever feelings I have for Chris will just dissipate. It's just a crush, it has to be.' Molly pulled a plastic tub out of her handbag, passing it to Saskia. 'I did some guilt baking last night. Here you go. Rocky road and chocolate cookies.'

Saskia took the tub from Molly. 'You're the best! You should cheat on Mark every weekend.'

'Could you keep your voice down?' Molly shook her head.

'Sorry.' Saskia winced. 'I think a change of subject might be in order. Did you get your tickets for opening night?'

'Bien sûr !' Molly replied. 'I can't wait. It'll be good to see Papa as well.'

'It will,' Saskia said. 'I've invited Scott to come too.' She flicked Molly a sly glance. 'Who are you inviting?'

Molly rolled her eyes. 'Sometimes you're the worst. Neither of them. Papa hates Mark and will know instantly that something happened between Chris and I if I invite him.'

'C'est vrai,' Saskia said. 'I'm slightly afraid of introducing Scott to Papa. He'll be analysing every movement, every word that Scott utters. Should I warn Scott? I never tell people who Papa is, but should I give him a heads up?'

'No,' Molly replied hurriedly. 'I think it might be best not to. It might make him anxious.'

'Good point.' Saskia checked her watch. 'Oh man, lunch is over. I need to go already.'

'I knew it would be brief, but it's so good to see you.' Molly stood up. 'And thanks for lunch.'

'You're welcome.' Saskia smiled. 'I owe you so many lunches. This is the first of many.'

Molly slipped her arm into Saskia's as they walked back across the road together. Sure, it had been a grilling, but a gentle one. And even though Saskia had asked some tricky questions, Molly wasn't changing her mind. She and Chris were friends, and their kiss was a drunken mistake.

Outside her building, Molly gave Saskia a hug. 'Thanks for lunch.' She paused. 'Tu me manques.'

Saskia smiled. 'I miss you too.'

Chapter Sixteen

November 2014, Canterbury, Kent, England

Chris ran his hands through Molly's hair. 'I can't believe I'm back here. Last night was incredible. Tonight's something else.'

Molly kissed him again, sliding her hands over his naked body. 'One night wasn't enough.'

'It wasn't enough for me either,' Chris said. 'I haven't been able to get you out of my head.'

A beeping sound made them both jump and Molly's eyes flew open. She rolled over, her breathing ragged. Unsure if she was alone, she switched off her alarm and flew out of bed, checking the bathroom.

It was empty. He wasn't there. For a second, she wasn't sure whether she was happy about that or not. She dragged herself into the shower, her heart still racing.

When she arrived at the station, right in front of her, was a man wearing a very familiar navy coat.

'Morning,' Chris said, a soft smile on his face.

'Morning,' Molly replied.

When the train arrived, she climbed on after him and followed him to a pair of empty seats.

'I dreamt about you last night,' she whispered as she sat down next to him.

'Was it another nightmare?' His brow creased with concern.

She shook her head. 'No. We carried on what we started the other night.'

He raised an eyebrow. 'Was I any good?'

'I don't know, I woke up before that bit,' she whispered.

He held her gaze. 'What a shame.'

She got her book out to distract herself from the way his eyes crinkled when he smiled. 'It's not funny. I can't even escape you in my dreams.'

'Do you want to escape me?' he asked, then bit his lip. 'I feel like I'm a bad influence on you.'

'You're not,' she insisted. 'You stopped it. I mean us, and from now on, we keep our hands and our lips away from each other. And we don't get drunk together. Deal?'

'Deal,' he said.

His words just confused her further. Why didn't this make her happy? Being his friend was what she wanted, wasn't it?

As they stood below the giant toucan outside her office, she turned to Chris.

'Did you want to walk back to the station later? Can we be trusted to spend that much time together?'

'It's a risk I'm willing to take. 'See you at five.' He gave her a nod and walked away.

Molly walked into the lobby of her building, worried that everyone would somehow know what she had done at the weekend. In the lift she twiddled her coat button around her fingers, waiting until she could sprint to her desk and hide from everyone.

Chris flew through the door of Molly's building, and out of the driving rain. Water dripped from the hood of his coat onto the doormat.

'My goodness!' the receptionist said. 'You're soaked.'

'I forgot my umbrella,' he said.

The cold was already penetrating through his coat. He usually had an umbrella. He was usually organised, but the two nights he'd spent in Molly's bed had fried his brain and he couldn't think about anything else.

'You're Molly's friend, aren't you?' she asked. 'I'm Sue. Do you want to borrow an umbrella? We have some spare ones.'

'Thank you, Sue, that's kind of you, but I think it might be bit too late for that.' He heard footsteps behind him and turned around.

'Oh my God!' Molly's hands flew to her face. 'Are you OK?'

'I'm a little cold,' he said, 'but if we walk fast, I'll be fine.'

Molly nodded and ushered him out of the door, waving to Sue as she went past the reception desk. He pulled open the glass door and Molly opened her umbrella.

'Can you carry this?' she asked. 'You're taller than me.'

'Sure,' he said, taking the umbrella.

She linked her arm through his and they hurried down the road to the station. Despite her heels, Molly kept up with his rapid pace. He was impressed. There was no way he'd be able to walk in them, let alone practically run.

They hurtled into the station, through the barriers and onto the train, scanning the carriages for empty seats. Locating two together, Chris offered Molly the window seat before sliding in next to her.

'You look really pale,' she said.

'I'm fine, just a bit wet and cold. We'll be home soon,' he replied. The train was cold, and he couldn't warm up, even though he was squashed up close against Molly.

She unwrapped the large blanket scarf she was wearing. 'Put that around your shoulders. It'll keep you warm.'

He took the scarf and wrapped it around himself. 'Thank you.'

'You're very welcome.' She got her book out of her bag, and he did the same.

They were almost back in Canterbury when Chris started to see the flashing lights in front of his eyes that signified that a migraine was imminent.

'Oh shit.' He pinched his eyes shut as a wave of nausea washed over him.

'Are you alright?' Molly whispered.

'It's a migraine,' he whispered back and opened his eyes, then rummaged through his bag. 'I forgot my tablets this morning.'

'What can I do?' she asked.

'Nothing,' he whispered back, as the pain started.

His head felt like it was being squashed in a vice and he wasn't sure if he was going to be sick or not. He laid his head back against the head rest and closed his eyes, smiling to himself as he felt her hand clasp his tightly.

When they arrived back in Canterbury, he stood up, fighting the nausea that was overwhelming him. Molly slid her arm through his and guided him off the train and through the station into the car park.

'Can I give you a lift home?' she asked as she pulled her car keys out of her bag.

'I live five minutes away,' he said, still shivering, the nausea swelling as they walked through the car park. 'I'll walk quickly.'

She raised her eyebrow. 'I don't think so. Get in the car.'

He nodded. There was no way he would have left her alone in the dark. She was just looking out for him. He followed her to her Green Mini and directed her to his apartment building.

'Thanks for the lift,' he said when Molly stopped in the visitor parking space.

He pulled his keys out of his bag and unclipped his seatbelt, then got out of the car. The fresh air hit him like a truck and the pain in his head intensified.

Molly flew out of her seat, shutting the car door behind her and locking the door. 'Give me your keys,' she said, holding out her hand.

'I'm fine,' he mumbled, but he didn't feel fine at all. He took another step before sighing and giving her the keys. 'Can you just help me to get inside?'

His clothes were soaked, and he felt so cold, colder than he'd ever felt before.

'Of course,' she said, taking the keys from him and sliding her arm into his, letting him guide her towards the door.

He pointed to the keys. 'The square one for this door.' He inhaled deeply. 'The Yale key for the front door.'

She nodded and put the key into the lock. He led her up the stairs and along the corridor to his apartment.

She unlocked the door. 'Do you need me to stay?'

'I don't think that's a very good idea,' he said, walking into his apartment and leaning against the wall.

He peeled off his coat, and threw it on the floor, groaning as it made a loud splat.

She took off her shoes and coat. 'I'm going to do my bossy older sister thing and help you out, alright? Let's go and get you some painkillers.'

He went into the kitchen and got his medication out of the drawer, swallowing it with a glass of water.

'You're still cold,' she said, pressing her fingers on his cheek. 'Can you manage a shower?'

'Yes. You're not helping me with that.'

Even in his current condition, the idea of Molly in the shower with him made him smile.

She laughed. 'I wasn't going to offer.'

'Make yourself at home,' he said. 'I'll be right back.'

Molly picked up Chris's wet jacket and ran her hand over the radiator. It was hot. She hung the jacket over it, then went into the living room, switching on one of the small lamps on the table next to the sofa, rather than the main light, knowing that he would need dim lighting when he came back. It was cosy, but in a different way to her living room. The walls were exposed brick, and the furniture was modern, but simple. The floorboards looked pretty old, judging by the nicks and scratches in them. The curtains were open, revealing the original sash window and a view across the city. Her mouth fell open at the collection of books on the bookcase. One shelf held the whole collection of Inspector Rousseau mysteries, even the rare ones from the 1980's. How had he managed to find them all? An oak coffee table was also covered with books. She picked up a book on the history of maps and flicked through it.

She heard the water running and decided to make them both a cup of tea, so she put the book down and went into the kitchen, running her hands over the wooden worktops which were immaculately clean. That must be Chris, she reasoned. There was no way Scott was that tidy. The cupboards were all painted pale green and there was a white ceramic sink just under the window.

She filled the kettle up and started opening cupboards until she found the mugs. On the worktop there were three glass jars, one with teabags, one with coffee granules and another with sugar. She made them both strong teas and added some sugar to Chris's, then took the cups into the living room, putting his mug down while she sipped hers.

He came into the living room in pale grey tracksuit bottoms, like the ones he'd been wearing Friday night at her house, and she felt the warmth rising in her stomach again, the giddy thrill she got whenever she saw him, even more so as his hair was still slightly damp and his t-shirt was slightly too tight.

He sat down next to her, and she handed him the mug of tea. 'I've added some sugar. It'll help.'

'Thank you.' He took a sip of it, then looked around the room. 'How did you know I'd need it dark in here?'

'My mum used to get migraines. The darker the better, right? Do you want me to switch this lamp off?' Her fingers slid over the lamp next to her.

'It'll be too dark for you,' he said.

Her eyes locked onto his and she switched the lamp off. The room was plunged into darkness, punctuated by the faint glow from the streetlights outside.

'I'm not afraid of the dark anymore,' she said. 'I'm braver now, thanks to you.'

'You were brave all along,' he replied. 'You just didn't realise it.'

Her breath caught in her throat. He was too humble, too kind. Too generous. She wished she hadn't dragged him into her chaotic, messy life, but at the same time, she couldn't imagine it without him in it. She put her empty mug down on the coffee table and rested her head back against the sofa. She could hear the sound of the traffic outside, and the rain lashing the windows, but she felt warm, safe, and content.

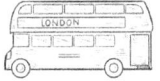

Molly opened her eyes and pulled herself upright on the sofa. She could just make out Chris's face in the darkness.

'I must have fallen asleep,' she said.

'Me too,' he replied.

'How do you feel?' she asked.

'Better,' he said. 'Hungry.' He switched on the lamp. 'Are you hungry? I'll make us some dinner.'

She blinked a couple of times as her eyes adjusted to the light. 'You can't cook for me. You're not well. I'll cook for you.'

She studied his face closely. He didn't look as pale, and the blue tinge had gone from his lips, although she didn't dare look at them for too long. The memory of them pressed against hers was still too new.

'I feel better than I did,' he said. 'Come on, let's see what we can find to eat.'

Twenty minutes later, Molly was sat next to Chris at his dining table. In front of her was a bowl of chicken noodle soup that they'd assembled from leftover roast chicken and vegetables, mixed with a miso broth. It was hot and aromatic, thanks to the generous helping of coriander that she'd added.

'Thanks for helping me cook,' he said. 'This is delicious.'

'I feel bad for *making* you cook,' she replied. 'You didn't need to feed me as well.'

He shrugged. 'It's late, it's dark and it's cold and I didn't want you going home hungry.'

'I appreciate it.' She paused, putting her spoon down. 'Is it OK that I'm here? I was scared it was going to be weird between us.'

His eyes flicked up to hers. 'Me too, and I do feel guilty about what happened. Are you OK?'

'I'm fine,' she assured him. 'I feel guilty about what happened too, but telling Mark would make things worse for all of us. We need to put it behind us, and move on, don't we?'

'We do, and we can.' He held her gaze. 'We're friends, Molly, and we're going to be fine.'

She nodded, and turned her attention back to her noodles. That niggling feeling had returned the second he had said that they were friends, but yet again, she ignored it.

After they'd eaten, she curled up on his sofa, as far away from him as possible His aftershave kept taking her back to Saturday night, when he had gazed into her eyes and told her that she was the most beautiful woman he had ever met. Had he meant that, or was he just drunk? She squashed those thoughts. This was not the time or the place.

'I like your place. It's cosy, and there's so much character in the exposed brick and the floorboards.'

'Thanks.' He smiled. 'It's bloody hard work. Scott and I bought this place when I moved back here and we completely renovated it.'

'Is there no end to your talents?' She raised her eyebrow.

'Scott did a lot of it. He's very good with tools. I just do as I'm told.' He shrugged.

'Sometimes,' she added. 'You were a little reluctant to accept my offer of help.'

'I'm glad I did,' he said. 'I'm dry and warm, and full of dinner. Thank you.'

She shrugged. 'I didn't do much. It's nothing compared to what you've done for me.'

'I'm not keeping score.' He smiled.

She sighed. 'I should go. It's late and you need to rest.'

The doorbell rang, and he frowned, then stood up. 'I'll be right back.'

She heard voices in the hall, and her stomach lurched. She shouldn't be here. She was intruding on his life. He came back into the room with a woman with dark curly hair, and bright, piercing blue eyes.

'Molly, this is Anne, my mum,' Chris said. 'Mum, this is Molly.'

'Lovely to meet you.' Molly stood up. 'I was just going.'

'Don't rush off on my account,' Anne said. 'I'm sorry to burst in on your evening. I had a feeling something was wrong with Chris.'

Molly nodded. 'Ah, you have your son's perceptive nature then?'

Anne shook her head. 'Oh no, it's just mother's intuition. I'm glad you were here tonight, Molly. He's not great at asking for help.'

'I know,' Molly said. 'I had to practically force him into the car.'

Chris shook his head. 'I'm sitting right here.'

'Sorry, love, I'm embarrassing you,' Anne said. 'I'll leave you to your evening.' She stood up and turned to Molly. 'So good to meet you. We've got tickets to see your sister in Peter Pan, and Scott's arranged for us to meet her afterwards.' She smiled. 'He seems really keen on her.'

'The feeling is very mutual,' Molly said. 'I'm so happy for them.'

'I can't wait to meet her,' Anne said. 'Anyway, I must go. I hope to see you again, Molly.'

'Same.' Molly swallowed hard. The fierce way that Anne cared for Chris reminded her of her own mum.

Chris went out into the hall with his mum. She tried not to listen to their conversation, but the sound echoed through the thin walls. She heard her tell Chris that she was worried about him getting hurt, and he reassured her that he wouldn't. It was the exact same conversation that she had had with Saskia.

'Your mum's so sweet,' she said when Chris returned.

He sat down next to her. 'She's great, but she worries too much.'

'I'd be like that if I had kids.' She stood up. 'I'm going to go home. You need to rest.'

'I'll walk you down to your car, hold on.' He pulled on a jacket and a pair of trainers, then grabbed his keys and opened the door. 'After you.'

She followed him down the stairs and into the stillness of the night. The rain had stopped, but the scent still hung in the air.

'Thanks for dinner,' she said.

'Thanks for looking after me.' He gave her a smile that didn't quite reach his eyes.

She drove home, still feeling the sensation of his face against hers, the soft swirl of hair that had brushed her cheek, the hint of stubble on his face. He was perfect. Too perfect for her. He would never cheat on his girlfriend. She sighed and drove home. When she let herself into the dark house, her mobile started ringing. Her heart leapt into her mouth as she pulled it out of her pocket, wondering if it was him ringing.

No, it was Liz.

'Hello darling, how are you doing?'

'I'm good, how are you?' Molly asked.

'I'm fine. I'm just checking in. Have you spoken to Chris?'

Molly cleared her throat. 'I've just got back from his flat, where we had a civilised dinner together as friends. Nothing else.'

'And that's what you want?'

'That's what I want.' Molly said firmly. It was so easy saying it, it was a lot harder believing it.

Chapter Seventeen

After work the following day, Molly applied some lipstick and took off her slippers, sliding her feet into her boots and zipping them up. She shut her laptop down and stuffed one of her new manuscripts into her tote bag. The next few days would be spent working in the quiet comfort of her living room, avoiding the damp cold weather, and the exhausting commute.

When she got to the lobby she spotted Chris chatting to Sue.

'Evening, Moll. Are you ready to brave the cold?' he asked.

She smiled at him and nodded. 'Yep, let's do it.' She waved to Sue, and they walked towards the door, pausing as someone else was coming through.

Molly's face dropped as the tall, dark figure walked towards her. 'Mark!' She squeaked. 'Hi.'

This was the scenario she had been dreading. Would Mark work out that something had happened between her and Chris?

'Hello, Molly.' Mark glared at Chris. 'Who's this?'

'This is Chris, my friend from the train,' Molly replied quickly.

Mark's eyes flicked back to Molly. 'What's he doing here?'

'Mark. We walk to the station together.' She could tell from Mark's narrowed eyes that he wasn't pleased to see Chris, and internally she was cringing at his rudeness.

'I'm gonna leave you guys to it. See you later.' Chris walked away from Molly and Mark, towards the revolving door.

'Chris, wait.' Leaving Mark, she hurried over to Chris. 'I'm so sorry. He was so rude, and didn't deserve that.'

'It's fine,' he said, but his tone, and the crease in his brow indicated that he was absolutely *not* fine. 'I'll see you tomorrow.' He turned away from her and walked through the door.

Molly stalked back over to Mark. 'Why did you have to be so rude to Chris?'

He glanced around. 'Let's not do this here.' He took her hand and led her out of the door.

She walked along the busy street, clutching his hand tightly as he led her through the crowds. Today had been a good day, and now it was all unravelling. Part of her wished she was on the train with Chris, not marching along the pavement with a silent Mark.

'Are you going to say something?' she asked.

He sighed. 'I've not seen you in two weeks, and I show up and *he's* the one meeting you from work?'

She chewed her lip. He had a point. 'I told you that we got the train together. He works around the corner from me, so we walk to the station together. After what happened to me, I don't like being on my own in the dark.'

He inodded. 'He's not what I pictured. He looks like he spends more time in the gym than behind a computer.'

This was dangerous ground. If she argued with him now, it would look like she *did* have feelings for Chris. On the other hand, he was equally dismissive of Saskia, and he had no reason to be jealous of her.

'The way he looks isn't relevant. He's a friend, and without him, going back to commuting would have been so hard.' She hoped her tone and her face were neutral, and she was aware that she was lying to him. Telling him the truth would only make this situation far worse, and cause more issues for Chris. Keeping the peace was the only way forward.

'I'm sorry,' he said. 'I didn't mean to embarrass you.'

She let out a long exhale. 'I don't care about you embarrassing me. I care about how you treat other people.' His obsession with appearances was starting to rile her.

'Again, I'm sorry.' He paused. 'I get that being on your own in the dark is probably hard for you.'

She smiled at him. This was the first time he had shown any real appreciation for what she had been through.

'It is hard,' she admitted, 'but I'm getting braver every day.'

Mark stopped outside the door of his favourite Japanese restaurant. 'How about we have some dinner and a proper catch up?'

'Sure.' She smiled at him. 'Sounds great.'

Damage control completed, now she could relax.

He pulled open the door and stepped inside the restaurant. Hurrying in before the door shut in her face, she gritted her teeth. He wasn't angry with her any more, but surely, he could have held the door for her?

The booth in the window was perfect for people watching, and for watching the stars sparkle in the inky sky. The chicken ramen was delicious, and the lemon green tea was perfect, but Mark had talked incessantly about his Luxembourg trip since they had sat down, and she hadn't said a single word. Not that he had noticed.

'Your trip sounds like a lot of fun,' she said diplomatically. In fact, it sounded like they spent a few hours working and the rest of the time partying.

'We work hard, and we play hard, Molly.' He shrugged. 'My job's extremely stressful and we need to let off steam. Your job's not as fast paced.'

'No, we just meander along like snails.' It wasn't the first time he'd suggested that her job wasn't as important as his. She put her chopsticks down in her empty bowl.

'Very funny. I've missed your sense of humour.' He looked at her intently.

She realised he was waiting for her to say that she'd missed him. The truth was that she'd been so caught up in Saskia leaving, and the situation with Chris, that she hadn't had time to miss him.

'Really?' she asked, laughing nervously. 'You don't always like my sense of humour.'

'It's *unique*, that's for sure.' He took his napkin from his lap and folded it, placing it next to his bowl. 'You didn't miss me then? I know you were angry with me.'

'You let me down right at the last minute.' She fiddled with one of the chopstick handles. She had a right to be angry with him, but if he knew what she had done that weekend, he would be furious.

He clasped her hands in his. 'I'm sorry. I won't do it again.'

'I'm sorry,' he said. 'I won't do it again.'

She nodded and decided that a subject change was for the best. 'How was the stag do? Did you all make it home?'

'It was good. *Obviously* I can't tell you too much about it.' He smiled at the waitress who took away their empty bowls, then turned back to Molly. 'How was your weekend? Was it weird being at home without Saskia?'

'Not at all. I went out with some friends on Saturday, then to Liz's on Sunday after yoga.' Her throat was dry, and she was terrified that he would realise she was hiding something.

'Sounds busy,' he said. 'Now that Saskia's in the city, maybe you'll want to come and live here too.'

'I can't.' She swallowed hard. They had been through this. 'It's Saskia's house too. I can't sell it.'

'You don't have to. You could just rent it out for a while.' He picked up the dessert menu. 'You could make a fortune.'

'I'm not renting out my house, Mark.' She was irritated by his nonchalance. 'Saskia's pantomime is only for a month. She'll be back home soon.'

He shrugged. 'Maybe. What if this is the start of her career? She might stay in the city.'

She couldn't even entertain that idea right now. Being apart from her for a month was hard enough. 'That doesn't matter. I'm still not leaving Canterbury. I thought you were thinking about moving there with me?'

'And how would that work with Saskia there too?' He raised an eyebrow. 'She can barely tolerate me for a dinner. There's no way she'd want to live with me.'

'We could find somewhere else in Canterbury?' she suggested, although she still couldn't imagine leaving her house. It was her only tie to her mum.

He put down his menu, and picked up her hand, squeezing it softly. 'Can't we just enjoy tonight? I don't want to plan out our entire lives right now.'

She felt a sharp pain in her chest. If she pushed him too much, would he run away? 'Of course.' Her heart rate slowed as he ran his thumb over the back of her hand. 'We don't have to talk about it right now.'

He smiled at her, then picked up his menu again. 'Are you going for chocolate, or lychee mochis today?'

And that was that. He had moved on from the conversation immediately, while she was left on edge, wondering what their future looked like, and if they even had one.

'I can't decide,' she said.

Making any decision felt too hard right now.

He nodded and caught the eye of the waitress, who came over to their table. 'Can we have the hazelnut chocolate and the lychee yuzu mochis please?'

She nodded, writing down their order and taking the menus away.

He sipped his green tea. 'You know, however many times we come here, I still can't get used to this stuff. I just tell myself it's good for me.' He shrugged. 'Are you coming back to my place tonight? It's been way too long.'

'I uh...sure,' she said. Being away from Canterbury, and Chris was probably a good thing right now. 'I haven't got any of my things there though. Can we stop at Boots so I can get a toothbrush?'

He smiled. 'Don't worry. I've got it covered. It'll be easier to get to work as well.'

'I was planning on working from home for the next couple of days,' she said. 'I've got my laptop and some manuscripts with me.'

'Even better. You can work at my place,' he said. 'We can go out after I finish work.'

'I'd like that.' Maybe this was what they needed, some time together. Maybe that would get rid of the slightly tense atmosphere between them.

'Good. Also, I've got something to ask you.'

Her stomach lurched. All of a sudden, the room felt too hot, and her clothes felt too tight. Hadn't he just said he didn't want to plan their entire future?

'Go on.'

He smiled at her. 'Would you like to come to my company's Christmas party with me?'

'Of course I will, I'd love to.'

She actually felt relieved, not sad that he hadn't asked her to marry him, and that thought bothered her. Surely that was what she wanted, wasn't it? She'd been terrified of blurting out that she'd kissed Chris, but as the evening had gone on, she'd pushed her thoughts about the weekend to the back of her mind.

After another cup of green tea, and some delicious mochis, Molly slipped her hand into Mark's as they walked back to the train station. When they arrived at Canary Wharf, she stopped and admired the reflection of the lights shimmering in the water, and the boats motoring slowly along the river.

'It's a beautiful view, isn't it?' Mark put his arms around her waist, and kissed her cheek.

'It is. It feels so peaceful here, but we're right in the heart of the city.' The steely giants of the financial district loomed over them, yet the gentle lap of the river against the walls of the bank was calming.

'Come on. You'll get cold.' He took her hand and led her to his apartment building.

Her heels echoed around the marble lobby, stark and clinical, a world away from her cosy, slightly shabby home.

Mark let her into his apartment and took her into the bedroom. Laid out on the bed were a couple of bags, and white boxes.

Molly frowned. 'What's this?'

'Open them,' he said.

She lifted the lid from the first box. Inside was the exact same toiletry bag as hers. She unzipped it. Inside was a tube of toothpaste, a toothbrush, and a pot of the exact organic rosewater moisturiser that she used.

She gasped. 'Did you do this?'

He nodded. 'Open the next one.'

Inside the next box were bottles of her shampoo, conditioner, and shower gel. One of the bags contained a white bathrobe and a pair of floral satin shorts and vest, just like she had at home. Inside a thin white cardboard box was a bra and several pairs of French knickers. The last bag contained a pair of yoga pants, a sweatshirt, and a couple of t-shirts.

'I said I would make it up to you,' he said. 'I'm sorry about last weekend. I thought that maybe the reason you didn't like staying here was that you didn't have any of your own things here.'

She didn't know what to say. He could have just given her a drawer to put her things in, that would have been enough. This was extravagant and overwhelming. 'This is so kind of you, thank you.' The pang of guilt in her stomach got stronger.

'This way you don't have to drag a big bag with you when you come here. You can have spares of all your things here.' He stood up. 'Come with me.'

She followed him into the kitchen where he opened a cupboard. 'We have granola, we have yoghurts in the fridge, and I got a yoga mat so you can do your class here at the weekend.'

Her eyes pricked with tears. 'You are so sweet.'

He wrapped his arms around her. 'I've been taking you for granted. I'm not doing that anymore.'

Chris traced a pattern on the condensation on his pint glass. Knowing Molly had a boyfriend was painful but meeting him had been something else. He'd disliked Mark instantly. His clothes and his mannerisms all screamed insecurity. The aggressive tone of Mark's voice had put him on edge and made him wonder if he spoke to Molly like that. Her face had been a mixture of embarrassment and regret as she'd walked away. Part of him had wanted to race after her, and tell her how he felt about her, plead with her to leave Mark and come with him, but they'd agreed that they were just friends, so he'd stuffed his feelings away and walked back to the station.

'What's up mate?' Scott smiled at him from the other side of the counter.

'Have you got a minute? I need to talk to you,' Chris said. 'I'm sorry to just turn up here, I know you're working.'

'Barely working,' Jo shouted over Scott's shoulder.

When Scott whipped his head around and glared at her, she laughed. 'I'm sorry. I didn't mean to butt in.'

'Can I leave you and Matt here for a minute while I go on a break?' Scott asked.

'Of course,' Jo replied. 'Take as long as you need.' She smiled at Chris. 'I hope you're alright. I've never seen you looking that bummed before.'

Chris gave her a thin smile. 'I've never been this bummed before.'

He followed Scott out of the back of the bar, to the tiny courtyard, then sat down on a bench, taking a sip of his beer. 'I met Molly's boyfriend after work.'

'Oof.' Scott winced. 'What was that like?'

'Not great. He's so...' He paused, searching for the right word.

'Arrogant, conceited, unpleasant...' Scott smiled. 'Am I right? Those are a few of the politer words that Saskia uses to describe him.'

'Yeah, he's all of those things,' Chris agreed. 'He looked at me like I was a piece of shit. He turned to Molly and said, "what's he doing here?" like I wasn't stood there. The worst part is that I came away feeling guilty because Molly and I have a secret that he knows nothing about.'

'Don't feel guilty,' Scott said. 'He doesn't deserve Molly, and you do. I'm hoping it's only a matter of time before she realises that.'

'She said she wants to be friends,' Chris reminded Scott. 'Clearly he's what she wants.'

'She told you that she was scared of *losing* both of you. She didn't say that she loved him, and from what Saskia has told me, I don't think she does. Not really. I think he's all she knows. And now this kiss has happened and it's thrown her. She doesn't know what to do, so she's clinging to *him* for some sense of normalcy, but she'll realise he's a douchebag.'

'Wow, that was all very insightful. Apart from the word douchebag.' Chris grinned at Scott.

Scott shrugged. 'Hey, my advice comes liberally sprinkled with expletives.'

'He seemed so *angry* when he saw me. The look he gave me was pure poison.' Chris sipped his beer. 'I think he was jealous too.'

'Of course he is!' Scott said. 'He turns up to surprise Molly and you're there, all handsome in your fancy coat, looking like the Hallmark dream boyfriend. I wonder if she'll tell him what you did?'

'She said she wouldn't and I believe her,' Chris replied. 'I didn't like the way he talked to her, or the way he reacted to me. I'm worried about her.'

'Not much you can do, mate.' Scott stood up. 'All you can do is be her friend, as that's what she's told you she needs. I get the feeling that their relationship is reaching the end of the track.'

'I love all the train puns.' Chris stood up. 'Thanks, mate. I appreciate your advice.'

'No worries.' Scott opened the door. 'Ladies first.' He gestured for Chris to go ahead of him.

Chris rolled his eyes. 'You're such a knob.'

The wonderful and perplexing thing about Scott was that he could do deep and meaningful, then instantly switch into being ridiculously annoying.

'That's why you love me.' Scott smacked Chris's ass, then walked into the bar, smiling at Jo.

Chapter Eighteen

The following evening. Molly sat in Mark's living room, snuggled in her sweatshirt, watching a film. It was almost eight pm and Mark still wasn't home. He had left for work over twelve hours ago, after they'd eaten breakfast together. He'd promised he would be home by six pm. Spending the day in his luxury apartment on her own was no issue, but she wasn't looking forward to spending the evening on her own. She called him again, but there was no answer. Her stomach rumbling, she walked into the kitchen and rummaged in his sparsely populated fridge. The front door slammed shut, and she flew into the hallway.

'I'm so sorry.' Mark kissed her cheek. 'I got caught up helping one of my colleagues fix a problem.'

'I was worried,' she said. 'I called you, but you didn't answer your phone.'

'I have my phone on silent when I'm at work. As I said, there was a problem that I had to fix.' He smiled. 'I'm here now though.'

He was home and that was great, but he didn't seem to have considered how she might have felt, being alone at his apartment.

She nodded. 'I was just about to make myself a dinner of toast and fruit.'

He laughed. 'We can do better than that. Do you want to go out or order in?'

'It's too late to go out.' By the time she had changed, and they had found somewhere and ordered it would be nearly nine. Turning away from him, she walked back into the living room, sitting down on the boxy sofa.

He sat down next to her. 'Let's order in then.'

'Sure.' She got her phone out of her pocket. 'What about Chinese? We can have some chow mein, prawn toast...'

He shook his head. 'Way too many carbs. My trainer has made some changes to my diet.'

'Right.' She wondered when he had got so worried about his appearance. 'I'm sure it wouldn't hurt once in a while.'

'Probably not,' he said, 'but we can't all eat cake every day, Molly.'

She bit her lip and continued scrolling through the app. 'I don't eat cake every day, but sometimes it's nice to have a treat.'

He shrugged. 'You don't have to worry about your figure. I do.'

You never used to, she thought, but refused to let herself entertain thoughts as to why he was so fixated on his body.

'OK, so what *would* you like?' she asked.

'Chinese sounds great, but I'll have the black bean beef and broccoli and a steamed rice,' he said. 'I might have one of your prawn toasts, as a treat.'

She smiled. 'If I let you.'

She ordered herself a sweet and sour chicken, egg fried rice, and the prawn toast, which she would definitely share.

'All done. It should be here in twenty minutes.' She put her phone down. 'Do you want to watch the rest of this film? It's a delightfully trashy rom com.'

'Mmm. My favourite.' He rolled his eyes.

'If you had been here earlier, you could have chosen the film,' she said pointedly.

'I don't think you understand how stressful my job is, Molly. I don't get to just shut my laptop and decide I'm done,' he huffed.

She nodded. 'I appreciate that. It's just difficult when you've asked me to come and stay and you aren't here.'

'I'm sorry. I should have let you know I would be late. I'm just not used to you being here. Let's see just how trashy this film is, shall we?' He moved closer and put his am around her.

Molly was sitting at the kitchen island, her fingers flying across the keyboard, although it was almost six pm, and she should have finished working an hour ago. She was still trying desperately to distract herself from her thoughts. Last night she'd fallen asleep on the sofa. She couldn't even remember watching the end of the film. When she woke up, in the middle of the night, she'd found herself alone in the dark living room. She'd tiptoed into his bedroom and climbed into bed next to Mark, but had been unable to sleep, her guilt weighing heavily on her.

In an attempt to impress Mark, she'd gone out at lunchtime and bought a new dress and heels to wear to his Christmas party, but now she had something else to feel guilty about. She'd opened his wardrobe to hang the dress up and spotted a ridiculously small black body con dress. He didn't like her vintage dresses, and this dress was a million miles away from them, sleek and modern, and all of the things that her wardrobe *wasn't*. Yet, she appreciated the gesture.

Glancing at her inbox, she spotted an email that she hadn't responded to yet, and typed out a reply as she sang along to today's playlist, a collection of her favourite Fall Out Boy songs.

'Molly? What the hell?' Mark appeared next to her.

She slid her headphones off. 'When did you get in? I didn't hear you.'

'I wonder why,' he said drily.

She glanced at the clock on her laptop. 'You're home early.'

'As promised.' He spun her around on the stool to face him. 'What shall we do with all of this extra time?'

'I need to finish my emails,' she said.

She could tell by the way that he was stroking her face that he wanted her, but her head was still a mess. Maybe coming here was a mistake.

'Right.' If he was annoyed, he didn't show it. He took off his tie and undid the top button of his shirt. 'I'll go and get changed. We have a table booked for seven somewhere in Butlers Wharf. Will you be finished by then?' He leaned against the island, studying her.

She nodded. 'I'll be as quick as I can.'

He nodded and left the kitchen, and for once she was relieved that he didn't talk about feelings. If he was upset or annoyed with her, he wouldn't say, and that thought made her feel slightly happier. She quickly replied to the last of her emails and put her laptop away. The uneasy feeling in her stomach was growing, but she ignored it, deciding that she needed to tell Mark what she'd seen in his wardrobe. She was carrying enough guilt as it was.

When he came out of the shower, a towel wrapped around his waist, she managed to avert her eyes from his toned body. 'Mark?'

He turned to her as he opened the wardrobe. 'Yes?'

She gestured to her dress, laid out on the bed. 'I hung this in your wardrobe earlier, and I saw something in there. I wasn't snooping, I just wanted to hang this up.'

He blushed and flicked through the wardrobe, until his fingers closed around the dress. He took out the hanger and held up the dress. 'Do you like it?'

'I do.'

She ran her eyes over the cut out panels on the side. Wearing it would involve revealing way more skin than she was used to. Then she noticed the tag. Not only was it a size too small, but it had also cost almost a thousand pounds, way more than she would ever have spent on a dress.

'I'm not sure if it'll fit. It's not my size.'

He cleared his throat. 'Right. I must have got your size wrong. Why don't you try it?'

She took off her t-shirt and leggings and breathed in as he slipped the dress out of the hanger and handed it to her. It was tight, but she wriggled into it, then walked over to the mirror in the corner of the bedroom, suddenly feeling self-conscious.

'Wow. It's tight. And short.' she pulled at the hem, which, unlike her calf skimming vintage dresses, stopped above her knee.

His eyes ran over her body as he dressed. 'It's hot. It shows off your curves.'

She turned around admiring herself from all angles in the mirror. 'I guess it does. It's a little too fancy for dinner tonight. I'll save it for tomorrow.'

'Tomorrow?' He frowned.

'Your Christmas party. It'll be perfect for that, won't it?' She could imagine it with a pair of statement earrings and heels. For once she would feel like she belonged amongst Mark's colleagues in her designer dress.

'It's a little revealing, isn't it?' He buttoned up his shirt, and she noticed the flush intensifying in his cheeks.

'If it's too revealing, why did you buy it?' she asked.

'I...' He rubbed his hand over the back of his neck. 'You should wear it. It looks hot. I just don't want any of my mates eyeing you up.'

'I'll be with you, not them.' She kissed his cheek. 'If you don't want me to wear it, I won't.'

She slid the dress off and put it back on the hanger, then put on the dress she'd bought earlier, the one she *was* going to wear to his Christmas party, a plum coloured skater dress with a floral print.

'That dress looks great too,' he said, then checked his watch. 'The taxi's here, are you nearly ready?'

'Sure, I just need to put some lipstick on.' She opened her make-up bag and her breath caught in her throat as her fingers closed around the scarlet lipstick that she'd worn the night she'd kissed Chris. Nope. Not that one. She took out a pink lipgloss and slicked some on. 'OK, I'm ready.'

Over steak, chips, and cocktails, Molly steered the conversation, telling him about her latest project, a book about a baby dragon, and he seemed to be listening intently. When he was sweet and kind, and asked thoughtful questions, she remembered why she loved him.

'Have you enjoyed working at my place this week?' he asked.

'I have,' she said. 'I got loads done, I liked being able to walk to the shops at lunchtime, and I get to see you every day.'

He smiled. 'Can I persuade you to stay a little longer?'

'I can stay tomorrow night but then I need to go home,' she said.

He stroked her hand. 'Why don't you stay until the weekend? Then you can go to Saskia's show from my place.'

'That would be great, but I need to go home. I've got no food or clean clothes. I need to do my laundry, my cleaning, and get some groceries.'

And she was starting to crave some time alone, something she thought she'd never want.

He wrinkled his nose. 'That all sounds so boring. Stay and we can have some fun. I'll wash your clothes.'

'Sometimes things are boring.' She shrugged. 'That's life. It can't always be exciting. Don't you ever have to do laundry or clean your flat?'

As the words came out of her mouth, she already knew the answers.

He shrugged. 'It's different when you work the hours I do. I take my suits to the dry cleaner, and Sheila keeps my flat clean.'

'She does a good job. It's spotless.' She took a sip of her drink. If she moved in, would she be expected to take on the role of cleaner?

He smirked. 'I guess you're used to the chaos Saskia leaves in her wake. It must be tidier now. That living room makes me feel so claustrophobic, all the stuff everywhere.'

'I did tidy up the day after she left,' Molly admitted. 'I love her so much, but she is so messy. You two are such extremes. She leaves a trail of chaos in her wake, and your place is so...sparse.'

'Sparse?' He snorted with laughter. 'I just like things clean. Minimal.'

She nodded, but something was nagging at her. He had photos of his friends and family dotted around his flat, but no photos of her or of them. That was what was annoying her. She took a sip of her drink, comforted by the knowledge that Mark would be oblivious to her inner turmoil.

'I guess we're all different.' This was as diplomatic as she could be.

'We are.' He let go of her hand and picked up his drink, taking a sip. 'So tomorrow's our last night together then?'

'I can come back next week?' she offered.

'I fly to Oslo on Tuesday,' he said.

'You could come to Saskia's opening night with me?' she asked hopefully.

'That would be my worst nightmare,' he said, laughing. 'Pantomime is for children. There's no way I'm going to one.'

She swallowed hard. 'It's a dream come true for Saskia.'

He nodded. 'I know. You said it yourself, we're all different.'

'We are.' She refused to let him spoil her excitement. 'And I'm excited to see her on the stage, doing what she loves. Pantomimes are a big part of Christmas for a lot of people, and I know she'll be incredible.'

'Speaking of Christmas,' he said, glossing over Saskia's role completely, 'you are going to come to my parents' on Christmas Day, aren't you? Mama is already hassling me about it.'

'Of course,' she replied, 'and you'll come to Kent with me on Boxing Day?'

'I don't think so.' He paused. 'Your dad's a bit much, Molly. He just goes on and on about his writing. Your sister just gets drunk and everyone speaks French. I don't feel like I fit in.'

She took a deep breath. 'Why didn't you ever tell me you felt like that?'

As much as it pained her to agree with him when he'd just torn her family to shreds, her dad *did* monopolise the conversation in group situations, and Saskia *did* drink way too much at Christmas.

'How could I?' He took a sip of his drink. 'They're your family. I'd be livid if someone came for my family.'

'Well, now I know, I can ensure that we don't just speak in French, and we do our best to include you. *If* you'll come to Kent and spend some time with us.' She smiled at him.

'I think I could do that.' He picked up her hand and kissed it. 'We can sort out the details nearer the time.'

This worried her. Was this his way of saying that he wasn't really going to come, or was she just reading too much into it?

The waitress arrived with the chocolate cake that Molly had forgotten she'd ordered, and she took a forkful, sighing happily.

'Oh my goodness, this is delicious. Want to try some?' she asked Mark.

'I don't really have refined sugar during the week...' He trailed off.

She found herself thinking about Chris, who leapt at any opportunity to try the cakes and biscuits she made. Watching Mark wrinkle his nose as if the sugar was somehow poisonous was a complete turn off. Especially compared to the groan of pleasure that Chris had made when he had tried her rocky road.

'Molly?'

Mark's voice brought her out of her thoughts. 'I said I'll have a little bit.'

'Sorry, I zoned out.' Feeling guilty, she held her fork out to him. She had to stop thinking about Chris. He was her friend and nothing more.

'That *is* good.' Mark nodded approvingly.

'Maybe you should allow yourself a treat every now and again. One piece of cake isn't going to throw your training regime off,' she said.

He wiped his mouth with a napkin. 'Maybe.'

She picked up her spoon and scooped up some of the chocolate ice cream on the plate, as well as the cake, but somehow on the way to her mouth, the ice cream ended up in her lap. 'Oh shit.' She scooped it off with her napkin and wiped the stain, which was spreading across her dress. The dress she had to wear tomorrow night.

'Leave it,' he said. 'We'll sort it later.'

She nodded, but felt irritated. The dress was dry clean only, so there was no way of washing it.

Putting more chocolatey cake into her mouth helped her to forget, and until she stood up, no one could see the stain anyway. She sipped the wine he had ordered them, and listened to him as he told her all about the deal in Oslo that he was working on.

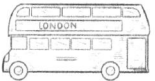

The following evening Molly pulled on the black body con dress. It was slightly tight and revealing, but it was designer, and so would impress Mark's colleagues. At last year's Christmas party, she'd felt so out of place, as Mark, who had only been in his job for a few months then, guided her around the room. The alcohol had flowed all night as they ate fancy, expensive food. She had no idea what tonight had in store but imagined it would be more of the same. She'd applied more make-up than she would usually wear, hoping to give the impression that she belonged there, belonged with him. As she glanced at herself in the mirror in his bedroom, she barely recognised herself. Was she losing herself to become who he wanted her to be, or was this the person she was always meant to be? She wasn't sure.

Mark walked into the room in his underwear, and his eyes widened. 'You're wearing that dress?'

'I spilt ice cream on the other one, remember,' she said. 'I couldn't get the stain off.'

He sighed. 'I wish you'd told me, I could have picked you up another dress today.'

'I didn't think it was a problem.' She frowned. 'Is the dress that bad? I don't have anything else to wear, only sweatpants and my work clothes.'

'It's fine.' His tone indicated that it was anything but fine, but she didn't have time to argue. Their taxi was on the way.

Now she felt self-conscious, and she was already anxious about tonight. She put her phone into the clutch bag she'd bought with the now ruined dress and walked out of the bedroom.

After taking a photo of herself in the full length mirror in Mark's hall, she sat down on the sofa and waited for him to appear. If he was already on edge and they hadn't even left the house, what did tonight have in store for them?

He walked in, looking yet again like a catalogue model in a black sweater and dark blue jeans. His hair was perfectly styled, and yet, she wasn't drawn to him. She felt herself craving someone else instead. Someone in a crumpled t-shirt, with messy, dark blonde hair. She closed her eyes for a second, blinking away the image of Chris, then opened them again, standing up and smoothing down her dress. 'Hey. You look good.'

'Thanks.' He gave her a tight smile. 'I'm sorry if I was short with you. You look stunning.'

The tense knot in her stomach dissipated as he walked over to her, then kissed her. Perhaps tonight wouldn't be so bad.

'The taxi's here. Are you ready?'

'As ready as I'll ever be.' Her stomach still swirling, she followed him out of the apartment and down to the taxi.

When they arrived at the restaurant, he got out of the taxi first, holding out a hand to her.

She took it, trying to make sure she didn't flash her underwear at anyone as she climbed out of the taxi.

As she had expected, the restaurant was lavish, a combination of glass, marble, and metal. Mark's hand pressed into her lower back and he guided her to the dimly lit bar, and ordered them both cocktails.

Molly took a sip of hers and her eyes watered. 'Wow. That's good. And strong. Don't let me drink too many of these. I'll either embarrass myself or you,' she whispered, the rum burning her throat.

'Please don't,' he whispered back, sliding his arm around her waist. 'Why don't we go and say hello to some people?'

She took another sip of her drink, hoping for a little Dutch courage.

Mark guided her over to a group at the other end of the bar. 'Molly, you remember Lewis and Craig? They work in my office.'

'Sure.' Molly smiled. 'Good to see you again.' She turned to Lewis. 'It was your stag do, wasn't it? Congratulations on your engagement.'

Lewis smiled back at her. 'Thanks, Molly. Hoping you guys can make it to the wedding. It's on Valentine's Day next year. Invites are going out soon.'

Molly glanced quickly at Mark. He hadn't mentioned it, but maybe it had slipped his mind? 'That would be great. Where are you getting married?'

Lewis's eyes lit up. 'Coxheath Hall. It's a manor house in Surrey. We've hired it for the whole weekend, and we have a packed itinerary. Think spa treatments and hot tubs for the girls, and golf tournaments for the guys.'

Mark gave him a high five. 'It's gonna be epic. So happy for you guys.'

A tall, slender woman with sleek black hair appeared next to Lewis. 'Molly? I almost didn't recognise you. That dress is fabulous.'

Molly racked her brain, trying to remember her name. *Erica*. It came back to her right when she needed it. 'Hi Erica, and thank you. Mark got it for me.' She flicked her eyes to him, but he was deep in conversation with Craig and Lewis.

'It's gorgeous.' Erica lowered her voice. 'These things are so tough. I'm desperate to be at home in my sweatpants right now.'

Molly giggled. 'I've been in mine all day. I've been working at Mark's place for the last few days.'

'Such a wrench to get dressed up at this time of year, isn't it? So dark and cold. Bring on the summer.' Erica turned away from Lewis.

'It was not my idea to get married in February. There's no place to hide the goosebumps in the dress I've got but he insisted on it. Said that Valentine's Day is the most romantic day of the year.' She glanced down at the tiny iceberg on her finger, then back at Molly. 'You're coming, aren't you?'

'I think so, yes.' Molly took a sip of her drink. 'Lewis just asked us.'

Erica nodded. 'So when are you and Mark getting married?'

Molly spluttered, almost spitting her drink all over Erica. She grabbed a napkin from the bar. 'Sorry. Didn't mean to be so dramatic. I have no idea. We're not engaged. We don't even live together, and I have no idea when or if we will.'

'My bad.' Erica put a hand on her chest, revealing her long, French manicured nails. 'I was sure you were engaged. Maybe I'm thinking of someone else.'

'Erica!'

A sharp voice rang out across the bar, and Erica was enveloped in a tight hug by a woman that Molly didn't recognise. Feeling awkward she stepped away, but the woman fixed her gaze on Molly.

'Molly, isn't it? I'm Beth. I work with Mark. I just started a few months ago.'

'Hi, lovely to meet you,' Molly said.

Why were these woman all so tall? She almost had to crane her neck to talk to Beth, whose bronzed skin was covered by a purple silk dress which draped over the floor like an artfully arranged puddle.

'And you. Is that a Delenner dress?' Beth asked, running over her eyes over Molly.

'Uh yes, Mark bought it for me.' Molly smoothed her free hand over the fabric. 'I like but I'm worried it's a little tight.'

Beth shook her head. 'No, not at all. What a *lucky* girl you are. Such a *thoughtful* gift.'

Molly took another sip of her drink and wondered where Mark was. Beth was giving off such a strange vibe.

'I hear you work in publishing.' Beth said. 'It must put pressure on your relationship with you both doing stressful jobs and him being away so much.'

'Beth!' Erica exclaimed. 'Don't grill the poor girl.'

'I'm sorry.' Beth laughed, a mean, tinny laugh that indicated that she wasn't sorry at all.

'Our relationship is just fine,' Molly assured Beth. 'We've been to-gether for a while and we trust each other.'

Beth raised an eyebrow. 'How refreshing.'

Molly flinched as she felt a hand on her waist, then relaxed as she saw it was Mark, who had a strange expression on his face.

'Molly.' He gripped her waist tightly. 'I see you've met Beth.'

'I was just admiring Molly's dress. What a special gift,' Beth said to Mark. 'She's got just the right figure for it.'

Mark's eyes flicked between Molly and Beth, and Molly heard him suck in a breath. 'She has, hasn't she.' He turned to Molly. 'They're just about to serve dinner, we should go and find our seats.' He nodded to Beth and Erica. 'See you later.'

'I'll catch up with you later,' Beth said to Mark, ignoring Molly.

As she sat down on one of the long tables in the restaurant, Molly leaned closer to Mark, making sure that she wouldn't be overheard. 'Well, that was odd. Beth was asking me lots of questions about our relationship.'

'Was she?' He pursed his lips. 'Don't know what that's about.'

Her gut instinct told her that there was more to this story, but this wasn't the time or place to discuss it.

With every mouthful, Molly regretted her outfit choice. The dress seemed to be getting even tighter, but the food was so good. She noticed that when slices of a rick dark chocolate torte were passed out for dessert, Mark dug into his enthusiastically.

'It's good, isn't it?' she said.

'Delicious. Could you make one of these?' he asked.

She took another mouthful, trying to assess what was in it. 'Possibly. I can try.'

'I'm sure you'd nail it. You're so good at baking.' He took another mouthful of the torte.

She smiled as she finished her own dessert. The awkward exchange with Beth was still niggling her, especially as, from the other end of the table, Beth was shooting pointed looks her way. However, she was in a fancy restaurant and had just eaten three courses of incredible food. Best still, Erica was opposite her, and they had spent the whole meal talking about her wedding.

Once the plates had been cleared, Molly followed Mark and the rest of the guests upstairs to a darkened room with a dancefloor and a DJ. The room seemed to fill up instantly, making Molly feel uncomfortable. She clung to Mark, putting her hand into his, but he was distracted, talking to one of his colleagues. Someone bumped into Molly's shoulder and she gasped, trying to ignore the fear rising in her stomach. In her mind, she was falling, hitting the concrete, clutching her grazed palms. Then another image came to her. Chris was wrapping his arms around her, calming her

'Molly!' Mark snapped. 'Did you hear what I said?'

Molly's eyes flew open. The room seemed louder, and the lights felt brighter, making her feel overwhelmed. 'I'm sorry. I zoned out. Can we get some fresh air?'

Mark opened his mouth to respond, but a man in a dark grey suit walked over to them, clapping Mark on the back.

'Richard, how are you?' Mark gestured to Molly. 'Yiou remember Molly, my girlfriend.'

'Of course, hello Molly,' Richard said.

Molly smiled. 'Hi.' She focused on her breathing, and tried to grab Mark's hand, but he away from her.

'Why don't you come and join me for a drink?' Richard asked.

'We'd love to,' Mark said. 'Excellent news about the Oslo deal, isn't it?'

Before she could say anything, Mark and Richard had disappeared into the crowd around the bar.

Molly hovered at the edge of the dancefloor, wishing she was back at home, wrapped on a blanket on her sofa with Chris, than here, in a room full of people, who, aside from Erica, didn't care about her at all.

Chapter Nineteen

December 2014, Canterbury, Kent, England

When Molly walked into the kitchen the following morning, Mark was sat on one of the stools at the kitchen island, already working. He looked up from his laptop as she walked in.

'Hey sleepyhead! You're up.'

'How long have you been awake?' she asked.

'An hour or so.' He shrugged. 'I wanted to get a head start.'

She nodded. 'Mark, about last night...'

'It was brilliant, wasn't it? Richard asked me to join his team for the Copenhagen deal. That's why I'm up so early, I need to get up to speed.' He started typing again, his eyes flicking between the laptop and her.

'That's good. I'm really pleased for you.' She swallowed hard, wondering how exactly to tackle him about the fact that he had forgotten all about her, in order to further his career.

'You seemed to be hitting it off with Erica,' he continued. 'She's a great girl, and their wedding will be something else. Lewis's parents have spent a fortune on it.'

'I really like her, and I agree, their wedding sounds incredible. It'll be quite an event.' She gritted her teeth. 'I didn't like being left alone while you went off with Richard.'

He rolled his eyes. 'Really? It's not as if I abandoned you in the middle of the city. You knew enough people there. Last night was really important for my career, why are you making it all about you?'

She sucked in a breath. 'I...I wasn't. I'm not. I just needed some air.'

'Well, then you didn't need me, did you?' He glanced at the laptop screen. 'Can you make some breakfast? I'm a little busy right now.'

His complete dismissal of her stung, but with a mild hangover, a lack of sleep, and a two hour train journey ahead of her, she didn't feel strong enough to tell him exactly how she felt. Unravelling her life was not on the cards for today. It could wait.

'I don't have time,' she said sharply. 'I need to catch my train.'

There was no point in asking him to walk her to the station. She knew he wouldn't.

He nodded. 'No problem.'

She left the kitchen, returning to the bedroom and throwing her clothes into her tote bag. She couldn't stay here a moment longer, and wasn't sure if she could ever come back here again. His apartment, like him, was stylish, but devoid of feeling.

Once her bag was packed, she put her shoes and coat on, and was just about to slip out of the door when he appeared in the hall.

'Is there something wrong?' he asked, frowning.

'I've got an early meeting.' This was a lie, but she felt far too emotional to admit to anything. If he snapped at her again, she would burst into tears, and for what she needed to say to him, she needed to be stronger than this.

'Right. I'll see you next week then.' He leaned forward to kiss her, then his phone started ringing. He pulled it out of his pocket. 'Sorry, Molly. I need to take this.'

She turned away from him, opened the door, and let herself out. Angrily she walked down the stairs and out of his building. She wanted to get as far away from him as possible, to try and make sense of the jumbled thoughts clattering around in her head. She caught the train back to Victoria and found a coffee shop where she ordered a strong black coffee and a croissant, hoping it would calm her head, and her empty stomach. After she'd eaten, she picked up her tote bag and walked to her office. She couldn't face another train journey right now, or being alone in her house with her feelings.

Molly let herself into her house that evening. She had spent the day plastering on a smile, and pretending that she'd enjoyed last night, which she hadn't and that she wasn't exhausted, and fed up, which she was. The house was cold and empty, and she shivered as she put the heating on, and walked into the kitchen. The fridge was pretty much empty, and it was too late to defrost anything. Instead, she ordered her favourite Thai green curry and sticky jasmine rice, then changed into her pyjamas.

When her food arrived, she put the curry and rice into a bowl and sat with it on the sofa. She tried to concentrate on the documentary on the TV, but her thoughts kept drifting back to Mark and the party. The strange vibe between Beth and Mark. The way that he had dismissed her when she told him that she felt uncomfortable. How out of place she felt there. She would never fit into his world, and he had no interest in fitting into hers. So where did that leave them? Stuck in a relationship that would never go anywhere. Her phone buzzed, and she picked it up.

> Are you OK? I KNOW something's off X

Molly sighed. She'd sent Liz a message last night when she'd been slightly drunk and very emotional.

> Am fine. Just hungover and Mark was a bit of a dick last night X

Liz's response made her laugh out loud.

> Mark was a dick? Shocker! It's a good thing he's hot because he's not got a lot else going for him X

> I feel like crap today and I couldn't face a row with him but I'm getting tired of his shit. When he gets back, I'm going to have it out with him X

> I would like ringside tickets to this please X

She put her phone down and flicked through the TV guide, choosing a channel showing a film that she had never seen before. John Williams' iconic introductory score started and the words "Star Wars" flashed across the screen. She wrapped herself in a blanket and as she lay down on the sofa, she felt a gentle rush of contentment. The doors were locked. The curtains were drawn for once, blocking out the darkness. She was safe.

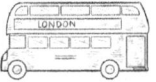

Molly woke up on the sofa the next morning and rubbed her eyes. She'd been asleep for almost twelve hours, and she felt so much better for it. She picked up her phone and checked her messages.

> I'm at the airport. My flight is on time. I will see you in London my darling girl. Papa X

She smiled. He would be sat in the airport, his glasses perched on his nose, his head stuck in a book. He would have had a strong coffee and a croissant or some toast and jam before he packed his battered leather suitcase and left his house. He always wore sunglasses outdoors, whatever the weather. He was stylish, but not fashionable. He'd worn the same straight legged blue jeans for the last twenty years, always paired with a shirt. A dress shirt when it was cold, with a cashmere sweater over the top, or a linen shirt in the summer, the top buttons open to reveal the thin silver chain her mum had bought him. His predictability was comforting but seeing him was bittersweet. All the while he wasn't there, she didn't miss him, but as soon as he had to leave, the heavy sense of longing came back. She replied to his message.

> Great news! I'll see you at Victoria at 4. Love you x

She put her phone down and ambled into the kitchen, making herself a cup of tea and warming a frozen croissant in the oven. Her dad wouldn't approve of a croissant that wasn't bought fresh from the boulangerie, but she didn't care. She slathered it in apricot jam and sat with a mug of tea at the dining table, watching the wind lashing the trees outside. Her phone buzzed and she picked it up, hoping her dad's flight hadn't been cancelled. It wasn't from him though. It was from Chris.

> Hey Molly, how are you? I don't know if Saskia told you but she invited me to come tonight. Is that OK? I haven't heard from you in a while. Is everything OK?

Before the kiss, before that night, it would have been fine for him to come, to be moral support for Scott, who would be under the scrutinising gaze of her dad, but now, it was a disaster waiting to happen. *Of course Saskia invited him*, Molly thought to herself. She loved to stir things up.

> I didn't know she had invited you! I'm sorry I've not been in touch. I've been busy with work, but I'm looking forward to seeing you later on.

She sent the message and the butterflies which had lay dormant in her stomach for the past few days came to life. Tonight she would see Chris again. And she would have to ensure that she didn't let on that anything had happened between them in front of the man who missed nothing.

Knowing that Chris was coming tonight, she toned her outfit down. She would have loved to have worn a dress and high heels, but she'd decided to play it safe, with wide legged black velvet trousers, high heels, and a black and white striped long sleeved top with a high neckline. She styled her hair to cover the scar on her eyebrow so that her father wouldn't see it as she hadn't told him about being mugged and didn't plan to.

With an overnight bag packed, Molly drove to the station and climbed onto the train. She was staying at Saskia's flat tonight after the show, and as the train sped towards London, a rush of excitement flooded through her.

When the train reached Victoria station, Molly got off the train and squealed as she spotted a familiar figure walking towards her.

'Papa !'

'Molly ! Ça va ?' His face lit up and he pulled her into a tight embrace.

'Tres bien, Papa, how are you?' It had only been a few months since she'd last seen him, but he seemed to have changed. He seemed older, more fragile somehow. As expected, his smart wool coat was finished with a thick red scarf and his long legs were clad in the usual dark blue jeans. His hair, a mass of grey and white curls, was as untamed as usual, hugging the slender frame of his face.

'I am very well, chérie,' he said. 'You're looking beautiful as always, my darling.'

'Thank you, Papa.' She smiled at him.

He let her go and straightened his scarf. 'Are you going to lead the way? I have no idea where we are going.'

'Of course, follow me.' She gripped his arm tightly in hers and led him out of the station and onto a bus. She had styled her hair to cover the scar on her eyebrow which had now faded from a deep purple to a pale silver. They took two empty seats at the back and Molly held onto his hand tightly as the bus joined the chaotic London traffic, and he began peppering her with questions.

'I still cannot believe my own daughter is in a West End show. I can't wait to see her. How is she? Is she enjoying living in London? Are you OK in that house on your own?'

She struggled to keep up with the flow of questions but knew that he wouldn't stop until he had got everything off his mind. That was just what he was like. They climbed off the bus, her hand still clutching his as they walked to the pub, where she pushed the door open and made her way to an empty seat at the bar.

'Papa, what are you having?' she asked.

'A glass of red wine, I think.' He squinted at the bottles on the counter. 'Whatever they've got, I'm not fussy.'

She smirked. He was fussy but he was just trying to be accommodating.

She ordered a wine for her dad and a rum and Coke for herself, which the barman placed onto the counter in front of them, giving her a broad smile.

'Santé,' she said, as she clinked her glass with her dad's.

'Santé.' He smiled. 'I have been waiting a long time for tonight. I think this will be Saskia's big break.'

'So do I, I'm so happy for her...'

Her breath left her body in a dramatic exhale as Chris walked in. He was wearing his navy silk bomber jacket with a dark t-shirt underneath and a pair of tight jeans. She imagined his arms sliding around her and forced herself to look away from him, noticing Scott following Chris into the pub. His scruffy stubble was gone, his hair was immaculately styled, and he wore a thick black cashmere jumper under his leather jacket. He clearly wanted to make a good impression on her dad, and she silently wished him luck. Her dad would not go easy on him. She waved them over and they made their way towards her.

'Scott, Chris, this is my dad, Gaspard.' Her eyes met Chris's and she saw the familiar twinkle in them. The one that made her stomach lurch. She looked away from him, and at Scott, whose hand was clasped in her dad's.

'Pleased to meet you, Gaspard,' Scott said.

Gaspard nodded. 'I have heard a lot about you from Saskia. It is good to put a face to the name.'

'Should I be worried?' Scott asked, with a nervous smile on his face.

'Not yet,' Gaspard turned to Chris. 'Good to meet you, Chris.'

Chris's jaw dropped. 'You're Gaspard Millot!'

Molly sighed heavily and took a big gulp of her drink.

Chris's eyes widened and he turned to Molly. 'Molly, you didn't tell me your dad was Gaspard Millot!'

Gaspard smiled at Chris. 'A fan! How wonderful.'

She shook her head. 'This is why I didn't tell you! I knew how much you liked his books. I thought you'd explode if you knew he was my dad.'

'I'm a massive fan of your books,' Chris said to Gaspard. 'They're phenomenal.'

Gaspard narrowed his eyes. 'You are much younger than most of my readers.'

'I found one of your books on my dad's bedside table when I was about ten. I read it twice and since then I've tried to find all of them,' Chris held out his hand. 'I can't believe I'm meeting you.'

Gaspard took Chris's hand and shook it. 'I am pleased you enjoy them. I am in the middle of writing one now. Perhaps you would like to see a draft of it when I am ready?'

'Of course I would!' Chris spluttered. 'Detective Rousseau is my hero.'

Gaspard grinned. 'Really?'

Molly nodded. 'I think he's learnt how to be a detective from your books. He's spookily accurate. He sees things almost everyone else would miss.'

'Ah, well you know I used to be a police detective?' Gaspard said to Chris. 'When Molly came along, I decided I needed a slightly less unpredictable career, and started writing instead.'

'You can tell that you know what you're talking about,' Chris replied. 'I've read a lot of crime thrillers, but they aren't as good as yours.'

Gaspard waved his hand. 'Thank you, I appreciate that. Perhaps you would like to become one of my advanced readers? You would get copies of my books before they are released.'

'I *would* love that,' Chris said excitedly.

Annoyed with her dad for taking over the conversation, as usual, Molly turned to the bartender. 'Hi, I've got a table reserved in the name of Millot and we're all here now.'

'Yes, I've got you on my list.' The bartender nodded to a passing waitress. 'Kat will show you to your table.'

When she sat down, her eyes met Chris's across the table. Why did he have to be so hot? Why did he have to be so kind? Why did he have to have a chest that she wanted to lay her head against?

Gaspard picked up his menu and put his glasses on, then turned to Molly. 'Pie and mash tonight then, Molly?'

'Bien sûr!' Molly said. Every time she'd been to London with her dad, they'd had pie and mash, something he didn't have at home in Provence.

To Molly's relief, the food arrived quickly. She kept her eye on her watch as they ate, knowing that they still had to walk to the theatre and find their seats, and she hated being late. Gaspard and Scott seemed far more relaxed. They were in the middle of a lengthy discussion about their favourite wines. She smiled to herself, wishing that Saskia could be here to see how Scott was holding his own against their dad. She leant over and stole one of Chris's chips, dipping it in his ketchup. He held her gaze for slightly too long. Just long enough for her heart to start pounding faster. Long enough for her to watch the light from the candle on the table flicker in his eyes. She took a deep breath and focused on her dinner, not daring to look at Chris.

As the waiter took their empty plates, Molly cleared her throat. 'We've probably got time for another drink if you want one?'

Scott shot out of his seat. 'I'll go and get them.'

Chris stood up too. 'I'll come and give you a hand, mate.'

Once they had left the table Gaspard turned to Molly. 'Molly, Je vois comment tu le regardes. Tu es amoureux, non ?'

'Non,' Molly replied quickly.

Her dad was speaking in French, meaning he didn't want to be easily overheard. As she had predicted, he had studied her and Chris, and had noticed that they had feelings for each other. But she wasn't in love with him, was she? No. She had to squash that thought, even though it kept bubbling to the surface.

'Nous sommes justes amis, Papa.' Chris had made it very clear that they were just friends, and so she said the same thing to her dad.

'Non, c'est ne pas vrai.' He shook his head and finished his glass of wine.

'Je te le dirai plus tard,' she said.

She would speak to him later. She didn't want to talk about it now, but he'd told her that that wasn't true and he was right. She'd been rumbled. He didn't believe her.

'Je veux être son ami mais j'ai des sentiments pour lui.'

This was the actual truth. He was her friend. And she had feelings for him.

Gaspard nodded. 'Comme je le pensais. Il ressent la même chose.'

Of course it was what he already thought. He missed nothing. But, Molly thought, it was interesting that her dad thought that Chris felt the same way.

She looked up, realising that Chris was standing next to her just at the moment that her dad told her that he thought Chris had feelings for her.

'Rum and Coke,' Chris said.

'Thank you,' she replied, wondering what he had heard, and if he had been able to interpret any of it.

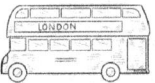

As the curtain dropped, Molly turned to Chris, who was sat next to her. 'What did you think?'

'She was incredible. Everyone was, but she was amazing. I had no idea she could sing like that.' Chris turned to Gaspard. 'Tu dois être très fier d'elle.'

'Ah oui, je suis tellement fier.' Gaspard nodded enthusiastically. 'Elle est très talentueuse.'

'I didn't know you spoke French,' Molly whispered to Chris as they walked to the theatre bar.

She was both impressed by his French, and the fact that he'd said that her dad must be proud of Saskia.

'Layers,' he whispered back, raising an eyebrow at her.

Molly stared back at him wide eyed. Before she had a chance to consider how much of her conversation with her dad Chris might have heard, the door opened and a bare faced Saskia, clad in a long dress, thick tights, and black boots flew in. She ran straight to her dad, wrapping her arms around him.

'Papa ! Qu'as-tu pensé ? As-tu aimé le spectacle ?'

'Incroyable !' Gaspard said, his words muffled in Saskia's hair.

'Can we grab a drink?' Saskia let her dad go. 'I'm on such a high. It was better than I'd expected. I cocked up my lines in rehearsal, and I was so nervous, but it went so well.'

'Of course. Champagne, I think, don't you?' Gaspard nodded to the bartender and ordered a bottle.

'One glass,' Saskia said. 'I've got to pace myself, it's only the first night.'

'You were just breathtaking, Saskia. I'm so proud of you.' Molly gave Saskia a hug.

'Thanks, Mole.' Her eyes shone with tears as she pulled away from Molly. 'I'm so glad you're here. I've missed you.'

'Me too,' Molly replied, then nodded to Scott, who was helping Gaspard pour the Champagne into glasses. 'I think someone else has missed you too.'

Saskia grinned as she walked up to Scott, sliding her arms around his neck. 'It's been forever since I last saw you.'

'Too long,' he said and pulled her towards him, kissing her.

'Wow,' Molly took a glass of Champagne from her dad. 'Probably best we leave them to it.'

'Saskia!' A husky voice rang out across the crowded bar.

Molly turned around. The husky voice belonged to Caro, who was wearing a turquoise coat, her make-up immaculate, her auburn curls bouncing across her shoulders. She wasn't alone. Her arm was tucked into the arm of a tall, dark-haired man. His tan leather brogues were expensive, like the ones that Mark wore, and as he raised a hand to greet Saskia, a gold signet ring sparkled on his little finger.

'That's Caro's boyfriend, Jeremy,' Saskia whispered as Caro and Jeremy walked towards them. 'They're very full on.'

'Full on?' Molly whispered back. 'What do you mean?'

Before Saskia could respond, Caro was in front of them.

'Hello Molly, darling.' Caro kissed Molly's cheek. 'What did you think?'

'It was brilliant!' Molly said. 'Your voice is stunning. '

'You're too kind,' Caro replied, then gestured to the man next to her. 'This is Jeremy, my boyfriend. Jeremy, this is Molly, Saskia's sister.'

'Wonderful to meet you.' Jeremy kissed Molly's cheek, making her smile. Was this how they all greeted each other in London?

'And you.' Molly was taken aback by just how handsome Jeremy was. He was like a sculpture, all chiselled cheekbones and strong jaw.

Saskia introduced Caro and Jeremy to her dad, Scott, and Chris. Jeremy ordered another bottle of Champagne and they all squeezed around the table together.

'Molly, I've missed you so much. What's it like in that house without me?' Saskia asked.

Molly raised her eyebrow. 'It's tidy.'

Everyone burst out laughing, and Saskia rolled her eyes.

'Seriously. I do miss you lots,' Mollyy said. 'It's been very quiet.'

'Oh really, I heard you'd had quite a lot going on.' Saskia smirked at Chris, who immediately blushed. She turned to Gaspard. 'How about you, Papa? Are you still writing your next book?'

Gaspard took a sip of his Champagne and smiled. 'I'm always still writing my book. One day it will be finished.' He nodded to Chris. 'I've met a fan tonight though, unlike my girls who never read my work.'

Molly glared at him. 'I read your books Papa. You know I do.'

As usual her dad's ego was taking over the room. She flicked her eyes to Saskia, alerting her to try and stop him.

'This is lovely, Papa,' Saskia said, 'but it is my night tonight, not yours. You can have your fan club night another night. Now, who is going to give me their honest review of tonight?'

After the second bottle of Champagne had disappeared, Caro and Jeremy got up.

'We're going to head off,' Caro said. 'Saskia, I'll see you tomorrow, everyone else, so lovely to meet you.'

Saskia nodded. 'See you tomorrow, babe.' As they left, she stood up. 'I hate to break up the party, but we'd better go too.'

Outside the bar, Molly directed her dad to the right Tube station for his hotel, after arranging to meet him for lunch the following day. To her left Saskia was wrapped around Scott, giggling as he whispered in her ear. To her right was Chris, bathed in the light coming from the theatre behind him.

'How are you?' he asked. 'It feels like I've not seen you for ages.'

'I know,' Molly said, nodding. 'I'm fine, I had a pretty eventful week, but all good.'

'Did you tell him?' he asked, his voice low.

'About us? No. I didn't see how that would benefit anyone. It was a one off, right?' Her mind flashed back to him kissing her and she felt her cheeks flush.

'Your words say one thing, but your eyes say another,' he whispered, then kissed her cheek.

She opened her mouth to reply, but she was interrupted by Scott and Saskia.

'You ready, mate?' Scott asked Chris. 'We need to go if we're going to make the last train back.'

Chris nodded and turned to Molly and Saskia. 'See you guys soon.'

Saskia slid her arm through Molly's. 'Right then, back to my beautiful little house Molly. Off we go. Please don't start tidying it up or moaning about the state of the place. We're barely there.'

'I'll keep my mouth shut. I promise. I'm too tired to do any tidying anyway,' Molly said as they walked along the brightly lit street. 'You took my breath away tonight, you know that?'

'Oh stop.' Saskia nudged Molly playfully. 'You'll have to squash my giant head through the door. I don't want an ego like Papa's.'

'Don't worry, I won't let you get one. I'm sure that when I get back to your filthy house, I'll be able to bring you right back down to earth.' Molly laughed.

'I'm slightly scared,' Saskia said. 'I don't think it's that bad, but I bet you'll have a different opinion. At least Caro's staying at Jeremy's place tonight, so it'll be quieter.'

'You were right about them,' Molly whispered. 'They are full on.'

'You try having a bedroom next to them,' Saskia raised her eyebrow. 'The first night he stayed over I could barely look them in the eye the next morning.'

Molly laughed and clung on to Saskia tightly all the way back to her flat.

'Can you believe your girlfriend is an actual West End star?' Chris said to Scott.

They'd just made it onto the last train home and his head was spinning from the Champagne.

'I can't believe she's spent all these years doing bit parts.' Scott shook his head. 'She belongs on a big stage.'

'How are you coping though?' Chris asked, studying Scott's face. 'It must be hard, not being able to see her.'

'We're trying to make it work,' Scott said. 'Right now, she needs to focus on this pantomime and our relationship has to work around it. I'm new to the whole relationship thing, but I know what *not* to do. How about you, what happened with you and Molly?'

'I'm confused,' Chris admitted, rubbing a hand through his hair. 'I set out tonight to prove that I can be Molly's friend, then I overheard her saying to her dad that she's got feelings for me. If that's true, then why is she still with Mark?'

Scott sighed. 'He's been a constant figure in her life. Even though he's a shitty boyfriend. I get it. I was the same with my dad, remember? Even though he was a complete arsehole, I didn't want to leave him.'

'I remember,' Chris said. 'I know how painful it was for you to walk away from him.'

'But I did, didn't I?' Scott paused. 'Are you trying to fix her? She's vulnerable- just like I was. You took me in and fixed me. Are you trying to do the same with her?'

Chris let out a long exhale. 'Scott, I didn't fix you. You were in a bad situation, and I did what I could – as a ten-year-old – to help you out of it.'

'Sorry.' Scott fiddled with the zip of his jacket. 'It's just that your mum is a counsellor, and it comes naturally to you, helping people, I just wondered if you were trying to help Molly.'

'No,' Chris said firmly. 'I'm not trying to fix her or help her. I love her.'

'Oh mate, I'm happy for you, but...' Scott took a deep breath before he continued. 'You absolutely *cannot* be her friend. It'll end in disaster. Does she know you love her?'

Chris lowered his voice. 'No, but her dad does. I overheard him telling Molly as much this evening in the restaurant.'

'Oh. What did she say?' Scott asked.

'She said that we were just friends, but when he pressed her on it, she said she'd speak to him later. They were both speaking in French so I didn't catch all of it.'

'Ever the detective.' Scott smirked. 'So what happens now?'

'I don't know,' Chris said. 'That's the worst part. Most problems I can solve. This one I can't.'

Chapter Twenty

The next morning Molly woke up hangover-free, but when she opened her eyes and surveyed the chaos around her, she groaned, and her stomach turned. Clothes were strewn over every surface, and across the armchair in the corner of the room, the wardrobe doors were inexplicably wide open, and pieces of paper, empty cans of soda and packets of gummy sweets littered every surface in the room.

It wasn't only her surroundings that were making her feel overwhelmed. She was still processing everything that had happened last night. Seeing Saskia giving it her all on the stage had made her feel overcome with emotion. She wondered if anyone on the cast knew how much courage it had taken Saskia to get back up there and perform. She was proof that you could conquer your fears. The other thing making her stomach lurch was the conversation she'd had with her dad, and the possibility that Chris had overheard it. If he had, he would know that she had feelings for him. The whole thing was just as much of a mess as Saskia's bedroom. She closed her eyes again, just as she heard Saskia stir next to her.

'Morning, love,' Saskia croaked. 'How did you sleep?'

'Really well,' Molly said opening her eyes, 'but I've woken up in a nightmare. This place is disgusting.'

Saskia cleared her throat. 'I know, but I've had no time to sort it out. Come, on, let's get up. You said you were going to buy me breakfast.'

'Why don't we ask Papa as well? Then you get to see him again before he goes,' Molly suggested. 'I was going to meet him for lunch, but if he comes now, you'll get to see him too.'

'Good idea. His hotel is only round the corner,' Saskia replied, tiptoeing over the mess. 'Can you text him and ask him to meet us in Café Floris? It's not far, and he'll love it.'

Molly raised her eyebrow and picked up her phone. 'Sure. How long do you need to get ready?'

Saskia looked at the clock on her bedside table. 'Give me half an hour.'

Molly showered in the surprisingly clean and tidy bathroom. When she returned to Saskia's bedroom, Saskia was still in bed, the duvet wrapped tightly around her.

'Come on, Sas. You need to get up.' Molly sat down on the bed, still wearing the towel she'd borrowed from the linen cupboard. 'You said half an hour. Now you only have twenty minutes.'

'Ugh, Twenty minutes is *not* long.' Saskia yawned and pulled back the duvet, sliding slowly out of the bed. 'Right. I'm up. If you want to have a tidy while I'm in the shower, you feel free.'

'You're the worst.' Molly shook her head.

'You love it,' Saskia said, then walked out of the room.

Molly dried herself and looked around the room, wondering where she'd put her clothes. She located her jeans draped over a chair but couldn't find her jumper. She opened Saskia's wardrobe and eyed the long-sleeved pink leopard print top that she'd always secretly longed to wear, and took it out, putting it on. Maybe wearing it would help her channel some of Saskia's confidence. She put some mascara on and had just put her make-up bag away when Saskia walked back in, her cheeks flushed red from the shower.

'Check you out!' Saskia said, running her eyes over Molly. She nodded approvingly. 'That suits you. Keep it. I can buy another one. I've got a proper job now.'

'Are you sure?' Molly asked. 'I've wanted to borrow it for ages, and I couldn't find my top anywhere.'

Saskia laughed. 'The bedroom has it now.'

Molly sighed. 'Get dressed.'

In Saskia's bold leopard print top, Molly felt confident striding into the café and sitting down at a table in the window next to Saskia. Her dad arrived a few minutes later, sitting opposite them.

'Morning, Papa,' Molly said. 'How's your head? We drank more than I thought we would last night.'

'I'm just fine, chérie.' He eyed two plates being delivered to the table next to them. 'Those croissants look almost as good as the ones I get from the boulangerie at home.'

'Oh, they are, Papa,' Saskia said. 'Get the almond one, c'est délicieux.'

He wrinkled his nose. 'Have I not brought you up to want fresh croissants, not yesterday's croissant with some frangipane stuffed inside?'

'These are way better, Papa, I promise you.' Saskia smiled at him.

Molly watched their exchange, smiling to herself. She loved the way that her dad and sister both knew their own minds and refused to settle. She needed some of that energy herself. She ordered the almond croissant, and when it arrived, she wasn't disappointed. The flaky pastry contrasted perfectly with the sweet almond filling.

Gaspard turned to Saskia. 'Now you can tell us, how is it going?'

Saskia wiped her mouth with a napkin. 'It's so intense, Papa. The schedule is relentless, but it's so worth it, and the friends I've made are so inspiring. Most of them have been in productions like this before. They're already going to auditions to line up their next jobs, and I keep thinking about how lazy I've been.'

Molly sighed. 'You aren't lazy Saskia. You were dealing with so much. The job at Ezio's was comfortable and secure, and you needed that.'

Saskia nodded. 'You're right, but I'm stronger now. I've got two auditions next week; one for a gin commercial and one for a play.'

Gaspard's face lit up. 'I am so proud of you, Saskia. I have been worried about you these last couple of years. I can see in your face that you're motivated. You will do well. I know it.'

'I'm so happy, honestly, I feel like pinching myself every day. The only downside is that I don't get to see Scott as much. I miss him. More than I thought I would. I love him.' Saskia's eyes filled with tears.

'Have you told him?' Molly asked.

'No.' Saskia shook her head. 'We're both kind of new at this whole relationship thing, we're taking things slowly. I want to tell him, but I also don't want to freak him out.'

'I don't think you need to worry about that,' Gaspard said. 'He's very much in love with you.'

'Do you think so?' Saskia wiped her eyes, then picked up the rest of her croissant and took a bite.

'Absolutement.' Gaspard nodded. 'I think he will tell you, but he is biding his time. He does not want to...clip your wings.'

'When I come back to Canterbury, I'm going to tell him,' Saskia said. 'It'll be our little secret for now.'

'You are not the only one keeping secrets.' Gaspard fixed his eyes on Molly. 'How long have you been in love with Chris?'

Molly almost choked on her tea. She put her cup down, spluttering. 'Papa, I'm not in love with him.'

Saskia snorted. 'Papa, you see it too? They are so smitten with each other, aren't they?'

'Can we not talk about this here?' Molly nudged Saskia who was giggling. 'It's not funny.'

'Admit it, Mole. Just to us,' Saskia whispered.

'No. We're friends.' Molly turned to her dad. 'Papa, I've not been honest with you. Back in October, I was mugged at the train station. I wasn't badly hurt, but I was too scared to get on the train for two weeks. When I did manage to get back on the train, there was a power cut and I freaked out. Chris was sitting next to me. He comforted me that night and we just...connected.'

Gaspard wiped his mouth with a napkin. 'I saw more affection from him in the few hours that I spent with him than your current boyfriend has shown you in the last four years. I don't believe that you are friends, you are too close, too intimate with each other.'

'We kissed each other,' Molly blurted out. 'Then the next day we both agreed that we were friends, nothing more. I put it behind me to focus on my relationship with Mark.'

'What relationship?' Gaspard said bluntly. 'There is no commitment, no future, just dates. You deserve more.'

Molly gulped down her tea. He was right. As usual. There was no future for her and Mark.

Saskia eyed Molly curiously. 'What happened when Chris and Mark bumped into each other? I would have loved to see that. I bet Mark was ready to explode with jealousy.'

'He was, and I was stuck in the middle of it all.' Molly paused. 'He was *right* to feel jealous, because there *is* something between Chris and I, however much I try to pretend that there isn't. So I was angry with Mark, but then I just... I didn't challenge him on it because *I'm* the one in the wrong. I'm the one who's been unfaithful.'

'Did you tell him?' Saskia asked.

Molly shook her head. 'No, because that won't benefit anyone. Chris and I agreed to forget it and put it behind us and I was all ready to try and move on with Mark, but the last week has shown me that the relationship will never be what either of us want or need. After we left Chris, we had dinner, and went back to his place. He'd bought me some clothes and toiletries to leave at his place, even made sure I had my favourite breakfast things. I felt *so* bad about kissing Chris, and I could start to see a future with Mark.'

'But...' Saskia prompted her. 'What happened at his Christmas party?'

Molly filled Saskia and Gaspard in on the last few days, then showed them the photo of her in *that* dress.

Saskia's eyebrows shot up. 'Crikey Molly, that doesn't leave much to the imagination. You do look gorgeous in it, but the question is, did he buy it for you?'

'I had my doubts when I saw it, and when I saw Beth's reaction to it, that confirmed my suspicions. I reckon he's cheating on me with her, and he bought it for her.' She glanced at her dad. 'Papa, qu'en penses-tu ?'

She wanted his opinion. He had listened intently to her, and he was rubbing a hand over his chin thoughtfully.

'If it walks like a duck...' Gaspard took a sip of his coffee. 'I believe that is the correct expression.'

Saskia snorted with laughter. 'Papa tells it like it is.'

'So Mark's a duck?' Molly giggled. 'If you both want the truth, which I know you won't rest until you get, then yes. I like Chris. A lot. And my relationship with Mark, or whatever you want to call it, is pretty much over. When he comes back from Oslo, I'll tell him.'

'Brilliant!' Saskia clapped her hands. 'Can I be there?'

'You have a pantomime, which is way more important,' Molly reminded her.

'Good point. I do.' Saskia drained her coffee. 'What about Chris? Are you going to tell him how you feel?'

Molly sucked in a breath. 'No. Yes. Maybe. It feels too *big* right now. I need to sort out the Mark thing first, then I'll have to work out how to tell him.'

'I do believe he feels the same way,' Gaspard said gently. 'He is a gentleman, and so there is no way he will tell you his true feelings all the while you are with someone else. He may be waiting for a sign from you that you have feelings for him.'

'Good point, Papa.' Saskia nodded. 'Molly needs to make the first move.'

'I did that a few weeks ago when I kissed him,' Molly whispered.

Saskia giggled. 'So you did! You might just have to brave it and put yourself out there again.'

Molly considered Saskia's words as she finished her tea. 'Thanks for the advice, both of you, I appreciate you.'

'You're welcome.' Saskia wiped her mouth on a napkin. 'I could sit here all day with you beauts, but I need to get to the theatre. Oh, I forgot to tell you, I've got two auditions this week, both for roles in plays here.'

'That's incredible! Are you thinking you might live here for a while then?' Molly's stomach lurched. She'd been hoping that Saskia would be coming back home once the pantomime wrapped.

'I don't know yet.' Saskia shrugged. 'You know me, I go with the flow.' She turned to Gaspard. 'It's been awesome to see you, Dad, will we see you over Christmas?'

'Oh yes,' he said. 'I've booked us a suite at the Devon Lane Hotel from Christmas Eve until Boxing Day. You will be backwards and forwards from the theatre, Saskia, but I saw this as the only way we could spend Christmas together.'

Molly and Saskia squealed 'Really?' at the same time, then laughed.

'Oh, Papa, thank you! A fancy hotel suite at Christmas.' Saskia's eyes lit up.

'That's so sweet of you, Papa,' Molly said. 'Thank you so much. Can we pay our share?'

'Non,' Gaspard replied firmly. 'Let me treat you both.'

'I'm looking forward to it already.' Saskia stood up. 'I need to go, but I love you both, and I'll see you soon.' She blew them both kisses, then hurried out of the café.

Molly walked with her dad back to his hotel, and as they reached the entrance, he smiled at her. 'I have been worrying about you too, Molly. You take on a lot, and you put yourself last.'

'Not anymore. I'm making myself a priority from now on.' Maybe it was the leopard print top, or a bigger sea change inside of her, she wasn't sure, but she knew she wasn't going to be walked over any longer.

'I can tell,' he said. 'I'm very much in favour of this. What I have learnt is that hearts are easy to break, and hard to mend. That includes your own.'

'Wise words as usual,' she replied. 'Has anyone ever told you that you should be a writer?'

'Plenty of people have told me that I shouldn't be. Mais, je m'en fous.' He shrugged.

'I might adopt that as my new motto.' She smiled. 'Maybe I won't give a shit either. Let them think what they want!'

'That's the spirit.' He kissed her cheek. 'Goodbye, my darling.'

She wrapped her arms around him. 'Thank you, Papa, for everything.'

'Je vous en prie.' He waved as he walked into the hotel, then blew her a kiss.

Chapter Twenty-One

As CHRIS STOOD IN the lobby of Molly's office building, his palms started sweating, and a prickly, uncomfortable feeling spread through his body. He'd spent the last few days thinking about Saturday night. About Molly, and her dad, and whether he'd overstepped the mark by insinuating that she hadn't been honest with him about how she felt about him. He hadn't contacted her, as he had no idea what to say.

She'd sent him a message last night asking him if he wanted to catch the train home together, so he'd walked over to her building when he finished work. He couldn't stop the smile spreading across his face as she walked into the lobby. Her blonde hair fell in loose curls, and her lips were, as always, scarlet red.

'Evening, Chris,' she said, a smile spreading across her face as she saw him.

'Evening, Miss *Millot*.' He raised an eyebrow.

She blushed. 'I'm sorry I didn't tell you, but sometimes when people find out my dad is a famous author, they assume I'm rich, or that I've only got where I have because of my name.'

He opened the door for her, and then followed her out into the darkness.

'I don't think that.' He shook his head. 'I see how hard you work. I understand why you didn't tell me and I'm so grateful to you for letting me meet him.'

She smiled. 'I miss him so much, but he is so French, like he couldn't live here, that's why he and Mum split up. He went back to France and we stayed here.'

'I'm sorry, that must have been hard for you,' he said as the bright lights of the station loomed ahead of them.

'It was,' she replied. 'We miss him loads, but we do get to have some pretty cool holidays in Provence, and he's so much happier in France.'

He followed her into the station, and his heart sank. The concourse was full of people with angry faces, all talking loudly. The colour drained from Molly's face and her eyes darted around nervously.

'What's going on?' she asked.

Knowing she would feel overwhelmed, he gripped her hand in his tightly and led her to the information board. Every train going back to Kent was delayed due to an accident.

'We might have a problem,' he said quietly to her.

'Can you get me out of here?' she whispered. 'I can't breathe.'

He tightened his grip on her hand, keeping his eyes on the station entrance, and guided her through the throng of people, out into the cold night air. Under the awning of the station, he held her tightly as she sunk her head into his shoulder and took several deep breaths, before pulling away from him.

'Are you alright?' he asked.

'I'm fine now,' she said, a steely determination in her voice. 'There are no trains, right? So I think we should go and get some dinner somewhere. We can always crash at Saskia's place if we can't actually get home.'

'Sounds like a good plan to me,' he said. 'Where do you want to go?'

She shrugged. 'You choose. I chose last time.'

'I think I know a place.'

He led her away from the chaos of the station, down Westminster Road and over the bridge, past Big Ben. They crossed over the road after the bridge and walked along the South Bank as the fairy lights draped between the streetlights twinkled above them.

'Where are we going?' she asked.

'You'll see. Mind the steps.' Down a flight of stone steps, just opposite the river, was a row of restaurants and shops. He pointed towards one of the restaurants. 'How about dim sum?'

Her eyes lit up. 'I'd love that!'

'That's a relief,' he said. 'It would be a bit awkward otherwise.'

She laughed and he pulled open the door and let her go in first. The restaurant was dimly lit, with bench seating. A waiter greeted them and showed them to an empty bench at the back of the restaurant, before handing menus to them. He took their drinks orders, then walked away.

She looked around the restaurant. 'I didn't even know this place was here. I like it.'

'I came here with Alex and Scott last summer, and I've been back a few times since then,' he said. 'I hope you're feeling proud of yourself right now. You took charge of that situation.'

'Thank you,' she replied. 'The last few times I've felt anxious, I've tried to stay focused on a solution and it helps. You helped too. As usual.'

'It's not a problem. Remember you had to look after me the other night.' He caught her eye. 'We're here for each other.'

'Right.' She held his gaze for just a second, before she looked away.

Guilt gnawed at his stomach. He'd overhead a conversation that wasn't meant for him, and he knew that she had feelings for him. He didn't want to make the evening awkward by bringing it up – and she clearly didn't want to either.

'You'll have to tell me what to order.' She looked at the menu. 'I've not been to a dim sum restaurant before.'

He picked up his menu and ran his eyes over it. 'I think we should get the chicken and the duck bao buns, vegetable gyoza, and char sui pork buns. Does that sound good?'

'I have no idea about any of it, but I'll try anything.'

Yet again, he bit back a smile.

After the waiter had taken their order, and delivered them glasses of jasmine iced tea, Chris turned his attention back to Molly.

'How's work? Have you been busy? I've not seen you on the train.'

She took a sip of her drink. 'It's been so busy. That's why I shut myself away to try and focus. I've got two deadlines to meet before Christmas and I'm running out of time. I'm sure I'll get there though. How about you?'

He nodded. 'Pretty much the same. New starters needing new laptops and system access at the same time as my sales guys needing new software. I'm counting down the days until Christmas.'

'Me too,' she said. 'Papa's coming over and he's booked us a suite in the Devon Lane Hotel. Me and Saskia, that is. We're staying there from Christmas Eve until Boxing Day.'

'Oh wow, that sounds incredible,' he said. 'I bet it'll be super luxurious.'

She smiled. 'It will. He likes the finer things in life. Good food, good wine, beautiful surroundings. It's no bad thing but I don't have the budget for it myself, so sometimes I feel guilty as he insists on treating us.'

'Don't,' he said. 'He wants to treat you guys. Let him. I bet if you had kids you would do the same.'

'I would.' She gave him a shy smile. 'I feel so much happier now you know he's my dad. Hiding it from you, it felt so massive.'

He smiled back at her. 'I understand why you didn't tell me, but I still think it's so cool.'

'It *is* cool. I'm so proud of him. When he first started writing, he didn't sell many books, and he was considering going back to the police force then they just took off, and now he's a bestseller.'

The waiter arrived at their table, bringing bamboo baskets full of buns and dumplings.

'Try a bao bun,' he said, passing her the basket.

She tentatively picked up a bun with her chopsticks and took a bite. 'Ooh, that's good.'

He took one for himself, and nodded approvingly as he took a bite. The duck was aromatic and the vegetables were slightly crunchy, just how he liked them. This wasn't how he'd planned on spending the evening, but he couldn't imagine anyone he'd rather be stuck in London with than her.

'I'm not the best with chopsticks,' she whispered. 'Please don't laugh at me.'

'I'm not much better,' he assured her. 'There's cutlery in that pot if you'd rather use that.'

'Absolutely not. The more practice I get, the better I'll be.' She carefully picked up a gyoza and took a bite. 'See!'

He smiled. Her determination was just one of the things that he loved about her. Not that he would tell her, even if he now had a feeling she might feel the same way.

'What are you doing for Christmas?' she asked.

He took a sip of his tea. 'We're going to the hotel that Alex and Sarah, my aunt, own. It's tucked away in the countryside near Barham, and it's so luxurious. It'll be closed on Christmas Day though as the whole family are going. All my cousins, aunts and uncles. It's gonna be noisy and brilliant.'

'Sounds wonderful.' She smiled. 'I wish I had cousins, aunts and uncles. Papa is, and Mama was, an only child.'

'You're welcome to share mine,' he offered. 'They're a little chaotic, and there's a lot of big personalities. Ben, Alex's brother, and Jake, our cousin, live in Cornwall so we don't see them that often. Christmas is one of the times where we all get together.'

He wished he could invite her to spend Christmas with them, but she had a boyfriend, and he had to take a step back from her.

'That's very sweet of you. If they're anything like you, I know we'll get on just fine.' She picked up another bao bun and took a bite.

They would all love her. Alex had contacted him after they'd left Mimosa the other night to check that Molly was alright. His protective side had come out in full force, as Chris knew it would. Scott saw Molly as *his* sister, mainly due to his relationship with Saskia, and was desperate for Chris to reveal his feelings to Molly, but right now, his focus was distracting her from the fact that they had no idea how they were getting home.

Molly had just paid the bill, despite his plea to split it, when his phone buzzed with a message. He read it, then looked up at Molly.

'There's a train in half an hour. If we miss it, we risk being stuck in London all night.'

'Let's go.' She finished the last of her green tea, and slipped on her coat.

He opened the door for her, bracing himself against the bitter December wind. He didn't reach for her hand although he wanted to, but she slipped her arm into his as they walked back to the station.

The crowds had dissipated somewhat, he noticed as he walked onto the station concourse, still gripping Molly tightly. She let go of his arm and swiped her ticket through the barrier, and he followed her through and onto the train, which was packed. He walked through carriage after carriage, searching for an empty seat, and in the last carriage, found two together, and paused, waiting for Molly to catch up.

She collapsed onto the seat. 'That was a bit of a race. I'm so glad we made it. Otherwise, we would have been stuck in London for the night.'

'That would have been...*awful*.' He raised an eyebrow.

'Not awful, just...inconvenient. I wouldn't mind being stuck anywhere with you. You know that.' Her cheeks flushed and he bit his lip to hide his smile. She *did* have feelings for him. He pulled his tablet out of his bag and switched it on. 'Your dad's sent me a draft of his book. You want to read it with me?'

'Wow, you are privileged,' she said. 'He hasn't sent it to me.' She moved closer and started to read over his shoulder.

He quickly became engrossed in the story, as he always did with Gaspard's books. When he looked up at Molly, he smiled. She was fast asleep, with her head on his shoulder. He stayed fixed in the same position, afraid to wake her, until they reached Canterbury, where he gently nudged her.

'Molly, we're home.'

Molly woke with a start. 'Oh no! I fell asleep on you!' she exclaimed, sitting up.

'It's fine, I don't mind. I've wiped the dribble off my shoulder,' he deadpanned.

She rolled her eyes. 'Very funny. That's the first time I've fallen asleep on the train since I got mugged.'

'I feel honoured. You must trust me.' He caught her eye.

'I do. Implicitly.'

Something moved between them, a shift, a change in the atmosphere, and for a second he could imagine his lips meeting hers. But then the bustle of commuters brought him out of his thoughts and he broke the eye contact, standing up and putting his coat on.

'Ready? I'll walk you to your car,' he said, squashing whatever it was to the back of his mind.

He decided not to question or examine it but followed her into the car park, which was lit by the full moon piercing its way through the darkness. When they reached her car, he bit his lip, aware of the isolated position that it was in.

'Why don't you park at my place tomorrow and we can walk to the station together?' he suggested. 'It'll save you some money and you won't have to be on your own.'

'Are you sure that's alright?' She chewed her lip. 'I can manage this on my own.'

'You can, but you don't have to,' he said.

'Thank you. She smiled. 'I had fun fun tonight. Maybe we can go again with Scott and Saskia after Christmas? We used to go to this Chinese restaurant when we were younger, and we'd always have to order more pancakes as she could eat so many we didn't get a look in.'

As she talked about her parents, a sadness swept across her face. He thought of his parents and how often he spoke to them or went over to their house. He thought about how hard it must be not to be able to do that.

'That's such a sweet memory,' he said. 'I wish your mum could see you now. She'd be so proud of you.'

Her eyes filled with tears. 'Why do you always do this to me? You always say the sweetest things, and it makes me cry.'

'I'm sorry.' He opened his satchel and handed her a packet of tissues. 'I didn't mean to make you cry. I just need you to know how incredible you are.'

'Thank you.' She pulled a tissue out of the packet, and wiped her eyes. 'Do you want a lift?'

He shook his head. 'It's a nice night for a walk. I'll see you tomorrow.'

She nodded and stood on her tip toes to kiss his cheek, before climbing into her car.

The walk back to his flat did nothing to clear his head. He was in love with her. It was inescapable. Even her dad had seen it. Did she feel the same way? He didn't know, and didn't know how to approach it with her. For the first time since he had known her, he was hiding something from her, and he didn't like it. He sat on the sofa in the dark, silent living room with his head in his hands. He wished he was at Molly's and that she wasn't going home alone to a cold dark house, but that they were together, drinking tea and wrapped in a blanket on her sofa. She would tell him she loved him as much as he loved her. He would tuck her under his arm so she could fall asleep, and he would hold her close. His chest felt tight, and he fought back the tears that threatened to push through the eyes that he'd closed tightly.

Chapter Twenty-Two

Molly carefully applied a flick of black liner to her eyes, then mascara, and a coat of scarlet red lipstick. 'How do I look?' she asked Liz, who was sat on her bed next to her.

'Gorgeous,' Liz said, as she put on her own lipstick.

'Thanks.' Molly smiled. 'That dress really suits you.'

'What are you wearing?' Liz asked.

Molly slid off the bed and opened her wardrobe. She ran her fingers over the dresses inside, debating over which one to choose. Why was it so hard to make any decision right now? She pulled out a pale blue dress, printed with sprinkle covered cupcakes. 'This one.' She pulled her t-shirt and jeans off and threw them on the bed, then slipped the dress over her head.

'Cake girl.' Liz smirked. 'Seems fitting.'

Molly sighed. 'Chris and I bonded over cake, so it would make sense that I reference that tonight, wouldn't it?'

She had been on edge all day. Not because tonight she would be in a packed bar, but because it was Chris's thirtieth birthday and she would be surrounded by his friends and family, and the knowledge that she was hiding a secret from all of them.

'I think you bonded over more than cake,' Liz said. 'He offered you something that you didn't even know you needed. Comfort, kindness.' She paused. 'Love.'

'Woah, hold up. We need to squash all that love talk right down,' Molly hissed. 'I cannot tell him and you can't either.'

'I wouldn't!' Liz insisted. 'And I know you won't until you've spoken to Mark. My lips are sealed.'

'Thank you. I know this whole situation is really messed up...'

Liz interrupted her. 'Life is messy. Do not apologise.' She checked her watch. 'Come on. We need to go.'

Molly sucked in a breath. 'I'm ready.'

She went downstairs to the kitchen and picked up the box of cakes from the counter, which she held on her lap as Liz drove them both into the city.

At Mimosa, Scott greeted her and Liz, taking the box of cakes from her. 'Can I take a peek?'

'Sure,' Molly said. 'There's brownies, school cake and rocky road in there.'

He lifted the lid and a sweet, sugary smell floated out. 'Do you need a taste tester? I'm happy to offer my services.'

'Nice try.' Molly shut the box. 'Let's save them for the birthday boy, huh?'

'Fine.' Scott handed the box to Jo. 'Can you put these somewhere far away from me, please?'

Smiling, she whisked the box away from him.

Molly gave him a hug, and a kiss on the cheek. 'That's from Saskia. She misses you.'

'I miss her too, but she's where she needs to be. On the stage.' He smiled. 'I'm so sure she's gonna get one of the parts she went for last week, and if she does, I'm a hundred per cent behind her, even if it means she stays in London for a little longer. It just means we have to make the most of the time we get together.' He raised his eyebrow.

Molly wrinkled her nose. 'Scott, that's my sister you're talking about!'

He winced. 'Sorry. No filter. Honestly, I keep thinking I'm gonna fuck this thing up, but for some reason, she seems to like me as much as I like her.'

'You're both the same brand of chaotic,' Liz quipped. 'Seems like you've both met your kindred spirit.'

Scott laughed. 'That's probably true. What can I get you ladies?'

'A virgin mojito, please, Scott. I'm driving,' Liz said.

'Same for me.' Molly felt too nervous to drink tonight.

'Coming right up.' Scott took a couple of glasses out of the rack.

Molly pulled out a stool and sat down, scanning the room even though she knew Chris hadn't arrived yet. She could see Kate and Alex, Chris's mum, and a man who she guessed was his dad, as he looked like an older version of Chris.

Liz sat down next to her. 'Are you OK?' she whispered.

'All good. You?' Molly whispered back.

'I will be once I've stuffed my face with your rocky road,' Liz said, giggling.

Scott put their drinks down on the counter and Molly handed him some money. 'When's Chris getting here?'

'Any moment now,' Scott said. 'He went for drinks with some of his team from work and got a later train back tonight.'

Molly lowered her voice. 'And he has no idea we're all here?'

She'd had a message from Scott, asking her to come tonight and not to tell anyone about it.

Scott shook his head. 'Nope. He thinks it's just me and him here tonight.' The door opened, and Scott looked up. 'Here he is!'

Chris's face broke out in a broad smile as the entire room cheered for him. 'Hey everyone.' He was immediately embraced by his mum, then his dad.

Molly watched as the rest of his family gave him a hug. There were two other men about his age who looked a little like Alex, who she assumed were his cousins, and a brunette, who all greeted him noisily. She couldn't help feel a pang of sadness that her family didn't look like that. She adored Saskia, but she had no idea what it must be like to have a big, close family. Scott piled in too, putting his arms around Chris and kissing his cheek, making the rest of his family laugh.

She turned her attention back to Liz. 'How was Martha's nativity play?'

'Adorable,' Liz said. 'I had no idea I was going to cry so much, but spoiler alert, I did.'

'She looked so cute in her sheep costume,' Molly replied. Liz had sent her a photo of a very smiley Martha wearing a fluffy white costume.

Liz rolled her eyes.'She did, but she didn't want to give the costume back to the pre-school. It took a lot of convincing and a little bribing to persuade her.'

Molly laughed, then stopped as she saw Chris walking towards them. Her heart leapt into her throat as she slid off her stool. 'Joyeux anniversaire mon amie !'

'Merci, mon cher.' He kissed her cheek. 'I love the dress.'

She smiled. 'Thank you. I thought it was perfect.'

'It is.' He turned to Liz. 'Hey! Nice to see you.'

'Happy birthday, cake boy!' Liz said. 'What's thirty like?'

'So far, so good,' he replied. 'I got taken out for lunch, then dessert, then drinks after work and now my entire family and all of my friends are here.' He looked around the room. 'It's a tiny bit overwhelming.'

'Birthday drink?' Scott put a glass in front of Chris with a smirk. 'It's an Old Fashioned.'

Chris laughed and took a sip. 'I don't know what you're smirking about, mate. You're going to be thirty in a couple of months.'

'Don't remind me,' Scott said, grimacing. 'I'm way too young to be turning thirty.'

Jo appeared next to Scott, and raised her eyebrows meaningfully at him. 'Can I borrow you for a second?'

'Oh.' Realisation dawned on him. 'I'll be right back, guys.'

When Scott returned, he had a large silver platter, with sparkler candles stuck in the top, and the entire bar crowded around Chris, singing "Happy Birthday."

'Thanks, guys. I love you all so much. These cakes look awesome.' He turned to Molly. 'You made these, right?'

She nodded. 'I added hazelnuts to the rocky road.'

He picked up a piece and took a bite. 'That was a good move.' He gestured to the cakes. 'Come on everyone, dig in.'

'Molly, this cake is delicious.' Kate held up her brownie, and Molly noticed a large diamond ring on her finger.

'Are you and Alex engaged?'

Kate nodded. 'He proposed last week. I don't know if Chris told you, but I'm a jewellery designer. I work at Correll's and Alex essentially tricked me into designing my own ring.' She laughed. 'David, the guy work with, asked me to help him design a ring for a customer. I had no idea it was for me.'

'Congratulations!' Molly gave Kate a hug. 'That's so romantic. How did he propose?'

'He's always been a bit extra but this time he went for it,' Kate said, sitting down next to Molly. 'We both love his mate's band, Future Proof. We had our first kiss at one of their gigs. They were playing at the Penny Theatre on our two-year anniversary, and he went on stage and held up a sign saying, 'Will You Marry Me?'

'I love that! It's so romantic! I'm so happy for you both.' Her eyes met Chris's and her heart started beating a little faster.

In that instant she knew. It was him that she wanted to marry. It was him she could see a future with. She sucked in a breath. Did he know? Could he tell? Did he feel the same? She stuffed some more cake into her mouth, and tried to concentrate on what Kate and Liz were saying.

'We're planning to get married next summer,' Kate said. 'Alex has booked the hotel for the weekend. Do you do wedding cakes, Molly?'

'I've never done one, but I'm sure I *could* make one, depending on what you wanted,' Molly replied.

'I'll have a think.' Kate put the last of her brownie into her mouth. 'I could eat at least five of these.'

'Well, you need to save some for everyone else,' Chris said, nudging her away from the platter. 'Like me.' He picked up a brownie and took a bite.

Kate snuck another brownie, raised her eyebrows at him, then walked away.

He shook his head. 'She's a law unto herself.'

'She's going to be your...' Molly paused. 'Cousin-in-law. Is that a thing?'

'Maybe?' Chris shrugged. 'I don't know. Let me introduce you guys to everyone else. Guys, this is Molly, and Liz. Molly, Liz, this is Ben, his wife Corinne, and Jake.'

Chris's cousins all greeted her and Liz, and before she knew it, she had been swept onto the dancefloor. Alex was in the DJ booth, Kate was doing a strange dance that made her look like a worm, making her friend Mia laugh. She caught Chris's eye and was immediately taken back to the last time they had been together, right before they went back to her house and kissed each other. There was no way he would be thinking about that, was there?

He held out a hand to her, and she took it, letting him twirl her around so her skirt flared out around her.

'Are you having a good time?' she asked as he pulled her closer.

'I am. Tonight's been fun. I'm so glad you're here too. It means a lot.'

She swallowed hard. 'Where else would I be? It's your big birthday, and Scott asked me to bring the cake, so...'

'It was amazing. Thank you.'

He held her gaze, and she felt for a second like they were the only people in the room. She longed to blurt out that she loved him, and she wanted to spend every single one of his birthdays by his side, but she couldn't.

When Alex's set finished, the bar was so full, Molly could barely see the door, and a prickly, anxious feeling flooded her. She was bumped and pushed as she searched the room for Liz, finally finding her talking to Corinne in one of the booths on the other side of the bar.

'Hey, love.' Liz smiled at her. 'You alright?'

'Uh huh.' Molly nodded and sat down next to Corinne.

Liz narrowed her eyes. 'It's too busy in here, and you're feeling overwhelmed, right?'

'Yes, that too,' Molly admitted, then turned to Corinne. 'I was mugged a few months ago. Crowded places make me feel a little anxious.'

This was the first time she had told a complete stranger this since she had told Chris, but the fear and stigma of talking about it were slowly dissipating.

'Oh Molly! How awful!' Corinne gave her a sympathetic smile. 'Can we do anything?'

'No, I'm just choosing to ignore it.' Instead of the relentless wave of anxiety, Molly felt empowered. She was here with her friends tonight. Friends who cared about her, and who would protect her. There was nothing to be afraid of.

'Wow, you're a badass. Huge credit to you.' Corinne nodded approvingly.

'So proud of you, Molly.' Liz blew her a kiss. 'Want another drink, or do you want to go?'

'I'll stay for another drink,' Molly said. 'What's everyone having?'

'Why don't I come with you?' Liz suggested. 'Corinne, we'll be right back.'

After another drink, this time one with a hit of rum, Molly felt more confident. She returned to the dancefloor with Liz, and danced until she felt like her legs might give way. As Jo called last orders, she ambled over to Chris.

'Goodnight birthday boy. We're gonna head off.'

He kissed her cheek. 'Thanks for coming tonight, and for the cake, which has been *devoured.*' He let out a dramatic sigh. 'I was hoping to take some home, but it's all gone!'

'I had two brownies and a rocky road,' Scott admitted. 'And I'd have had more if there had been any left.'

Molly laughed. 'I'll make you guys some more.'

She slipped her arm into Liz's and they walked out of the bar together, into the cobbled streets of the city, which sparkled under the strings of fairy lights above them.

'Molly, you did so well tonight,' Liz whispered. 'I saw the anxiety coming over you, and you just *fought* back against it.'

'I did.' Molly smiled. 'And I feel good for doing it.'

When they reached Liz's car, Molly climbed in. Now they were in a private, quiet space, she had to let it out.

'If I was in any doubt about the fact that I'm in love with Chris, tonight has proved it to me, completely, inescapably.' Molly let out a long exhale. 'I love him, but I cannot lose him as a friend, Liz, I just can't.'

Liz cocked her head to the side. 'What if he feels the same way? Maybe he feels the same way and has the exact same fears as you.'

'He might, but I need to deal with Mark first.' Molly grimaced. 'That's not going to be pretty. Or maybe it'll be fine? Maybe *he* feels the same as me too. He's clearly cheating on me.'

'Did you feel jealous of Beth?' Liz asked.

Molly shook her head. 'Not a bit. I just felt annoyed by her. I think that was a sign that the relationship was over. I just need to rip off the plaster.'

'I know it's scary but I'm proud of you for taking charge of your life.' Liz clipped her seatbelt on. 'Let's get you home.'

'Thanks for listening, and for not judging me,' Molly said. 'I appreciate it.'

'Why would I judge you? You're my friend, and I love you. And I never liked Mark. Sure, I wouldn't *recommmend* cheating on anyone, but life isn't black and white, it's all kinds of grey.'

'Morally grey?' Molly asked.

Liz laughed. 'Maybe. Is that so bad? If you kissing Chris means that you're finally ditching Mark, then I don't see it as a bad thing. And if it means that you and Chris live happily ever after, even better.'

Molly considered Liz's words. Was there such a thing as happy ever after? Or was that only in the fairy tales she edited?

Chapter Twenty-Three

Molly paced the floor of her living room. When she'd told Mark that she needed to see him, she'd been surprised that he had chosen to come to Canterbury, but he would be arriving at her house any minute. After his Oslo trip, he'd gone to Copenhagen, so it had taken longer to have this conversation than she would have liked, which had increased her anxiety. *Mark knows*, she thought to herself. He obviously knows. She was certain that he knew she was planning to break up with him or he was planning to break up with her. She felt mean doing it right before Christmas, but there was no way she could go through another Christmas, or even another date with him. An expletive laden pep talk from Saskia had helped, and now she was ready. The doorbell rang and she rushed to answer it.

'Mark. Hi.' She gulped nervously. 'How are you?'

'I'm fine.' He kissed her on the cheek. 'Can I come in?'

She stepped back to let him in. 'Sure, sorry.'

He frowned as his eyes raked over her. 'I've booked us a table at Riad. Did you want to get changed?'

'What's wrong with my outfit?' In her black jeans and cashmere jumper she was ready for the death of her relationship. She led him into the living room and perched on the edge of the sofa.

He sat down next to her, stretching his long, chino clad legs out. 'Oh, nothing, I guess. It's just a bit...dark.'

'Did you say you'd booked Riad? It's so good in there.' She chose to ignore his comment about her outfit. This was what she was wearing, and she didn't care what he thought about that.

'You've been already?' he asked, his voice heavy with disappointment. 'It's only been open a few months.'

'I went last month. I didn't expect you to come back here for a Moroccan restaurant. You love the one in Chiswick.' She kept her tone neutral. Best not to rile him now.

'I do, but this one has really good reviews, and I wanted to try it out.'

She studied him closely. His jaw was tight, and he had beads of sweat forming on his brow. He was going to break up with her. At least she knew the food would be good, and if they were in a public place there wouldn't be an argument. They could just amicably go their separate ways. He had never raised his voice in all the time she'd known him. He would probably be relieved. It would mean he could get together with Beth.

'What time did you book the table for?' she asked.

'Seven, so we should get going now.' He stood up and smoothed down his trousers.

He was quiet as he drove her into the city, but as they walked to the restaurant, he complained about the cobbled streets. Molly smiled to herself. After tonight, she wouldn't have to listen to him talking about how Canterbury wasn't half the city that London was.

Inside Riad, the lights were dim, and the waiter showed them to a table at the back of the restaurant, before taking their drinks order.

'What are you going to have?' she asked. 'I had the lamb tagine, and it was really good.'

'I'll go with that then.' He shut his menu.

When the waiter brought their mint tea, she took a sip, wondering when Mark was planning on breaking up with her. Would it be during the meal? Afterwards? She hped she'd at least get to enjoy her tagine before it all imploded.

'How was Copenhagen?' she asked, plastering a smile onto her face.

'Cold,' he said. 'But the deal was successful, we impressed the client, and we had a laugh in Tivoli Gardens. The rides were a bit tame, but

Beth was still scared.' He chuckled. 'I also secured a second client in Oslo, so it was worth it. There's a promotion on the cards for me now as a result.'

'Great. What does it involve?' she asked.

'It's a step up and a move to a different team.' He waved his hand. 'It's complicated.'

'Right. I probably wouldn't understand anyway.'

'I doubt it, no.'

She plastered on a smile. His condescending tone would no longer be her problem after tonight.

Their tagines arrived, and she managed to make minimal conversation as she ate. He didn't ask her a single question about what she had been doing, or how she was, but that just made what she had to do even easier. He seemed unusually nervous. His eyes kept wandering around the room, and his cheeks were flushed.

He swallowed another mouthful of tea as the waiter took their plates away.

'Did you want a dessert?' she asked.

She was baffled. Why hadn't he broken up with her yet? Maybe he was building up to it.

He pulled at the collar of his shirt, and she could see the fear in his eyes. *Come on, just do it,* she thought to herself. Rip the plaster off. Get it over with.

'I called ahead and arranged something special,' he said.

She frowned, puzzled, as the waiter returned with two plates. 'Homemade baklava, with honey and yoghurt.' He set them down on the table.

'Thank you,' she said, smiling politely at Mark. 'This is really thoughtful.'

She picked up her fork, noticing for the first time what was on her plate. Written in swirly chocolate writing, were the words *Will You Marry Me?*

She gasped. 'Are you serious? Is this for real?'

'Well, yes,' he said. 'I didn't think that would be the first thing you'd say.'

'Oh, Mark...' she trailed off.

'Molly, we've been together for four years, and you spent pretty much *all* of my Christmas party talking to Erica about her wedding, telling her how much you loved weddings.'

She lowered her voice. 'I said that I love weddings, but...' she paused. 'I can't marry you.'

His eyes narrowed. 'Excuse me? Would you care to elaborate?'

'I thought you were bringing me here tonight to break up with me,' she whispered.

He shook his head. 'Why would you think that?'

Her words stuck in her throat. 'We're just too different,' she said eventually, as he glared at her. 'I need someone who will be there for me. Not just physically, but emotionally.'

'You're a little needy at the moment, and that's OK,' he said. 'Once you've had some more counselling, you'll be fine. You were like this after your mum died.'

She sucked in a breath, remembering Saskia's words. *You're not needy, you just need me,* she had said. Mark would never understand that.

'When my mum died, I needed you, and you weren't there for me. I got on with it then, but I can't do it any longer. I ask you for *nothing*. And the things I do ask you to do, like walking me to the station, you don't even do.'

'I didn't know that walking you to the station was such a big deal,' he said sulkily.

'I was still scared, Mark. I thought you might want to be there for me. You just don't get it. You won't ever get it.' She glared right back at him.

He rolled his eyes. 'I don't know what you want from me. I thought you wanted to get married, and now I've proposed, you're breaking up with me?'

She felt a hot flash of anger course through her body. 'You don't even want to marry me?'

There had been no ring, and he hadn't got down on bended knee. He clearly didn't want this either.

'That's not what I meant,' he said quickly. 'I just thought it was time. All the guys in my office are getting married.'

'That is the least romantic thing I've ever heard. How could you possibly expect me to marry you?' She paused, narrowing her eyes. 'Does this have anything to do with your promotion?'

He studied his napkin intently.

She stood up, her body shaking with rage. 'I wanted to do this amicably, but I can't. I'm too angry. You proposed to me just to impress your boss?'

She grabbed her coat and bag and walked to the front door, flinging it open and walking out into the street. Taking a lungful of the cold night air helped calm her burning cheeks. The door flew open, and Mark came out, rounding on her.

'How could you do that to me?' His eyes burnt into hers. 'You really embarrassed me.'

'Is that all you care about?' She backed away from him. 'Being embarrassed is more of an issue to you than the end of our four-year relationship?'

He glared at her, then at the bar on the other side of the road. 'You need to calm down. People are staring.'

'Calm down?' She shook her head. 'I've spent our whole relationship biting my lip and not saying what was on my mind.'

He moved closer to her. 'Molly, listen, I think you're overreacting. Can't we talk about this?'

Her heart started beating faster and she suddenly felt unsafe. She didn't like the way his eyes had darkened, his brows almost touching.

'No, I don't think so.'

'What? You mean I've spent three hours driving here tonight for nothing?' He frowned at her. 'You're not even prepared to talk about this?'

She swallowed hard. 'What is there to talk about?'

'This is about him, isn't it?' he said, his eyes narrowing. 'You've been led astray by that nerdy gym freak, haven't you? Have you been sleeping with him?'

'No.' This was the truth, and she was sticking to it.

'So you're telling me there is nothing going on between you?' He raised an eyebrow.

She wrestled with her conscience before she responded. 'I kissed him. We'd been out drinking, and I kissed him, but he stopped it and we both agreed that it couldn't happen again.'

'Bullshit,' he said, folding his arms. 'You're a liar, and a cheat, Molly. I don't believe you for a minute.'

'I don't care,' she responded, feeling empowered. 'That's the truth.' There was no way she was going to tell him that she was in love with Chris. 'Maybe you've got a guilty conscience yourself. Are you going to tell me that the only thing Beth rode while you were in Copenhagen together was a rollercoaster?'

'You're disgusting.' He looked away from her.

'Am I wrong?' she asked. 'Look me in the eyes and tell me you didn't sleep with her in Copenhagen.'

'I didn't,' he snapped. 'I slept with her in Belgium. It was a mistake. One I'm still paying for. She won't leave me alone.'

She sucked in a breath, before narrowing her eyes. 'You mean the trip where you presented me with a ridiculously expensive bag when you got back. Was that a guilt present?'

He sighed. 'Yes.'

'That stupid bag that I was assaulted for was a gift because you had slept with someone else?' she shouted.

'Keep your voice down,' he hissed. 'I'm not discussing this here. Let's go back to your place and we can talk about this rationally.'

'I don't think so.' Her heart was pounding so furiously she could almost hear it. 'I'm not going anywhere with you.'

'You're being stupid, Molly,' he spat. 'Come with me.' He grabbed hold of her arm, pulling her towards him.

'Let me go!' She gasped as she heard the seam of her coat rip. As she stepped backwards, she tripped, sending her stumbling onto the pavement and into a muddy puddle.

'Oi, what's going on here?' The man who had been standing outside the bar was now in front of Mark, and he had an angry expression on his face.

'This is none of your business.' Mark turned away from her, to face the man.

Molly pulled herself to her feet. The city was full of people coming out of the bars and restaurants. Running away would mean running towards these people, but she didn't want to stay with Mark either. Leaving Mark and the man arguing, she turned and ran as fast as her heels would carry her, her tears falling onto the cobbled street.

Chapter Twenty-Four

Mimosa's neon sign appeared in front of Molly. Pushing open the door, she almost fell in, her chest heaving as she tried to catch her breath. She scanned the bar, but Scott wasn't there. Her body shaking, she walked unsteadily to the counter, then scanned the room again, hoping he was here somewhere.

Jo hurried over to her. 'Oh love, do you need some help?'

Molly nodded. 'Is Scott in tonight?'

'Yes, darling, he's in the back. I'll call him for you.' Her brow furrowed as she ran her eyes over Molly. 'Are you alright here for a minute while I get him?'

'Yes,' Molly said. 'Thank you.' She pulled a tissue out of her bag and wiped her eyes.

'Molly?' Scott came around to her side of the bar, his eyes widening. 'What's going on?'

'Mark...' Molly tried to swallow the lump in her throat. 'I ran.' The tears flooded down her cheeks again.

'Let's go somewhere quieter. Is that OK?'

She nodded and followed him out of the back of the bar, into a tiny office. The desk was cluttered with papers and a laptop.

'Sorry about the mess,' he said and pulled out the chair from the desk. 'Have a seat.'

'I, uh, I fell.' She gestured to the muddy patch on her jeans.

'Doesn't matter. Sit down.'

She sat, trying to avoid getting the chair dirty.

He leant against the desk. 'What happened to you? Do you want to talk about it?'

'Yes, but I don't want to drag you into this.' She bit her lip.

'You aren't. We're friends, and you can talk to me. Or if you don't want to, I'll get you to wherever you need to be, and whoever you need to be with.'

'You're so kind.' She wiped the fresh tears from her cheek. 'I don't know what Chris told you about Mark...'

He folded his arms. 'He told me enough that I'm not surprised that you're here right now.'

She nodded. 'Then I'll fill you in on the rest.'

He listened intently, saying nothing, his brow furrow deepening as she spoke.

When she finished, he gripped the edge of the desk tightly. 'I get it, Molly. I know why you stayed with him. You thought he would change. You thought things would be better, right?'

'Yes,' she said. 'How did you know?'

'You're not the only one who's been there,' he replied. 'Only for me, it was my dad. It took Chris and his mum a while to convince me that I would be better off without him, and do you know what? I was.'

'I'm so sorry, Scott.' She put her hand on his. 'You deserved better.'

'So do you,' he said, 'and I hope you know that.'

She nodded. 'I thought things could be different. I *wanted* things to be different, but he's showed me who he really is. I'm so sorry to just barge in here, but I'm scared to go back home in case he's there.'

His eyes met hers. 'So don't. Tell me where I need to get you to, and who I need to get you to.'

She didn't want to have to say it out loud, but there was only one person she wanted. 'I need Chris. He...I just need him.'

'Understood. I'll take you there.'

'You're working,' she said. 'I can't ask you to leave work.'

He stood up. 'Jo will understand. She'd be furious with me if I put you in a taxi right now. I can drop you there and come right back to work.'

She nodded. 'Thank you.'

'Come on. Let's get you out of here.' He led her back into the bar, where he sidled up to Jo. 'Can I borrow your car keys?' He nodded to Molly. 'I need to get my friend somewhere safe.'

Jo pulled her keys out of her pocket, handing them to Scott. 'For her, sure. Do not damage my car. Got it?' She gave Scott a pointed look.

'Thank you. I will not damage your car.' He paused. 'Again.'

'What did you do to Jo's car?' Molly asked as Scott drove them back to his flat.

'I might have hit a kerb and scratched her brand-new alloy wheels when I borrowed it to collect a delivery.' Scott winced. 'I paid to have them repaired, but she hasn't forgiven me.'

'Oh no,' Molly said. 'I bet she felt like she couldn't say no to you tonight. I'm so sorry.'

Why did everything she did cause hassle for everyone else around her?

'You don't need to apologise, Molly. You're not to blame here.'

'I feel bad for dragging you both into this,' she said. 'I just didn't know where else to go.' She bit her lip.

'Listen, you came to the bar, because you knew me or Chris, or both of us would be there and you knew we would help you get through this.' He gripped the steering wheel tightly. 'I know what it's like when your world falls apart and you have to put your trust in someone else. I put my trust in Chris and his family and they've never let me down. Chris and I will never let you down. I promise you that.'

'I know you won't.' She swallowed hard. 'I knew I could trust Chris the minute I met him. I don't know why or how, I just did.'

'I felt exactly the same.' He parked outside their apartment building. 'Look, we're here. Let's hope Chris isn't asleep, or naked.' He let out a wild laugh as he got out of the car.

She fell into step with him as he walked to the door of their building, and unlocked it. Once she was inside, she finally breathed a sigh of relief. She was safe now. No one knew where she was, or who she was with.

Scott unlocked the door to his and Chris's flat and pushed it open. 'After you.'

Molly took off her heels and followed Scott into the living room.

'We have a guest,' Scott said.

Chris, who had been sprawled out on the sofa, leapt to his feet. 'Oh shit! Molly, what's happened to to you?'

She cleared her throat. 'It's a long story. Can I stay here for a bit?'

'Of course you can,' Chris said.

'I need to get back to work.' Scott looked at Molly. 'You OK?'

She nodded. 'Thank you so much. You're awesome.'

'I need to get back to work,' Scott said. 'I'll see you later, guys.'

'Thank you for bringing me here, Scott. You're amazing.' Her voice cracked as she spoke, and she knew the tears were not far away, so she bit her lip.

He shrugged. 'I didn't do anything. I'm glad you're safe.'

He left the room, and Molly heard the front door shut behind him. She hovered by the sofa, not wanting to sit down on it. She was cold, tired and emotionally drained.

'You don't have to talk about it if you don't want to,' Chris said. 'Just tell me what you need from me.'

She put her arms around him, and rested her head on his chest. 'I just need this.'

Just hold me and don't ever let go of me, she thought to herself.

'You're wet,' he said. 'Your jacket is wet.' He let her go. 'And you're shivering.'

Slowly and carefully he took her jacket off. 'How does a shower and some clean dry clothes sound?'

'Really good.' The cold was seeping through to her bones.

She followed him down the hall to the bathroom. He took a towel from the linen cupboard and put it on the heated rail below the other two. 'That'll be warm by the time you come out.' He switched the shower on. 'Help yourself to whatever you want in there, and you can adjust the temperature with the buttons on the right. My bedroom's the next room on the left. I'll leave some clothes out for you. They'll be massive, but they'll keep you warm.'

She folded the towel under her arm. 'Thank you. I'm so sorry to gatecrash your Friday night.'

'You haven't. I just wish I wasn't seeing you like this. I'll make you some tea. Rooibos or regular?'

To him, she was never too needy, too much. He was too good, too kind. She felt like her heart might burst and she needed him to leave the room so she could cry without him seeing her.

'Rooibos would be great, thanks. I'll be right out.'

He nodded. 'If you leave your clothes in here, I'll put them in the washing machine once you're done.'

He left the room and closed the door behind him. Struggling with the buttons on her damp jeans, she pulled them off and folded them neatly, tucking them next to the bath. The back of her jumper was damp too, thanks to the stupid thin jacket she'd grabbed to go out in tonight. The thin, *ripped* jacket that she loved. As she took off her jumper and underwear she realised that if Chris was going to wash her clothes he was going to *see* her underwear. At least it was a fancy, lacy set, but she was still cringing at the idea.

She stepped into the shower and let her tears fall, swirling away down the drain with the warm water that was caressing her cold skin. She picked up the shower gel and squeezed some into her palm. It smelt of fresh lemons, just like Chris. His shampoo had a musky, masculine scent, and as she washed herself, her whole body began to relax. His scent made her think of watching films on the sofa with him, of being held tightly on the dancefloor. Of his hand clasped firmly around hers. He had always shown her that he could be there for her exactly where and how she needed him to, and never asked for anything in return.

Once she was clean, she stepped out of the shower and rubbed herself dry with the towel, then cracked the door open and tiptoed down the hall to Chris's room. Laid out on the bed was a t-shirt, a pair of sweatpants, a hoodie, and some long black woolly socks. She burst out laughing as she put the sweatpants on. They were about a foot too long, but they were warm and dry, and that was what mattered. She pulled the t-shirt and hoodie on, instantly feeling warmer, then slipped the socks on.

She flicked her eyes around the room, noticing the pile of books on his bedside table, the neatly ironed bedsheets. She wasn't going to rummage in his wardrobe, but she was fairly sure it was all full of immaculately pressed clothes as well as good quality sportswear, judging by the sweatpants he'd given her. Her socks slipping across the floor, she walked into the kitchen.

'Oh wow,' Chris said, running his eyes over her. 'I thought they'd be a little big, but...'

She flapped the long arms of the hoodie like a penguin. 'Is it ridiculous?' She laughed. 'I feel ridiculous.'

Yet, she didn't feel self-conscious. He was familiar, someone she could trust.

'No, not at all.' He handed her a cup of tea. 'Let's go and sit down.' He picked up his own cup and led her into the living room.

She sat down on the sofa and took a sip of her tea. 'Mmm, this is good, thank you.'

'No problem.' He picked up the TV remote. 'If you want to talk, I'll switch this off.' He gestured to the Star Wars film which was paused. 'If you need to switch off, we can watch this, or whatever you want.'

She nodded and picked up her phone, wincing as she unlocked it. There were ten missed calls. She sighed and opened her messages.

> Where are you? I'm at your house. I need to talk to you.

Her stomach lurched. How long had he been there? Would he stay there? Before she could think about it, she replied.

> I have nothing to say to you. Go home and don't contact me again.

She stuffed her phone back into her bag and took a sip of her tea. All the while she was here, she was safe. He had no idea where Chris lived.

'I broke up with Mark tonight.' She looked up at him.

He swallowed hard. 'You did?'

'I did.' She paused. 'It didn't go well.'

'What did he do to you?' His eyes darkened. 'Did he hurt you?'

'No. Yes. Sort of. I thought he was going to break up with me, but then he *proposed*. I said I couldn't marry him and when I walked out of the restaurant, he followed me. He admitted he'd slept with someone else. I admitted that I'd kissed you. I guess I wanted to be honest with him. He wanted to go back to my place so we could *talk,* and when I said no, he grabbed me, tore my coat, and I fell over. Some guy came over from the bar over the road and I just got up and ran until I got to Mimosa. Jo and Scott were there...' Her eyes filled with tears and she wiped them away.

'I hate that he did this to you,' he said, through gritted teeth. 'How could he? After everything you've been through? Where is he now?'

She nodded to her bag. 'He's just messaged me telling that he's waiting for me at my house. I've told him to go home.'

His jaw tightened and he picked up his phone. 'I can ask Scott to send some of his mates round there and make sure he leaves.'

Her phone buzzed with another message and she picked it up, holding her breath as she opened it.

> I meant what I said. You're a liar and a cheat, and I can't believe I asked you to marry me.

She showed it to Chris. 'I don't want to go back to my house tonight.'

You don't have to,' he said. 'You can stay here as long as you need to.'

'Thank you.' His kindness prompted another flood of tears. 'I'm sorry to drag you into all of this.'

He shook his head. 'Don't apologise. You haven't done anything wrong. He didn't deserve you. You deserve someone who proposes to you because they want to spend the rest of their life with you, because they can't imagine their life without you in it.'

Her breath caught in her throat as their eyes met. She wanted to tell him that this was how she felt about him, but now was just not the time. 'You're such a romantic... I like that.'

He nodded. 'I can't deny it. I love happy endings.'

'Me too.' She sat back on the sofa and rested her head against his shoulder. He made her feel safer than anyone else ever could, and she so desperately wanted him to be her happy ending. She just couldn't bring herself to tell him that. 'What are you watching? Is this the film with the Ewoks? I've not seen that one yet.'

'Yes, this is Return of the Jedi. I'll start it from the beginning.' He stood up, pulling a blanket off the armchair next to the sofa and handing it to her. 'Let's see who's still awake at the end.'

Chapter Twenty-Six

DECEMBER 2014, CANTERBURY, KENT, England

Molly's eyes flew open and she gasped for breath. In her dreams, it had been Mark mugging her this time, and she'd woken up just as he'd pushed her to the floor. She was sprawled out on the sofa and Chris was asleep next to her. Taking some deep breaths, she closed her eyes. *You're safe. You're safe,* she told herself. As she settled herself back down pulling the blanket back over them, Chris stirred next to her.

'Come here,' he whispered, lifting his arm.

She snuggled underneath it, her heartbeat slowing, her eyes closing again.

When she woke up again, the sunlight was streaming through the window, making her squint. Her throat felt dry, and her stomach was still churning from the night before. Trying not to wake Chris, she tiptoed out of the room and into the kitchen, and poured herself a glass of water, then another one for Chris. When she walked back into the living room, Chris was awake.

'Morning,' he said. 'How are you feeling?'

'Honestly?' She handed him the glass of water, then sat down on the sofa next to him. 'I've been better. How about you? Did you get back to sleep after...?'

'The nightmare?' He nodded. 'I slept fine.' He looked at his watch. 'It's eight am. That's a lie in for me.'

'Same,' she said. 'Those six am alarms are so shit, aren't they?'

'Who is this Molly?' He smiled. 'She wears jeans and sweatpants. She has slightly messed up hair and she swears.'

She laughed. 'You're unpeeling a few more layers.'

'I am. I can't wait to see what you reveal next.' His lips curved into a smile.

'I think I've done enough revealing for now,' she said. 'Do you mind if I use the bathroom?'

He shook his head. 'No, you go first, but let me come and do what I should have done last night. I didn't realise then that you'd be staying at Hotel Parker, and we always look after our guests here.'

He led her to the bathroom and opened a cupboard on the wall, taking out a new toothbrush, a tiny tube of face wash and a small brown jar. 'A few things to make you feel at home.' He picked up the jar. 'This is my moisturiser, but you're welcome to use some. And as last night, help yourself to whatever you want in the shower.'

'Thank you. I like Hotel Parker.' She smiled. 'The staff are so helpful and they give the best advice. And they know how to hold you so tight that you don't feel scared any more.'

He didn't respond right away. Instead he pursed his lips and looked down at the floor for a second, before he met her gaze.

'I only ever wanted to make you feel safe. I care about you so much.' His voice cracked and for a second she thought she saw his eyes filling up, but then he blinked, and the moment was gone. 'I'll leave you to it.'

He closed the door behind him, and she leaned against it. What was that? What had passed between them? It was brief, fleeting, even, but it had been there.

If she was an onion, then so was he. They both had so many layers. She thought about what Liz had said. Life wasn't black and white. It was all kinds of grey. Yes, she had cheated on Mark with Chris, and maybe that made her and Chris the villains of their story, but she couldn't see Chris as anything other than a humble, somewhat reluctant hero.

She washed her face and cleaned her teeth, then applied some of the moisturiser from the tiny jar. It had a strong botanical smell, and she realised it was another facet of Chris's overall scent. Citrus, musk, and something vaguely herby. A scent she was addicted to. Her hair had got damp in the shower last night, and she wrinkled her nose at her reflection in the mirror. It resembled a tangled blonde mane, and she ran her fingers through it, trying to tame it. Satisfied that she looked as presentable as she was going to, she returned to the living room.

'Are you OK?' Chris asked as she sat down on the sofa. 'I'm just going to grab a shower, then I'll make breakfast, unless you want something to eat now?'

She shook her head. 'No, I'm fine.'

Her stomach still felt unsettled after last night. The first thing she'd thought about when she'd woken up was the look on Mark's face as he shouted at her outside the restaurant. A look of pure hatred. How had she let him manipulate her for four years? Four years of doing what he wanted, when he wanted her to do it. No one else would ever take advantage of her like that again.

She picked up her phone and cautiously unlocked it, letting out a sigh of relief when she saw that there were no calls or messages from Mark. Putting her phone back in her handbag, she rummaged through it and pulled out her make-up bag. After applying a smear of concealer, a little blush and a coat of mascara, she brushed her hair and tied a silk bandana around her head, disguising her messy hair.

'Morning, Mole!' Scott called cheerfully as he walked into the room. He was wearing a pair of checked pyjama bottoms, a crumpled blue t-shirt and his dark hair was sticking up in all directions.

She laughed. 'Hey, Scott.'

'Am I allowed to call you Mole, or is that reserved just for Saskia?' he asked as he sat down on the sofa.

'No, you can use it too. I like it, it makes me think of her.' She smiled.

He nodded. 'How are you doing?'

'I'm alright. Much better now I'm here.'

'Good. I love your outfit,' he said.

She looked down at the hoodie which came almost to her knees. 'It's very warm and cosy, but it looks like I shrunk overnight.' She laughed, but what came out wasn't a laugh. It was a cackle.

He laughed. 'You do that too? Saskia does that. You two are so alike.'

'You think so?' she asked. 'I think we're total opposites.'

'You're more alike than you think.' He paused. 'In a good way. You're both fun, kind, and sweet. And you love your family and friends.'

'We do.' She smiled and picked up the blanket that she and Chris had slept in last night, folding it up and putting it back on the arm-chair. 'Can I make you guys some breakfast? I want to thank you for looking after me last night.'

He shook his head. 'You don't need to do that. No one else makes us breakfast when they stay over. Mainly because we don't let them.'

She laughed. 'I like this hotel more and more.'

'We provide a security service too.' He stood up, pausing by the doorway to the kitchen. 'I drove past your house after I dropped you off to make sure that Mark wasn't there.'

She gasped. 'Oh Scott, I didn't want to drag you into this even more.'

'Chris wouldn't have been happy unless I did.' His eyes darkened. 'And neither would I. Luckily for Mark, he wasn't there.'

She shuddered. 'I hope I never see him again.'

'Let's hope you don't, but if he ever does show up, you call me.' His face softened. 'I'm on breakfast duty today, which means eggs, bacon and pancakes. Are you good with that?'

'I am, but can I help?' She stood up, unable to allow herself to be waited on.

He seemed to consider it for a second. 'Well, seeing as my sous chef is in the shower, sure, why not?'

She had expected him to be like Saskia in the kitchen, overwhelmed and disorganised, but within minutes he was cooking sausages and bacon while making up a pancake batter. She'd been tasked with making him a very strong coffee, and tea for herself and Scott, something she felt more than capable of doing.

When Chris walked in, the pancakes were done, and Scott was just serving the eggs and bacon onto the plates.

'Thanks, Moll.' Chris took the cup of tea that she offered him. 'This looks good, thanks guys.'

'It was all Scott,' Molly said. 'I just made the tea.'

'You did the scrambled eggs too,' Scott reminded her.

'Badly.' She groaned. 'If there's any shell in there...'

'Then we'll pick it out and we won't say anything,' Scott assured her, then handed her a plate. 'Come and sit and eat your breakfast.'

'He's bossy,' she whispered to Chris.

'We take it in turns being the bossy one,' he whispered back.

She enjoyed this little glimpse into their domestic life way too much, and wondered if Saskia had seen this side of them too. Taking her plate, she let Scott and Chris sit down at the table first, so that she didn't take *their* seats, then sat down next to Chris.

'The eggs are really good, Molly,' Chris said. 'No shell in sight. I hope you know that you can stay here without having to make breakfast for us.'

She shrugged. 'You made breakfast at my place.'

'There's a lot of things he did at your place,' Scott blurted out.

Chris sighed. 'Dude. Now is not the time.'

'I'm so sorry, Molly. I know it's not an excuse, but I have no filter.' He poured a little more syrup onto his pancake. 'Sometimes this stuff just *comes* out. I can't help it.'

'It's fine. I live with Saskia, remember? And I don't want you guys to tiptoe around me.' She smiled at them. 'I've dodged a bullet with Mark. I've got the best friends, and, in a few days, I'll get to see my dad and sister in London.'

'Thanks for being cool about it.' Scott gave her a sheepish smile. 'You're right, Saskia does do it too.'

'I'm slightly scared of what she's going to do once she finds out about last night,' she said. 'She already hated Mark before all of this even happened.'

'She is pretty scary. I'm doing everything I can to stay on her good side,' Scott assured her.

'She's like a Rottweiler, but I'm not, so we balance each other out.' She smiled at Scott. He was a good match for Saskia.

'Same with us,' Chris said. 'I'm the peacekeeper.' He gestured to Scott. 'He's the guard dog.'

Scott put down his cutlery and drained his coffee. 'I need a shower. I might be a dog, but I don't want to smell like one.' He stood up and took his plate and cup with him and walked to the kitchen.

Molly insisted on cleaning the kitchen up, despite Chris's protests. It helped calm her nerves, but once it was done, and she was sat on the sofa, staring out of the window, her anxiety kicked in. She needed to go home, but a part of her was still scared that Mark would turn up. Her phone buzzed and she picked it up cautiously.

> How did it go last night? Did you break up with him? Or did he get there first?

She took a deep breath. Unless she replied to Liz, she would worry, or turn up at her house, looking for her.

> I broke up with him. It's all over. I'll call you later and fill you in. I'm with Scott and Chris right now. Everything's OK. X

She put her phone away, and turned to Chris. 'I should go home.'

'You don't have to if you don't want to,' he said.

'Don't say that.' She smiled. 'I can't stay here forever. I need to face it at some point, and I'm interrupting your weekend. Don't you usually go to the gym on a Saturday morning?'

He shrugged. 'I can skip it, or go later. It's no big deal. Scott will be bummed that he can't roast me for the entire session today, but that works out well for me.'

She laughed. 'You guys are so funny together. I can't thank you both enough for last night. You both made me feel so much better.'

'That's what we're here for.' He switched on the laptop on the coffee table. 'You want to help me plan my set at Mimosa? You love music as much as me. I could use your input.'

'Sure.' She nodded. 'Show me what you've got so far.'

He opened the set list and turned the laptop around so that she could see it. 'What do you think?'

She scanned the set list. 'I approve. I'd be on the dancefloor for pretty much every one of these songs.'

'Good to know.' He shut the set list. 'I've been working on something for you. I'd planned on giving you this for your birthday, but I feel like you might need it right now.'

'What's that?' she asked, as he opened a software program she hadn't seen before.

'It's mixing software,' he replied. 'I made you a kind of emo-punk-grunge mix.' He paused. 'Do you want to hear it?'

Her heart leapt into her throat. Music was *his* thing, and it was how they'd bonded. That he'd taken the time to make her her own mix meant more to her than he would ever realise. 'Of course! I don't know what to say, I'm so touched.'

He handed her a set of headphones and she put them on as he pressed play.

She listened to a few songs before taking off the headphones. 'It's so good!'

He smiled. 'I'm glad you like it. I'll convert the file and put it onto a flash drive for you so you can take it home.'

It was too much. He was too much. Not only had he remembered all of her favourite bands, but he'd somehow made an amazing playlist with all of their best tracks.

'Thank you.' She swallowed the lump in her throat. 'Would you mind giving me a lift home? I'd rather do it in the daylight. Once it gets dark...'

'It's harder, right?' He stood up. 'Your clothes from last night are still wet, and your jacket's a little ripped. My mum's pretty good with her sewing machine, shall I ask her to take a look at it?'

Her heart skipped happily. 'Would she mind? I love that jacket. I was so sad when I heard the seam rip.'

'Oh she loves a project,' he said. 'I'm sure she wouldn't mind. I'll bring back the rest of your clothes when they're dry if you don't mind going home in mine?'

'Not at all. They're so cosy. I've never had a hoodie before.' She followed him out to the hall.

'You've never had a hoodie?' He frowned. 'You're twenty-six and you've never had a hoodie?'

She shook her head. 'Just not part of my wardrobe.'

'Ah well, keep that one. I've got loads of them,' he said picking up his car keys. 'You ready?'

She nodded and put her high heeled boots on, bursting out laughing at how ridiculous they looked under her tracksuit trousers. 'This is quite a look.'

'You can pull it off.' He opened the door. 'On y va !'

She walked down the stairs and out of the building, into bright, if chilly, sunshine. The dark, harsh rain of last night had disappeared, making it all feel like a horrible nightmare. As she climbed into Chris's car she wished that it had been a nightmare, but it wasn't. It was real, and she would have to face her fears now.

When she got out of the car at her house, there was a man standing outside. He wore a shiny suit, and had a large folder tucked under his arm. She and Chris looked at each other at the same time.

'That's not Mark,' he said. 'What's going on?'

'I don't know, but I'm going to find out,' she whispered.

The man smiled as she walked up to him. 'Ah, you must be Molly.' He smiled at Chris. 'And you're Mark, is that right? I've been calling you all morning, but you weren't answering your phone.'

Molly frowned. 'I'm sorry, who are you?'

'I'm Liam, from Hawksmoor Estate Agents,' he said. 'Your fiancé contacted me to ask me to come over to assess your property for letting.'

'Letting?' Molly shrieked. 'I'm not letting my house out.' She gestured to Chris. 'And he's not Mark.' She folded her arms. 'I think you should leave.'

'It seems like there's been some misunderstanding here,' Liam said nervously. 'Mark told me that you were moving to London and that you wanted to let the property out. It's a beautiful house.'

A hot burst of anger flooded through her body. 'I'm not moving to London, and I am not letting my house out!'

'Yes, I kind of got that impression. I'll leave you to your Saturday. Sorry to bother you.' Liam gave Molly and Chris a nervous smile and walked off, the heels of his brogues clipping along the pavement.

'He contacted an estate agent behind my back?' She let out a long exhale. Pulling the keys from her bag, she unlocked the front door. 'I bet he thought I'd be all loved up and would just agree to whatever he wanted as we were engaged.'

'What an entitled, arrogant...' he trailed off. 'Sorry. I just can't believe he did this.'

'I can't decide whether to ring him and shout at him, or just ignore it.' She paced the hall angrily, then walked into the living room and sat on the sofa.

He sat down next to her. 'Do you want me to stay or go?'

'Can you stay for a while.' She shivered and rubbed her arms. 'Why did all of this feel so much easier when I was at your house?'

Glaring at the empty fireplace, she stood up, wishing Saskia was here. She was far better at getting the fire going.

'Do you want a hand getting the fire lit?' he asked.

'Probably.' She crouched down next to the fireplace. 'Saskia usually does it as I always burn my fingers.'

He crouched down next to her and within a few minutes, the fire was roaring.

'Brilliant, thanks for helping me. Sorr for being *needy*.' She sat cross legged on the rug, her cheeks warmed by the flames.

'You're not needy. He's emotionally devoid,' he said darkly.

'Papa said that we didn't have a relationship, we just went on dates, and he was so right.' She gazed into the fire, mesmerised.

'He's very perceptive.'

She turned to look at him. 'They say don't meet your heroes, but I'm still starstruck.'

'I'm sure he would be delighted to hear that.' She smiled at him. 'I have no idea what this fancy suite he's booked will be like, but everything he does is very...lavish.'

'I can believe that.' He yawned. 'The fire's making me sleepy.'

'You should go and get some rest.' She felt warmer now, and not just because of the fire. Her proximity to him was setting her body alight. She wanted to lean her body into his, and let him wrap his arms around her.

He frowned. 'Are you sure? I can stay if you want me to.'

'I always want you to.' She smiled. 'I should call Saskia, and I need to sleep.'

'Sure. Both of those things are a good idea.' He stood up. 'If you change your mind and need company, you know where I am.'

She nodded. 'You're amazing. You deserve a drama-free friend, not someone like me.'

He slid his arms around her, one gripping her waist, the other stroking her hair. 'You are amazing. Don't listen to anyone who tells you otherwise.'

She let him go and wiped her eyes. 'Thanks for the pep talk.'

'I meant it.' He opened the front door. 'Good luck with Saskia.'

'Thanks. She is going to be apoplectic.' She sighed. 'I'll see you on Monday.'

'If it gets dark and you get scared, ring me, and I'll be straight over.'

She closed the door behind him and leant against it, to stop herself from running after him and asking him to come back because she missed him already. She buried her face in her hoodie and breathed in his scent as tears sprang to her eyes again. He was the kindest, sweetest human being and she dreamed of a day that she could tell him that she loved him. Now that he'd gone, the only sound was the clanking of the radiators as they warmed up. She wiped her eyes and walked back into the living room, keen for noise and distraction from the swirl of emotions in her mind.

She sat down on the sofa and picked up her phone. It was almost midday. This would be the best time of day to catch Saskia. She sighed and dialled her number.

'Hey, Mole! How are you doing?'

Saskia's voice made Molly smile. 'Hey, Sas. I need to tell you something and it is good news, but it might not sound like it at first, so just bear with me.'

'Oh God, Molly, what's going on?' Saskia sounded concerned.

'I'll start at the beginning.'

The second that Molly finished her blow-by-blow account of the last twenty-four hours, Saskia exploded. 'That stuck up, lying, deceitful, sack of shit!'

'I know,' Molly said. 'I'm so glad it's over. I feel like I can be me again.'

'You actually said that to him? About Beth riding him in Copenhagen?' Saskia let out a cackle. 'I love it.'

'I think I was channelling a bit of my inner Saskia,' Molly said drily. 'I don't know what's worse, that argument or the fact that he thought he could just persuade me to rent out our house.' She paused. 'I hadn't had a nightmare for a while, and I had one last night at Chris's.'

'He's crossed a line. I won't allow it.'

Molly could imagine the expression on Saskia's face. Eyes narrowed and full of fury.

'Saskia,' she warned. 'Don't get involved. He's not worth it.'

'He's got away with too much for too long. No one hurts my sister.' Her tone was still laced with venom.

Molly sighed. 'Don't jeopardise everything you've worked so hard for.'

'I won't. I've matured.'

Molly wasn't sure if she believed Saskia. 'You should know that your boyfriend saved the day last night. He knew what I needed even when I didn't.'

'He is a sweetheart,' Saskia said. 'I'm so glad you we were with them last night. The only thing that's stopping me from getting on a train to be with you right now is knowing that you've got those guys just around the corner. I bet Chris didn't leave your side all night did he?'

'No he didn't.' Molly replied. 'Saskia. I love him. Not as a friend. More like I want to marry him, and have his babies, and grow old with him.'

'I knew it!' Saskia exclaimed. 'Have you told him?'

'No, of course not.' Molly thought about last night, about the way he had held her on the sofa when she woke up from her nightmare. 'He had to hold me, literally, through another nightmare last night. He needs someone less...complicated than me.'

'Why don't you let him decide what he needs?'

Molly considered this for a second. 'I'm not ready yet. I need to move on from what happened with Mark, I need time...'

'Take all the time you need. I have a feeling he'll wait.'

'Saskia, do you know something I don't?' Molly asked.

'I have to go, Mole. My break's over now.'

Molly smiled. What perfect timing. 'I'll see you next week. Love you.'

'Love you too. If that douchebag contacts you again, tell me.'

'He can't contact me. I blocked his number and I'm going to change mine today,' Molly said. 'I'm not giving him any more opportunities to hurt me.'

Chapter Twenty-Seven

December 2014, Canterbury, Kent, England

Molly opened her eyes and yawned. last night she had fallen into a deep, uninterrupted sleep, wrapped in Chris's hoodie, his scent comforting her. She looked at her watch. It was almost midday, which meant that she'd slept for almost twelve hours. Slowly, she climbed out of bed. Her left hip was aching, which it had since she'd fallen over on Friday night. A bath with some Epsom salts would fix that, but first, she needed food.

She went downstairs and pulled a croissant out of the freezer, switching the oven on to heat it. The warm buttery smell made her feel hungry, and as it cooked, she gazed at the bare branches of the trees and the frost hardened grass.

The oven timer pinged, and she turned her attention away from the garden to add some jam to her croissant. As she sat down, a pang of loneliness hit her. The dining table felt far too big for one person, but it wasn't Saskia that she wanted to share her table with. It was Chris. Having breakfast with him yesterday at his flat had felt so natural, but every time she allowed herself to dare to dream that he might love her too, she heard Mark's words in her head. *You're needy. You're a liar and a cheat.* Every word felt like a knife in her heart. She ate the last of her croissant and sipped her tea. When her phone buzzed, her stomach didn't lurch. There was no way that Mark could contact her. Hoping it was Chris, she picked it up and unlocked it.

> Morning, Mole! How are you doing? Love you
> Sx

Molly smiled and typed a reply.

> I'm fine. I slept well and although I keep thinking about what happened, I won't let him get into my head. I can't wait to see you next week. Love you too x

She put her phone down and sighed. Christmas was almost here, and she still hadn't decorated the house, or put the Christmas tree up. It had been a big deal when her mum was alive. They would get the boxes out of the loft, turn on some Christmas classics and turn their house into a festive wonderland. Her mum would make a yule log, which she and Molly would decorate, then once the house was decorated, they'd watch Christmas films on the sofa in their pyjamas while they ate fish and chips. Christmas in France was very different. Her dad didn't like a lot of decorations. He preferred a simple, real tree with some fairy lights and a few handmade glass baubles. His Christmas Day feast included oysters, chestnuts, turkey, goose, and lots of delicious cheese. Last year her dad had come to stay for a week, and he'd joined in with decorating the house, glass of wine in hand, casting his critical eye over the tree.

Today she would be doing it alone. Deciding that she could still make it fun, she found a Christmas playlist on her phone, then she made a thin chocolate sponge cake, and rolled it up tightly to decorate later. She might not have her sister, or her dad, but she could still have cake.

Once she had cleaned the kitchen, she took herself upstairs and ran a bath. Propped on the shelf in the bathroom was the spicy novel she'd read the night she kissed Chris and she smiled at it, then picked it up. She needed to know how this one turned out. Was there a happy ending? Or did it all go down in flames? She added a scoop of Epsom salts into the bath and climbed in, then opened the book.

She lost herself in the book, and it was only when the bath got cold, and her skin wrinkled like a prune, that she climbed out, still going over the ending in her mind. There had been drama, tension and then the bodyguard had literally driven off into the sunset with his love. Could this happen to her and Chris? Could she risk their friendship to find out if they could be more? Maybe. But not right now. Not while the ghosts of her past were still looming over her.

The grey hoodie went right back on over her jeans and t-shirt, and then Molly got the boxes of Christmas decorations and the tree out of the loft and stacked them in the hall. The doorbell rang and she froze, her heart pounding. Slowly, she tiptoed to her bedroom window, and looked out of it, letting out a sigh of relief as she saw Liz and Martha stood outside her front door. She hurtled down the stairs and let them in.

'Hey guys, come in.'

'Hello, love,' Liz kissed Molly on the cheek. 'I just wanted to check in on you.'

'That's so sweet of you.' Molly gave her a hug. 'I'm fine.'

'Hello, Auntie Molly.' Martha sat on the floor and removed her little boots.

Liz nodded to the pile of boxes. 'Do you need a hand decorating? I'm sure my little elf wouldn't mind.'

Molly nodded. 'I could do with a hand.'

'Molly Millot asking for help? Wonders will never cease.' Liz raised an eyebrow. 'Put the kettle on and we'll make a start.'

Molly led them into the kitchen. 'Actually, I've got another job that I need some help with first and it involves chocolate cake. Are you in?'

'Uh yes,' Liz said. 'What do we need to do?'

'Get your hands washed girls. We've got a yule log to make.'

Molly let Martha help measure out the ingredients for the buttercream into the bowl of her stand mixer, then she put all the utensils they would need onto the dining table and opened the dresser to get her mum's holly printed plate out. She lifted Martha onto one of the chairs and called Liz, who was making them all cups of tea in the kitchen.

Carefully, she peeled the chocolate sponge away from the baking paper and unrolled it onto the plate, then handed a palette knife to Martha. 'You need to spread it with buttercream, sweetie, just like this.' She swiped the other palette knife into the buttercream and smoothed it over the surface of the sponge cake. 'Got it?'

'I got it.' Martha put the knife into the buttercream, before spreading it over the cake.

Once Martha had covered it in buttercream, Molly rolled up the sponge, cut the ends off and attached them to the log to make branches, then handed her palette knife to Liz. 'You want to have a go?'

Liz dipped the knife into the bowl of buttercream and smoothed it onto the sponge. 'Ooh, this is satisfying.'

'I know, right?' Molly turned to Martha. 'You're doing a great job, Martha.'

'It's really easy.' Martha continued to smear buttercream over the yule log.

'Have you taken Chris's hoodie off since you got back from his place?' Liz, asked Molly.

Molly felt her cheeks colour. 'How did you know it was Chris's?'

'He was wearing it that morning I came over after he'd stayed over.' Liz cocked her head to the side. 'You didn't answer the question.'

'I haven't taken it off,' Molly admitted. 'It smells like him, and it makes me feel happy. So, it's staying on.'

'You went to him last night and you let him be there for you. That's big.'

Molly put down her palette knife. 'It is. He's become more than my friend. I let him see every single side of me, I can be myself with him and know that he'll accept me for who I am. I've fallen hard.'

'I guessed this might happen when you guys kissed,' Liz said. 'I could see you both falling for each other, despite how much you insisted you weren't.'

'You know me too well.' Molly paused. 'I did fall for him, I *have* fallen for him, but I'm still not ready to tell him yet.'

Liz nodded. 'Sure. You've been through so much. And it's safer to keep him as a friend until you feel brave enough to tell him how you feel. Are you sure you're OK after...everything?'

'I still can't believe how *quickly* it all just fell apart between Mark and I.' Molly was aware that Martha was listening, so chose her words carefully. 'It's gonna take a little while to process what happened, but he's out of my life now, and I'm so happy about that.'

'Me too!' Liz's eyes lit up. 'I've disliked Mark since I first met him, and I'm so glad you're not together any more. I hated the way he treated you, always expecting you to do whatever he wanted.'

'I won't let anyone treat me like that again,' Molly insisted.

'So happy to hear that.' Liz reached over and took the palette knife from Martha, who was licking it. 'I think that's enough, sweetie.'

Molly cast her eye over the cake. 'It looks perfect guys, well done. I'll get some plates and we can have a piece.'

After they'd eaten their slices of cake, Molly took Liz and Martha into the living room, and sat on the floor to do a jigsaw puzzle with Martha.

'Check these out.' Liz opened her large canvas shopping bag and showed Molly the reindeer pyjamas she'd bought for Martha.

Molly squealed. 'I love them. Do they make them in my size?'

Liz laughed. 'I thought you'd say that.' She pulled out a larger pair of pyjamas and handed them to Molly. 'Here you go. An early Christmas present.'

'Thank you so much!' Molly stood up and gave Liz a hug. 'I've got your presents upstairs, hold on.' She ran upstairs and returned with two neatly wrapped boxes, which she handed to Liz. 'You can open them if you like, it's not long until Christmas.'

'Can I, Mummy?' Martha asked.

Liz nodded and Martha tore off the paper.

'It's the new Boulangerie Bleue book!' Martha said excitedly, waving the book at Liz.

Molly smiled at Martha. 'Do you like it? It's not out yet, but I managed to get you an advance copy.'

'Thanks, love, you know how much she loves that series.' Liz opened her own present. 'Ooh, just what I need.' She slipped the gloves on and wrapped the scarf around her neck. 'Thank you. I know this time of year is hard for you without your mum and Saskia, but we're all here for you.'

'I love you guys so much.' Molly gave Liz another hug.

'No need to thank me. That's what friends are for.' Liz stood up. 'Now, are we going to get this place decorated?'

'Hold on.' Molly picked up her phone and selected her Christmas playlist, before pairing it with her speakers. 'Now we're all set.'

Molly tasked Liz and Martha with choosing which baubles to go on the tree from the huge collection in the boxes, while she wrapped the tree in lights. She hung three knitted stockings from the mantelpiece, one for her, her mum and Saskia, before adding her LED candles, which gave the room a cosy glow.

'I've switched from regular candles,' Molly said to Liz. 'If I'm on my own, I feel safer with LED ones. If I fall asleep, they won't burn the house down.'

'Very sensible, but that's no surprise. You've always been risk averse,' Liz replied.

'This year I've done just the opposite,' Molly reflected. 'I got drunk in a Halloween costume. I fell in love with a stranger, and I ran through a dark city on my own late at night.'

Liz's eyes widened. 'Thats true. Let's hope next year is less dramatic.'

When the tree was finished, Molly got her phone out and took a picture of her, Liz, and Martha in front of it. 'I'll send that to Saskia so that she knows I've kept the tradition going.'

'I'm very honoured that we've been allowed to join in,' Liz said. 'We'd better go home. I need to cook dinner as Jacob's working.'

'Why don't you stay for dinner? We used to have fish and chips in our pyjamas after we'd decorated the tree. Want to do that?'

Liz turned at Martha. 'What do you think?'

'Can we, Mummy?' Martha asked.

'I think we could,' Liz said.

Molly gestured to the pyjamas on the sofa. 'I've even got new pyjamas to wear. Did you get yourself a pair?'

Liz walked over to her bag and pulled out another pair. 'Of course.'

'Brilliant. You guys go and put your pyjamas on. I'll run to the fish and chip shop, then we can watch a film.' Molly handed Liz the TV remote. 'Choose whatever you like.'

'Are you sure you don't mind going? It's dark out there, and you don't love the dark,' Liz said, biting her lip.

'I'll be fine. Get yourselves ready and I'll be back soon.' Molly pulled on her coat over Chris's hoodie and put on her boots, shutting the door behind her.

Twenty minutes later, Molly was back home, where Liz had got plates and cutlery out. Molly changed into her pyjamas, and nestled herself on the sofa next to Liz. 'Which film did you guys pick?'

'The Snowman,' Martha said. 'It's my favourite.'

As she ate her fish and chips, Molly realised that family wasn't just the people you were related to. It was the people you loved.

After the film finished, Liz nudged Molly. 'I think I'd better get this one home.' Martha was half asleep, curled up in her lap.'

'You're welcome to stay,' Molly offered.

Liz shook her head. 'That's very sweet of you, but you need to rest, and Martha will be awake before six am.'

Molly wrinkled her nose. 'Ugh, that's early.'

'Tell me about it. I've got used to it though.' Liz stroked Martha's hair. 'Time to go home, Martha.'

Martha nodded and sat up. 'I'm not even sleepy.' She yawned.

Molly stifled a giggle. 'Maybe not, but Mummy is and she needs to drive you home.'

'OK then, come on, Mummy.' Martha slid off the sofa.

In the hall, Molly helped Martha put on her boots, then gave Liz a hug. 'Thanks for coming over, and for helping me keep my decorating tradition alive.'

'You're welcome, I loved it.' Liz let go of Molly and picked up her shopping bag. 'Thanks for the cake.'

Molly had cut a couple more slices and put them in a box for Liz to take home. 'You're welcome. See you soon.'

'Sleep well.' Liz smirked. 'In that hoodie, I bet.'

Molly felt her cheeks colour. 'He said I could keep it.'

'He's a good man,' Liz took Martha's hand as Molly opened the front door for them. 'You're just as good. Don't let yourself think otherwise.'

Molly nodded. 'I won't.' She waved Liz and Martha off, then shut the door.

Before she went up to bed, Molly sent the Christmas tree photo to Saskia, and to Chris. Wrapped in his hoodie, with the fire glowing and the Christmas tree lights twinkling in the corner of the room, she didn't feel so scared anymore.

Chapter Twenty-Eight

On Christmas Eve, Molly made her way to London with her suitcase. She wished she had Chris by her side, but he was working back in Canterbury. He'd come over a couple of days ago, and she had been so close to telling him how she felt about him, but she just couldn't get the words out. Instead, they had fallen asleep on the sofa together again. She had woken up in the morning, still nestled under his arm, and decided that she didn't want to wake up any other way. She just had to work up the courage to tell him that.

She breathed a sigh of relief when she reached London safely, and crossed the station concourse, climbing into a taxi. Without knowing what her dad had planned, it had been difficult to pack, but she'd brought her best dresses, heels, and warm clothes for walks around the city. Also squashed into her suitcase were two pairs of brand-new brogues for her dad. She hadn't been able to choose between tan and navy-blue, so she'd bought both.

At the Devon Lane Hotel, she was welcomed by a doorman with a suit, tails, and immaculate white gloves. He showed her through the vast lobby, past the guests drinking expensive cocktails to the reception desk, gilded, and lit with a glittering chandelier.

'Are you checking in with us today?' A receptionist with lipstick the same scarlet red as Molly's, smiled at her.

'Yes,' Molly said, quietly, overwhelmed by the grandeur of this hotel. 'Molly Millot. It's a suite. I think it will be in the name of Gaspard
Millot.'

The receptionist smiled. 'I'm afraid there is no one here with that
name.'

Molly sighed. What was the name he used? She racked her brains
but couldn't remember. 'Hold on, let me call him.' His mobile rang
and rang, but there was no answer. She felt hot and embarrassed. Just
as she was about to give up and order herself one of the expensive
cocktails at the bar, a familiar face appeared. 'Papa, I'm so glad you're
here. I couldn't remember the name you use to book the hotels.'

Her dad smiled at her, then turned to the receptionist. 'This is my
daughter, Molly. She will be staying with me. Her sister, Saskia will
also check in later.'

'Thank you, Mr. Blanc,' the receptionist smiled at him.

'Mr. Blanc! That's it. I knew it was a colour,' Molly said, clapping
her palm to her forehead.

The receptionist handed Molly a key card. 'Welcome to the Devon
Lane. I hope you enjoy your stay.'

'Thank you so much,' Molly replied.

'Come on, let me show you the room,' he said, putting his arm
around Molly's shoulders and taking her bag for her.

Molly's jaw dropped as he unlocked the door. It was the grandest
hotel room she had ever seen. She slipped off her boots and took her
case from her dad, tucking it away into the luggage rack in the hall.
Walking across the plush carpet to the cream sofas, she ran her hands
over the soft fabric, a world away from her own scruffy furniture. On
the glass coffee table between them was a large basket of fruit and two
vases of fresh flowers. She walked past the sofas, to the highly polished
dining table, pulling out a chair and sitting down, gazing out of the
French doors behind the table.

'What do you think?' he asked, sitting down next to her, following
her gaze.

'Oh Papa, it's wonderful. It's so fancy.' She stood up and walked to
the French doors. 'Do we have a balcony?'

'Oui, bien sûr. Let me show you.' He walked over to the doors and
flung them open dramatically. 'Voilà!'

Molly stepped out onto the balcony, which was tiled, with a small table and two chairs to one side. She leant on the wrought iron railings as she took in the view of the street below and the designer shops over the road. It was noisy and busy, sirens blaring, taxis and cars all stalled in traffic.

'This is an incredibly special place,' he said softly. 'It was the first hotel I took your mother to when I published my first bestseller. We had one of the smaller rooms, but it was wonderful. They could not do enough for us.'

'Do you miss her?' Molly asked.

'Very much,' he said. 'We could not live together, but we could not be apart. It was an extremely complicated relationship.' He smiled at Molly. 'I have many happy memories of her, and I have you and Saskia too. I consider myself incredibly lucky.'

Molly smiled, watching the cars crawling along the street below her. She knew that her parents had always loved each other. He had held her mother's hand and told her that he loved her right before she died, and she had repeated his words back to him before she closed her eyes.

She slid her arms around her dad's waist and gave him a squeeze. 'I'm lucky, too. I have you and Saskia and you are more than I could ever wish for.'

'Perhaps,' he said, turning to face her. 'What is it that you are not telling me?'

She let out a long exhale. 'I don't know if I'm ready to talk about it yet.'

'Then I will say nothing else until you are,' he said. 'You know I'm here for you, and when you have processed your thoughts, perhaps I can be of some assistance.'

'Thank you, Papa.' He hadn't asked her a thousand questions, as he usually did. The likelihood was that he knew what was going on anyway and was choosing to wait until she was ready to tell him. She followed him back into the room.

He turned the handle on one of the two doors facing each other in the hall beyond the living room. 'Here is your bedroom. You'll have to share with Saskia, is that alright?'

'Of course!' she squealed. 'We love sharing a room.' She followed him into the room, watching as he ran his finger over the furniture, as if checking for dust.

He nodded. 'I'll go and ask for some tea to be sent up while you unpack. Rooibos, I'm guessing?'

'Yes please, Papa, that would be wonderful.' She kissed him on the cheek. 'I'm still pinching myself that I'm actually here.'

'I'm very glad that you are,' he said. 'I've booked a table at the French bistro in Covent Garden for dinner tonight. I forget the name, but I know we've been there before.'

'You forgot the name?' Her eyes widened. 'You never forget anything.'

'I have the occasional slip,' he said. 'I am an old man. A few months off seventy, remember.'

'Your mind is sharper than mine has ever been.' She unzipped her suitcase. 'I'll be right out.'

She hung up her clothes in the wardrobe, before pulling open the door to the ensuite bathroom and gasping as she flicked the lights on, illuminating the marble walls and floors. Every surface was polished to a mirror-like shine. Thick fluffy towels were slotted into the heated towel rail, and a large wicker basket held bottles, tubes, and jars of luxury toiletries. She picked up the beeswax lip balm and applied some, then a squeeze of camomile hand cream, the floral scent filling the air. Closing the door, she walked back into the living room.

'Papa, the bathroom is beautiful. This place is incredible.' She sat down next to him on the sofa, noticing the silver tray on the coffee table, with bone china cups and saucers. 'Thank you for the tea. I'm slightly scared to pick one of those cups up. I bet they are extremely expensive.'

He shrugged. 'Relax and enjoy yourself, Molly. For the next few days, you don't need to worry about anything. That is my Christmas gift to you.'

Chris had wrapped all the presents for his family and was waiting for Scott to get back from work. He'd tried to make the flat more festive with a small tree and some lights strung around the kitchen, then with some Christmas music playing, he'd made burgers for himself and

Scott, knowing that they were going out tonight and that having a full stomach would avoid a Christmas Day hangover.

'Evening, mate! It smells good in here,' Scott said as he walked into the kitchen.

'Good,' Chris said. 'I hope you're hungry.'

Scott washed his hands and turned back to Chris. 'Of course I am. What can I do?'

Chris nodded to the fridge. 'Can you grab the beers? We're good to go.'

Scott was already diving into the fridge.

As they sat at the dining table, Chris raised his beer to Scott. 'Merry Christmas mate, the fun can start now.'

'Merry Christmas! And thanks for dinner.' Scott picked up the burger and took a huge bite, letting out a moan of pleasure. 'This is so good,' he mumbled, his mouth full.

'You're welcome,' Chris said. 'What have you got planned for tonight?'

Scott swallowed his mouthful. 'There's a band at the Five Barrels. I doubt they're as good as Future Proof, but we should go check them out. Jo and her girlfriend might join us for a drink.' He dipped a fry into the dollop of ketchup on his plate and stuck it into his mouth. 'Sound good?'

Chris nodded. 'We should set some ground rules for tonight. We stick to one pub. We leave before midnight and no shots.'

'Agreed,' Scott said. 'We're definitely not ending up like we did a few years ago. Mum was furious.'

Chris laughed. 'Do you remember us trying to force down that turkey and roast potatoes?'

'Dad kept trying to give us another beer, saying that hair of the dog was the best cure.' Scott shook his head. 'That was the worst. We are not doing that again.'

'Never again,' Chris agreed. 'Have you heard from Saskia today?'

'Yeah, she's excited about seeing her dad and Molly later on.' Scott paused. 'Have you heard from Molly?'

'She sent me some photos of their hotel suite. Check this out.' Chris handed his phone to Scott.

'That's the fanciest hotel room I've ever seen.' Scott smiled at Chris. 'You're missing her, aren't you?'

Chris nodded. 'I am.'

'You have to tell her, Chris.' Scott said. 'At some point, she's going to get another boyfriend, and you'll have to go through the agony of watching that again, unless you tell her how you feel.'

Taking a gulp of his beer, Chris considered this. 'I can't just be her friend. I can't keep pretending.' He sighed. 'It's exhausting.'

'Then stop pretending. Pick your moment and take a leap of faith.' Scott smiled at Chris. 'I've seen you two together. I feel like she does have feelings for you and she's trying to hide it, just like you are.'

Chris took a bite of his burger and chewed thoughtfully. 'I'll tell her,' he said after he swallowed. 'The next time I see her, I'll tell her. What is it the French say? Qui vivra verra.'

'What does that mean? Scott asked.

'Roughly translated, who will live, will see,' Chris replied. 'It's the French version of que sera sera.'

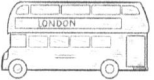

Molly and Gaspard walked arm in arm to Covent Garden after they left the restaurant, so that they could see the Christmas decorations. When the freezing wind got too much to bear they walked until the lights of the Devon Lane welcomed them in.

Molly changed into her festive pyjamas and joined her dad in the living room, her bare feet padding across the thick carpet. Gaspard was reclined on one of the sofas, his eyes closed. 'Are you alright, Papa?'

'Yes, I'm fine. Just closing my eyes. That was an excellent meal, thank you.' He sighed happily. 'I'm hopeful there will still be chestnuts and oysters tomorrow.'

She flicked her eyes over the gilt-edged lamps, the embroidered cushions on the sofa and the immaculately polished furniture. 'I think in this place you could probably have anything you asked for.' She stretched out next to her dad. 'Thank you for coming here to be with us, Papa.'

'It is my pleasure.' He smiled at her. 'It is a wonderful adventure, is it not?'

At that moment there was a clattering sound at the door and Saskia flew in, suitcase in tow. 'I hate these key cards. They never work for me,' She put her bag down. 'Hi, Mole, Hi, Papa.'

Molly flew off the sofa and gave her sister a hug. 'Come and see this place, you won't believe it.'

Saskia looked around the room. 'Woah, this is immense.'

'It is good, isn't it? Happy Christmas my little one.' Gaspard put his arms around Saskia.

'Happy Christmas! It's so good to see you, Papa,' Saskia squealed.

'Now you are here, Christmas can begin. What do you need? Have you eaten? Would you like some tea?'

'I'm fine, Papa,' Saskia sat down on the sofa next to Molly. 'I'm just happy to be here.'

'Good,' Gaspard said. 'I have all sorts of treats planned tomorrow.'

Molly and Saskia's eyes lit up. 'Like what?' they both said at the same time.

'You'll have to wait and see.' He raised an eyebrow.

Saskia snorted with laughter. 'Oh Papa, you're so dramatic! I love it.'

'I'm creating an air of mystery.' He picked up his coffee, taking a sip.

'Come and see our room,' Molly said to Saskia, taking her hand and pulling her to her feet.

Saskia picked up her bag, and Molly led her to their bedroom. 'Woah, this place is *nice*. Do you remember what it was like before Papa's books took off? That Christmas where we had no heating and no money to pay to fix the damp patch on our ceiling?'

'I remember,' Molly said, nodding. 'We were all huddled around the fire in the living room and Mama and Papa took us for an extra-long walk that day to warm us up.'

'Did you ever believe we would be spending Christmas here one day?' Saskia asked.

'No.' Molly shook her head. 'But even then, they still gave everything they had to make us happy. You had a princess dress that year and I had a boxset of books.'

'I still have the dress,' Saskia said.

Tears sprang to Molly's eyes. 'I still have the books.'

Chapter Twenty-Nine

Molly was the first to wake up the following morning. Saskia was sprawled out next to her, snoring loudly and taking up most of the bed. She got up and pulled on one of the thick bathrobes from the wardrobe, tucking her phone into the pocket, before tiptoeing out of the bedroom. She could hear loud snoring coming from the room opposite, meaning that her dad was still asleep too.

Pulling back the heavy curtains and opening one of the French doors, she crept out onto the balcony. It was a crisp, clear Christmas morning. The street below was empty, and a light dusting of snow covered the ground. She breathed in the cold air and exhaled, watching her breath swirl up into the sky. It had been a chaotic, rollercoaster of a year, but she suddenly felt a wave of contentment wash over her. She was here in London with her family, who loved her, and when she got back to Canterbury, she was going to tell Chris that she loved him. She had no idea what his response would be, but she knew that she couldn't go on pretending any longer. She pulled her phone out of her pocket and typed out a message to him.

> Merry Christmas! I hope you guys have the BEST day today!

She smiled, wondering what he and Scott were doing. His reply came quickly.

> Same to you! What was it like sleeping in that suite? Do you feel like the Queen?

> Pretty much. It's a world away from my bedroom!

He sent back a photo of a haphazardly decorated Christmas tree, in the middle of his living room, where Scott was lying, face down on the sofa.

> This was Scott's bed last night! So much for having a quiet one. I bet your evening was much more civilised. Say hi to your dad for me and I'll see you when you get back.

She stared at her phone and smiled. She couldn't wait to see him.

> I will! We'll catch up when I get back

Her reply was way more relaxed than she actually felt. When she got back to Canterbury she was going to tell him that she loved him and that thought provoked a mixture of nerves and excitement. Did he feel the same? Would he have to politely tell her that he didn't?

'Merry Christmas my darling.' A voice came from behind her, making her jump.

'Merry Christmas, Papa,' Molly said, turning around and kissing him on the cheek. 'Isn't it a beautiful day?'

'It is.' He came to stand next to her. 'Clear and still. Just like it was on your first Christmas. And Saskia's too.'

She smiled. 'You still remember our first Christmases?'

'Of course I do.' He put an arm around her. 'Christmas became magical when you were born, and even more so when Saskia arrived.'

She rested her head against her dad's shoulder. 'I'm so glad we're all here together.'

'So am I. How does room service breakfast sound? Pancakes, toast, eggs, bacon, fresh fruit.' He frowned. 'I forget what else. Maybe some fruit juice.'

'That sounds delicious.' Her stomach rumbled, as if agreeing with her.

'Good, I ordered it already. It will be here in half an hour.'

'I'd better go and get dressed and wake Saskia up.' She slid out of her dad's embrace. 'I'll be back in a minute.'

When Molly opened the bedroom door, Saskia was just waking up.

'Morning, Mole. I slept so well.' She smoothed her hands over the duvet. 'This place is so fancy they probably fill the duvets with swan feathers.'

Molly laughed. 'How are you this funny the minute you wake up?'

Saskia shrugged. 'Just talented, I guess. How long have you been up?'

'Not long,' Molly said. 'Papa's ordered breakfast, and it sounds pretty epic.'

Saskia flew out of bed. 'Room service breakfast? Say less. Do I have time for a shower?'

'Probably not.' She handed Saskia the other bathrobe from the wardrobe. 'Just chuck this on. We can get dressed later.'

The room service breakfast was, as Molly had expected, delicious. Fresh flowers adorned the plates, the pancakes were fluffy, the eggs perfectly cooked, and there were some fruits on the platter that she had never even seen before.

Saskia wiped her mouth with her napkin. 'I think that was the best breakfast I've ever had. And I bet lunch will be the best Christmas dinner I've ever had too.'

Molly carefully stacked the empty plates. 'This is so luxurious. And I'm here in my bathrobe with bed hair.'

Saskia giggled. 'It's our room, we can do what we like. Can we do presents now? I'm so impressed with myself for actually remembering to bring them with me.'

Molly laughed. 'Of course we can.' She stood up and found her bag of gifts, handing two gifts to her dad.

He tore off the paper from his strangely shaped presents, and ran his hands over the shoes, nodding approvingly. 'My last pair are getting a little battered. Thank you darling.'

Saskia handed her present to her dad and sat back down on the sofa.

'Oh, this is wonderful.' He smiled and held up the cream cashmere sweater. 'Thank you, cherie.' He leant over and kissed her on the cheek.

Molly handed Saskia her gift, and perched on the edge of the sofa as she opened it.

'Oh my God! This is brilliant, I love it.' Saskia held the pink leopard print top against herself. 'This is way better than the one you pinched from me.' She pulled Molly in for a hug, then let her go, handing her the last brightly wrapped present on the sofa.

Molly took the paper off, revealing several bars of expensive chocolate. 'Oh Saskia, thank you, I've wanted to try this for ages.

'I know! I won't be offended if you want to chop it up to make brownies,' Saskia said. 'As long as you let me taste them.'

'Of course I will.' Molly put the bars of chocolate onto the coffee table.

'I do have another present for you, well for both of us.' Saskia handed Molly another gift.

Molly opened it, and two cerise berets fell out. 'These are cute.' She put one on. 'Is the other one for you?'

'Yes, but they aren't the gift.' Saskia put the other beret on. 'I'm taking you to Paris for the weekend. You name the date and I'm booking us into the fanciest hotel, for a weekend of sightseeing. Papa, will you join us?'

'I do not want to, how do you say, cramp your style, but I can perhaps join you for a meal,' he suggested.

'It would have to be L'Esapdon, though, wouldn't it?' Molly said.

The last time she'd been in Paris with her dad, he'd insisted on taking her and Saskia to the chandelier draped dining room of the Ritz Hotel.

He scoffed. 'I would be just as happy with steak frites in a bistro, you know.'

Saskia laughed. 'I'd love to see that.' She turned to Molly. 'What do you think?'

'I don't know what to say. It's such a great gift.' She gave Saskia a hug. 'Thank you. I can't wait.'

'You're so welcome. I want to thank you for everything you've done for me.' Saskia let Molly go, then adjusted her beret. 'Paris had better watch out. The Millot sisters are coming!'

Molly got out her phone and took a photo of her and Saskia in their berets.

Saskia's phone started ringing and she picked it up. Molly saw Scott's face on the screen, just before Saskia whisked herself away to the balcony.

'Ah, young love,' Gaspard said. 'Do you need to call Mark?'

Molly shook her head. 'We broke up.'

He nodded, and she was sure he was biting back a smile. 'I'm sorry to hear that. I suspected that was the case. Are you alright?'

'I am. I knew you'd know what was going on.' She smiled at him. 'I had an epiphany when one of Chris's friends got engaged. It made me realise that Mark wasn't the one I wanted, and that I was holding onto a fantasy of what I thought we were to each other. You were right. It wasn't a relationship, and he showed me his true colours when I broke up with him.'

'Did he hurt you?' He frowned.

Molly shook her head. 'No more than he had been for the last four years. He called me all kinds of things, but I don't care. I know who I am.'

'Good for you.' He smiled. 'He was not the right person for you. You seem happier now. This was a good decision, no?'

'It was.' She took a deep breath. 'Papa, I love Chris, and when I go back to Canterbury I'm going to tell him that.'

His eyes lit up. 'Now this is a match I approve of. He has character, warmth, depth. He's also given me some very insightful feedback on my novel. He suggested that I...' He stopped. 'Sorry. We're talking about you. I'm almost certain that he feels the same way.'

'I can't let myself believe that he does,' Molly said quietly, 'but I'm still going to tell him.'

'That is brave. I'm so proud of you.' He smiled at her.

Saskia walked back into the room with a huge grin on her face and gave Molly a hug. 'That's from Chris and Scott.'

'How are they?' Molly asked.

'Slightly hungover,' Saskia said, laughing. 'They went out with Alex and some of his friends last night. It was supposed to be a quiet one, but Scott persuaded them to go to see a band and it got a bit messy.'

Molly smiled. 'I bet you can't wait to see him.'

'Yeah, but I'm not the only one desperate to get back to Canterbury.' Saskia waggled her eyebrows. 'Chris even looks hot when he's hungover.'

Molly's heart skipped a beat, imagining his rumpled hair. He would look good in anything. Or nothing. She stood up. 'I guess we should get dressed.'

'Nice subject change, Mole. You're so into him.' She paused. 'Did you tell Papa about Mark?'

Molly nodded. 'I did.'

Saskia rubbed her hands together gleefully. 'Oh good, now I can tell you both about the little acting job that Caro and I did the other day.'

Molly cringed. She had no idea what was going to come out of her sister's mouth. 'What acting job?'

Saskia started giggling before she even started talking. 'So I was telling Caro about Mark, and how you'd said not to get involved. We decided to ignore that. Caro has some expensive power suits, so we dressed in those and went to his office. He was *not* pleased to see me.'

Molly gasped. 'What did you do?'

'I just wanted to be sure that he wasn't ever going to contact you again. I told him that we had the CCTV footage from Riad. Scott knows the owner, who was more than happy to let Scott take a look at it. Caro implied that we would be keeping an eye on him on your behalf, and he didn't like that very much. Instead of being a good boy and admitting that he'd done wrong, he laid into me in the foyer. It is *very* echoey in there, and it was such a shame that his boss appeared. And Beth.' Saskia giggled. 'I think he can kiss that promotion goodbye.'

Molly stared at her sister, speechless.

'I wasn't going to ruin his career, Molly, I really wasn't. I just wanted him to know that we knew what he'd done and that if he *did* ever contact you again, we'd make sure that everyone knew who he was. It worked out better than I could have expected. He showed himself up in front of everyone.' Saskia laughed. 'Are you cross?'

'No, I just don't know what to say,' Molly wasn't surprised that Saskia had gone after Mark, and she was touched that Caro had joined in to, but she feared that encouraging her too much might not be the best idea. 'What you did was really sweet, but it could have backfired. You and Caro could have jeopardised your careers, or your safety.'

Saskia waved a hand. 'We risk assessed it. We were considering going to his apartment but we decided that going to his work was safer. More people.' Her eyes sparkled. 'More onlookers.' She giggled.

'I'm so proud of you, my darling.' Gaspard smiled at Saskia. 'I should not encourage you, but sometimes what is wrong and what is right is not that easy to determine.'

Molly smiled thinking about Liz's words. Life was not black and white. 'Very wise words, Papa.'

'I can be wise on occasion. Why don't we have a walk before lunch?' Gaspard suggested.

'Good idea.' Molly stood up. 'Come on Sas, time to get out of the bathrobe.'

'I'm comfy.' Saskia pulled her robe tighter around her and sipped her coffee. 'I need time to unwind. I'm a very busy actress.'

Molly stifled a laugh She knew exactly what had happened. 'You've got into the sit pit. A very *luxurious* sit pit, but it's still a sit pit.' She thought for a second.'If you come and get dressed and showered, I'll wear the pink beret on our walk. And I'll speak in French.' Offering to embarrass herself was a surefire way to get Saskia to do anything.

'Done.' Saskia stood up, grinning. 'I'll wear mine too.'

After a walk around the city pretending to be a French tourist, Molly put on a scarlet velvet skater dress, and her heels, then slipped her arm into her sister's. 'Are we French or English now?'

'French,' Saskia's eyes lit up. 'Shall we wear the berets to lunch?'

'Absolutely not,' Gaspard said. 'Enough silliness.'

'Je suis suis désolée, Papa.' Saskia fluttered her eyelashes. 'I'll behave.'

'Moi aussi,' Molly added.

'Wonderful. Shall we go?' He opened the door and ushered Molly and Saskia out of their room.

The restaurant was as opulent as the rest of the hotel. Hand painted murals graced the walls, and everything Molly could see was edged with gold. Gaspard and Saskia had oysters to start, while Molly chose soup. She'd tried an oyster once and vowed to never do it again. When they'd finished their starters, the waiters served turkey with every imaginable trimming and Molly wished she had chosen a dress with a looser waistband.

As their plates were taken away, her dad lifted his glass. 'Mery Christmas to you both. I'm so proud to be your father. Molly, you are kind, smart, and strong, and Saskia, you are eternally positive, creative, and passionate. May you both have a wonderful year and be successful in whatever you choose to do.'

'Lovely speech, Papa,' Molly said, 'We think you're wonderful too.'

'Merci.' Gaspard took a sip of his coffee. 'You are very kind.'

'We love you, Papa,' Saskia added. 'Can I make a toast to myself? You know the two auditions I told you about? Well, one of them I didn't get, but the other one I did, and I'm flying out to LA in March for a very small part in a film.' She lowered her voice. 'That's about all I can tell you. Well, I could tell you more, but I'm not supposed to.'

'Congratulations!' Molly lifted her glass. 'Don't tell us anything else until you can, we can wait.'

'My little girl is going to be a Hollywood star!' Gaspard said. 'After your first nativity play, I said to Nancy, that girl is meant to be on the stage. This is wonderful news.'

'I don't know about a Hollywood *star,* but I will be *starring* in a film in Hollywood.' Saskia turned to Molly. 'I'll come back to Canterbury once the pantomime has wrapped, so we'll have a few months together before I go to the US.'

'I'm so proud of you, Sas. I knew you were destined for big things. How long will you be in LA for?' Molly asked.

'I don't know yet.' Saskia chewed her lip. 'I feel bad for leaving you.'

Molly shook her head. 'You don't need to worry about me. I'm braver than I've ever been.'

'You are, and I'm so proud of *you.*' Saskia blew her a kiss, then took a sip of her Champagne. 'Here's to us strong, independent women, and our strong, independent Papa!'

Chris was struggling to stay awake. The quiet evening that he and Scott had planned had got derailed when Alex persuaded them to go backstage with the band, then follow them to another bar. Now, almost twelve hours later, he had eaten the best Christmas dinner he'd ever had, and all he wanted was to go to sleep, but he was surrounded by all of his family at the hotel that Alex and his mum, Sarah, owned.

'More wine, Chris?' his mum asked, holding a bottle over his glass.

'No thanks.' Chris lowered his voice. 'I might fall asleep if I drink any more.'

She laughed. 'I thought you were only going to have a few drinks last night.'

'He did, but I persuaded him to go and hang out with George and Ed and we got in really late,' Scott confessed. 'That's why I'm not drinking today. I drank way too much last night.'

'It was my fault too,' Alex admitted. 'We stayed out later than I'd planned to.'

'This happens to us a lot,' Kate added. 'We go out, thinking it's going to be a quiet night, then we end up staying out until two am.' She laughed. 'That's what happens when you date a DJ.'

'We aren't dating,' Alex reminded her. 'We're engaged.'

Sarah smiled. 'So you are!' She stood up. 'Can we all raise our glasses to my wonderful son Alex, and his beautiful wife-to-be, Kate.'

'To Kate and Alex!' Chris cheered, then sipped his coffee.

Kate had blushed scarlet and was also gulping down her coffee. Alex winked at her, and she beamed at him.

'Are you guys still going to come out and party with us when you're married?' Scott asked.

'Of course we are,' Kate assured him. 'I love hanging out with you lot.'

'Us getting married isn't going to change who we are,' Alex added. 'We're still going to want to see you all, and we're gonna need all of you to help us plan this. We have no idea what we're doing.'

Kate laughed. 'We really don't. We've got the venue sorted, and that's about it.' She turned to Chris. 'I asked Molly if she would make the cake. Her cakes are *so good.'*

'What did she say?' he asked.

'She said she would.'

He smiled. Of course she did. She was always helping everyone else out, while insisting she was too needy herself. The night they'd spent together last week had been perfect. She'd fallen asleep in his arms, and he'd had to fight the urge to blurt out that he was in love with her.

'So glad she's broken up with her boyfriend, he sounds like a *tool.'* Kate grimaced. 'Good for her.' She paused. 'I know what it's like when other people interfere in your relationship, *but* I hope you guys get together as I think you're *perfect* for each other.'

'So do I,' Chris said, 'but she she needs me to be her friend right now.'

He wished that things were different, but there was no way he would jeopardise what they had. She trusted him and he wouldn't take that for granted.

'Got it.' Kate nodded. 'Sorry for overstepping. I just care about you. And her.'

'It's fine, Chris said. 'You weren't overstepping. I've been in love with her for a while, but I'm going to wait for the right time to tell her.'

Kate clasped her hands to her chest. '*That* is the right approach. This is why she trusts you, Chris. You tread carefully with her.'

'I wouldn't know any other way.' He glanced at his parents. 'I've learnt from the best. Kindness and respect are the only way to build a relationship with someone. I want and need her in my life, and I know she feels the same way. Whether or not she loves me back, I don't know.'

There had been many moments over the last few weeks where he'd thought she might love him too, but he hadn't allowed himself to believe it. He couldn't let himself think what it might be like to kiss her any time he wanted to, to run his hands over her soft skin, and hold her as they fell asleep together.

Chapter Thirty

December 2014, London, England

'Where are we going?' Molly asked Saskia. 'You know I don't like surprises.'

'Do you trust me?' Saskia asked, cocking her head to the side.

Molly closed her eye so that Saskia could do her eyeliner, then opened it, examining the perfect flick in the mirror. 'Do I trust you? Hmm. Not sure.'

Saskia pouted. 'Rude.' She handed Molly a tube of mascara. 'Put this on, but do it carefully. I don't want you smudging my perfectly applied eyeliner.'

Molly applied a coat of mascara. 'Will that do? Are you going to give me a clue about what we're doing?'

'Nope,' Saskia said. 'All you need to know is that it's New Year's Eve, so we're going to kick this year firmly in the arse, send it on its way and embrace whatever next year has in store for us.'

Molly laughed. 'You have such a way with words. You should think about stand up.'

'Caro and I are considering doing it,' Saskia said. 'If you think I'm funny, you need to spend an evening with her.'

'I'd love to.' Molly raised an eyebrow. 'Add it to the list of things we're going to do this year.'

'I love this new, confident Molly.' Saskia brushed some blusher across Molly's cheeks. 'You're good to go. What are you going to wear?'

'I have no idea, because I don't even know where we're *going*,' Molly said pointedly.

'We're going to a party,' Saskia replied. 'Dress like you're a Bond girl in a casino.'

Molly wrinkled her nose. 'I don't think I have anything like that.'

Saskia jumped off Molly's bed. 'Hold on, I'll be right back.' She disappeared out of the room and returned holding their mum's navy blue jumpsuit. 'I think you should wear this.'

Molly stood up and took the hanger from Saskia, running her fingers over the navy-blue velvet. 'It does need some new memories.'

'Exactly,' Saskia said. 'Put it on and I'll fix your hair.'

The taxi arrived outside just as Molly had put on the glittery high heels that she'd borrowed from Saskia. She checked her reflection in the mirror. The jumpsuit wrapped across her chest, revealing a hint of cleavage, and clung tightly to her waist and hips before the trousers tapered to her ankles. 'Does it suit me?' she asked.

'It does. Like it was made for you. Are you ready for this?' A huge smile spread across Saskia's face.

'I have no idea, but I'm going to trust you.' Molly ran her eyes over Saskia, who was wearing a silver, Grecian style dress. Her hair was swept dramatically to one side and fixed with a jewelled clip. 'You look stunning as always.'

'I haven't decided if I'm Bond villain, or Bond girl yet, though.' Saskia glanced at her reflection in the mirror. 'Definitely a villain.' She opened the front door, ushering Molly out.

The taxi drove out of the city and into the darkness of the country-side. The further they went, the more confused Molly got. Eventually they came to a long drive, which led to a car park. As the taxi parked, Molly gasped at the stunning stately home in front of them.

'Where are we?' Molly asked.

'Come with me.' Saskia paid the driver and waved him off, before slipping her arm into Molly's. 'Mind your heels on the gravel.'

Molly frowned, puzzled, and walked along the gravel lined drive with Saskia at her side, until she reached a path which led to the front door of the house. Saskia let go of Molly's arm, and pulled it open. 'After you.'

Molly could hear voices and glasses clinking as they walked down a long hallway. Saskia opened the glass door at the end of the hall, and Molly's eyes widened as she walked into the upmarket bar, with velvet upholstered furniture, and Victorian tiled floors. On one side of the bar, a band were setting up.

Alex, dressed in a tuxedo, appeared, handing them both a glass of Champagne. 'Welcome to the Woodlands Hotel. I hope you enjoy tonight.'

'Alex?' Molly frowned, puzzled. 'Is this your hotel?'

'Sort of,' he said. 'It was our family home, but my mum and I converted it a few years ago.'

Saskia looked around the room. 'It's beautiful. I can't believe we haven't been here before.'

'I think you'll be back.' He gestured to the guests behind him. 'Most of the people here tonight were here for our first New Year's Eve party two years ago.'

'Including me,' Kate said, appearing by Alex's side. 'Molly, Saskia, lovely to see you.' She ran her eyes over Molly. 'I love your jumpsuit. Is Biba?'

'It is,' Molly replied. 'It was my mum's.'

'It's gorgeous.' Kate gave her a sympathetic smile. 'It's wonderful that you're keeping her memory alive.'

'Thank you.' Molly bit her lip. 'Thank you for inviting us tonight, I mean I assume we're invited and not just gatecrashing.' She flicked her eyes to Saskia.

'You were definitely invited,' Alex replied. 'Come and get a drink.'

As Alex led them to the bar, Molly pulled Saskia towards her. 'Is he here? You told me he was DJing at an exclusive party!'

'Yes,' Saskia said slowly. '*This* one.'

Alex handed them both glasses of Champagne. 'Welcome, ladies. We have an Italian buffet, a swing band, and DJ sets later on. I'll leave you to it, but if you need anything, come find me.'

'Or me,' Kate added. 'I'll grab you guys for a dance later.' She winked at Molly.

'Oh, she's lovely,' Saskia whispered as Kate walked away.

Molly took a sip of her Champagne. 'I know, I really like her. Did I tell you that she asked me to make her wedding cake?'

'No!' Saskia exclaimed. 'That's exciting! I love a wedding.'

'Me too. And Kate and Alex's will be here. They're getting married next summer.' Molly took a sip of her Champagne.

Saskia's smile disappeared. 'I dont know where I'll be next summer.'

'Does that worry you?' Molly asked. 'I would hate that, but you've always been so much better than me at flying by the seat of your pants.'

'I am a little worried, but I have a new motto,' Saskia said. '*Trust the process*. I'm going to believe that things will all work out, and maybe they will.'

Molly wondered if this applied to her and Chris. 'I love that motto.'

'I thought you might.' Saskia sipped her Champagne. 'Tell me, are you furious with me, or do you think I'm a genius? You said you were going to talk to Chris, but knowing you, you would overthink it and drag it out for months. I'm just speeding up the process.'

'And you chose to do this on New Year's Eve, where I could make an idiot of myself in front of all of his family and friends?' Molly took a deep breath, thankful for the stretchy velvet fabric of her jumpsuit. 'Where is he?'

'Relax. He's not here yet. Scott's working at Mimosa until ten, then they're both coming up here.' Saskia paused, studying her nails. 'He doesn't know that we're here. He thinks we're still in London.'

'I wondered why I hadn't heard from him.' Molly shook her head. 'Why didn't you tell him that I was coming?'

'I wanted it to be a surprise. I had this vision of your eyes meeting across the room, and you running towards each other.' Saskia's eyes filled with tears. 'I didn't believe in love until I met Scott. I finally understand what those shitty rom coms are all about. And I can see it when you and Chris are in the same room.'

'Sas, come here.' Molly put her glass down on the bar and put her arm around her sister. 'I love him, and I'm going to tell him that. If it ruins our friendship, so be it. I can't hide how I feel any longer.'

'Yes!' Saskia kissed Molly's cheek. 'So you're not angry with me?'

Molly shook her head. 'No. You had my best interests at heart. As you always do.'

'I do.' Saskia glanced away from Molly, at a woman sitting down at the next table with a plate of food. 'Now that we've got everything out in the open, can we get something to eat?'

'Why not?' Molly finished her Champagne, and she wasn't sure if it was that, or the thought of seeing Chris that made her feel slightly light headed.

In the restaurant opposite the bar, white shirted waiters and waitresses were serving guests a selection of Italian meats, cheeses, breads, olives and grilled peppers. Molly and Saskia joined the queue of people, then took their plates to an empty table and sat down. Despite her nerves, Molly devoured her food, as did Saskia, who always ate like she hadn't been fed for weeks.

'Do you know what you're going to say?' Saskia asked.

'I have no idea,' Molly said. 'I'm going to trust the process.'

'That's my girl.' Saskia smiled. 'Who knew that *I'd* be the one with the words of wisdom?'

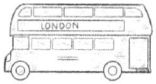

Chris walked into the bar, spotting Alex. 'Hello mate, looking sharp as usual.'

'Thank you. Nice tux.' Alex smirked.

Chris shook his head. 'I knew the blue velvet was a mistake.'

'Oh no, it definitely wasn't a mistake.' Alex smiled knowingly, then turned to Scott and high fived him. 'Hey man, how are you doing? Love the tux. Velvet not your thing?'

Scott shook his head. 'I prefer to stick with the classics.' He smoothed down the jacket of his black tuxedo.

'Grab a drink,' Alex said, patting Scott on the back. 'I'll catch up with you later.'

Chris nodded, then walked over to the counter with Scott. 'Hey, Mel.' He greeted the barmaid with a smile.

'Chris, and Scott! Good to see you.' Mel handed them both glasses of Champagne. 'You're both looking very dashing.'

Chris laughed. 'Dashing? I like that word.'

'I think it's a relic from like a hundred years ago, but I still like it.' Mel shrugged, then nodded to a customer further along the bar. 'Duty calls. I'll catch you later.'

Chris took a sip of his Champagne, then noticed who was walking towards him. Everything seemed to slow down for a moment as he ran his eyes over her. Her hair curled over one eye, and her jumpsuit was the same navy-blue velvet as his tuxedo. He put down his Champagne and walked towards her. Every sound, every person faded away as he approached her.

'Molly,' he said. 'You're here.'

'I'm here.'

He could tell by the wobble in her voice that she was nervous.

'I thought you were in London,' he said.

'I'm not.' She bit her lip. 'I'm here. I love...your tuxedo.' She ran her fingers over the lapel. 'So soft.'

'We match,' he said. Her nerves were rubbing off on him. This was Molly. His friend. Molly, who he sat on the sofa and watched films with. Who he ate dim sum and read books with. It was like he was seeing her for the first time tonight.

'Saskia told me that you were DJing at an exclusive party tonight,' she said.

'She was right.' He wanted to tell her how much he'd missed her, but the band had just started playing. 'Want to dance?' He offered her his hand.

'Sure.' She took his hand, and he led her to the dance floor.

She seemed different tonight, and he couldn't work out why. Everything felt different tonight. Flickers of colour from the disco ball above them flashed across her face as they danced, and he tried to work out what was different. Was it her? Was it him? And why had Scott and Saskia lied to them? He span her around, watched her curls bounce across her shoulders, then pulled her close again. She pressed her hand against his chest, and his heart started beating faster. It had been just over a week since he had last seen her, but it felt like a lifetime.

One song finished, another began, yet he didn't move away from her, and she showed no intention of moving from him. He noticed Scott and Saskia in each other's arms on the other side of the dance-floor, and smiled at Scott, who gave him a thumbs up in return.

When the band stopped playing, he finally let her go. 'Do you want to get a drink?'

She nodded. 'Yes, but can I talk to you first?' She glanced around the room. 'Somewhere quiet.'

His stomach lurched. What was she going to say? 'Of course. Come with me.' He led her out of the bar, and along the corridor.

'Where are we going?' she asked.

'You'll see.' He pushed open a door next to the grand staircase and flicked the lights on.

Molly walked in first. 'Wow.' She turned away from him, towards the bookshelves full of leather-bound classics, paperbacks, and reference books.

'I thought you might like it in here,' he said. 'They're all my aunt and uncle's books,' he said. 'Kate helped Alex renovate it. You need to see the library at her house. It's probably five times the size of this.'

'It's amazing. I could probably spend hours in here.' She walked towards one of the bookshelves, running her eyes over it.

He closed the door. 'Is this private enough?'

'It is.' She turned to face him. 'I need to tell you someting, but it could change everything.' He recognised the look in her eyes, and the crease of her brow. She was scared.

He reached out and took her hands in his. 'It's me. You can tell me anything.'

'I know. But this is big.' She took a deep breath. 'I broke up with Mark because he wasn't right for me, and I would never have the kind of relationship I wanted with him. The kind of relationship I didn't even know that I wanted...until I met you.'

He bit his lip. 'I didn't know that.'

'I didn't realise it, and then I did, and I tried to pretend that I didn't.' She paused. 'Chris, I love you. I've loved you for a long time.'

He swallowed hard as a rush of excitement flooded through him. 'You love me?'

She nodded. 'I love you. So much.'

He smiled so hard his face hurt. 'I love you too.' He cupped her face in his hands and kissed her. 'I've tried so hard to be your friend, but instead I fell in love with you.'

'You did?' Her face softened. 'I didn't know.'

'I couldn't tell you.' He spoke slowly, choosing each word carefully. 'You were with someone else, and I was afraid that if I told you, I would lose you as a friend.'

'I thought you regretted that kiss,' she whispered. 'If I had known how you really felt...'

'I'd never felt anything like it in my life.' His voice cracked. 'I never will again, not for anyone else. Only for you.'

She pulled him towards her, kissing him again, her hands pressed against his chest. 'I feel the same way.'

'So, how would you feel about not being friends?' he asked.

'I would love to *not* be friends with you.' She paused. 'I love you, I want you and I've never wanted anything more than I want this, us.'

'Then I'm all yours.' He held her gaze. 'You can do whatever you like with me.'

'Really?' she raised an eyebrow. 'I have a few ideas, but I kind of hoped that *you'd* be the one in charge.'

'I can take charge.' He paused. 'If that's what you're into.'

She nodded. 'I'd do whatever you asked.'

He kissed her again, pressing her against the bookcases, feeling her murmur of pleasure vibrate between them, before pulling away. 'I guess we should get back to the party.'

'I like how you always leave me wanting more,' she said.

'I'll keep that in mind,' he replied, taking her hand in his, and guiding her back down the corridor into the bar.

'You told him!' Saskia squealed as Molly and Chris walked back into the bar, hand in hand.

'I did!' Molly squealed back at her.

Scott smiled at Saskia, then turned to Chris. 'You told her?'

Chris nodded. 'I told her.'

Had she really not known? He wasn't sure, but now he could tell her that he loved her whenever he liked. And it felt amazing.

'We know you set us up,' Molly said to Saskia and Scott.

'It worked, didn't it?' Scott shrugged. 'We knew you were both in love with each other, you just needed a little...help.'

'Thanks, man.' Chris smiled. 'I can't even put into words what I'm feeling right now.'

'I bet,' Scott said, then stepped back. 'Don't waste your time with me, go get her.'

Chris left Scott, and went back to Molly, kissing her cheek. 'Hey.'

'Hey.' She slipped her hand into his.

'*Stop.* You two are so cute, I can't.' Saskia clasped her hands together. 'You had your rom com moment!'

Chris frowned. 'Rom com moment?'

Molly smiled. 'We walked towards each other in a crowded room, which is exactly what Saskia imagined us doing.'

'You masterminded this whole thing?' Chris shook his head.

Saskia took a bow. 'I know, brains and beauty, I've got it all.' She flicked her hair dramatically away from her face, and her elbow caught her glass, knocking her drink all over the counter. 'Maybe not,' she said, laughing.

'Oh no.' Molly grabbed a handful of napkins.

Saskia took them from her. 'I'm good. I can clear up my own mess.' She mopped up the spilt cocktail, as Scott swooped in with a cloth.

Molly held out her hand to Chris. 'The band's playing again.'

'So they are.' He took her hand and led her onto the crowded dancefloor.

When the countdown to midnight began, Chris gazed into Molly's eyes. As everyone around them cheered, welcoming in the New Year, he kissed her.

'Wow.' She pulled away from him. 'That kiss was... phenomenal. Can we do it again?'

'I can do this all night,' he breathed against her cheek.

'I'd like that,' she whispered.

'Then stay. Stay with me here tonight.' He held her gaze. 'I don't want to let you go yet.'

Her eyes filled with tears. 'I don't want to let you go either.'

And now, he didn't have to. She was his, and he was hers. As they danced, he held her close against him, her heart beating in time with his.

Epilogue

June 2016, Canterbury, Kent, England

Molly pushed open the door of the hotel bar, and gasped. It had been decorated with strings of bunting in teal and mint green and there were floral arrangements everywhere. Her stomach fluttered nervously, as if it were her wedding day, not Kate and Alex's. Saskia followed her in, letting out a loud whistle at the decorations.

'They've gone all out for today, huh?' She nudged Molly. 'Come on, we need to go see the bride-to-be.'

Saskia marched through the bar, and Molly followed her up the stairs and along the corridor to the room where Kate and her bridesmaids were getting ready. Molly knocked on the door, and it flew open a few seconds later.

'Morning!' Kate said, beaming at Molly and Saskia. Her face was bare, and her strawberry blonde hair was in rollers on the top of her head. She ushered them into the room and closed the door behind them.

'How are you?' Saskia gushed. 'You're getting married today!'

'I know! I'm so excited! I didn't sleep at all last night.' Kate gestured to the bottle on the coffee table. 'Grab a glass of Champagne.'

While Saskia started doing Kate's make up, Molly sat down on the sofa and sipped her Champagne, suddenly feeling nervous. What if the cake collapsed? Or it tasted awful?

When Saskia moved onto Kate's best friend Hannah's make up, Molly slipped downstairs and into the kitchen, where Stefan, the hotel's chef, was waiting for her. His eyes crinkled as he embraced her, giving her a kiss on each cheek. She'd spent the previous day at the hotel baking the cake, and she'd already grown pretty fond of him. He reminded her of her dad, as they were from the same region of France. Today the kitchen was a hive of activity, with Stefan, his kitchen assistant Ed, and Alex's cousin Jake, who was a chef, all working together in the small space.

'I've set you up a little spot here.' Stefan patted a clear area of stainless-steel counter next to the fridge. It had been his idea to make and assemble the cake at the hotel, and Molly had accepted his offer gratefully. 'I've set up the stand mixer for you. Help yourself.'

'Thank you,' Molly replied, before she washed her hands and slipped on her apron over her jeans and jumper.

She carefully unwrapped the cling film covered layers of cake. The sweet aromas of vanilla, lemon and chocolate filled the kitchen. With the radio in the kitchen blaring, she made the buttercream and put it in the fridge to chill. Carefully, she dowelled and stacked the layers of cake, smoothing the buttercream over the top. Once the cake was assembled, she decorated it with summer berries and fresh flowers.

Stefan nodded approvingly. 'Good job, Molly. It looks wonderful.'

'Molly, that's awesome,' Jake said, smiling at her.

'Thanks,' Molly said, then checked her watch. 'There's less than an hour until the ceremony. I'd better go and find Saskia.' She slipped off her apron and folded it up. 'Good luck guys, I'll see you later on.'

She hurried out of the kitchen, through the restaurant and into the corridor, where she barrelled straight into Chris.

'Hey, slow down.' He smiled. 'Are you alright?'

'I am now.' She kissed him, and then stepped back so she could admire him. His navy-blue suit was perfectly cut, and his hair was swept back like a film star. 'You look so hot.'

'Why thank you.' He smiled. 'I'm guessing you've just finished with the cake. You're wearing some buttercream.'

'Am I?' She looked down at her jeans. 'Where?'

'Here.' He leant forwards and licked her cheek. 'Mmm, lemon. My favourite. Is there any more left? Maybe we could put it to good use later?' He raised an eyebrow.

She laughed. 'Keep it in your pants, Parker. You've got responsibilities.'

'True. How did it go with the cake? Are you happy with it or are you overthinking it?'

He knew her so well. 'Both. Obviously. Once everyone's eaten it and I know that they like it, then I can relax.' She adjusted his tie. 'How's the groom holding up?'

'Ah, he's his usual mysterious self,' he said. 'He's not saying much, but he can't stop smiling.'

'How sweet. I love that he's managing to be mysterious *and* excited.' She pressed her hands against his chest. 'I need to go and get changed. I'll see you later.'

'Before you go...' He slid his arms around her waist and kissed her again. When he pulled away, he smiled at her. 'You taste delicious. Like chocolate and lemon.'

'You taste like whisky and cigars, like some dude from the 1950's.' Blowing him a kiss, she went up to Kate's room.

'Perfect timing,' Hannah said as she opened the door. 'Can you help us get our dresses on?'

'Of course.' Molly walked into the room, which seemed even more cluttered than she'd left it, with dress covers, and shoes everywhere. Mia's children were sprawled out on the middle of the floor, immersed in a colouring book.

Hannah let out a loud whistle. 'Right people, we need to get dressed. Let's go!' She picked up one of the dress covers and read out the label on it. 'Lucy, this is yours.' She handed it to Kate's friend, Lucy. 'Mia, this one is yours, and this one is mine.'

Molly nodded approvingly. Hannah was taking her role of maid of honour very seriously. She and Hannah were very alike, both eldest siblings, and both risk averse overthinkers.

While the bridesmaids dressed, Molly helped Mia to find her son's shoes, then helped Saskia to finish Kate's mum, Amelie's hair.

The bridesmaids had just put their dresses on, when Hannah let Leon, Kate's friend, and dress designer into the room. He wore a pale blue suit, the lapels piped in dark blue, matching his tie. His browns curls were artistically arranged, and he smiled as he saw Kate, wrapped in a cream silk robe. 'Well, aren't you the most beautiful bride-to-be! How are you doing?'

'So much better now you're here.' Kate gave him a hug. 'I can't believe you've made me wait until now for my dress.'

'I wanted to make sure it was perfect,' he said. 'I've been up all night sewing on more beads.'

He held up the dress cover he was carrying and unzipped it. Everyone gasped as he revealed the gown. The sleeves were long and covered in hundreds of tiny beads in shades of white, cream and ivory, with sparkling crystals dotted between them. The fitted bodice had a trail of crystals which spread out across the silky skirt.

Kate's eyes filled with tears. 'I love it! Thank you so much.'

Leon smiled. 'I'll wait outside while you get the dress on, but you might need my help to get all the buttons done up.'

Once Kate was in her dress, Hannah and Lucy started fastening the buttons at the back of Kate's neck, while Leon did up the tiny buttons on her cuffs. Molly and Mia helped Kate step into her white satin peep toe heels, while Amelie carefully adjusted Kate's veil. As the last button was fastened, everyone stood back.

Amelie wiped her eyes. 'Kate, you look absolutely beautiful. Alex is going to faint when he sees you.'

'I hope not.' Kate walked slowly over to the mirror. 'Oh wow, maybe he will. I'll have to give him the kiss of life.' She turned to Leon. 'You did such a good job. I can't thank you enough.'

Amelie handed her a tissue and Kate wiped her eyes, the crystals on her sleeve sparkling.

Hannah checked her watch, then clapped her hands. 'Places, everyone. Mia, grab the bags, Lucy, take Kate's handbag...'

Molly ushered Saskia out of the room and back into their own room. She changed as quickly as she could, then put on her heels. 'You ready, Sas?'

Saskia nodded. 'All good. Let's go.'

When they arrived at the church, Molly smiled as she walked up to the door. Chris was stood there, greeting the guests. She kissed his cheek. 'Good luck.'

She couldn't shake the thought that this could be them one day, that she could be walking down the aisle towards him.

'I'll see you afterwards.' He stroked her cheek, holding her gaze, and she wondered if he was thinking the same thing.

Molly slipped her arm into Saskia's and led her to an empty pew in the church. When Chris took his position at the front of the altar next to Alex, he winked at her, and she smiled back.

The church fell silent, and Molly turned around in her seat. Mia walked slowly to the front of the aisle, holding her children's hands. Hannah and Lucy followed, then there was a pause before Kate and her dad walked to the front of the aisle. Kate's smile spread across her face as she saw Alex, his ocean-like eyes accentuated by his navy-blue suit. When she reached him, he took her hands in his and held them tightly.

'Can you see the way he's looking at her?' Molly whispered to Saskia.

'Ugh, I know. Those eyes,' Saskia whispered back. 'I know he's literally getting married right now, but you have to admit he's hot. Not hot hot, but kind of cool, aloof hot.'

Molly stifled a giggle. Alex's serious, intense personality was a contrast to Saskia's bubbly one. 'You can't say that in church,' she whispered back.

As they repeated their marriage vows, Kate and Alex's eyes stayed fixed on each other. They smiled and wiped away each other's tears and when they were declared husband and wife, he swept her into his arms and kissed her to cheers from everyone around them.

Molly pulled a tissue from her bag and wiped her eyes, before handing one to Saskia. 'Well, that was emotional,' she whispered as Kate and Alex disappeared to sign the register. 'I sobbed the entire way through Hannah's reading.'

'Me too,' Saskia whispered. 'I already know what I'm going to read at your wedding.'

'I dread to think,' Molly hissed. 'I'd have to check it thoroughly first.'

'Is there a wedding on the cards then?' Saskia raised her eyebrow.

'We've only been together for a year,' Molly whispered, 'but if he asked, I'd say yes in a heartbeat. How about you and Scott?'

Saskia chewed her lip. 'I don't know. We're apart a lot with work, and neither of us like planning ahead. I'm happy with things the way they are for now.'

Molly nodded. 'Come on, it's time to chuck some confetti.'

She slid out of her seat and followed the rest of the guests out into the churchyard. Alex and Kate came out of the church, hand in hand, and were showered with confetti as they walked along the narrow path to the road, where a vintage Jaguar was waiting for them. Alex opened the door for Kate and helped her in, before sliding in next to her. They both waved as it drove off.

'Now the fun can begin,' Saskia said, her eyes lighting up.

'Saskia,' Molly rolled her eyes. 'The ceremony is the most important part of the wedding.'

'I think I like parties better than weddings,' Saskia mused.

Molly smiled. 'Well, let's get to the party then.'

Once she arrived back at the hotel, Molly slipped into the kitchen, and, with Stefan's help, set up the cake in the restaurant, which had been decorated for the wedding breakfast. Each table had a cactus in a china pot on it, as Kate loved them.

Chris carried a large cardboard box into the restaurant and set it on one of the chairs. 'I didn't eat any, I promise.'

Molly laughed. 'I made a few extra in case they got broken.' She had baked a hundred tiny shortbread cacti as favours, then enlisted Saskia, Scott and Chris to help her decorate them and put them into tiny cellophane bags. 'Can you help me put them on the tables.'

'Of course,' he said, and opened the box. Together, they put the cacti onto each linen napkin, and once they were finished, he went over to the cake, running his eyes over it. 'It looks incredible, Molly.'

'Thank you. I hope it tastes as good.' She crossed her fingers. 'At least I don't have long to wait to find out now.'

'Do you want a drink?' he asked.

'I don't want one, but I think I *need* one,' she said, and followed Chris out of the restaurant.

After a gin and tonic, she went back into the restaurant, where a taco bar had been set up.

'Now, this is my kind of wedding breakfast,' Saskia said to Molly as they joined the queue.

'I agree,' Molly replied. 'They didn't want anything formal, and this is perfect. Apparently they had tacos on their first date.'

'They are *too* cute,' Saskia whispered.

Instead of circular tables, and a top table, long, rectangular tables lined the restaurant. Molly found her seat next to Chris, and opposite Scott. The tacos were spicy, but delicious, and totally different to anything she'd ever had at a wedding before. Molly wiped her mouth with a napkin. It was almost time for the cake to be cut, as it was being served as dessert. She squashed her nerves as Alex stood up.

'I want to thank you all for coming today. There are some people that we wish could be here, especially my dad.' He turned to Kate. 'I know he would have loved you. Thank you to our bridesmaids, Mia, Hannah, and Lucy. We're so lucky to have you in our lives. Thank you to our families, and to my wonderful mother who has let us host our wedding in her hotel.' He paused as Sarah blew him a kiss. Turning to Kate again, he smiled at her. 'Kate. When I met you, I had a feeling you were going to change my life forever, and you did, in the best way possible. You see the good in everyone, and I love that about you.'

Molly squeezed Chris's hand under the table, as Kate stood up and wrapped her arms around Alex.

'I love you so much,' Kate said, her eyes filled with tears. 'I knew my life would change forever when I met you too.' She turned to face their guests. 'I love you guys too. I'm so glad you're all here with us.' She sat back down, and Alex discretely passed her a tissue.

Alex smiled. 'I'll hand over to my brother and hope he doesn't embarrass me. Ben, the floor is yours, but I would just like to remind you how *kind* I was to you at your wedding.'

As Ben started his speech, Chris leant over to Molly. 'Are you alright?'

'Yes,' Molly whispered. 'They're so perfect for each other.'

'They are,' he whispered back. 'I watched them fall in love, and I knew I'd be here one day, watching them marry each other.'

'I love how romantic you are.' She kissed his cheek.

'Congratulations to the bride and groom,' Ben said, 'who I believe are now going to cut the cake.'

He sat down and Alex stood up, holding out a hand to Kate, who took it.

Molly held her breath as they approached the cake. Stefan handed Alex a large silver knife, which he offered to Kate, and together they cut into the bottom tier of the cake.

Putting down the knife, Alex picked up a small plate and Kate slid a slice of the chocolate cake onto it, then broke off a piece and put it into Alex's mouth. He offered her a piece and her eyes lit up as she ate it.

'Now you can relax, Mole,' Saskia whispered.

'Not yet,' Molly whispered back.

When she took a bite from her own slice of cake, she finally relaxed. The chocolate was sweet and heady, and she could taste the hint of vanilla and coffee in it. She'd just finished her slice when Kate and Alex came over to their table.

'Great work on the cake, Molly,' Kate said. 'It was delicious. We've asked Stefan to save us some.'

Molly smiled. 'I'm so glad you like it! I've been so nervous for the last few days.'

'I don't have a sweet tooth,' Alex said, 'but I intend to spend the next few days eating it. I think you might be getting a few more orders after today.'

'I might just get you to make one for me every week.' Kate looked down at her dress, gasping as she noticed a chocolatey stain. 'I need to find Mia. She'll know how to get the stain out.' She held up her dress and hurried over to the other end of the table.

'You ready for tonight?' Chris asked Alex. 'You're really going to do this?'

'What, play a set on my wedding night? Hell, yeah. Alex raised his eyebrow. 'My wife and I have worked on our own mix of the song I wrote for her.'

Saskia slid her arm around Molly. 'I love that. *My wife*. There is nothing more romantic than that.'

Molly laughed. 'I know, right?'

'I need to go and check that the band have got set up. I'll catch up with you guys later.' Alex gave Chris and Scott a high five before walking away.

After a couple of mojitos in the hotel bar, Molly felt even more relaxed. Chris's arm was wrapped around her waist as she listened to one of Saskia's stories, peppered with expletives. The lights in the bar dimmed around them, and Molly turned around, beaming as she saw Future Proof, Alex's friend's band, take to the stage.

'Good evening, everyone!' A man with long dark hair, and a guitar slung around his waist shouted. 'I'm George, and this is Future Proof. My band and I would like to be the first people to congratulate the new Mr and Mrs Compson!' He paused while a cheer went up around the room. 'We don't normally do covers, but we'd do anything for Alex and Kate, so here goes.'

Alex took Kate's hand and guided her onto the dancefloor, sliding his arms around her as George started singing Candi Staton's *You Got the Love*. His haunting vocals echoed around the high ceilings, as below him, Kate and Alex danced, wrapped in each other's arms until the song finished.

'Aren't they beautiful?' George gestured to Kate and Alex. 'They look a bit lonely out there don't they? You guys need to come and join them.' He started playing another song, and the dancefloor slowly filled up.

Molly took Chris's hand, and when they reached the middle of the floor, he slid his arms around her waist. '*Now* you look relaxed. Everyone loved your cake.'

Molly nodded. Every single plate she'd seen had been empty. 'I'm so happy! I didn't sleep at all last night worrying about it collapsing.'

'I know,' he said. 'I didn't either.'

'I'm sorry.' She pressed her hand against his chest.

'It doesn't matter. I'd rather not sleep next to you, than sleep anywhere else.' He kissed her cheek.

'I do love you.' She smiled. 'And I loved today. The ceremony was perfect, and the whole day has felt like *them*. You know? Even the cacti and the taco bar. It's all been so personal, and not *stuffy*, and dull like some of the weddings I've been to.'

'Our family don't do stuffy, or formal, or dull.' He smiled. 'As you know.'

'Oh I know.' She laughed. 'That's why I love you all.'

'So is this the kind of wedding you'd want?' he asked.

Her heart started pounding faster. Her parents' divorce had tainted her view of marriage, even though they'd remained friends. 'I'd never really thought about what kind of wedding I'd want. As long as you were there, on the other side of the altar, that's all I'd need.

'That's all I need to know.' He pressed her closer against him.

'What kind of wedding do you want?' she asked.

'Something relaxed and low-key, maybe in France, in a tiny little church, with an outdoor reception...' He trailed off. 'What's up?'

'You've thought about this a lot.' She smiled.

'Is it too soon? Too much?' His brow creased.

'No, and no. It sounds wonderful.' She could picture it already. 'And we could have a swing band, cocktails, a cake buffet...'

'I love the sound of all of those things.'

She couldn't have pictured this before now, before him, but now it was crystal clear. 'So do I.'

'There's no hurry,' he assured her. 'We're taking this slowly, right?'

'Right,' she said, but in her head, she kept the image of her walking into a church in a flowing white gown towards him.

A few songs later, Molly squeezed her way through the dancefloor, and out into the corridor, stopping by the door of the ladies bathroom.

In front of her, Kate's friend Lucy was kissing Mel, the barmaid. They sprang apart as she walked towards them.

'I'm so sorry, I was just going to the ladies.' Molly squeezed past the, and once she was shut in the safety of the toilet cubicle, she wished Saskia was there so that she could tell her. Why were they kissing in secret?

Before she left the bathroom, she paused, listening for voices in the corridor. Hearing nothing, she opened the door, and seeing the corridor empty, she walked back to the bar, where Chris was talking to Sarah.

'Oh, hello love,' Sarah said. 'I was just telling Chris what a *marvellous* place this is to get married in.'

Chris laughed. 'You're about as subtle as a sledgehammer.'

'I'm just saying, it's gorgeous here in the summer.' Sarah took a sip of her drink. 'The rose beds are really beautiful.' She raised her eyebrow.

As she walked off, Chris shook his head. 'I'm so sorry. My mum and my aunts are super nosy. They mean well, but they're terrifying.' He laughed. 'She'll go and interrogate Scott now.'

'What about Jake?' she asked. 'What happened with him and Cora? He said they weren't together anymore.'

He lowered his voice. 'Her parents didn't approve of their relationship and she married someone else. It's been so hard on him. He's been in France for the last year or so, but his mum and my aunts persuaded him to come back for this.'

'Oh wow, he must be heartbroken,' she whispered.

'He still thinks they'll get back together,' he said. 'He doesn't think her husband is good enough for her.'

'Star crossed lovers.' Her eyes widened. 'I love it. Have the band stopped playing?' It was quiet in the bar.

'For now.' He pointed to the back of the bar, where Alex was setting up his decks. 'It's our turn now. Are you coming to dance?'

'Of course.' She spotted Saskia at a table with Kate and Mia. 'See you there.'

A few minutes later, the dancefloor was packed again, as Chris and Alex played an eclectic mix of songs. Saskia twirled Molly under her arm under the disco ball, and as Molly tried to return the favour, she bumped straight into Hannah, whose arms were wrapped around George, from Future Proof. 'I'm so sorry.'

'No worries,' Hannah said, barely looking at Molly. George stroked her cheek and kissed her again.

Molly looked at Saskia, who stifled a giggle, and they stepped back to give them some privacy. She dragged Saskia to the edge of the dancefloor. 'This wedding is wild! Not only did we just bump into Hannah and the rock god, but I caught Lucy and Mel making out in the corridor.'

'Really? Good for them.' Saskia nudged Molly. 'Oh, look. I don't know if my waterproof mascara is strong enough to deal with this.'

Molly followed her gaze to the stage. Kate and Alex were sharing a set of headphones, as the slowed down remix of *Shattered Hearts* played. 'Can you believe he wrote that for her?'

'I know,' Saskia said. 'Absolute husband goals.'

Alex put down the headphones, holding out his hand to Kate, who carefully stepped off the stage with him. They made their way to the middle of the dancefloor, their eyes locked on each other's.

Scott appeared, sliding an arm around Saskia. 'You guys alright?'

'Would you write a song for me?' Saskia asked.

Scott smiled. 'If I could write songs, of course I would. I named a cocktail after you, didn't I?'

'You did,' Saskia turned to Molly. 'I can't remember what's in it, but it's boozy and fiery, and so good.'

'Sounds just like you,' Molly said, laughing. Leaving Scott and Saskia on the dancefloor, she snuck up to the stage.

'Hey,' she said as Chris slid off his headphones. 'Can I be your groupie?'

'Of course. My one and *only* groupie.' He put his arm around her waist.

When the next song finished, Ben stepped up onto the stage with a microphone. 'Can we have the single ladies to the front please? Kate is going to throw her bouquet.'

Molly looked down onto the dancefloor, which was emptying. Saskia marched over to the stage and held her hand out. 'Come on, Mole. Get down here!'

Molly carefully stepped off the stage, and Saskia pushed her to the front of the group of women forming on the dancefloor. Molly was more focused on Kate's stunning dress than her hand as she threw the bouquet across the room, but as it flew through the air, she stuck her hand up, and gasped as the stems of the bouquet hit her outstretched fingers. As she clasped her hand around it, she felt her cheeks colour. She looked back at Chris, who was staring open mouthed at her. Around her, everyone was cheering. She walked back to Chris, in a daze.

'So much for taking it slowly, huh?' she laughed and shook her head.

'Maybe fate is trying to tell us something,' he said, putting his arms around her. 'You told me you wanted forever, and I want that too.'

Her eyes filled with tears. 'I've learnt that you don't always get forever.' She thought about her parents, who she was sure would have got back together if her mum hadn't passed away.

'Then what are we waiting for?' He wiped her tears from her cheek with his thumb. 'Let's start our forever now.'

The End

Acknowledgements

There are so many people I need to thank for their help with this book!

Firstly, my alpha readers, who got hold of this book when it was literally still being written. Katie, your continuous support, promotion and love of this book has meant the world to me.

Natalie, I loved your hatred of Mark and insta-love of Chris. Thank you so much for all your suggestions. You helped amp Mark show his true villain nature. Huge thanks as always to Cherry for your insight. Bring on Book 3! Thanks to Hannah, and Gen for being there and encouraging me onwards. Miley, your comments have spurred me on to make my characters funnier, and wilder, so thank you!

Stefanie, thank you for delving deep into the story and getting me to focus on interiority. Anne, you are a legend. Thank you for checking my French, teaching me some brilliant new words, and taking Chris to your heart!

Thank you to my editor, Juli, who leapt at the chance to revisit Kate and Alex and get to know the rest of his family. I can't wait to work with you again.

To Kate, thank you for your eagle eyes, and sage advice.

Thank you to all of my ARC team, you have been incredible at promoting and getting excited for the story, even when all I could share were tiny snippets.

A massive thank you to Claire, the Molly to my Saskia. I love you. Your support means the world to me.

To my wonderful husband, thank you for encouraging me to be brave enough to follow my dreams, and my parents who inspire me to push myself. Thank you to my son, who is too young to read my books, but loves to hear about all the characters. I know you're going to be an awesome writer.

Last, but not least, thank you to every single person who picks up a copy of this book. I am so grateful that you did.

About the Author

Laura Elise Bishop is a romance novelist from South East England, where she lives with her husband and son. She was the kid in the corner with a book for most of her childhood and she's been writing ever since.

Her favourite place is the beach and her hobbies are sea swimming, baking, embroidery and watching romantic comedies.

Also by

Incomplete Strangers is the second part of the Wilder Hearts Series. If you enjoyed this, you might like the other books in this series, which are available now

The Ivy House (Book One)

Kate Barton is a woman who gets what she wants. Fresh out of university, she's secured her dream job as a jewellery designer. However, it involves returning to her imposing family home, The Ivy House and the chaos she left there. When she falls for a tall, dark, mysterious stranger, she's shocked to learn that he's linked to every part of her life.

Alex Compson is a man who never sits still. Clever, secretive, but vulnerable, he's built a fortress around his heart. A chance encounter with a beautiful woman forces him out of his comfort zone and deeper into her life.

The Ivy House is forbidding and protective of its inhabitants, with the power to tear relationships apart, or secure them forever. With both Kate and Alex keeping secrets from each other, which threaten to collapse their relationship, will the house come to their rescue or force them apart?

An Alpine Proposal (Book Three)

Caro Brown's life is chaotic. As an ex-West End actress with a famous family, dealing with paparazzi, fake friends and endless parties is par for the course. All that glitters isn't gold though. Her friends are never there for her, her dates are selling stories, and she can't stop thinking about the man she stormed out on a year ago.

Jeremy Hawksworth has spent the last year trying to put his life back together after his relationship with Caro went down in flames. While she parties with the Mayfair set, he keeps himself out of the limelight, throwing himself into his work.

When Caro loses her beloved grandfather, she's shocked to discover he left her his Alpine chalet in his will. However, it comes with a caveat, one that forces her to rethink her lifestyle. When her path crosses with Jeremy again, it sets of a chain of events that makes him question everything he's ever known.

Buried Treasure (Book Four)

ra Trevellyn is on a high from her first book tour when the woman who unknowingly slept with her husband turns up at her door. Leaving him, Cora flees London for Cornwall, to find solace in the town she grew up in. It's not plain sailing though. The only man she has ever truly loved is there, and there's stormy waters between them.

Jake Curnow is speechless when the red haired siren he has never stopped loving walks into his pub. Their relationship had always been secret, because of a mysterious centuries long feud between their families, but Cora is determined to find out what caused it, and she's taking Jake along for the ride.

When their feelings for each other resurface, is their love for each other strong enough to withstand the storm ahead of them? Or will it sink like the treasure they're seeking?

Buried Treasure will be available on the 1st August 2025

Printed in Dunstable, United Kingdom